PRAISE FOR *THE GOD PATENT*

"What distinguishes this classic ... its unusually deft infusion of legitin ... ıbi-tious first novel that uses Stephen ... a particle physicist, director of patents, public speaker and single father in a narrative that sings of the heart and the scientific method as two parts of the same song."

–*San Francisco Chronicle*

"*The God Patent* tackles the biggest question in the universe in a brand new way. Who knew science could be this entertaining? Stephens takes on technology, existentialism, and confronts religious dogma, in a novel that will provoke the ultimate water cooler conversation."

– Kemble Scott, bestselling author of ...d *SoMa*

"When ... le is a science ... ise to unloc ... ıto an Exxoı ... ıer multi ... me hung ... he bad g

ase

"The ... rg-ing p ... ɔed arouı ... sus faith ... ers. Inste ... ves us bu

r of *ted.*

"Thi ... You won' ... see the v

ı of *xult*

THE GOD PATENT

THE GOD PATENT

A Novel

RANSOM W. STEPHENS

The characters and events portrayed in this book are fictitious. Any similarity to real persons, living or dead, is coincidental and not intended by the author.

Printed in the United States of America.

Published by 47North
P.O. Box 400818
Las Vegas, NV 89140

ISBN-13: 9781611099126
ISBN-10: 1611099129
Library of Congress Control Number: 2012951473

For Karen, who both

loved and tolerated me the

whole time I wrote this.

In memory of Uncle Sherman,

whose tail went thump,

thump, thump after every

revision…except this one.

The constable set the arrest warrant on the counter between them.

Ryan, stalling for something to say, scraped dirty oil from under his thumbnail with a screwdriver. Jail meant he had no other options. It was tempting to relax in this pool of defeat, but no, he never wanted to be that man again.

The constable said, "Don't make sense to me how jailing you helps anybody. If you can't pay your child support changin' oil, how you gonna do it from jail?"

"Officer, the judge won't reduce my child support, and there aren't any jobs that pay anything close to what I was making when Linda threw me out." His words flowed together. "I'm not allowed within a hundred feet of my son, I want my wife back, I want my family back, but I can't even—"

The constable, well over six feet tall, had to lean forward on the counter to make his eyes level with Ryan's, and, as he did, his eyes narrowed in recognition. "Ryan McNear. Didn't you used to coach peanut league football?"

"Um, yeah." Struggling to recover some poise, Ryan forced himself to speak slowly. "I coached my son's team two years ago, the Shorthorns." He licked his lips into a smile. Framed by his chisel-cut jaw, and in the light of blue eyes and auburn wire-brush hair, his smile looked calm and warm, and sometimes it was, but not now. Ryan's wet-lipped grin was his response to stress. As a boy, he used that smile to soften arguments between his sisters; in school it broke up fights; in business it brought opposing sides together. It gave the appearance that he saw humor in the situation, that he couldn't be rattled, and, in so doing, it disarmed conflict. Pretending to look down at the counter, he stole a glance at the name tag above the constable's badge. "Holcomb? Bill Holcomb?" And as he spoke the name he remembered, "Your son—Willie, right? Didn't he get hurt in our first game?"

"Yes sir, he did."

Ryan leaned back on his heels and set the screwdriver next to the cash register. Along with his smile, the movement gave the illusion of confidence, but the memory of Willie Holcomb screaming in pain felt like another count against him.

"After the cast come off, my boy wanted nothing to do with football," Holcomb said. "Nothing I could say would get him back on the field—until you called. I don't know what you said, but he's turning into quite a linebacker." He squinted at Ryan's name tag. "Assistant manager? I thought you were an engineer. What happened?"

Ryan shut the door to the garage, directed Holcomb to the waiting room, then sat next to him and told the story. Not the complete story—that would have sent him straight to jail—but he couldn't have described all his failures in ten minutes anyway. Holcomb nodded occasionally and barely blinked. Ryan finished with the words he'd said to a judge six months ago. They hadn't helped then. "I made plenty of mistakes, but all I can do is keep trying to fix them."

"And I'm here to arrest you." Holcomb, with his elbows on his knees, rested his face in his hands and started speaking. He didn't stop for fifteen minutes. He talked about what it takes to break a man. Maybe he'd seen it in his job, but it sounded to Ryan as though he had walked close to the line himself. For Ryan, it had been a line of white powder, a line that he'd crossed. As the constable spoke, he looked out the window past the cars waiting to have their oil changed to the used car lots down the street, and by the time he focused on the tired cinder-block saloon next door, he was talking about his wife and children and how the smallest decisions can destroy the greatest dreams.

Finally, he looked at Ryan. "Sometimes it just don't seem like justice is very just." He stood, handed Ryan the arrest warrant, and ran his hand along his belt, over his sidearm, past the radio module. "I have to cuff you," he said and stared deep into Ryan's eyes.

Ryan's smile disappeared.

"You see, I have to handcuff you," Holcomb continued, "but danged if I didn't leave my cuffs out in the cruiser. I'll have to go back out and get them and, before I come back in, I think I'll call my wife just to hear her say she loves me, just to check in. A man only gets so many chances in life, you know what I'm sayin'?" He paused for a second, shook his head, and added, "What you're going through scares hell out of me." Then he tipped his hat as though offering a farewell, turned his back, and stepped toward the front door.

Ryan looked down at the arrest warrant and wondered if he'd ever get a chance to put his life back together. For the hundredth time that day, like every day, he recalled the last time he'd seen Sean, his son, and how the look of disappointment on the boy's face had turned to scorn and then to tears. Only one thing could dull the pain of that memory, but Ryan had sworn he'd never surrender to that desire again.

He looked up, out the shop window, and saw Holcomb open the cruiser door and climb in.

Ryan did a double take.

He could see Holcomb's handcuffs dangling from his waist as he climbed into the car.

Ryan set down the screwdriver, picked up the arrest warrant, took a deep breath, and decided to make his second chance count.

Driving away from everything you love is hard. Driving away in a Ford Probe with over two hundred thousand miles on it is almost impossible. A tire blew fifteen miles from Oklahoma City. It was hot and dirty on the side of the interstate but a good place to stop and think. When he got to Interstate 40, he'd have a decision to make.

The two relevant things to keep in mind when you run away are, first, you have to choose a direction and, second, since you can't run away from your problems, you might as well run toward their solutions.

Ryan had enough gas money to get to the coast, either coast, but not enough for a deposit and first and last months' rent on an apartment. It was autumn of 2003, and unemployment in high tech was over 25 percent nationwide, higher back in Dallas and with more layoffs being announced every day.

He could go back east to Andover, the Boston suburb where he grew up. They all still lived there—Mom, his sisters, and the huge marginally functional network that is every Catholic kid's birthright. He wouldn't have to pay rent for a while, and Andover was sort of a mini Silicon Valley. He could probably land some contract work hacking software and build from that when things turned around. It wasn't a bad idea. Mom would be happy to see him too. But he'd have to tell her what happened, and she'd get that look. Her chin would crumple, her eyes would sink, and her hands would reach out and shake—the same look that had burned into his memory when he was ten years old and she'd told him his father was dead.

After installing the donut spare tire, he stood off the highway in the shade of an oak tree and fidgeted with an acorn. He pictured himself driving into his hometown. When he got in trouble as a boy, he used to run to his grandma's house. If she were still alive, he'd go there now. He tugged the acorn from the branch, and a funny thing happened—a simple, obvious thing, but it startled Ryan. He knew exactly what Grandma would say. He could even hear her light Irish brogue, "What sort of man would you be then?"

Grandma always made these decisions easy. He smiled up to the sky and winked at her.

In Oklahoma City he sent a postcard to Mom: "I love you. Try not to worry, I'm healthy and strong. Sean and I will visit after I fix things." As he wrote it, he even believed that last sentence, could almost picture Sean smiling up in admiration the way he'd done before it all went to hell.

He went west on I-40—headed for Silicon Valley, the electrical engineer's mecca.

Two days after leaving Texas, Ryan emerged from the fertile valleys of central California to the San Francisco Bay Area. He landed in a semipermanent traffic jam at the junction of four different freeways. A new VW Beetle whose license plate read "D BUGGED" sat in the next lane. The driver, a man in his early thirties, about the same age as Ryan, glared back.

Ryan knew the look of a software jock whose code was crashing. The familiarity was comforting.

Ryan couldn't know it, but that little distraction would change everything.

He had been to Silicon Valley for conferences and customer meetings. He thought he knew his way around, but he went north when he should have gone south, and an hour later, instead of arriving in mecca, he was stuck in a traffic jam in Oakland.

The sun was setting across the bay beyond the Golden Gate Bridge. It really was gold, and it really did look like a gate—a gate to a better place.

Before everything collapsed, Ryan had a buddy named Foster Reed. Foster always insisted that everything happens for a reason. Ryan wasn't sure whether it was born of stupid hope or divine revelation, but he now believed that the little quirks in life are more like guideposts than accidents. The version of Ryan McNear who had visited Silicon Valley on business would have cussed and turned around. The revised version smiled inside and followed the signs to the Golden Gate.

By the time he pulled onto the Golden Gate Bridge, a cool blanket of fog covered the great suspension cables rising up to the towers. When he got to the other side of the bridge, he just kept going. The highway narrowed through rolling hills and, as the distance between each town grew, Ryan started to wonder about the "reason" for that wrong turn. Before the guy in the Beetle glared at him, his destination had at least been vague, but now it was a total mystery, and he was also on his last tank of gas. After a long stretch between off-ramps, he pulled onto a dark, rough road and parked between two big rigs. Lights in the distance reflected from a river flowing parallel to the road.

Ryan reclined in the front seat, the only hotel he could afford.

Rays of sunlight pushed Ryan's eyes open. The big rigs were gone, the muddy river rolled south, and the sun was rising over a mountain ridge clothed in a plaid of vineyards. With fingers crossed, he turned the key—it started on the first try. A steady stream of cars drifted in the opposite direction: a few expensive sedans, lots of minivans and SUVs, but mostly Japanese imports driven by sleepy white people—it looked like the California version of his commute back in Dallas.

The street curled under the freeway along the river. He passed a sign: "Petaluma City Limits, Pop. 55,900." The density of buildings increased, old Victorians on the left and warehouses on the right. He drove up to a park with public restrooms. The feeling that everything was arranged came back—the wrong turn that led him to the Golden Gate was one thing, but having the fuel light come on just as he pulled up to "McNear Park" clinched it.

He ducked into the restroom with a change of clothes and his shaving kit and emerged ten minutes later looking and smelling civilized.

He found a coffee shop among the mid-nineteenth-century buildings, got a cup of black tea, and sat at a table near a boulevard-facing window. A man sat at the table next to him reading a newspaper. He had long gray hair tied in a ponytail and was wearing sandals with socks and a purple T-shirt that read "Keep Sonoma Grapes Monsanto Free." Ryan looked out the window, then back at the man. He fidgeted with the teaspoon, tapping it against his thumb and then against his chin. When he started tapping the table, the man grunted and handed Ryan the sports section and classifieds.

He looked at a small map in the apartment rental section. Most apartments were within three blocks of town. Most of the jobs were across the river. There were a handful of engineering jobs farther north in Santa Rosa, a few back south in San Francisco, but of course most were down in Silicon Valley.

With the paper tucked under his arm, Ryan headed out to find an apartment. He passed McNear's Restaurant and Saloon and walked up McNear Avenue toward McNear Landing. That tenuous hint that he had been drawn here for a reason was getting out of hand. God might as well have put up a billboard: "Ryan McNear! Rebuild Your Life in Petaluma."

Filled with confidence he hadn't felt in years, he walked the tree-lined streets. A woman with long dark hair on an old bicycle that had shiny chrome fenders waited next to him at a stoplight, muttering to herself. The darkness of her ankle-length black skirt was amplified by her pale skin. When she pedaled away, her hair and skirt swirled behind her.

At an apartment manager's office, Ryan discovered that his lack of immediate cash would be a greater impediment to getting housing than he'd hoped. Plus, rents were twice what they'd been in Texas. Finding a hole in that soft blanket of arranged destiny was strangely comforting. Ryan didn't want the solutions to be handed to him.

An "apartment for rent" sign hanging from an expansive but drooping porch on one of the old craftsman-style mansions directed Ryan to an elderly lady sitting at an iron table. He filled out a rental application and licked his lips into that disarming smile. She was apologetic but wouldn't take a renter without the standard deposit plus first and last months' rent. Instead, she offered a suggestion. "Go up Liberty Street to the black-and-red Victorian. Dodge Nutter might rent you something."

Ryan walked up a short, steep hill to a Victorian with fire-engine-red siding and twin black turrets topped with conic spires. The carpenter's lace trim sparkled in gold with tiny but screaming slivers of lime green.

Most of the other Victorians at the top of the hill were partitioned into apartments too, but they had multiple entrances and tasteful paint. The red-and-black monstrosity at the corner towered over them and had just the one entrance, ten-foot-high double doors. An "apartment for rent" sign was duct-taped to the porch's iron railing. As he climbed the stairs, Ryan decided that the place must be haunted, and, by the time he reached the porch, he could picture Grandpa Munster resurrecting Herman in the basement.

Four mailboxes were mounted on the wall. Instead of a doorbell, under a little window, the sort of window you'd expect in the door of an abbey, was a huge goat-head knocker. He let it fall an inch, and the iron-on-iron clap shook the porch and echoed around the neighborhood.

After a couple of minutes, Ryan peeked through the little window. It took a few seconds for his eyes to adjust, and, just as he could make out some details inside, he heard scuffling behind him.

A girl with long dark hair combed to one side so that it hung over her left eye dragged a huge skateboard up the stairs. "Scammin' the crib?"

It cracked the seriousness right out of Ryan. "I am scammin' the crib. Lookin' for diamonds, a major stash. You got any diamonds in there?"

In addition to the skateboard, the girl was struggling under a full knapsack.

Ryan said, "You need a hand with that?"

She cast Ryan a quick glare and scampered the rest of the way up to the porch. She was wearing black sneakers with striped socks and a black skirt that hung down to her scratched-up knees. Graffiti was scrawled along the hem in white paint, and her tank top was closer to gray than white. She looked a little younger than his son, at least one year on the child side of adolescence.

"I'm looking for an apartment to rent," Ryan said.

She set her skateboard under a bench and let her backpack fall off her shoulders onto the porch. She knelt down and dug through it. "Deal with Dodge, then."

"Yeah, that's what I was told," Ryan said.

"Sucks to be you." She pulled out a key.

"Do you know where he is?"

"He'll waddle out of his cave eventually."

The way she talked was refreshing, no child-to-adult pretense. Ryan said, "I have a kid about your age."

"Six billion people on this planet—I'm thinking that's not such a coinkydink."

"I suppose." He held out his hand. "Ryan McNear…"

She opened the door, dashed through the foyer, and bolted up an oak staircase without returning his look or saying another word. Ryan followed as far as the base of the stairs. A door slammed above, and a few seconds later, loud music vibrated the walls.

Another odd thing about this Victorian-turned-apartment-complex: the foyer opened to someone's living room. An antique couch, diamond-tuck red velvet with sloping arms and lion feet, was set in the center of the room on a matching Persian rug. Ryan leaned against the wall and stared across the room out a picture window at the rolling hills across the valley. The reverberation of the girl's music reminded him of his sisters at that age, and the smell of the well-oiled hardwood floor was just like his grandma's house. Home had never been exactly comfortable, but it was home, and this wasn't too far off.

After about ten minutes, the bass line of whatever music the girl was playing had faded into the background, and Ryan heard a voice that sounded like an a.m. disc jockey who'd mixed black coffee, scotch, and cigarettes until his tone could define the word *gruff*.

"You got a job, McNear?"

Ryan looked up the stairs and around the living room but couldn't tell where the voice came from. "Sir?" Surprised that whoever was behind that voice knew his name, he forced himself to relax against the wall.

A man walked in and sat at the edge of the couch. He was several inches shorter than Ryan, about fifty, bald but with curly hair over his ears and thin glasses perched at the end of a long pointy nose. He set a thick stack of paper on the table in front of the couch, looked over his glasses at Ryan, and patted the velvet upholstery next to him.

Ryan eased into the room and sat as directed. The top sheet was a faxed copy of the rental agreement he'd filled out on the elderly lady's porch half an hour ago. It explained how the man knew Ryan's name.

"You got a job, McNear?"

Ryan put on a facade of confidence and spoke the way he would to a business colleague in a boardroom. "I just got to town. I'm an electrical engineer—should have a position by the end of the week."

Dodge waited, holding his hands together so that the fingertips of one hand just touched those of the other. There was something deeply obnoxious about his extended silence and unwavering stare. Eventually Ryan gave in and, for no reason he could fathom, started explaining his situation, just the details a reasonable landlord might need: the job situation in Dallas and that he'd come to California to find an executive engineering position.

Dodge laughed, a raspy but screeching chuckle that seemed to echo between the tip of his nose and the paunch of his belly. "Did you bring a shovel, McNear? The gold rush ended a hundred and fifty years ago."

Ryan's instinct was to laugh along, but he resisted. The days of avoiding confrontation at any cost ended when the constable showed him that arrest warrant. This time, he let indignation temper his words. "I was the director of a Fortune 100 company. I've led a staff of fifty software jocks developing new technology—"

"Software's written in India now. What have you done—"

"I hold half a dozen patents, from artificial intelligence to energy production to networking technology." At the mention of patents, Dodge's eyes opened wider, just for a second, but long enough to bolster Ryan's tenuous confidence. "In my last engineering gig, I brought home six figures."

"And now you don't have enough for first and last on a studio apartment." Dodge leaned back and put his hands behind his head. "What did you burn that cash on, Irish boy? Meth? Hookers? Gambling?"

"Child support."

"Now we're getting somewhere. So why'd she throw you out? Meth? Hookers? Gambling?"

"None of your fuckin' business." Ryan stood and walked out the door.

As it swung shut, Dodge called after him, "You're homeless without me."

Ryan gritted his teeth. Those words hurt. He slumped onto the bench and put his feet on the girl's skateboard. Even if everything bounced his way, he was at least a few months from an executive engineering position. He looked across the valley. Things happen for a reason. Maybe having a landlord who could see through his bullshit wasn't such a bad thing.

He walked back inside. "Are you going to rent me an apartment or not?"

Dodge said, "I have some ideas for how you might compensate me for the deposit and first and last and a few of my other fees…"

The way Dodge said this, smooth and just above a whisper, pegged Ryan's bullshit meter. "What do you mean?"

"I want to help you," Dodge said, but he spoke like a bad salesman. "Really, I'm a man of goodwill. I care for the downtrodden. I'm a do-gooder. Don't I look like a do-gooder? It's not all about profit to me, really."

Ryan started to laugh. He said, "How full of shit are you?"

"Okay, I lied. It is all about profit to me. So shoot me for being an entrepreneur." Dodge laughed with him. His laughter came out as a long, loose, liquid cough. When he got hold of himself, he said, "Tell me about your patents."

Ryan countered with, "Let me see the apartment."

Dodge led Ryan upstairs to a good-sized studio set in the corner of the building. It included one of the two cylindrical towers that framed the Victorian and had a curved glass window with a 270-degree view across the valley to the mountains along the horizon. The kitchenette had one long counter along the interior wall and old but clean appliances. Ryan stared out the window, southeast toward Texas. "I don't have first and last. I might not have second." He turned to Dodge. "But I'll have third."

This time Dodge threw a wink in with his raspy snicker. "Well, I'll need to do better collecting from you than your wife does." As he led Ryan back downstairs, he said, "There are a few things you'll have to sign. Several things, actually. Are you familiar with contract law?"

Ryan felt a few butterflies waft around his stomach as the notion of indentured servitude passed through his mind. With all defenses in position but a complete realization of his bargaining position, he sat next to Dodge on the diamond-tuck couch.

Dodge scrawled on a clipboard that held a thick sheaf of pages. Ryan took a pen from the coffee table and thumped it on his ankle as he looked over Dodge's shoulder. Dodge repositioned himself so that Ryan couldn't see what was on the clipboard.

Dodge snickered and said, "Why'd your wife throw you out?"

"You don't need to know that."

"I need to know what I'm buying." Dodge coughed again. "I think you get me, McNear. I sense an opportunity here, maybe even a partnership. You need me and I don't need you—just the way I like partnerships. But I do need information. I like information. So tell me, you were cheatin', right? It's nothing to me—a man has needs. Monogamy is for the birds."

"No." Ryan spoke louder than the situation warranted, but his nerves were raw. He had never broken a promise to his wife—ex-wife. Never. He had clung to that knowledge through the pain of reality. There was more to it, of course, but the tipping point came when Linda found what she thought was proof he'd cheated. Ryan stood and took a step away from Dodge. "I never cheated on her. Never. She's the love of my life. I wouldn't—"

"Throw me a bone, McNear. What mess are you in?" He set the clipboard on his lap and put the pen behind his ear.

Ryan paced, trying to walk off the vision of Linda sobbing and asking him to leave their home. He clenched every muscle, fighting the urge to walk away. The tension in his body absorbed the tension in his mind, and he realized that swallowing his pride wouldn't be the hardest part of rebuilding his life. He sat back on the couch.

Dodge responded with the most offensive smirk Ryan had ever seen.

"Okay," Ryan said, "I'm in debt. Wading in debt, debt up to my fuckin' eyeballs."

"Closer." Dodge wheezed. "How'd you get in debt?"

"They set my child support payments when I was a company director, and six months later the economy crashed and I got laid off—there was no way I could keep up." He stood again and walked across the room. The farther he got from Dodge, the easier it was to talk. "If I'd gone to the judge sooner, he might have reduced my payments, but I didn't. I kept thinking there'd be another job, and my debt kept building."

The bass line from upstairs came to an abrupt stop, a door slammed, and the girl ran down the stairs. Dodge hollered, "Where you goin', Kat?"

"Forced mentoring with the bitch."

Dodge said, "Your mom know where you're goin'?"

She slammed the door behind her.

Through the window, Ryan watched the girl jump on her skateboard and zip down the hill. "Is she your kid?"

"Mine? No. I don't reproduce," Dodge said. "She's a brilliant kid, damaged, though. Her father died a few years back. Mother should have, for all the good she does. If I let you move in, they'll be your neighbors down the hall."

"How many apartments do you have?"

"Three. The studio you just saw, a two-bedroom where Kat and her mom live, and a two-bedroom that you don't need and can't afford."

"Does someone live in the other one?"

"Do I look like a font of information?" Dodge picked up the clipboard and continued, "Child support, huh? How many kids?"

"Just my son."

Dodge scribbled on the form. "When did you last see him?"

Adding up the months, Ryan released a long sigh. "Over a year now, almost two."

Dodge leaned back, and that nasty chuckle erupted into another coughing attack until a chunk of something hit the back of his teeth. "So, along with deadbeat dad, you can add poor excuse for a father to your résumé."

"Fuck you!" Ryan took two hard steps toward Dodge and stopped. "I tried to see him, but I couldn't." Then, under his breath, "My wife got a restraining order, and the judge granted her sole custody."

Dodge pushed his glasses up his nose and scribbled on the rental documents. "You realize that without any money you're not buying, you're selling, and you're not a very good salesman." He smiled up at Ryan. "Why would a judge prevent a pillar of society like you from seeing his son?"

Ryan tried not to choke on the bitter taste of the last of his pride. An image came back to him, the first picture in his album of shame. It was at his best friend's bachelor party. His duty as best man was to organize the traditional strip-joint celebration. He had just stumbled out of the men's room, staggering drunk but experiencing a moment of warm clarity. A perfectly voluptuous woman wearing a light-blue lace bikini top and g-string caught him by the shoulders. Ryan slipped her a fifty and pointed at the groom, his buddy Foster, and told her to give him the lap dance of his life. It was a bachelor party tradition.

That was the moment Ryan's life started to cave in. The next morning his wife found a piece of paper with a phone number in his pants pocket. Six months later they were divorced, and a month after that, he got laid off. It had taken only three years to lose everything. How long would it take to get it back?

Ryan looked away from Dodge, through the window and across the valley to the mountain. "I made some big mistakes. Unemployment, divorce." He started to speak, started to describe the bachelor party as a "tradition" again, but fought the impulse to rationalize. He'd organized that party, and the day he was laid off he'd walked straight into his own personal hell. He said, "A few months after the divorce, the day I got laid off, I met a woman who made me feel better. Well, no. Not better, worse really—but she definitely made me feel." He turned back to Dodge. "She did something horrible to my son, and before I had any idea, I was served a restraining order."

"So, was it meth, hookers, or gambling?"

Ryan sunk back onto the couch and leaned forward with his elbows on his knees. He hung his head and mumbled, "Well, it wasn't gambling."

Dodge let fly an especially loud version of his raspy laughter, this one with a trace of genuine humor.

With the clipboard on Dodge's lap, Ryan caught a glimpse of his notes. The word *patents* was circled over and over.

"Okay," Dodge said, "a five-thousand-dollar good-faith fee to pay for my risk, and if it even crosses my mind that you're using methamphetamine, you're out. Your rent starts at twice what your apartment is worth—make rent four months in a row and it comes down to market rate. If you miss a month, we start over. If you're five days late, there's a ten percent fee—that's the most the state will allow—"

"That's robbery."

"—and I'll have to type up a separate form, but in exchange for renting an apartment without first and last, I'm taking an interest in any future income derived from your patents. Do you have a car?"

Ryan noticed how Dodge had slipped in the phrase about patents. It didn't make sense. Those patents weren't worth anything. He set the thought aside and answered the question. "Sort of, a twelve-year-old Probe that's clicked over twice."

Dodge shuffled through his folder. "Sign this too. I'm putting a lien on it."

Ryan grabbed the growing pile of contracts as if to stem the tide. "Does the state allow this?"

"Strangely, it does. Even here in Commie-fornia—did I mention I'm an attorney? I don't practice law anymore—bad for my liver—but I had a tenant sue me a couple of years ago. The judge was amazed at how well I work the system." He rambled from one tenant anecdote to another, speeding through pointless stories as though trying to confuse things.

Ryan read through the documents. With each page, outrage pushed shards of his pride to the surface. "Give me a pen."

Dodge offered a blue ballpoint, but instead of signing, Ryan scratched out a few lines and made edits between a few others. As Ryan set the marked-up pages aside, Dodge picked them up, initialed some of Ryan's modifications, scribbled through others, and set the pages in yet another pile. As the sun set, the two men passed the documents back and forth, sometimes laughing, saying "yeah right," sometimes grunting "cold day in hell."

As Ryan read the last page, its margins already scribbled and initialed several times over, Dodge leaned against him. Ryan pushed back with an elbow. He put the last sheet on top of the stack and rubbed his eyes.

Dodge assembled the contracts and stood. "You can bring your stuff in while I retype this."

As the bluster of negotiating started to subside, Ryan felt puzzled. He had no bargaining position, yet Dodge had negotiated. Yes, he'd agreed to absurd rental terms, but there was no way for Dodge to enforce them. Then Ryan recalled Dodge asking if he was familiar with contract law. All the details in the contracts had to be a ruse, had to be covering up a greater con. And that con was somehow related to his old patents—or maybe something deeper. Ryan made a mental note to comb through the documents before signing.

The front door opened, and the girl walked through the foyer. She stopped at the stairs. "Is the woman in the house?"

Dodge said, "No, your *mother* isn't home—learn anything from your mentor?"

"That she is freakishly weird." She started up the stairs.

"Stop. Come here. Meet your new neighbor."

"Can't. Already did. Meeting is a one-time thrill."

Ryan said, "But I didn't meet you." He walked over, smiled, and held out his hand. "Ryan McNear."

The girl performed an exaggerated curtsy and said, "Katarina Ariadne, pleased to meet you. My friends call me Kat; you can call me Katarina." She stomped up the stairs.

Dodge yelled after her, "If I find any more paint on your walls—"

A door slammed, and a few seconds later, the bass line to some heavy-metal music leaked through the ceiling.

Ryan turned back to Dodge. "She's brilliant, huh?"

"Character judgment isn't one of your strengths, is it?"

Ryan put a toothy grin on his face. "Strong enough to know you're an asshole."

"Heh, heh, I like you." Dodge headed deeper into his apartment as Ryan opened the front door.

As Ryan headed out to find his car, fog rolled over the Nutter House towers the same way it had the Golden Gate Bridge. He wondered about the girl, Katarina. Funny, Ryan was fighting to rebuild his life just so he could be a dad to his son, and here was Katarina, loud and clear, but with a dead father. At least Sean had a stepfather.

He passed an old theater whose marquee was covered with Day-Glo writing in the style you might expect to see spray-painted on a New York subway car: "Skate-n-Shred." Teenagers huddled around the entrance. It looked like a natural habitat for a kid like Katarina.

The fog worked its way into his bones, and he picked up his pace. By the time he found the Probe, he was shivering. He started the car and flipped on the heat. As the engine warmed, the car filled with the smell of tired antifreeze. That smell reminded him how far he had to go, but he'd made the first step. He had a place to live.

He drove through town along the boulevard, paused at a stop sign, and then turned up the hill toward Nutter House.

Something darted in front of him—he hit the brakes hard.

A woman on a bike headed straight for him, her long black skirt trailing behind. Did she have a death wish? If not for her pale skin, he'd never have seen her.

In the instant that her face crossed his headlights, she looked at him with a blank stare and then pedaled off.

The Probe sputtered to a stop in front of the garish Victorian. He took a deep breath of the moist air and stared up at his new home. He put his outdated computer atop a box of books and carried it upstairs. Being an engineer whose computer had a squeaky fan, whiny disk drive, and hardly any memory was embarrassing. He didn't have a cell phone, not even a pager—no reasonable technology at all.

Ryan opened the door to his new apartment, stepped in, and fell over a pile of contracts. He managed to cradle the monitor so that it didn't break as he went down.

One more trip up the stairs and everything Ryan owned was in the apartment. He set the tiny student desk in the rounded corner facing out the curved windows and unrolled his sleeping bag between his lamp and an aluminum beach chair that would double as a nightstand. Then he grabbed his most valuable possession: a football.

Sean had scored his first touchdown with that ball. The memory shaded his outlook. Ryan used to live in a real house in a nice neighborhood with a loving wife, a fine son, and a good job. He'd always been happy. Even now, he wasn't really unhappy. It was just that memories like this, when he was alone and undistracted, gave him a case of what his grandma used to call "the melancholies."

He grabbed the stack of contracts and leaned back on the beach chair with his feet propped on the windowsill. There it was: in exchange for the deposit and first month's rent, Dodge would take half of any income that Ryan made from his patents.

Ryan didn't get it. The company he'd worked for when he formulated the inventions held all the rights. Engineers have to sign the patent waiver before they can even interview for a job. But there was something about Dodge; the only way any of this made sense was if the old bastard knew something that Ryan didn't. Ryan scratched out the 50 percent and wrote in 25 percent, initialed it, and took the papers downstairs.

Uncomfortable stepping into Dodge's living room, he stopped in the foyer. There was a wide offset floorboard where a door should have separated Dodge's apartment from the rest of the house. A huge flat-screen TV across from the couch was tuned to a crime show, but no one was watching.

With no door to knock on, Ryan walked through the living room, looked around a corner, and started quietly down a hall. He felt like a burglar until he realized that this was exactly how Dodge wanted him to feel.

He called down the hallway, "Hey, Nutter, we need to talk." There was no answer.

At the end of the hall, he walked into a brightly lit kitchen. Dodge sat at a round Formica table wearing headphones and plinking away on an electric piano. He glanced at Ryan but kept playing.

Ryan waited.

Except for copper pots and pans hanging from the ceiling, everything in the kitchen was starkly white. After a few minutes, Ryan set the pile of documents on the table and eased into a chair. Just as he settled down, Dodge pulled off the headphones, stood, and said, "In my office—now that we're business partners, it's time to chat."

Ryan followed him back down the hall. The term *business partners* churned in his belly like sour milk. Dodge walked into his office—a sprightly walk, nearly a dance. It did nothing to reduce Ryan's emotional nausea.

Dodge sat behind a desk the size of a twin bed and flicked on a lamp. It had a green shade that cast an olive pall, not a pleasant match to Dodge's skin tone. In addition to a blotter, an alarming ornament rested on the desk. Set on a judge's gavel pad was a snub-nosed pistol.

Dodge flipped through the documents, adding his signature. "You can stay in the hallway, McNear, or take a seat." He motioned to a rocking chair—upholstered in the same diamond-tuck red velvet as the couch.

Ryan pulled the chair closer to the desk. "Is the gun loaded?"

"There's no such thing as an unloaded gun." Dodge pulled a bottle of Irish whiskey out of a desk drawer and two tumblers. "Sorry, I don't have any meth."

"Funny." Ryan sipped from the glass, sinking into the sweet-scented fluid—it reminded him of his father.

"All right, you have six patents that are owned, as far as you know, by GoldCon, a cable manufacturing company whose stock skyrocketed when they introduced fiber-optic technology in 1999." Dodge looked over his glasses for confirmation.

Ryan watched his whiskey swirl around in the glass, unsurprised that Dodge could find the information but noting how fast he'd assembled it.

"I don't care about the 'Novel Multi-Tasking, Multi-Threading Tool,' or the 'Self-Optimizing Optical Network.' No, it's these two patents that interest me—the ones you coinvented with Foster Reed: 'Application of Fundamental Uncertainty to the Generation of Energy' and 'Method of Multiple Feedback for Neural Network Self-Generation of Artificial Intelligence'—remember those?"

"I remember them."

"Talk to me."

"Not much to say. A couple of ideas my friend and I played around with. We never expected the patents to be granted."

"Tell me about the patents."

Ryan sipped the whiskey and glanced from the revolver to Dodge. He took another sip. "What's with the gun?"

"Go ahead," Dodge said. "Pick it up. Shoot it if you want." With his bald head sticking up behind the huge desk, he looked ridiculous. "Come on, McNear, tell me about the patents or the deal's off."

Ryan pushed the gun aside along with its little platform. "Do you know anything about GoldCon?"

"The patents, McNear."

"Well, it started out as Golden Conductors. They've been manufacturing wires and cable in Texas since the advent of electric power. In 1998, they renamed the company GoldCon and got into high tech. During the tech buildup, lots of companies jumped on the telecom locomotive. I was hired along with a hundred electrical, optical, and computer engineers from tech powerhouses like Bell Labs and WorldCom. We were all in our late twenties, the perfect age for high productivity and low salary, and some of us, like Foster Reed and me, had worked together before. We'd been on the same development teams since we graduated from college."

"The patents, McNear—get to the point."

"We wrote those patents on our first day at GoldCon..."

Ryan dropped a box of books on the desk of his new cubicle. "Why is everything in this business blue? I feel like a bee in a huge blue honeycomb."

In the neighboring cube, Foster positioned his monitor at the perfect angle and then stepped back. "I love it; smells like a new car." The cubicles didn't have doors and the partitions were just chest high. Foster attached a Christian fish symbol to the entrance of his cube and started unpacking his things.

Ryan booted up his computer, leaned back in his chair, and sorted through the pile of memos in the welcome packet. “Hey, did you see this patent award bonus thing?”

Foster leaned over the wall between their cubes. He had light brown hair precisely parted on one side with a little flip over his forehead. “I saw the subject header in an e-mail.”

“They’re offering a five-hundred-dollar bonus for filling out a patent submission form.”

“So?” Foster pursed his lips the way he did when confused. “You have an invention?”

“Dude, you’re not getting it. We fill out the form, put it in internal mail, and some lawyer who knows jack-shit about high tech cuts us a check.”

Foster sat down, adjusted his glasses, and opened his packet. “I see a foosball tournament, a barbecue for the whole engineering team.” He laughed and added, “Perhaps they’ll even have a slumber party. Wouldn’t that be great?”

Ryan said, “It’s the same game they play at all the big tech firms. Whether the patents are useful or not doesn’t even matter. They just want to trot out a ridiculous number of applications to impress investors.” He stood and looked over to Foster. “What are you doing?”

“Signing up for aerobics—if there are any women in this company, that’s where to find them.”

Ryan and Foster had met during orientation at their first jobs and were assigned to the same product development teams, Foster on hardware design and Ryan in software. Ryan had moved to Texas from Massachusetts for that job, and Foster was his first buddy.

"Come on, Foster, let's fill out patent applications. It's easy money. If we come up with a real idea and the patent's granted we get five thousand dollars!"

Foster made a *tsk* sound. "Okay, Mr. Edison, what's your brilliant invention?"

"My brilliant invention is to fill out as many of these forms as I can before the patent attorney clues in. Remember that guy at Bell Labs who has a hundred patents? He told me that most of them were lame ideas dressed up in enough jargon to confuse attorneys at the patent office. He holds a patent for drilling a hole through a chunk of circuit board—called it an optic waveguide."

"There is already a name for holes in circuit boards. The *via* has a grand history."

"Yeah, but this one was for a *horizontal* hole."

In a whining, übergeek tone of pure sarcasm, Foster said, "I consider that patentable."

Ryan tapped a mechanical pencil on his keyboard and then put the pencil between his teeth and started typing at full speed. He stopped long enough to pull a book, *Fuzzy Thinking*, out of his backpack, dug around in the boxes he'd just set down, and found another, *Neural Networks*. "We're in. The down payment for the metal-flake blue Ski Nautique will be in hand shortly."

A few months earlier, Foster and Ryan had rented a boat on Lake Texoma. They caught largemouth bass as the sun rose and skied around the lake all day. When they returned the boat, they vowed, complete with pinkie-shake, that someday they would buy a boat together.

With the two books on his lap, Ryan resumed typing. Foster wheeled his chair over, and Ryan moved aside so that Foster could scroll through the document. A smile separated Foster's pursed lips. "I see what you're doing, translating English into engineering—this is a Dilbert moment—except, hold it. This might not be such a bad idea."

Ryan chewed his pencil and stared at the ceiling for almost a minute. "You think?" He resumed typing again. A few minutes later Ryan said, "There are tons of patents for artificial intelligence and stuff like neural networks—I want to patent something special or maybe something ridiculous." He typed for a while longer and then stopped. "I've got it."

"What are you doing?"

"I'm submitting a patent for the soul."

"Pardon me?"

"Yeah, free will, sentience, the soul. I'll write an algorithm that does something that, at least to an uneducated observer, would do the same thing that the Bible says a soul does."

"Scroll through that again." Ryan scrolled and Foster read, "…a software algorithm that makes decisions based on a preconceived concept of right and wrong."

"Yes," Ryan said, "and to the computer, right and wrong means making the best choice for the user—after all, the user is God. Get it?"

"Yeah, I get it." He cocked his head to one side. "Ryan, you're on ice so thin you're about to fall into H-E-double-hockey-sticks." He read more of the patent submission and added, "This is okay. You know, it might even work."

"I'm glad you approve," Ryan said. "Get a price on the blue Ski Nautique—and a slip. Where should we keep it?"

Ryan resumed typing with Foster looking on. He stopped and asked, "What does the Bible say about the soul, anyway?"

"If you'd ever read the Bible, you'd know that it doesn't say much about the soul." Foster wheeled his chair back into his cube and took a worn black leather Bible from a shelf. "There's something in Ecclesiastes." He flipped to a page and read aloud:

"'Then shall the dust return to the earth as it was: and the spirit shall return unto God who gave it.'" Flipping to another page, he said, "And, of course, there's a psalm—there's a psalm for everything—'By the Lord's Word the heavens were made; by the breath of his mouth all their host.' The word *soul* is used a lot to refer to people, but that's about as much as there is distinguishing the physical, His Word, from the spiritual, His Breath." Foster leaned over and dug through a box and then held up an old paperback, *The Philosophy of Man and Spirit*. "Fortunately for you, other misguided Catholics, Saint Thomas Aquinas and Saint Augustine, spent a lot of time trying to figure it out." He handed the paperback to Ryan but hugged the Bible to his chest.

"If they grant this patent," Ryan said, "I'll hold the rights to every thought any Christian ever had."

"I wish you wouldn't say things like that."

Two hours later, Ryan sent the patent submission form to the printer. On his way to pick up the hard copy, he leaned into Foster's cube. Foster was typing away with the Bible open in his lap and two paperbacks, each written by a physicist, Steven Weinberg's *The First Three Minutes* and George Smoot's *Wrinkles in Time*, on his desk.

Ryan read the file name. "A power generator?"

Foster said, "Yes, this is something that's bothered me for a long time. Back in college my physics professor used to go on and on about energy and time. These books do too. They use the word *symmetry* a lot, as though energy and time are somehow like left and right, as if you can't have one without the other." He looked up at Ryan. "God created the universe from nothing, but physics insists that you can't get something from nothing. Think about it. The universe had to come from somewhere, so there must be conditions that allow energy to come from nothing—the conditions of Creation, the perfect power generator!"

"Is there anything in Genesis other than 'and God said, let there be this, that, or the other'?"

"It was 'this, that, *and* the other,'" Foster said, shaking his head and smiling. "Genesis may be short on details, but it's irrefutable."

"Doesn't the Bible say that the universe is like six thousand years old?" Two vertical lines formed in Ryan's brow.

"If you add up the ages of everyone from Adam, yes, you get about six thousand years. And, also yes, these physicists have evidence that the universe is almost fourteen billion years old. The thing is, though, Genesis is the Word of God and the Big Bang is a theory that's still being developed." He tossed *Wrinkles in Time* to Ryan. "Have you heard of *inflation*? It's one of the things they had to add to the Big Bang theory, an epoch when the universe expanded really fast. Surprise! Science discovers something that shortens their measurement of the age of the universe and moves the theory closer to the description in Genesis. It's still got a long way to go, but the scientists will get it right eventually."

Ryan balanced the book on the partition between their cubicles, hesitating before broaching the sensitive topic. "Why are you obsessed with the Bible being literally true?"

Foster and Ryan had been close friends for five years. They shared affection for boats, cars, and sports. Ryan understood that Foster was a devout Christian. It seemed as though Foster was okay with Ryan's essential indifference to religion until this topic came up.

"Even if it was inspired by God, the Bible was still written by men," Ryan said, "men who didn't know the first thing about quantum physics or relativity or evolution. Even if God had told them the whole story, how could those guys have written it down?"

"The Bible is the Word of God, verbatim." Foster looked back at his monitor and resumed typing. A few minutes later, he looked back at Ryan and added, as if to make peace, "Though it would be convenient if the description were more mathematical, and please don't get me started about evolution."

Dodge refilled Ryan's glass and said, "So you and your buddy developed these patents so you could buy a boat?"

"Yeah," Ryan said. "Even if they had any value, GoldCon has all the rights."

"Are they totally bogus?"

"Actually, the one I wrote, my patent of the everlasting soul," he laughed at the thought and the memory of Foster looking aghast at the concept before proceeding to write his own version of Creation, "has some neat ideas in it about training neural networks and some cool optimization algorithms, but I never got a chance to develop them."

"What about the other one?"

"I never really understood it. Whenever religion came up, Foster got kind of weird, so when he tried to explain it, I just sort of nodded. But he's a smart guy—who knows?"

Dodge looked at the desk. He slid the revolver over and spun it around. When it stopped spinning it was pointing at his empty glass. He said, "Last week, someone bought the rights to those two patents—a university."

"What university?"

"Does Evangelical Word University ring a bell?"

"No."

Ryan lay awake in his sleeping bag that first night in Nutter House. When cars drove by, lights flashed off the tarnished copper work on the ceiling. It reminded him of the day GoldCon's CEO had presented a plaque to each of them. That the patents were granted had caught Ryan by surprise. At first he'd felt uncomfortable cashing the big checks—the company split the $5,000 for each patent between them; together they had four checks for $2,500—but it didn't bother Foster. He said they should trust the patent office, that it had happened for a reason. They were skiing off that blue boat the following weekend.

Ryan listened to the sleepy old house creak and settle. It was hard to get comfortable, not just because the foam under his sleeping bag was lumpy, but because he wanted to go home.

He started dozing off, and a vision of Linda and Sean woke him. He thrashed around, trying to think of something else, anything that could shake off the melancholies. It was harder at night. These internal battles always ended the same way: an image of Sean—half daydream, half nightmare. He'd be thirteen by now, wearing cleats, pads, and a helmet, walking home after being cut from the team and blaming his absent father for not being there to teach him football's *X*s and *O*s. Ryan couldn't stand the fact that he had abandoned Sean, just like his father had abandoned him. Linda had thrown Ryan out when Sean was about the same age Ryan had been when his father died.

Someone coughed down the hall. Ryan got up, put on his pants, and stepped toward the door. He opened it and looked down the dim hallway, up at the ornate crown molding, and realized what he was doing. Without even considering it, something lurking in his brain, the monkey on his back, was requesting a few hits of meth to make everything all better.

He hung his head and sighed. Would it ever get any easier?

Stepping inside his apartment, he closed the door and paced in front of the window. He listed everything in his life that was getting better. Every step that took him closer to a life where he could be with Sean and make a living solving technical puzzles was a good step. Any step out that door in search of a chemical nightmare was a bad step. When he finished, one thing stood out: he had a room in a nice house in a good town and, if not a bed, at least a soft, warm place to sleep.

Ryan lay back down and pulled the sleeping bag around him. Visions of the past mixed with hope for the future. He thought of his old friend and wondered where Foster was now. Probably sleeping peacefully with his wife—he ended up marrying the aerobics instructor. Ryan wondered if Foster knew that a university had bought the rights to their patents.

The way that mathematical symmetry appears in nature is as elegant and beautiful a thing as there is in the universe." Professor Emmy Nutter loved teaching the first term of senior-level quantum physics. Thirty of the University of California's finest faced her in an auditorium with a capacity for three hundred.

"We're going to take our time with this derivation, okay? I want you to feel this. It's what art students feel when they study Renoir, what music students feel the first time they play Brahms, what computer science students feel when they learn—I don't know—queuing theory?" Emmy smiled, giving the class permission to laugh. Turning back to the board, she tossed her long wavy hair out of her eyes. Her hair was currently brown with blonde streaks. She'd been dyeing it different colors since she was ten and wasn't sure what its natural color might be—blonde like her mother's, brown like her father's, or black like her brother's.

She drew symbols on the whiteboard with a black pen, symbols in a language as arcane to most people as druidical runes, but this really was the language of nature. It was this mathematical purity that had drawn Emmy to physics.

"We start with a general wave function." She scribbled a Greek letter on the whiteboard. "Let this symbol describe the evolution of a system in space and time. It could be a hydrogen atom, a black hole, the mold growing on your roommate's pillow, anything you want. Now watch, multiply it by this function of time." She turned back to face her class. Two young men, Mike and Rob, sat in the front row, overachieving A-students wearing Society of Physics Students sweatshirts with an image of Einstein and the caption "I'd have written this in four dimensions, but I didn't have the space-time." To Emmy's left, Tran, a thin, pale Asian man in a pressed Oxford shirt with a razor-sharp part in his hair, stared back. A month ago Tran had been tentative, afraid to demonstrate ignorance. Now, when he had a question, he blurted it out as a challenge without even raising his hand. Lori, the only female student, sat ten rows back in the center of a cluster of young men. Lori disappointed Emmy. No stranger to being the only woman in a room of men, she hoped Lori would grow into a scientist. Instead, she sat there playing soap opera games with her boyfriends.

Emmy said, "The function of time resets the clock. That's all. You can think of it like daylight savings time. Can you think of a reason that the system should behave differently by resetting the clock?" She watched the class, encouraging them with a smile here, a little nod there.

Mike and Rob whispered to each other.

Emmy turned back to the board. "Let's see what happens when we apply the principle of least action—remember from last year? The universe is lazy. In going from one state to another, a system takes the easiest way possible. Balls roll downhill, frat boys barf at parties, stars cool as they expand."

Mike and Rob nodded. Lori stared at her notes, pencil poised, and Tran pulled a second notebook from his briefcase.

Emmy wove calculus and algebra across three whiteboards. Most of the students copied it to their notes verbatim, but a few raced her to the result. Finally, the symbols boiled down to a compact equation.

This was it.

She could feel her students' minds working. A wave of affection welled up. She spoke softly so that they had to strain to hear. "Consider *how* everything simplifies."

"Whoa," Mike mumbled. "Conservation of energy?"

Emmy danced up on her tiptoes and clapped. Mike's eyes flashed understanding. She wanted to hug him. "You've just accomplished one of the most noble goals of humanity. You *derived* the first law of thermodynamics: energy is neither created nor destroyed, it merely changes form."

She waited, staring at Tran. He took a little longer than the others, but when comprehension came to him, it was so complete that he could reformulate and expand a theory in ways that few others could. She skipped across the room to the first symbols she'd written. "We've related the single most fundamental law of nature directly to the way that time passes."

Tran's brow furrowed and he scribbled furiously. Rob leaned over to Mike and whispered. Across the room, some of the students flipped through their notes, some stared intently, and one read a newspaper.

Finally, Tran raised his hand. Tran hadn't raised his hand in a month. Emmy held her arms out to him. He said, "Dr. Nutter, does this mean that it's not energy that's special, but time?"

Emmy felt the familiar thrill, the reason she taught. He got it. She scanned her kids, waiting for them to look up. "Yes, the laws of nature are not dictated by the matter that fills the universe, but by the geometry of space and time." She leaned against the center of the whiteboard and spread out her arms. "Look what we did: we're just a bunch of organic matter, but we proved—*proved!*—that the law of conservation of energy, that the total energy in a system is fixed, is a direct consequence of the fact that if we do an experiment on Tuesday, we'll get the same results on Thursday, or Saturday, or next year."

Emmy bounced up and down. "This special relationship between energy and time is a mathematical symmetry. Energy and time are like mathematical reflections of each other. Any questions?" She made eye contact with every student.

Tran interrupted. "Does this mean that for every mathematical symmetry there is also a fundamental law of nature?"

Emmy wondered if you could pass out from joy.

Mike whispered, "Wow."

In full lecture form, she said, "Let me give you an example where it doesn't work—you're going to love this." She erased a section of whiteboard and drew a stick figure looking at itself in a mirror. "What do you see when you look in a mirror?"

Tran said, "Your reflection with left and right reversed."

"Exactly. Switching left and right is a symmetry transformation. If we were to study the mirror image of the universe, which amounts to switching the positive and negative *x*-axes, would anything change? If not, then there is an unbroken symmetry, and for every unbroken symmetry, there is a corresponding law of nature.

"Think of time as a line, one dimension stretching from past to future. That the geometry of time itself is the same anywhere on that line leads to the law of conservation of energy." She walked up the aisle and leaned toward Lori as if to share a secret. "Our universe is symmetric between the past and future, but it's *not* symmetric under a switch of right and left. If it were, there might be equal amounts of matter and antimatter. Trying to understand how this works is the point of my research across the bay at the Stanford Linear Accelerator Center—SLAC."

The clock ticked to 10:50. The student in the top row tossed aside his newspaper and walked out of the room. The other students packed their notebooks and laptops into their backpacks.

Fifteen minutes later, Emmy was in her office on the hill over the Cal campus at Lawrence Berkeley Lab. She had three offices around the Bay Area; this one, where she spent most of her time, one in the physics department on campus that she only visited to hold office hours, and one at SLAC. She set her notes between the latest edition of *Physical Review Letters*, the premier research journal, and a prototype circuit board and saw her phone's message light blinking.

She picked up the phone and punched in her PIN. The message was from her brother, Dodge. She could guess that he'd called for a favor. Dodge was almost fifteen years older than Emmy and somewhat of a mystery to her. Though he had doted on her since the day she was born, her parents always tried to keep them separate. She was aware that he'd had some trouble with the law but didn't know any of the details. Dodge would only joke about it when asked. He once told her that he considered suicide every day, that everyone should consider it, and that most people ought to act on it. He was a weird guy, all right, with that gun out on his desk. He was always up to some ridiculous, though mostly harmless, plot to generate wealth. She'd been caught in her share of his schemes over the years, but at thirty-four she thought she'd matured beyond his reach.

Dodge answered on the first ring and didn't waste time with pleasantries. "Can you read a couple of patents for me?"

Instead of replying, she sipped her coffee and relaxed at her desk. She was pleased to hear his voice but knew better than to encourage him.

After a few seconds, Dodge launched into the sad story of his new tenant: a good guy but down on his luck, a talented engineer burned by his employer who had a couple of inventions whose rights had been purchased by a university.

When he finished, she said, "So you conned this poor guy into giving you a piece of the action on patents that he doesn't even own." She dropped down a few octaves when she said "a piece of the action," mimicking her brother.

"The contract hasn't been written that doesn't have a hole that I can't find," Dodge said. "Between the four winds of menace, fraud, undue influence, and mistake, I'll find a way to get a piece of the action." He went up an octave to mock her. "It's a great case." Then his voice took a different turn, a turn that she'd heard before and should have recognized. "Especially if I can get it in front of a jury."

"What university bought them?"

"Now I've got you." Dodge chuckled. "See, that's the weirdest thing about it—Evangelical Word University, somewhere in Texas."

"Evangelical Word University? Never heard of it. Okay, Dodge, I have real work to do..."

"Five minutes, that's all I want. A quick look at these patents, no more."

Emmy groaned but brought up a web browser and surfed to the patent office web page. Dodge told her the patent numbers. She downloaded the text and started skimming. "Dodge I'm not an engineer, I don't know what this—wait a minute. This is kind of interesting. No." She started to giggle. In contrast to her brother's raspy chuckle, Emmy's rang with the song of a schoolgirl, but the overall effect, mixed with her sharp blue eyes and accompanied by just the wisp of a smile, conveyed the same sense of ironic amusement. "Okay, here's the giveaway line: realization of the symmetric conditions of the Big Bang allow energy release through vacuum fluctuations." She stopped laughing. "Please tell me this is a bad joke."

Dodge said, “Why would anyone invest in them?”

“Remember cold fusion?”

“What about it?”

“It was totally debunked over fifteen years ago, but people still invest in it.” The memory of the cold fusion debacle brought a flush of embarrassment. She had been a first-year graduate student at Caltech when Pons and Fleischman announced their results: unlimited cheap energy produced by nuclear fusion at room temperature on a tabletop. At that point in her career, she had known enough to understand how it might work but hadn’t yet developed the scientific acumen to question the important details. In the excitement, she designed an experiment to reproduce the results. Then she manipulated a fellow graduate student into putting her on the Physics Department Colloquium agenda. She proposed her experiment with unvarnished naïve confidence to the entire department. A Nobel laureate professor, obviously impatient, had interrupted her: “Why have you no gamma-ray detectors?” She would never forget standing in front of all those distinguished men floundering for an answer. She had missed the point. And it was the only point that mattered: nuclear fusion is characterized by emission of gamma rays, essentially ultra-ultraviolet light. No gamma rays meant no fusion. It was the most embarrassing moment of her life. After the colloquium, he had come to her and said, “The beauty of physics is that you can understand it yourself. You don’t need faith in anything, but you have to think it all the way through.”

Emmy dispelled the memory by focusing on the patent. “These guys were totally clever. This one on energy creation—the name alone should have set off alarms at the patent office. I like the other one better, it’s subtle.” She took her time reading through the preferred embodiment section of the patent disclosure. “In a way, it’s brilliant. If I’d read it without seeing the energy creation one first…it's a delightful idea for a neural network." Then she laughed—a real laugh, not her version of the family chortle. "Except for this one line: 'Further sentience is created through conception of another intelligence, for example, by insemination of one network, by said original network, resulting in, as detailed below, a proliferation of intelligences, each possessing the ability to choose with progressively greater liberty.' I've heard about engineers toying with the patent office like this."

"But why a university?"

"Dodge, please call me sometime when you aren't scheming, okay? Please?"

"Will you testify as an expert witness if I go to court?"

He said it with that tone again, and this time Emmy noticed, but instead of amplifying her suspicion, she was distracted by the image of herself in court teaching the legal system that science is beyond political interpretation. "If you get that far, I'll testify—for sure. But listen, Dodge, no meetings in smoke-filled rooms. I will only participate to prevent those charlatans from deceiving the scientifically illiterate." She paused for a second to make sure he was listening and then spoke loud and clear: "Everything I say has to be public. Do you understand?"

Dodge liked to think of himself as a card shark, and what he liked best in life was to stack the deck. The trick was to assure that nothing, no change, no nuance, not the slightest fluctuation, occurred without his knowledge, therefore allowing him to react with the appropriate check or bet. Over the years, he'd played lots of hands; not only had he developed a wide network of associates, he was an expert at developing new sources of information.

He made calls to Evangelical Word University until he found something that resembled the science and engineering department. A woman with a thick Texas twang answered. Dodge sensed that this woman, Mabel Watson, wore a constant nervous smile. When he asked about the patents, she directed him to a company called Creation Energy. She gave him the number and laughed as she hung up. Dodge dialed it, and the same woman answered the phone—still laughing. Creation Energy wasn't just related to Evangelical Word University, it was wholly owned and operated right there in the Department of Earthly Science.

Dodge asked about investment opportunities, and she gave him the phone number of the chief financial officer, a guy named Blair Keene. He thanked her but then, instead of hanging up, cultivated her as an informant. The first step was to ask her about the weather. She went on a long boring trek along the lines of "if you don't like the weather 'roun' here, jus' wait ten minutes." Then he got her talking about family and found out she had a son who was some kind of modern cowboy on a ranch between San Antonio and Austin.

Dodge liked the idea of hiring some muscle in the neighborhood, so he told her a lie about being interested in buying a West Texas ranch. He said that he needed a consultant and asked if her son might help. Dodge tried not to chuckle as she gave him her son's contact information; his name was Dale Watson.

Since the cards were hot, he went with the direct approach. Seeing as he was "investing down there," he told her that he'd need some information periodically. She took the hint literally and spewed university gossip covering rumors from the chancellor to the janitor. It took a good hour, but he learned that she was Foster Reed's secretary—Dodge skimmed his notes to double-check the name of Ryan McNear's old pal. He managed to resist laughing at that tidbit.

When she finally let him off the phone, he contacted her son, Dale, found out where he lived, asked some irrelevant questions, and sent him fifty bucks to establish that he was on the payroll. A phone call to an old associate in Houston returned more information on the chief financial officer, Blair Keene: a trial attorney who dumped money into right-wing Christian causes and was well connected in local government, especially high-tech regulation—i.e., the patent office.

Monitoring the company website turned out to be the easiest way to watch their progress. When something changed he'd call Mabel, flirt with her a little, listen, take notes, and then, after hanging up, send her a fifty.

His plan required two simple steps: wait until Creation Energy had attracted enough investment that it would be worthwhile to sue, and cultivate Ryan's sense of greed and injustice to a frothy anger. Dodge rubbed his hands together, yearning for the day that Ryan would storm into his office demanding that they "sue the bastards."

The excitement of escaping arrest in Texas, then zipping across the country and landing in Northern California's wine country, left a reality hangover. Ryan was farther from his son than ever, and as hard as he tried to deny it, he even caught himself missing Tammi—the poison he'd fallen for in his weakest moment.

With the sun rising over the valley, Ryan booted up his tired old PC and put the kettle on. He was stirring sugar into a cup of tea when Nutter House awoke to the sound of Katarina's stereo. Ryan combed through Internet job sites and listened to Katarina yelling at her mother. He had the same feeling he got on long airplane flights. Right after sitting down and buckling in, he'd wonder about the people sitting next to him, energized by the knowledge that they'd be friends by the end of the flight.

He polished off his second cup of tea, scrawled the addresses of some nearby tech companies onto a pad of paper, and headed for the door. As he started down the stairs, Katarina slid down the wide smooth banister behind him and almost bowled him over. In one seamless motion she descended the stairs, jumped out the door, and hopped onto her skateboard.

Ryan spent the day stuttering in front of impatient human resources officers. He had no answer to the first question they asked: Why have you been out of high tech for three years? When he got back to Nutter House, he surrendered to the desire to call home, what he thought of as home, anyway.

His ex-wife, Linda, answered but wouldn't let him talk to Sean. She rubbed it in pretty well too. "Sean has a better daddy now. He's finished with you, sperm donor." Then she hung up.

Over the next few weeks, he tried phoning the house at different times. If Linda answered she hung up immediately. One time her new husband answered, a man twenty years older than Linda and Ryan, and said, "Sean is fine and the three of us are very happy. Don't worry about him and please leave us alone."

Early one Sunday morning, Sean answered. Ryan said what he'd always said, "How's it goin', buddy?" and Sean said, "Buddy? You calling *me* buddy? You're no buddy—nobody to me." That Sean's voice was changing stretched the feeling of distance even farther than his words.

Ryan stopped calling. Instead, he found an old e-mail distribution list for the neighborhood. He sent a note asking if anyone would let him know how Sean was doing, kind of a desperate message, but someone actually replied. Ryan couldn't quite place the guy, whose name was Ward. He replied every week with a single-sentence report: he'd seen Sean at a church fund-raiser or getting home from a football/baseball/soccer game. It was just enough information for Ryan to feel connected.

A month after Ryan moved in, Dodge invited him down to his office for a drink. Dodge sensed that something was missing, as though he needed to call a bet to see the next card. Dodge thought Ryan was an interesting case, outwardly calm and easygoing, but he couldn't tell whether Ryan's constantly tapping fingers were nerves or excess energy. There was a difference. So he poured them each a tumbler of whiskey and then waited.

Ryan swirled his drink in one hand and tapped his fingers in time with the reverberation of music from upstairs. Dodge set his fingertips together and pretended to stare at them but kept an eye on the revolver he left out on the desk.

Obviously not realizing what he was doing, Ryan started rubbing his fingers along the short barrel. Dodge tried not to laugh. The instant that Ryan realized he was touching the gun, he jerked his fingers away. Dodge couldn't hold it any longer. His laughter finished in a cough.

He started asking questions about GoldCon, about Foster, and about the patents. Nothing triggered his intuition until he backed up and said, "Review for me how you were compensated for your patents. What did you sign? What were you paid and when? I need details."

"Well, we had to sign the standard waiver. The same thing every engineer signs when they take a job: anything you invent is the intellectual property of your employer."

"What about the money?"

"When the patents were granted, I got two checks for twenty-five hundred dollars because I'd coauthored two patents. Foster got two checks too. Get it? We split the five thousand for each patent."

"But for *submitting* the patents, you each got checks for five hundred dollars?"

"Right."

Dodge wasn't one to draw on an inside straight, but every now and then, instinct or intuition or plain stupidity encouraged him to go for it. As Ryan spoke those words, Dodge knew he'd gotten the card he wanted. "Let me get this straight: they gave each of you the full award when the patents were submitted but split the awards between you when they were granted?"

Lines formed in Ryan's brow, arcing up to the sharp widow's peak of his dark auburn wire-bristle hair. "Yeah, but it was fair enough; two authors on each, after all. We were psyched that they didn't split the submission bonus too." His forehead relaxed. "We got our boat."

"Do you remember anything—anything—in the documentation describing the patent award bonus about splitting the award for multiple authors?"

"I don't think so."

"You're not sure."

Ryan shrugged.

Dodge said, "Was there any difference between the phrasing of the bonus for submitting the patents and the phrasing of the bonus for when the patents were granted?"

Ryan shook his head. "No. I'm sure of that. It definitely said the same thing for submitting as it did for granting."

"Did you get the patent-submission bonus before you got the patent-granted bonus?"

"Yeah, it took over a year for the patents to go through."

Dodge leaned back in his chair. Glee filled his stomach. If he played it right, there would be a quick settlement with just enough rancor to make it sporting. Nice.

Dodge said, "I don't suppose you still have that document." Ryan shook his head. Dodge continued, "They paid you in full for both patent submissions but only gave you half when they were granted. In legal terms, by giving you the full amount for the submission they defined an *implied contract*. The implied contract guaranteed you each the full amount when the patents were granted. They didn't deliver. Bingo. Fraud marries mistake and gives birth to an implied contract. That patent rights waiver you signed is out the window. You still have rights to those patents. God, I love this."

Ryan said, "What difference does it make?"

"Just leave it to me."

Dodge flicked his wrist at Ryan, waving him out of the office.

"You think I have a case?"

"I think I'm monitoring my investments. Now go away. I have work to do."

"What are you going to do?"

"I'm going to ask you to walk out that door."

"Don't they have to develop the patents and make a profit before my interest has any value?"

Dodge picked up the revolver. "Walk out that door or I am going to shoot you."

Ryan walked upstairs to his apartment shaking his head. Every interaction with Dodge was more complicated than the previous. For Ryan, the discussion had brought back bad memories. Last he had heard, Foster Reed was a graduate student at some podunk school in West Texas.

Ryan did a web search on Foster's name, and it brought up Evangelical Word University, the place that bought rights to the patents from GoldCon. Two clicks later, he was staring at a list of the EWU Department of Earthly Science faculty. There he was: Foster Reed, PhD, Associate Professor of Physics and Cosmology. Along with his research interests—Creation-based energy generation and cosmology—it listed his e-mail address and phone number.

Ryan picked up the phone and dialed. Everything in this house, everything associated with Dodge, had to have some twist to it. Ryan hadn't used a phone with a dial since his grandma died.

A woman with a vibrant Texas twang answered, "Dr. Reed's office." He had his own secretary? Not bad.

Ryan asked for Foster, told the lady he was an old friend, and sat on hold for a few seconds. There was a clicking sound, and then a familiar voice said, "Ryan?" There was another click on the line. "Ryan, oh my! Where are you, man? What are you doing?"

Ryan leaned back and grinned. Foster. The guy was always trying to sound cool but could never pull it off. The crazy thing was that, down deep, Foster wasn't nearly as uptight as he seemed, and when you least expected it, he'd come up with an idea that would totally blow you away. Plus, he was loyal. Hound-dog loyal.

"Hey man, what kind of goofball school would make you a professor?"

"Ryan, I found it. It's like I told you—we got laid off for a reason. I followed the path and here I am, a physics professor at the coolest, most righteous university in the world." Foster rambled on about his wonderful wife, career, and religion. Ryan recognized jealousy and fought it by picturing his own path, the sun setting behind the Golden Gate.

Foster's voice turned serious. "Ryan, are things getting better? Do you need help?"

"Things are starting to come together. I landed in California last month."

"Why California?"

Ryan thought it was obvious—what better place to jump back on the high-tech gravy train—but couldn't resist telling the more immediate truth. "Runnin' from the law."

Foster laughed. "Hold it, what're you up to? Hacking code in Silicon Valley?"

"Well, I just got here, but that's the idea. Actually, I'm a couple of hours north of Silicon Valley in the wine country—but the big question is, what are you doing, Professor?"

"Being the luckiest guy in the world," Foster said. "After we got laid off, I came here to EWU and did my PhD in physics. I'm the world's leading expert on the cosmology of Creation—the university published my dissertation as a book; you can download it from the website." He waited a second before continuing, as though debating whether or not to fill Ryan in. "Ryan, I made an important discovery. Those two patents we did the first day at GoldCon fit together like a divine jigsaw puzzle. It's amazing. It can save humanity. We can generate essentially free energy. No greenhouse gases and no waste. But when I say it can save humanity I mean that it can save our souls. By developing this technology, we'll *prove* that God created man and earth and that there is eternal life. We're building the power generator right now."

Foster had always been both ridiculously enthusiastic about his work and a man of tremendous faith. The enthusiasm had always infected Ryan, but right now Ryan was uncomfortable. Minutes before, he had watched Dodge rub his hands together like a cartoon villain. Ryan felt like a spy. "Yeah, I heard that a university bought the rights to those patents—that's why I called. Do you really think that—"

"I believe it to the very core of my spirit. Look, I spent the last few years studying relativistic quantum field theory. It's amazing how our two patents fit together."

Typical Foster: the enthusiasm freight train blew right by Ryan's admission that he knew something was cooking. He tried to spell it out. "Do we have any rights to those patents?"

"Rights? What do you mean?" Ryan thought he heard a suspicious edge in Foster's voice.

"That's sort of why I called. I signed this lease and—"

Foster made his confused *tsk* sound and said, "No, we have no rights—they're owned by the university. We both signed the patent rights waiver, remember?"

"Yeah, I know, it's just that I have this crazy landlord and—"

"But you know what?" Foster's confusion converted back to enthusiasm. "We're going to need a software director. Funding is kind of short right now, but we're getting calls from investors all the time."

"I just got here, signed a lease." Part of him wanted to level with Foster and admit that he couldn't go back to Texas because he'd go to jail, but pride got in the way. "I need to stand on my own two, you know?"

"This is the opportunity of a lifetime."

"Yeah, that's what my stockbroker said when I bought WorldCom at fifty bucks a share."

They both laughed.

"Ryan, God was watching over our shoulders that day."

"Foster, listen." Ryan took a breath. "I signed a lease that gave my landlord twenty-five percent of my rights to those patents—"

"You don't have rights to them."

"I thought so too, but this guy—"

"We're going to get major funding, and I'm going to need your help." Foster paused, and Ryan could practically hear him look at his watch. "I have to go to a meeting now, but keep it in mind. This is big, Ryan. I understand that you need to prove a few things to yourself, but remember, I'll be praying for you."

"Foster, wait—my landlord thinks that—"

"Ryan, I have to go. E-mail me your address. I'll mail you my book."

It took his computer almost a full minute to bring up an e-mail window, and by the time it got there, Ryan was scrolling through the patents. He'd always felt funny about them, and now he realized why. It wasn't because he thought they were bogus—it was because he'd always had this niggling feeling that they might not be bogus.

In his office downstairs, Dodge hung up the phone. He picked up the revolver and tapped it on the gavel pad a few times.

He loved watching the cards being dealt. Two new ones: the ace, that Foster Reed thought the technology could actually be developed, could mean a lot more money; and the deuce, that Foster might offer Ryan a job, could blow the whole scam.

His sister, Emmy, was the wild card.

He twirled the pistol on his finger like a gunslinger. "Timing. Timing and patience. Wait until these bozos smell cash, show them the wild card, let them sweat, and then pull the trigger while the pot is full.

"Bang."

Professor Foster Reed waited backstage, back-sanctuary really. This was the sixth huge church he'd been invited to. The ten-thousand-strong Greatest Good Christian Center in Alexandria, Virginia, had video screens showing the preacher from every angle, spotlights, and an acoustically tuned ceiling. Foster, like a paladin adjusting his armor before battle, tightened his tie and made sure his shirt was tucked in and his coat properly buttoned. The internal battle between faith in God and doubt in himself was a sure sign that he would be introduced soon. Every congregation he'd visited had been thrilled to welcome him, Foster Reed, a scientist defending Genesis on the atheists' turf, but that initial excitement always dissolved into boredom, if not contempt, by the time he finished. At home, up in Evangelical Word University's ivory tower, this sermon, more like a lecture really, seemed guaranteed to deliver the support he would need when the battle grew pitched.

The battle itself, though—that was a different problem. The project could survive but couldn't move forward without substantial financial support. He knew better than to doubt that the right support would arrive at the right time. Not the time he thought was right, but at the time God made right. He would wait. Through Foster's entire life, every seeming coincidence had pushed him farther along this path. It was this knowledge, so certain in his heart, that impaled him with shame when self-doubt tried to possess him.

The preacher, a man in his sixties with big eyes and a bigger smile, spoke softly. “We are under attack.” His voice got louder with each word. “The courts tear down the commandments, evolutionists and homosexuals demean the Bible, and the humanists silence prayer in the schools you pay for.” He paused between sentences to let the audience know it was time to yell a “Hallelujah!” or an “Amen!” And when that crowd responded, it was probably loud enough to be heard clear to Washington, DC. Foster hoped so, anyway.

The preacher paused, scanning every row of the stadium, and then spoke softly. “Today, I present to you the man who will return the Word of God to science…”

The word *science* brought Foster to his feet.

A few scattered *Amens* echoed up to the stage. “…Professor Foster Reed.” The preacher turned to face Foster and applauded.

The congregation joined in applause as Foster walked out. He shook hands with the preacher and, though he considered applause inappropriate in God’s House, beamed at the congregation. One woman who had sung loud enough for Foster to make out her voice among the thousands, looked content but determined, her jaw clenched so that her lips made a horizontal line. In a row behind her, a black man with a shaved head wearing a brown three-piece suit was scowling.

He waited for the woman to make eye contact. A thin older gentleman in the front row wearing a bow tie but looking as though he’d be more comfortable in coveralls returned a welcoming smile. Foster switched on the headset microphone. The lights, too bright to see past the first dozen rows, warmed his skin to a righteous glow. He took his time, glanced at his notes, and absorbed the congregation's faith. He felt his jaw tighten and the muscles down his back grow rigid. The inspiration, like everything else in his life, was there, not when he wanted it but when he needed it.

"Several years ago, when I was an engineer at a high-tech company, God guided me to a discovery. Like Paul on the road to Damascus, I was confused…" He told the story of the day he and Ryan had written the patent submissions, trying to impart his belief that they'd been guided by the Lord that day—but the thin old man's eyes narrowed as though he were dozing off, the woman looked past him into the sanctuary, and the black man shook his head.

Foster stopped. It just wasn't working. He fought a feeling of contempt for these people—they should embrace science, but instead, science offended them. He looked through his notes. The woman finally looked back at him, but she wasn't happy. The black man snickered and looked away.

In that instant, Foster felt alone, a foreign feeling that contradicted his faith. He hadn't felt this way since he was a child. Back in first grade he'd gotten lost during a field trip to a museum. He'd been meandering along, and when he turned around, no one was there. He went back the way he'd come but took a wrong turn and ended up alone in a huge room of gothic portraits. With all those strange faces staring down at him, he started to cry. Staring at the floor, he moped to another room and nearly walked into a wall. There, in front of him, as though greeting him personally, was a painting with a boy about his age being guided by two people in robes. As he sat in front of that painting, his fear and loneliness were replaced by warmth and strength. He talked to the boy in the painting, and when he asked the boy a question, the answer came to him. In that presence he could feel no loneliness. Finally, his classmates entered the room. His teacher, surprised that she'd found him before realizing he had been missing, read the title, *Jesus Found in the Temple*, and told him it was painted by a man named Tissot.

Foster fumbled his notes. The pages fluttered around the stage, and he staggered about trying to collect them. Then he caught himself. On one knee with the pages a mess in his hand, the image of Jesus in that painting came back to him. As though something were lifting him up, he stood. The sheets of paper scattered about the stage, and he said one word: "Science."

He waited.

The black man turned away and the woman scowled.

This time he yelled: "Science!"

A few muffled hems and haws echoed in response.

"Why don't we embrace science? Why can't you embrace science?"

The black man responded in a full-volume baritone, "Because it violates the Word."

Foster dropped the pages still in his hand and stepped to the edge of the stage. "Science is the ultimate expression of God's work. It can't violate the Word." The room went silent. "He gave us minds so that we could understand. The intellectual thieves of the scientific establishment stole science from us. They reject God, and in response we reject science." He paced across the stage. "Do you believe in the Big Bang?"

The parish chanted, "No."

Foster said, "The Bible is infallible, but it leaves out a lot of detail. My lab is filling in those details. The Big Bang is a fine theory, but it's not finished." Foster reached out. "When it's all said and done, science will verify everything in the Bible. There can be no contradictions."

Scattered voices responded, "Amen."

He looked down and shuffled his feet. "Those scientists, they don't believe." Then he looked up and spoke with conviction. "But they will.

"That day in that Dallas laboratory, the Lord guided me to the key—the key that will unlock the glory of God as written in the laws of nature. In the coming months, you'll hear from both sides in the battle between good and evil, the moral and the amoral, between faith and atheism. As I bring this new discovery into the world and demonstrate how God acts in the material world, as I submit proof to the faithless, we will face great opposition. I will be challenged and we will face doubt, but our faith must guide us. You know this to be true. As God grants us His power in a culture that has been ruled by the cold, sterile, faithless tools of science for the last century, that world will rise against us, and we must be prepared."

Foster paused, crossed his arms, and raised his head so that he spoke to the rafters. "I will fight for you, for God, for Jesus." Then he dropped his gaze straight into the lights and panned across the crowd. "But I can't do it alone. I'll call on you to fight this battle, this culture war. Driving the faithless out of our institutions takes more than one man, however well armed. When the entrenched atheists in the scientific establishment raise doubt, I'll call on you. I'll rely on you. Raising the power of the Lord from the forces of nature will not be easy. It will not be a spectator sport."

He leveled his right arm and pointed at the crowd. "I need you at my side. Can I count on you?"

The audience responded with scattered responses of "Yes," "Amen," and "Hallelujah."

"You can count on me," Foster bellowed. "Can I count on you?"

It generated a louder response: "You can count on me."

He pointed in another direction. "Can I count on you?" And another. "Can I count on you?" Each iteration generated a louder, more coherent response: "You can count on me!"

He repeated the process until he'd indicated every section of the stadium and then stepped off the stage with the entire auditorium in perfect synch, chanting, "You can count on me!"

The ad-lib lecture took half the time of the one he'd prepared, and as he left the stage, he felt a rush like none he'd felt before. He'd won them over. Ten thousand people in fervent support, whether for letters to Congress, phone calls to newspapers, or e-mails to TV shows, His troops were lining up for battle.

An hour later, exhausted but triumphant, a question danced into his mind. He'd given that lecture half a dozen times, so why did it finally come out the way he'd wanted today? He chuckled to himself, certain that the answer would come soon.

On a table in the church bookstore, Foster set out copies of his book, *The Cosmology of Creation*. The black man from the audience brought him a cup of coffee and bought a signed copy. The woman asked, "What is it like to discover what He did?"

After the congregation reassembled, as Foster packed up the remaining books, a trio of men approached. One of them, in a solid black suit, pitched in to help with the books. Another in pinstripes, who looked like a businessman, offered Foster an outstretched hand. "What a terrific story, Dr. Reed. As an engineer, a businessman, and a Christian, I had a difficult time restraining my applause until you were finished."

Foster smiled, not at the introduction or compliment, but at the recognition of why he'd gotten the lecture right today. He accepted the man's hand and looked him in the eye.

The man put his other arm on Foster's shoulder as though they were fraternity brothers. "My name is Bill Smythe. I'm with America's largest engineering contractor. I'm sure you're familiar with National Engineering Group, NEG, and, like I said, you inspired me."

Foster didn't let go of the man's hand until they made eye contact. Smythe's eyes were gray, and Foster couldn't help but think they were empty. Still, Foster knew better than to question moments like these. He let go of the man's hand and reached down for his briefcase. One of the hinges strained under the pressure of Foster's notebooks and files. Bill Smythe reached it first, but he didn't lift it carefully, and that hinge popped. Foster managed to clamp the sides shut before everything fell out. Once his briefcase was under control, he asked Smythe if he'd discussed investing with Blair Keene.

"I talked to Blair last week. We've got a team of engineers combing through your book. I'm based here in Washington. Blair suggested I come out today."

Foster smiled on the man, recognizing that he was a weapon in God's war, not a soldier. If NEG invested in Creation Energy, nothing could stop them. "A team of engineers? I'd be happy to extend my trip to address any technical questions."

Smythe said, "There are a few hurdles that Keene and I need to jump, but let me tell you this: we think there is synergy between NEG and Creation Energy that can make America safer, stronger, and more righteous."

Smythe squeezed Foster's shoulder and motioned to the man who'd helped with Foster's briefcase. "This is Steven Jones, the project leader for our Alternative Energy Group. He'll be your NEG liaison in the development of Creation Energy."

Foster took the man's hand. In a navy blue blazer, khaki pants, and a black polo shirt with the NEG logo, Jones looked like an engineer, a company man. Jones gave him a firm handshake.

"Do you have time to get lunch?" Jones said. "I have some questions about the project, the intellectual property, and the development plan." Foster noticed that the man had a copy of *The Cosmology of Creation* in his other hand. He also noticed that the copy looked fresh from the printer. In the face of all this enthusiasm, the near-commitment of a huge financial backer, Foster would have preferred to see a thoroughly dog-eared copy.

Smythe said, "Of course you have time. Let's get a nice meal, and you two can talk shop." He applied enough pressure to Foster's shoulder to encourage him to step toward the door but not so much that Foster felt coerced.

The first man held the door open. In addition to the black suit, he was wearing a wire in his ear and a pair of sunglasses that were straight from the movie *Men in Black*.

True to his word, Ryan made rent on the third month. He'd scored a six-month contract as a technician at a big fiber-optics company just across the river, FiberSpec Communications. When Ryan handed him the check, Dodge said, "You should be working off the books." Ryan didn't understand the reference and didn't want to start a conversation with Dodge, so he didn't ask.

He took on any extra work he could find too. He filled in at the Tea Café or Copperfield's Bookstore when someone called in sick, and he did odd jobs for Dodge. Each month, he paid rent, kept $200 to live on, and sent the rest to Linda—barely a third of his child support payment but hopefully enough to show he was trying.

In those first three months, Ryan still hadn't seen Katarina's mother. Other than a few rapidly shut doors, the only sign that she existed at all was the sound of Katarina arguing with her. Ryan was sympathetic, though; it had taken his mother five years to recover from his father's death. Of course, Ryan had had Grandma and his sisters to fill the gap.

Katarina only had Dodge. Yikes.

When Ryan got home from work, Katarina was usually sitting on that ridiculous red velvet couch watching TV in Dodge's living room. Ryan would sit at the other end of the couch, and after a few weeks, the two of them were exchanging wisecracks about the quality of the music videos and skateboard competitions that Katarina watched. It brought Ryan up to speed on pop music, and he learned more about extreme skateboarding than he thought there was to know. That part was scary; Katarina was bound to try those stunts. That the kid had no boundaries made him angry with her mother. He knew what his grandma would say; he could hear her voice. "We mustn't waste our time on the dead."

In December, Dodge put a huge plastic Christmas tree topped with a Star of David in the foyer and set gift boxes wrapped in red, green, and blue beneath it. Ryan was surprised that Dodge would bother. Katarina said, "He's pretending to be a human being. Appropriately, all the gift boxes are empty, like the man's soul."

Ryan pointed at one of the boxes. Its reindeer wrapping paper made it stand out. "What about that one?"

Katarina picked it up and looked at the tag: "For Katarina, From Ryan." She looked at him with mock distrust. "It's not going to blow up, is it?"

Then she tore it open and found a skating helmet and wrist guards. Ryan could tell by the way she looked at them and then back at him that she appreciated the gesture, but she didn't say "thank you." Ryan figured that she didn't know any better.

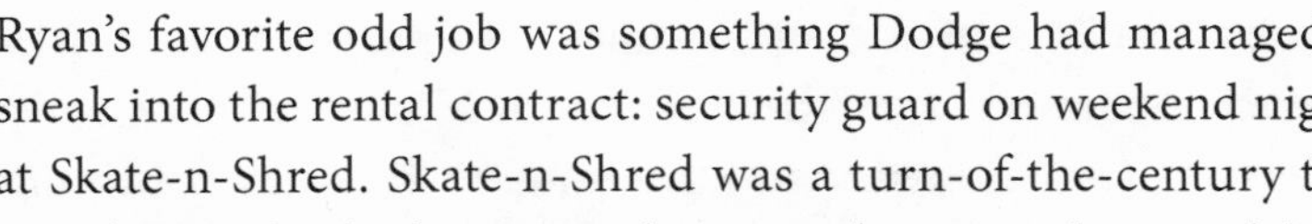

Ryan's favorite odd job was something Dodge had managed to sneak into the rental contract: security guard on weekend nights at Skate-n-Shred. Skate-n-Shred was a turn-of-the-century theater that Dodge had converted to a combination skate park/concert venue catering to Petaluma's teenage population. Two blocks down the hill from Nutter House, the building occupied the corner of a busy street a block from the boulevard. Katarina spent most of her waking hours there.

Ryan felt more like Margaret Mead in New Guinea than a security guard. He enjoyed getting to know the kids. Mostly, though, he felt responsible to watch out for Katarina. Skate-n-Shred wasn't the safest place in town for a twelve-year-old girl with no curfew.

On a cool, dry Friday night, he passed a few kids out front smoking cigarettes, their skateboards leaning against the wall. One wore a "Surf 707" hoodie, another had on a patch-covered denim jacket, and a few sat on a bench strumming guitars. Inside, the walls of the lobby were covered in graffiti of varying levels of artistic promise. Dodge left a box of markers, some acrylic paints, and brushes to encourage his patrons to release their creative angst. To him, it was a device to convince parents and police officers that Skate-n-Shred served a public purpose.

Katarina stood on an old stained couch working on a mural. Her black skirt was decorated with Celtic knots along the hem and a crucifix on the seam in what could have been the same paint she was using. A smiling black dragon, smoke shooting from its nostrils and a few random flames leaking between its fangs, looked like it was jumping out of the wall and over the couch.

Ryan sat on the sofa's armrest. "Whatcha doin'?"

"Painting death."

He stared at the painting for a second. The dragon only looked black at a glance. Colors swirled into its skin and the spiny structure of its neck, with shades of purple on its belly. She'd included shadows that made it look three-dimensional. It was a happy-looking dragon.

He said, "Shouldn't death look more, um, dead?"

"No." Katarina stepped up on the back of the couch and brushed white paint above the dragon, covering the wall's olive drab up and onto the ceiling.

On the wall directly across the lobby, a much larger dragon looked back at the little smiling dragon. The small one was vivid and sharp. The larger was dun brown and mottled. "Did you paint that one too?"

"Uh-huh."

He went across the room and looked closely at the larger dragon. The mottles were from the olive drab of the wall leaking through. Where the little dragon sparkled, its layers of acrylic reflecting the fluorescent light, the big dragon's flat latex absorbed the light. A few wisps of smoke curled straight up from the big, old-looking shadow of a dragon. "This guy looks pretty beaten down."

"He's not *beaten down*," she snapped. "He's doing the best that he can."

"Oh." Ryan noticed that the little dragon's eyes, complete with little stars in their irises twinkling like emeralds—the same color as Katarina's eyes—were aimed directly at the old dragon, but the old dragon was looking up at the ceiling.

"If you were dead, you'd look beaten down too."

"Sorry, Katarina." Ryan went back to the couch. "What do I know from art?"

Reaching her brush farther out on the ceiling, she lost her balance and had to step down from the couch. Ryan caught her arm, steadying her. She pushed away. "I don't need your help."

Ryan shrugged. "Sorry." He noticed that, incorporated in the dragon's breath, there were little symbols and some writing. He pointed at them and said, "What are these things?"

"These *things* are what's left over after death—would you please leave me alone?"

As he walked from the lobby to the theater, he heard Katarina mumble, "People are so fucking stupid." That she was such an ornery little wretch amused him. It reminded him of the youngest of his three sisters at that age. Ryan didn't like her saying *fuck*, though.

Inside the theater, a dozen skate rats flew up and down the ramps while a band called Broken Skeg set up on stage. As he passed, the kids held out their skate-cards. Ryan pretended to scrutinize them but gave most of his attention to whether they had their helmets strapped on and wrist guards tight.

Backstage, Broken Skeg's junior groupies, two fifteen-year-old girls wearing lots of black lace, flirted with the band's front man. Make that "front boy"—he was barely sixteen. Sitting in the center of the couch, he had his arm around one of the girls and pulled her close. She whispered in his ear and snuggled against him.

Ryan leaned over to listen. She glared at him. To the front boy, Ryan said, "Go tune a guitar or something."

The next time Ryan passed through the lobby, he noticed that Katarina had painted the ceiling white with gray puffy edges from one end of the room to the other, connecting the two dragons—there were more of the little symbols and words, like tiny graffiti, embedded in the clouds. He looked around for her, but it was crowded and she was small.

Around eleven o'clock, Ryan wandered through the alley in back. Three teenagers, two older boys and one smaller kid, huddled behind the Dumpster in the shadows of the security lights.

One of the boys abruptly threw his smoke into the gutter. He wore a black leather vest over a torn T-shirt and had a spiked collar around his neck.

Ryan sniffed the air and groaned. "I really wish you'd get stoned someplace else." Ryan recognized one of the two bigger kids. Alex, the ultimate poseur; he made the other kids call him The Ace, and the force of his personality was strong enough to pull it off.

The smaller kid's face was turned away, but Ryan recognized the skateboard—it was nearly as long as she was tall.

"Katarina?"

She started to take off.

"Wait up—Katarina!"

She stopped and turned around, her face aimed at the ground between them, but her eyes turned up at him. Ryan knew adolescent-surly when he saw it. She kicked her skate up to her hand. "What?"

His impulse was to snap at her for hanging out with a bunch of losers, but he'd already pissed her off once that night. He searched for something to say. It was too late for her to be out, but she wouldn't listen if he told her to go home. He got an idea. Raising a hand to his head and squinting, he said, "Could you do me a huge favor?"

She took a step toward him.

He lowered himself to the curb and said, "Major sinus headache."

"Are you okay?" Her eyes widened. "My dad used to get headaches."

"It's just allergies, no big deal—I mean, they suck, but—could you go up to the house and get my medicine?"

"Give me your keys."

"What?"

"To get your medicine, McDoofus."

"Oh yeah." Ryan handed her the keys to his apartment and directed her to the shoe box in his bathroom. "Thanks, Katarina. Sorry I didn't get your painting—I like it, though, even so."

She jumped on her skateboard and took off. She wasn't wearing her helmet.

Ryan resumed his circuit. As he walked toward the lobby, he saw the lady on the bicycle again. The way her hair and skirt floated behind made her look like a witch on a broom. He caught her eye the instant a streetlight illuminated her. Then, as if making eye contact was somehow forbidden, she rode away.

"McNear!" Dodge yelled from the lobby. "Get in here! Some punk-ass motherfucker is stage diving—get him out of my theater!"

Fifteen minutes later, Ryan dragged a drunk teenage boy outside, encouraged him to hand over his cell phone, found "mom" in his contacts, and called her to come pick him up. On his way back in, Dodge tossed him his medicine. Ryan asked, "Where's Katarina?"

Without looking up, Dodge said, "Not in here."

Ryan took a quick patrol through the alley and around the block. The boy who called himself The Ace sat on the curb smoking. Ryan asked if he'd seen Katarina. He answered by flicking his cigarette into a Dumpster.

Ryan said, "Alex, leave her alone."

He scowled. "Chill, dude, I don't know who you're talkin' about."

Ryan took a closer look around the alley, the fire escape, and the parking lot. Katarina must have gone home.

An hour later, when Ryan finally headed up the hill, a crescent moon was peeking from behind a long, narrow cloud. At the door, he realized Katarina hadn't returned his keys. It was locked. He knocked a few times but didn't expect much. There was no doorbell, and the door was too thick to generate enough resonance for knocking to be heard upstairs. Besides, Ryan didn't want to wake anyone up.

He looked around for an open window and went around back, but that door was locked too. On the second floor, Katarina's light was on. He threw some pebbles up, and a minute later she stuck her head out.

"Could you let me in?"

She came downstairs, sock-footed and in a dirty nightshirt, and opened the door.

"Do you have my keys?"

"The woman said she'd give them to you."

"Your mom?"

"Yeah."

They walked inside together. "Really? I've never actually seen her…"

Katarina stopped at the foot of the stairs with a confused look. "You have to." Turning up the stairs she added, "And if you haven't yet, be afraid. Be very afraid."

Ryan closed and locked the door. A reddish glow from a sconce lit the stairs. Katarina was already back in her room, door closed. He paused to knock—he'd need his key to get in his apartment—but, looking down the hall, he saw that his door was cracked open. It smelled sweet, sort of like cotton candy. He pushed open the door and flicked on the overhead light.

A woman was seated at his desk, facing the window.

For an instant Ryan felt like apologizing for intruding, but it was his apartment. Still, he said, "Excuse me?"

She turned to him.

"You're Katarina's mom?" He looked both ways, at the kitchenette and his bed. He went in the kitchen. There was something familiar about her. "Do you want coffee or something?"

She didn't respond.

He reached into the fridge. "Beer?" She still didn't respond. He twisted the cap off a bottle and leaned against the counter. His keys were sitting there.

She was at least a decade older than Ryan, had long dark wavy hair, and wore a similarly dark skirt. That was it—she was the woman on the bike. Katarina had the same jawline and smooth course to her cheek, though her nose and eyes were different. It was definitely the face that Katarina would grow into.

She finally looked away, back at the window.

All he could think of to say was, "Thanks for bringing me my keys."

She nodded and the quiet strained a while longer.

Ryan finally said, "I love Katarina. You have a wonderful kid."

That was the trigger. "Katarina was a fine child. We loved her so much." Looking at the floor in front of her, she walked toward him. One step onto the kitchen's linoleum, she stopped one foot away. Close enough to be uncomfortable.

She said, "My name was Jane," and offered a hand. It was cold, and as he closed his hand around hers, she stiffened and her eyes seemed to focus for the first time. "It's nice that you watch TV with Kat; her father and I can't."

"It's cool," Ryan said. "I like hanging with her. I have a son about her age back in Texas."

"Is your wife dead?"

"What?" Ryan stepped to the side. "No, she lives in Texas with my son."

Her eyes tracked him but she didn't move. Her words flowed in a monotone, and she told him about her husband's fight with brain cancer. "That was our sad-glad time. As we watched our world dry up and blow away, our pain blew away too. I wanted to go with him, but he wouldn't let me. He told me to stay here with Kat. As soon as I'm finished with Kat, I'm going to him."

When Ryan's father died, he learned that hugging his mother helped; not that he had enough hugs to fill her loss, but they helped. Ryan stepped toward her.

Jane's face jerked toward him. "Don't comfort me. Only he could comfort me. I held onto him, you know. Even when he was cold and rigid, I didn't let go. It was Katarina. Katarina made me let go of him. She pulled my arms away. She made me let go. I wouldn't have let go, but she made me. Someday, when she's ready, then I'll go. Dodge is going to help me."

Any sympathy he felt for this woman was washed away in anger and jealousy. "My son is two thousand miles away. I'm not allowed near him." She didn't seem to be listening, so he grabbed her shoulders. "Listen to me, Jane. You're wasting time. He's dead and you're alive. Katarina needs—"

"No, I'm not."

"What?"

"I'm not alive." Her eyes were blank, empty, even empty of tears. "I died with him. I'm just here until Kat is ready."

He let her shrink out of his grasp. Her response struck him as the opposite of what a parent should say. He said, "Katarina needs you," but it was like speaking to a closed window.

She shuffled out the door, drawing in on herself with each step. Ryan held the door for her and watched her work her way down the hall in uncomfortable silence. She opened the door to the apartment she shared with Katarina and stepped inside.

Katarina leaned out the door and made a face at Ryan. With raised eyebrows she whispered, "Be afraid. Be very afraid."

He smiled at Katarina and waved off the drama, but once he closed his door, Katarina's mother's words echoed in his head: "I died with him. I'm just here until Kat is ready." He believed it.

Ryan was rebuilding his career and his life according to plan. His rent was on time nine months straight. Plus, he paid all of Dodge's fees and sent Linda over $5,000. When his contract with FiberSpec Communications expired, the manager offered him an electrical engineering staff position. Technician to staff engineer was three rungs up the career ladder. He had business cards, health insurance, a 401(k), and a new blue cubicle. With the steady success, Ryan's confidence filled him up, crowding out the ever-present but now diminishing appetite for meth and its destruction.

Maybe he should have done more research into the legal aspects of his predicament; maybe he should have listened to Dodge, but he didn't.

Six months ago, when FiberSpec first hired him, human resources had filed all the standard forms, including one with the Directory of New Hires. The Office of Child Support Enforcement eventually matched Ryan's name to a list submitted by the DNH. The OCSE filed a standard form with FiberSpec human resources, and they generated a memo saying that child support would be garnished from Ryan's pay. Since the child support had been set at 20 percent of his pay when he was software director at GoldCon, he would take home less than half his rent.

When he saw the first check with all the deductions, he thought it was a mistake. He kept his cool as the HR administrator explained all the policies. He didn't say a word, except to thank her for her time. He went back to his cube and his job.

That night, Ryan digested the news and decided that it was just another part of the rebuilding process. After all, he'd made the mistakes. He hadn't earned any favors. Besides, he could make enough on the side to keep Dodge off his back and to put enough food in the cupboard for his meals and Katarina's snacks. He even convinced himself that it was better this way, better to have everything go through the proper channels.

After a few months paying full child support, he figured he could go to court in Texas, argue that he'd demonstrated ability and willingness, get the amount reduced, and have that arrest warrant rescinded.

But Ryan still didn't understand the extent of his predicament.

Of course, Dodge had a complete understanding of Ryan's situation. If Ryan had asked, Dodge might have even filled in all the details. Probably not, it was more fun this way, but he could have asked.

It came as no surprise when the OCSE agent knocked on the door. Dodge invited the tired-looking man in for coffee and tried not to chuckle as he followed him down the hall. It wasn't a complete hand yet, but his down cards looked good. Apparently, the raspy laughter leaked out. The agent flashed a suspicious look as he entered the kitchen. While brewing a fresh pot, Dodge said that yes, a man named Ryan McNear lived there, but no, it didn't sound like the man he was looking for.

"McNear, a deadbeat dad? I don't think so." He offered a seat at the kitchen table. "You're looking for a bald man? About fifty?"

The agent opened a folder, took out two envelopes, confirmed the address, and said, "Ryan McNear, thirty-seven years old, auburn hair, blue eyes, not quite six feet tall?"

"Naw, the guy that lives here isn't any taller than me and, if his eyes were ever blue, he's full of shit now." Dodge laughed extra loud at his own joke, loud enough that the agent had to join in the laughter or appear rude.

Dodge poured coffee while the agent puzzled over the contents of an envelope. "I should really talk to your Mr. McNear before reporting that we have a bad address—will he be home soon?"

Dodge couldn't help but smile—is stupidity a requirement for government work? You know where the guy works, you know what he does, and you come to his house in the middle of the workday. "Nope, the Ryan McNear who lives here is out of town—don't expect him back for a couple of weeks."

"Does your Mr. McNear work for"—he scanned a page in his folder—"FiberSpec Communications?"

"FiberSpec? No, this guy is a traveling salesman—sells raincoats or something."

"I have to leave a notice for your Mr. McNear, just in case. I sure hate going into a place of business and dragging someone out..."

Dodge gestured surrender with his hands. "Wish I could help."

The agent took a sheet of paper from the folder. Dodge leaned over, close enough to make the man uncomfortable. The page was a map of Petaluma with both Nutter House and FiberSpec marked.

"Going over to FiberSpec then?"

"I have to."

The agent took a long drink and set the coffee mug down. As he lifted the map, Dodge put his thumb on it and said, "Best way to get over there is to take the Rainier connector. It's not on the map, but it'll save you fifteen minutes and is much easier to get to."

Dodge took a pen from the man and drew a nonexistent street on the map. The Petaluma City Council had been discussing construction of another freeway off-ramp and connector between the west and east sides of town for a decade but never built one. In the process, Dodge got enough ink on the map that there was no way the OCSE agent could reconstruct reasonable directions. The diversion would add at least twenty minutes to what was otherwise a ten-minute drive.

The agent gave a halfhearted thank-you, and Dodge walked him to the door.

Dodge was on the phone within seconds of the door shutting. Ryan picked up on the third ring. Dodge said, "There's a federal agent on his way to arrest you."

Ryan said, "What are you talking about? Arrest? What for?"

"McNear, you fucking idiot. Don't you know that crossing state lines to avoid paying child support is a felony?"

"I didn't cross state lines to avoid paying child support. I crossed them so that it would be possible for me to pay child support."

"Maybe so, but the eyes of justice are blind to that sort of nuance."

"The police are coming here?"

"McNear, you need to leave right now."

"I'm in the middle of a—"

"Leave right now. You won't be going back anyway, so just go. Tell them something has come up. Tell them the feds are onto your ass and you need to leave."

"Why should I believe you?"

"Because in fifteen, maybe ten minutes, you'll be in handcuffs."

As Ryan hung up the phone, Dodge heard him whine, "Oh fuck."

Less than ten minutes later, Ryan walked in the door and threw his tired, patched-up briefcase against the stairwell.

"If I don't work, I can't pay my child support. Everything was coming back together. Why would they destroy me? How can I pay child support from jail? What do they expect me to do? Why on earth would…"

Dodge stopped listening. It all ran together anyway. He bent over and rubbed the tiny scratch from the briefcase collision out of the hardwood with a little piece of lapping paper that he kept in his pocket. As Ryan threw his temper tantrum, Dodge tried to give the appearance that he was listening. Staring at Ryan's nose, he added together everything he knew. National Engineering Group, the conglomerate best known for supplying hardware to the world's oil companies and refineries, was getting a larger and larger share of weapons research contracts since 9/11 and had met with Foster Reed. It was a nice card but not good enough to start the betting.

Finally, Ryan leaned against the wall and let loose a long sigh. With his tantrum complete, he was guided into the office by Dodge, who sat him down and said, "How many times have I told you that you have to work off the books?"

Faint lines etched up Ryan's forehead, connecting the bridge of his nose to his widow's peak. They added ten years. Perfect.

"McNear, understand this: I'm an attorney, an expert on these things. You know that IRS form, the W-4, you fill out before an honest employer can pay you?"

Ryan nodded.

"Next time you fill that out, you're going to jail. It doesn't matter whether you do it here or in Texas, you're going to the big house."

Ryan said, "What if I—"

"The slammer, the cooler, the hoosegow, the pokey, the pen—of course, you and your husband will call it home."

"But if I got a job in Texas, at least—"

"Don't drop the soap, Ryan. Your fine Irish ass is at stake." Dodge waited for it to sink in and then tried not to laugh at *sink in*.

Ryan stared into the shadows under the desk. His fingers stopped tapping, and he let loose a long sigh, as though he were exhaling the last wisps of hope. Dodge tried not to smile, but it was impossible. Fortunately, Ryan didn't seem to notice.

"This is how you'll get your money," Dodge said as earnestly as he could manage. "Your friend's company, Creation Energy, is going to get some contracts for their technology, and, when they do, we will sue them and all your problems will disappear." Dodge snapped his fingers. "Just like that—all you have to do is be patient and let me take care of it."

"I'm not suing Foster Reed," Ryan said.

"Of course you are. Otherwise you go to jail. Don't you want to see your son? Besides, they're your inventions. You have a right to that money." Dodge still saw doubt in Ryan's eyes. The solution was simple: stack the deck. It was time to con his science-zealot sister, Emmy, into coming up for a visit. She could beat any belief out of Ryan.

"You mean that I can't get a job?"

"I mean you're unemployable. But don't worry about it. You can earn your money the old-fashioned way, through litigation."

"What about my rent?"

"I'll keep track of your debts."

“What’s the point?” The line in his forehead looked more like a crease now.

“Listen, McNear, I’m going to have my sister visit. She’s a physics professor—a real physics professor, at a real university. She can help us understand what your chum is trying to do.” The best part of dabbling in the lives of others is setting them up and then watching them betray their desires. “She’s a beautiful girl. Course you probably wouldn’t be interested—she comes with a brain.” Ryan didn’t take the bait, though. He just sat there staring under the desk, a human-shaped pool of hopelessness.

Freshly unemployed and basically unemployable, Ryan was spending his fifth straight day on Dodge's couch when he heard someone walk up to the porch. Maybe it would be for the best. Maybe this federal deadbeat-dad office had a program to help guys like him get their shit together. Then he heard the muffled thump of Katarina tossing her skateboard under the bench.

Katarina walked in and tossed her backpack to the bottom of the stairs, took the TV remote from Ryan, switched it to MTV2, and sat down. Ryan stared out the window and pondered his next move. There weren't many available. Waiting for a federal agent would be stupid. It would be much better to get busted trying to solve his problems than hiding. He laughed at himself—so this is how martyrs are made.

"What's so funny?" Katarina asked.

He looked at the TV, a heavy-metal video that, for no discernible reason, was on MTV2's heavy rotation. "How does a song this bad ever get on TV?"

"Trivium kicks ass," she said, but she turned off the TV. "Doesn't matter, though. I'm late for mentor torture." She picked up her backpack again and headed for the door but stopped and looked back at Ryan. "Why do I have to go to a *mentor*? All she does is bitch at me about my clothes."

Still staring out the window, Ryan said, "Being bitched at by adults is an important part of your childhood."

"I'm not a *child*."

"Sorry, I meant, adolescent-hood."

"You should be my mentor."

"What?" He looked at her. "I'm not qualified. I don't like to bitch at people."

"You already *are* my mentor."

"What mentoring have I done?"

"You delivered the helmet and wrist guards."

"You don't wear them."

She stepped away from the door and climbed back out from under her backpack. "You can do this, Ryan O'you-think-you-can-ahan. Mentoring is one part fake homework help; two parts complaining about my clothes, friends, the music I listen to, the amount of TV I watch; and one generous helping of philosophical criticism about my being 'obsessed with death'—she even said I was spiritually empty. Deliver me, Ryan, deliver me from that bitch."

"That bitch? Isn't your mentor the lady who does yoga with homeless people?"

"Uh-huh."

"Katarina, that woman would never criticize a child—"

"I'm not a child."

"—the yoga lady is the most tolerant person on Earth, how could she possibly annoy you?"

"Hearing how wonderful the world is, how lucky we are to be alive, how she doesn't want me to make the mistakes she made with drugs and sex—she's beyond freakishly annoying." Dragging her backpack into the living room, she flopped down hard on the couch. "I could actually benefit from some homework aid…"

"You need more than that." His tone was flippant.

"Please?" She opened her backpack and pulled out a binder.

He'd known Katarina for a year but still didn't know how her mind worked. She wasn't any more or less "obsessed with death" than any other kid who'd watched her father die. Ryan considered it. He did have flexible hours, after all. "If I were your mentor, you'd have to agree to a few things. First, you have to wear your helmet; second, no late homework—"

"Never mind." She started up the stairs. "And don't try to be my fucking father—he's dead."

Ryan called after her, "Third, don't say fuck."

An upstairs door slammed her response, and as it did, Ryan realized the magnitude of this moment. Katarina had just peeled back her obnoxious-kid veneer, and as she laid herself bare, he'd maintained the same banter they used to discuss bad music videos. He groaned, mentally kicked himself, and then scrambled to recover.

Her backpack was still next to the couch, and a binder was sticking out. He grabbed it and flipped through: one half-completed math assignment after another. She was doing algebra in eighth grade, already starting analytic geometry—she must have aced the placement exam. A sheet of paper was folded into her math textbook, an old homework assignment that she obviously hadn't turned in. The chapter's exercises were all word problems, the hard part of algebra. She'd drawn little curlicues and dragons in the margins. He noticed that she had set up most of the problems but hadn't bothered to finish them.

Except for one that was worked out in detail.

He found the problem in her textbook. It was marked with three red stars, extra difficult. And it was.

Since Ryan's college degree was in applied math, he should have been able to figure out how she'd solved it, but he didn't recognize her notation, much less her technique. He glanced through the text; it used standard notation.

He took a blank sheet of paper and tried to solve it. It was hard, even when he used calculus. Without calculus, it looked impossible. He looked at the cover of the book—yep, algebra. He went back to Katarina's solution and followed it step by step. Her solution was shorter than his—half a page to his two pages. Then he recognized it. She had set up the problem as a differential equation: an elegant linear nonhomogeneous differential equation with nonconstant coefficients. She used neither Newton's nor Leibniz's notation; she'd invented her own.

He stared at the ceiling, as though he could see through it to Katarina's apartment. That kid had intuited calculus. Invented it for herself. It's one thing to write down a DE, altogether another to solve it.

Brilliant wasn't a strong enough word.

Ryan grabbed her binder and the textbook and went upstairs. He knocked on her apartment door.

Katarina said, "What do you want?"

The sound came from behind him, down the hall a dozen steps. She was in Ryan's apartment. He walked over and opened his door. She was sitting on the kitchen counter with Sean's football in her lap.

Ryan held the book and binder out like a waiter with trays of food, turned on a big fake grin, and said, "I'm your guy. BS applied math, UMass." He set the books on his desk and pulled the beach chair out like a maître d' seating a debutante.

She slumped off the counter, said "Whatever," and sat at the desk. She opened her binder and pointed at a pencil scrawl. "How can this one equation describe every one of those things?"

He looked over her shoulder. It was the expression for conic sections, not easy stuff but should be trivial for someone who could invent calculus. He looked at Katarina from the corner of his eye as though expecting her to have transformed into some sort of math-breathing dragon. It was just Katarina being lazy, though. "You mean the bowl-ofs?"

"What?"

"You don't know about bowl-ofs?" He knelt next to her and opened the textbook. "You know, hyper-bowl-ofs, para-bowl-ofs…"

Katarina elbowed him. "Ryan van Dweeben, they're called parabolas and hyperbolas."

Ryan elbowed her back. "No, *you're* saying it wrong. They're bowl-ofs."

"Never mind, you don't even know."

He took a mechanical pencil from a tray and demonstrated the algebraic steps to convert the expressions for each shape into the common form. Then he asked, "Did you read the book?"

She curled her lip. "The math book?"

"Yeah, the *math* book. Math books make great reading." He picked up the text and took it to a tired couch he'd pilfered from Skate-n-Shred. "It's story time, children!"

She rolled her eyes and stayed at the desk, but the corners of her lips sneaked up into a smile.

Ryan held it out like a picture book, pointing to the equations as he read the text, emphasizing the *if-thens* and *if-and-only-ifs*, the way kindergarten teachers emphasize the morals of fables.

Katarina said, "That's not human speech." There was ridicule in her voice, but he noticed that those bright green eyes didn't leave the book. A few seconds later, she reached over and turned the page.

14

It took a couple of weeks of self-pity, but Ryan's goodwill reasserted itself, and he pushed forward. He added more off-the-books work, safe from the OCSE. He got a job watering the potted plants that decorated Petaluma's sidewalks. Most days, he also joined the Central American migrant laborers who stood in front of the mini-mart hoping for an honest day of work at a decent off-the-books wage. At first his freckled arms, auburn hair, and inability to speak Spanish kept him on the fringe of the day-labor subculture, but soon his easy wisecracks and disarming smile were welcomed by his comrades. He kept pushing—picking grapes, fixing fences, and laying concrete—kept stashing his pay, kept his confidence that the money would accumulate. He made sure he was home twice a week for Katarina after school. Watching Katarina reformulate algebra and geometry and helping her address questions in set theory and topology provided the intellectual stimulation that Ryan had always gotten from solving high-tech puzzles.

Then the rains came and drowned the day-labor work. It rained through December and January. He had to dip into his savings to make rent. He made some money during a rain-free week in February clearing vineyards of brush, but that was it. The storms blew through the rest of February and into March.

His funds deteriorated, and reality clashed with his drive to succeed. He had too much time to himself, too much time to think.

On the first day of spring, he got an e-mail from his old neighbor, Ward. It included a link to a newspaper story. Sean, who was in his first year of high school, had hit the game-winning home run on opening day.

Wind-driven rain pummeled the copper turret, and Ryan stared into the storm. As the hours passed, any joy he'd felt for his son's accomplishment faded behind a great screaming message: your boy doesn't need you!

He stood and his bones felt heavy. There was no bounce left in him. He slumped under his coat and trudged out the door. He was halfway downstairs when he realized what he was doing. That same old desire—would it ever go away?

He was going to score some meth.

He stopped and shook like a wet dog, turned around, went back to his apartment, and grabbed a beer from the refrigerator. As he took a swig, beer for breakfast, he smiled at the irony. He looked around the apartment, from the frumpy couch to the pile of foam he called a bed. It sure didn't look as though he'd made any progress. Time was wasting. As long as his child support was pegged to an executive income, it would be impossible to get forward on the wages of a working man. As frustration engulfed him, he felt something in his spine. Gently, from deep inside, Grandma spoke to him: "What sort of man would you be then?"

"Not the kind who sits around waiting to win the lottery," he said to himself.

He paced back and forth in front of the rain-streaked window. The valley was fogged in. He could barely see across the street.

There were only two ways that he could reclaim his life, and they both sucked. He trotted out the idea of suing Creation

Energy. Fighting had tremendous appeal, but fighting Foster—well, Foster wasn't his enemy. He finished the beer and tossed the bottle across the apartment to the recycling bin. He missed, but it didn't break; it just rolled around the kitchen floor.

The second option was no better. Dodge was right: if he took a real job, he'd be arrested. In California, he'd be arrested for a federal crime, leaving Texas to avoid paying child support. At least if he got a job in Texas it would come with one less count against him.

He leaned his head against the window. It was cool against his skin. Listening to the rain, a thought came to him. It came to him in his father's voice: "Do you want to do it on their terms or yours?"

No matter what he did, he would eventually have to face a judge in Texas.

It took almost ten minutes to boot up his computer. He sent an e-mail to Foster, phrasing it as though they were in adjacent cubicles. "Have you got funding for that project? I might have some breathing room next month." He didn't even sign his name at the bottom. There was something ecstatically normal about that note.

A few seconds later, his phone rang. It was Foster. "Ryan, I got your note." The phone made a series of clicking noises, probably caused by the weather. It cleared up as Foster said, "Are you really interested? If you are, I won't interview anyone else."

"Yeah," Ryan said, "I'm interested."

"It's the software director position," Foster said. "The pay is pretty good, about what you were making at GoldCon before we got laid off."

If Ryan were making that kind of money, it would only take a couple of months to accumulate enough cash to put a dent in his child support. He might even be able to appear in court before the payroll information made it to the deadbeat-dad office. The charges would at least be suspended. Like Constable Holcomb had said, "Can't pay child support from jail." A few months after that, there had to be a way to repeal the legal mess that kept him away from Sean.

"Yeah, yeah, I'm interested," Ryan said. "When can you put together an offer?"

"We're really close to having funding—a couple of months? Two or three? Three max."

When Ryan hung up the phone, he didn't feel the relief that he thought he should. Foster had changed. Everything had changed. Going back to Texas felt off balance, like going backward when the solutions to his problem should be forward. It all nagged at him. What had led him to Petaluma in the first place? It sure had seemed like he was here for a reason.

⌒

Something nagged at Dodge when he hung up the phone too. Why would Ryan choose to be arrested when he could just sue the bastard? This one was getting away from him. He had to play a card.

Dodge picked up the phone and called his sister, Emmy, or, more properly, Professor Amolie Nutter, Department of Physics, UC Berkeley.

⌒

Upstairs, Ryan dug up the book Foster had sent him months before, *The Cosmology of Creation*. As he read, the mix of religion and science both tugged his curiosity and ticked his bullshit meter. Ryan couldn't tell where the science ended and the religion began, but he knew that Foster wouldn't budge on biblical literalism. Was it just a big scientific-seeming rationalization of religion or a genuine treatise of discovery? By midnight, barely halfway through, the math and physics were completely over his head. Still, it convinced him of one thing for certain: Foster believed that he'd discovered a link between science and spirituality.

As he went to sleep, a question kept ringing in his head: which came first, matter or consciousness?

Five hours later he awoke to someone pounding on his door. He jerked up from a nightmare, the same nightmare he always had, another view of his past, the part that had led to the restraining order that kept him away from Sean. Tammi. Damn Tammi. You'd think that, at least in his dreams, she'd have found her way to hell. He looked around, not sure where he was.

Katarina yelled through the door, "I need a ride to school. It's raining."

Ryan grabbed his trousers, glad to be among the awake.

"Come on! I'll miss a test, fail eighth grade, never recover, and become a junkie. Do you want that on your head?"

Katarina was sitting in the hallway opposite his room when Ryan stepped out the door.

Ryan said, "Are we late?"

"A smidge." She stood and handed Ryan her backpack.

Ryan ran down the stairs and Katarina launched down the banister—a slope of polished oak. The two of them reached the bottom at the same time. Ryan caught her around the waist, kept going, and pretended like he was going to ram her head in the door. Katarina let out a high-pitched shriek. Ryan set her on her feet and pretended to dust off her shoulders.

Once they were in the car, Ryan told Katarina that he might be going to Texas for business.

She said, "Business? Is there a city there that needs you to water their plants?"

"Yeah, watering plants is the next big thing, sort of like the Internet." The old Probe stuttered and threatened to stall in the long, slow procession of minivans depositing eighth graders at the school entrance.

Katarina stared straight ahead.

"It seems like the only way I can get my shit together and see my son again."

"You don't even know your son."

"Thanks for reminding me of that." He elbowed her. "Too bad I know you."

"You wish."

Emmy was finally visiting her brother in Petaluma. This time, at least he'd pretended that he wanted to see her. She would reward any positive step, no matter how small—sort of like domesticating a dingo. Besides, she was curious.

As her car climbed the hill to the black-and-red Victorian, she caught herself laughing. Dodge must have blackmailed one of the ladies on the Heritage Homes Committee into allowing those colors. She could picture him hiring a private investigator to turn up some ancient dirt and then threatening to "go public." Dodge, please. Why did he work so hard to suppress his innate decency?

She parked, and when she was halfway up the porch stairs, the door opened. Dodge waited at the threshold in a ratty beige sweater, the frown lines etched into his cheeks cracked into a smile, and all at once she felt like a five-year-old.

"You're going to love McNear. He's like an overgrown leprechaun. You'll want to pack him up and take him home."

"Dodge, I'm here to see *you*." Walking through the living room and down the hall, Emmy looked back. He was older and fatter and balder than the last time she'd seen him. At least he'd quit smoking.

In the kitchen, Emmy turned on a burner under an old iron kettle, and Dodge assembled an antique bone china tea set—the very tea set their grandmother had given the two of them when Emmy was three and Dodge was eighteen.

They talked about their parents, still living in Los Angeles, still in need of help around the house and too proud to admit it, and still sending Emmy a card every month telling her how proud they were. Maybe that was it. Maybe she worshipped her mean old brother out of guilt. The second she was born, all attention had focused on the brilliant baby girl. Dodge must have been jealous, but then, Dodge had lavished more attention on her than either of their parents.

Dodge snickered. "I have a brilliant plan to make a ton of money. Are you in?"

"Dodge, please be nice to the other children."

"You'll love this caper. It's right up your alley." The kettle whistled, and Dodge hopped out of his chair cackling like a yenta with fresh gossip. "We're going to screw a bunch of fundamentalist right-wing Bible-thumpers and help a really decent guy put his life together." He poured tea into their cups. "Creation Energy is about to get major corporate funding. They'll have the resources to sell the public on bogus science. You think it's tough to get intelligent design out of the schools? Wait until the Department of Energy starts investing in Creation and the soul."

Dodge knew that the DOE funded her research. She stirred some milk into her tea and took a sip, trying to withhold her response.

Dodge continued his con. "All you have to do is fight the mock-science—you're doing that anyway."

"And you?"

"As Mr. McNear's attorney, I'll file a suit naming Creation Energy in a conspiracy to defraud Mr. McNear of the income resulting from his intellectual property." He looked away from her and added, "At the trial, you'll be my star witness—think about it, the perfect stage for you to tear them down."

"You're leaving something out." She waited until he looked at her. "Dodge, those patents will never produce income."

"Then why is Creation Energy investing in them?"

"Simple: they believe their own propaganda. They're like, so greedy—whether for money or fame or maybe just recognition—that they talk themselves into absurdity. Pons and Fleischman are still pushing cold fusion. There's a doctor named Robert Miller who doesn't understand the basic principles of physics, and he's gotten over twenty million in venture capital to produce energy by forcing hydrogen atoms into energy states *below* the ground state. If he remembered his freshman chemistry, he'd know how absurd the idea is."

She sipped her tea, and it occurred to her that she might be using this opportunity to dispel the ghost of embarrassment she had suffered when she proposed that cold fusion experiment in front of the whole physics department back when she was a student.

She said, "I'll testify," and stared at Dodge. He looked back at her. She knew that he wasn't telling her everything. "Dodge, everything I say is on the record."

"Emmy, we'll do it however you want. Have I ever led you astray?"

She laughed. "Please. If you try to trick me…"

Dodge poured himself another cup of tea, stirred in some sugar, and spoke very softly. "Ryan believes they can do it. In fact, just before I called you, he said that he's worried Creation Energy will start a matter-antimatter reaction that will get out of control…"

Emmy could tell that he was lying, but his words were so well chosen that they touched all her buttons—buttons that, mostly, he had programmed. She sighed. "Don't say it, please, don't."

"…he thinks they're going to start the apocalypse, and he's worried that he won't have a chance for repentance. Of course, he's impressionable, what with his string of bad luck. It's really a shame to see a gifted engineer, a former company director, a handsome man, fall for something like that."

"Someday I'm going to visit you and we're going to talk about our lives, things that actually matter to us." She finished her tea, amused by her own reaction. "Okay, I'll talk to him. Where is he?"

Dodge let loose his raspy chortle. "I control you."

Emmy reached over and pretended to slap him. "I hate you."

Ryan started up the stairs, but a sound stopped him. He noticed a light, sweet fragrance, like honeysuckle. Dodge was in the kitchen talking to someone. He'd never heard Dodge actually laugh before. Laugh as if he were happy. He went the rest of the way upstairs to his apartment. The notes he'd scribbled from Foster's book the day before were piled next to Katarina's scratch paper. He caught himself musing on an image of Katarina: her dirty brown hair tied in a series of random ponytails and a pencil dangling from her mouth, her feet tapping along without any rhythm in those goofy black sneakers. He mentally kicked himself, stood up, dipped into his rapidly waning savings for a twenty, and headed back out.

The bookstore had three used calculus textbooks, including a really old one for three dollars. Bound in red and just under three hundred pages, it was written by an Oxford professor in a formal style that concentrated on theorems with short, elegant proofs—a purist's math book. After paying for it, Ryan walked along the river. Wind blew the clouds south, and the river carried away the morning rain.

Three blocks from the river, he walked onto the courtyard of a Catholic church. The creamy white steeple reached into the sky, and stained-glass windows told the story. He went inside. It was quiet and cool and smelled of frankincense and myrrh, the smell of Sunday morning. He sat in a center pew. There were candles burning, and someone sat at the bench of a pipe organ. Other than that, he was alone.

The calculus book's red binding was worn at the corners, and cardboard showed through. He pulled a prayer book from the back of the pew in front of him and weighed the two books, one in each hand. Each book was filled with short passages—prayers and theorems, hymns and proofs. The arcane symbols and language of each was perfect and elegant. Ryan wondered about mathematical prayers. Was that what Foster's book was?

He set the prayer book back in the stand, tapping it down with affection, then tucked the math book under his arm and walked outside.

Crossing the street in front of a brand-new BMW, he felt a familiar pang. He should be at work in a cubicle pounding a software program through a debugger, not wandering around town in the middle of the day.

Katarina was walking home from school, dragging her skateboard and lugging her backpack. Meandering up the hill, she stopped every few feet to look at flowers or birds or trees or the little concrete statue of an owl at the old school that had been converted to condos. She saw Ryan waiting. When she passed, he fell in step with her.

Half a block later, he said, "Nice day at school?"

It sounded more like something to say than a question. She looked up at him, squinted in the sunlight, and turned away.

His arms swung as he walked, and he had a book tucked under one of them. His square chin had little red stubble on it. He glanced down at her and put his hand on her shoulder as though it were a reflex. It was the sort of thing her father used to do. Katarina avoided thinking about her dad and Ryan at the same time. She didn't want to jinx Ryan. There was always that nagging feeling that if she'd done something different, avoided cracks in the sidewalk or something, that her father wouldn't have died.

"Can I carry your backpack for you?"

"No."

They passed a shiny red Acura parked next to Ryan's beat-up car and went up on the porch. Ryan said, "I got you a book." He handed it to her.

She opened it close to her face and took a deep breath. It smelled like old paper and floor wax, the way a library smells, the smell of cool and quiet, like something separate from life and death and people. She set her skateboard under the bench and let her backpack slide off. Flipping through the pages, she paused on symbols she'd never seen. She wanted to inhale them, and she would too. The great thing about math books, the thing that makes them better than any other kind of book, is that when they prove something, that's it. She looked in the first chapter. Under the proof of the first theorem, it said *quod erat demonstrandum*. To Katarina it meant "end of discussion."

"Isn't it weird how math works?" she said, but Ryan obviously didn't understand what she meant. Big surprise. She tried to define it for him. "If people spoke mathematically, there wouldn't be any arguments. Just long proofs with tons of scratch paper and then one guy going 'See?' and the other guy going 'Well, I guess,' and that's that."

Ryan shrugged. "You'll love this book. Old math books are way more elegant than new ones. Nowadays they try to spoon-feed people as if everyone's afraid of math."

"Hate that."

"Me too. Mathematical wusses."

"Word," Katarina said and opened the door. "Know what's best about math?"

"What?" Ryan said, holding the door for her.

"It's neither alive nor dead."

16

Ryan's eyes took a second to make the transition from daylight to Nutter House dim. He noticed that smell again. Not like honeysuckle after all, more like those purple flowers that hang from wisteria but with a bit of earth to it, almost salty.

Dodge was sitting on the couch next to a woman. "McNear, this is my sister. She's a real physicist at a real university, and she has offered to help you." At the word *help*, the woman cast a quick glance at Dodge. He added, "She'll tell you how full of crap your Bible-thumping pal is."

She looked almost frail but had a serious countenance, as though she knew what you were thinking and didn't care. She had thick, wavy black hair with brown streaks that framed her broad forehead and long sharp nose—very much like Dodge's, but that was the extent of their resemblance. She wore jeans, white tennis shoes, and a tight black T-shirt with the image of a galaxy and an arrow pointing to a spot with the words "you are here" that drew Ryan's eye to her right breast and then, naturally, to her left breast.

She held out her hand. "I got a kick out of your patents." In the time it took her smile to form, she transformed from a serious professional to one of God's cutest creatures. "It was some of the most amusing nonsense I've ever read." Her voice was strong and direct, a total contrast to her fragile-looking self.

"Thanks. I guess." Ryan felt his face start to heat up. Hopefully it was dark enough in the room that she wouldn't notice.

"My name is Emmy."

Ryan realized that she'd been holding her hand out to him for far longer than was socially acceptable.

Katarina punched him lightly in the back.

He leaned over and took her hand. "Ryan McNear. Nice to meet you."

Dodge said, "And this is Kat."

Emmy nodded to Katarina with the look of someone who had little time for children. Ryan felt immediately defensive. Katarina responded by walking across the room, taking a seat at the opposite end of the couch, and opening the book.

"Your colleague, Foster Reed, has formed a company that claims to be able to develop a power generator, right?"

"My friend Foster is a pretty sharp guy." He took a quick look at Dodge, who didn't seem to be listening. "He sent me a book based on his PhD thesis—I don't really understand it, but it sure looks like Foster knows what he's talking about."

"Do you understand that he's trying to violate the first law of thermodynamics?"

Ryan dug through his brain. Thermodynamics covered temperature, heat, energy, and entropy, but he couldn't remember the first law.

Katarina rescued him. "You say that as though we all know about this so-called first law of thermodynamics."

"I'm sorry," Emmy said. "The first law states that energy is neither created nor destroyed, it can only change form. It means that there's no way to create energy; it has to come from somewhere. For example, the energy released by burning wood comes from the energy that was required to form the chemical bonds that make up the wood."

Ryan pulled a chair closer to the couch and sat down. Standing in front of him, Emmy was only a few inches taller than he was sitting, but when she spoke, she looked larger. Katarina had the math book in her lap, conspicuously pointing the spine in a direction so Emmy could see it.

Katarina said, "Then where does it come from?"

Dodge said, "Stay out of this."

Almost simultaneously, Emmy and Katarina said, "Shut up, Dodge," and then looked at each other. Dodge let loose a raspy chuckle and, for an instant, Ryan felt very much at home.

"Energy," Katarina said. "It has to come from somewhere."

"Matter began forming from the energy of the Big Bang." Emmy talked to Katarina the same way that Ryan did, not like an adult to a kid, but as two people with similar interests. The difference was that Emmy sounded like a professor giving a lecture. Then, to Dodge, she said, "Do you have a whiteboard or something that I can use?"

"A whiteboard? Sure Emmy, right next to the lecture hall over by the bowling alley."

Ryan said, "He's got a huge desk blotter."

Emmy motioned to Katarina to lead the way.

"Hold it," Dodge said. "We don't all find physics so damn fascinating. Can you just give me the punch line?"

Emmy stopped. "If you don't understand it, how can you—"

"Because the judge won't understand it either—no one understands it. The executive summary, please?"

She looked at Katarina and then Ryan.

Ryan said, "I'm interested."

And Katarina, "I'll understand it."

Then Emmy turned to Dodge. "Okay, this is all you need to know: They claim to be able to make a power generator that converts spiritual energy to physical energy. They will say that it proves the existence of a deity. It would also violate several established principles of physics."

Dodge leaned back and turned on the TV. "That's all I need."

"That's it?" Ryan said. "You're dismissing Foster, just like that?"

"That's like, all you really need to know," Emmy said. She motioned for Katarina to lead them to Dodge's office. "Come on, you'll love the physics, and once you understand, you'll see why your friend's idea can't work."

Ryan followed them down the hall, immediately mesmerized by the wiggle in Emmy's walk.

Katarina flipped the light switch on the wall. A nightlight near the floor went on. Ryan turned on the desk lamp and quickly grabbed the revolver. He set it on top of a bookcase, hoping that Katarina hadn't noticed it.

Emmy stood next to Katarina, across from Ryan. "Okay, the basic idea is this: everything was everywhere—all at once."

Katarina looked baffled too. She said, "Huh? If everything was everywhere…"

Emmy smiled. "Without a universe, there is nothing anywhere or any*when*—without a universe, there is no space or time. It gets tricky without the math—"

"Then use the math." Katarina stepped closer to Emmy.

Emmy put a hand on her shoulder. "It took me ten years of college to learn this. You can learn the whole story and more, but it will take a long time."

"I am learning it." Katarina set the calculus book on the desk.

Emmy picked it up. "You're only thirteen and already doing calculus? I didn't get to calculus until I was seventeen."

Ryan said, "Katarina and I do math together. It's kind of a hobby, huh Kat?" Saying it out loud to this woman felt like a pickup line. Okay, it *was* a pickup line. His face heated up.

Katarina cocked her head at him. Emmy looked from one to the other. Ryan could feel another blush coming on and had to defuse it. "Is anyone else hungry?"

Emmy said, "I can make Dodge get us a pizza."

"Pepperoni and shroomage," Katarina said.

"And beer," Ryan added.

After Emmy walked out, Katarina said, "Ryan McPlayer. You're hitting on her."

Ryan responded, "Duh."

Emmy came back in. "Pizza in half an hour." She picked up her pencil. "Whenever language is used instead of math, we have to be careful to distinguish questions that are worth asking from those that sound interesting but don't make sense. For example, the question 'what was there before the origin of the universe?' is meaningless. The word *before* implies that time was passing, but without a universe, there isn't any time. When I say everything was everywhere all at once, what I mean is that at the instant of the Big Bang, the universe formed and whatever space and time it contained was all the space and time that there is, ever was, and ever will be. The Big Bang is a great burst of energy expanding outward. The character of the universe has changed with time, but it settled down within a few minutes and has been expanding for almost fourteen billion years now."

Katarina tapped her shoe against the desk, much the way Ryan did when he was nervous. "And that's forever."

"Hmm?"

"Forever. If there was nothing before, no time or space, then however old the universe is, that's forever."

"Yes! Exactly," Emmy said.

Katarina perched herself on the corner of the desk where the revolver and gavel pad had been, the calculus text in her lap.

Emmy faced both of them. "At the beginning, there was an incredible amount of energy concentrated at one point." She took a mechanical pencil from her jeans pocket and carefully put a dot in the center of the blotter. "When I say *a point* I mean an infinitely small spot, so small that it doesn't take up any space at all." Then she wrote $E=mc^2$ at the top of the sheet. "You've seen this before. It's Einstein's energy-mass relation. It means that energy can be converted to matter and that matter can be converted to energy, okay?"

Katarina said, "If it doesn't take up any space, does it take up any time?"

Emmy's eyebrows arched. She stared at Katarina for an instant. "Something only exists in time if it also exists in space. If so, then it exists in time the same way that we do, always in one spot, its present." She indicated the dot. "The Big Bang describes how the energy expanded into space, how it evolved into matter, and how stars and planets formed."

"And again, where did that energy come from?" Katarina asked.

Emmy set the pencil down. "It is what formed the universe. There was no universe before the Big Bang—no *from* and no *before*. It's impossible to talk about anything outside of spacetime."

Katarina nodded. It didn't look like a sincere nod to Ryan. Katarina would never accept being shut down like that. Had it been just she and Ryan, her response would have been loud and fast.

Emmy seemed to pick up on it too. "Okay, maybe it would help if I point out something about how science is done and how it differs from religion. When we do anything, we start with assumptions. If the assumptions are wrong, then everything we do is probably wrong too. If they're right, then, since we use this perfectly consistent language—mathematics—the results must also be right. So it's the assumptions we have to worry about. In science, we demand that our initial assumptions be as simple as possible because that's where we're investing faith. In religion, people start with faith—huge leaps of faith, belief in gods and ghosts, saints, resurrection—things for which there is no physical evidence. In physics, we have to start with something, at least the belief that our senses aren't lying to us. I think of this as a small step of faith rather than a leap."

Katarina smiled with her mouth open, as though she were swallowing something big and sweet. "I like that," she said. "If you keep looking, and something is really true, then the more you learn, the smaller your leaps of faith until they're just steps and then not steps at all."

"Yes! That's it exactly." Emmy pumped her fist as though she'd just won something. "You nailed it: the scientific method is nothing but watching your step."

She and Katarina looked very happy in that instant. Then Emmy turned back to the desk. "I'm going to describe a totally simple model of a big bang—just to get a couple of points across." She picked the pencil back up and drew a wavy line from the dot to the right. "The wavy line represents the energy in this little universe. So far, it's just sitting there and time is passing." She ended the wavy line with another dot and drew two lines connected to the second dot. "At this point, the energy converts into matter. The straight lines represent particles, point-like pieces of matter."

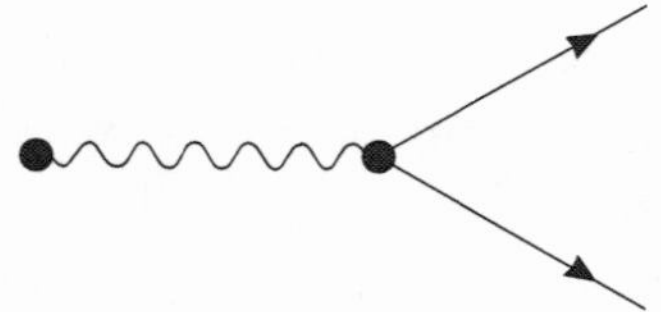

Emmy looked up at them again. Ryan had the distinct impression that if she caught him spacing out, she would whack his knuckles with a ruler. He couldn't quite hold back a smile. She smiled back. It was the last thing he expected. And her smile was warm and sweet.

Emmy underlined $E=mc^2$ and said, "Remember, Einstein told us that matter is a form of energy." She wrote *e-* next to one of the straight lines and *e+* next to the other. "In this little universe, the *little bang* formed two particles. This one"—she pointed at the *e-* —"is an electron. Electrons carry one unit of negative electric charge. The other one is called a positron, and it carries one unit of positive electric charge." She looked up again. It distracted Ryan. She was saying things that he'd read about in Foster's book, and he wanted to pay attention, so he concentrated on the diagram. He hoped she was disappointed that he looked away.

She said, "The laws of nature come from different types of symmetry, and this is an example of one. When matter forms, an equal amount of antimatter also forms. The electron is matter and the positron is its antimatter equivalent—a positron is exactly like an electron except that it carries the opposite charge."

Katarina said, "Is every electron and positron the same?"

"Very good." As Emmy nodded, her hair floated against her cheeks and, before continuing, she tossed it back in one graceful motion. "Yes, every electron is exactly like every other electron, and every positron is exactly like every other positron—we call them identical particles."

"How do you know? You can't check every one of them."

"If they differed, the universe wouldn't look the way it does."

Katarina looked at Ryan, and they nodded at each other. A big grin formed on Katarina's face. "Wow…*the universe would look different*, that is *so fucking cool*."

Ryan said, "Don't say *fuck*."

Katarina glared at him. "Lay off, *Ryan*."

Emmy tore the sheet of paper from the blotter and handed it to Ryan. He rolled it into a tube. She started drawing again. "In this diagram, we start with an electron and a positron moving forward in time. When they meet, they annihilate into pure energy."

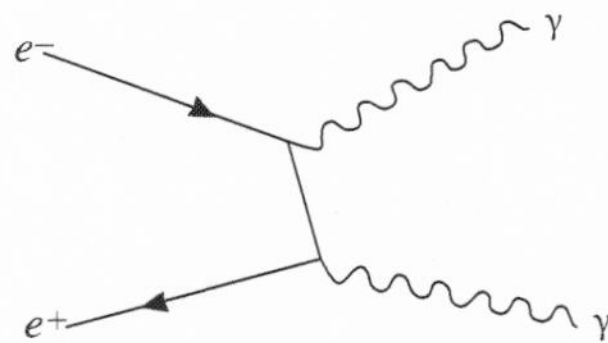

"This is called a Feynman diagram. Richard Feynman was a physicist at Caltech who made this subject understandable. It's called QED, quantum electrodynamics. In this case, the pure energy is represented by the wavy lines—they are called photons. Light, radio waves, X-rays are all examples of photons. The only difference between them is the amount of energy they carry. But it gets better." She drew more diagrams under the first one.

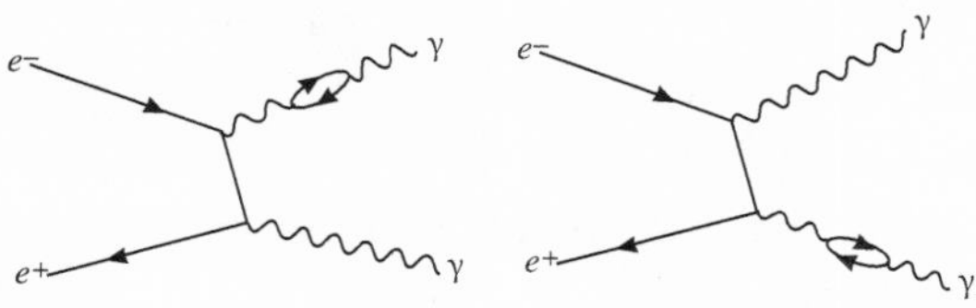

"To predict what happens when the electron and positron annihilate, we have to include every possible way that the reaction can proceed, and there is an infinite number of them. This is where quantum physics comes in and makes things seem bizarre."

Katarina shook her head, finally looking more like the surly adolescent that Ryan knew. "You can't add up an infinite number of things."

Emmy turned to Katarina and said, "Adding up all the diagrams is tricky, but it can be done, and the results of this theory are the most accurate of anything humanity has ever produced. If the universe behaved the same way at very small distance scales as it does in our world, where men like Ryan are two meters tall, then we could actually see the single process through which the reaction evolves. Instead, it's as though the end result is caused by contributions from every possible process."

She pointed at each of the new diagrams. "Look at the closed loops in these diagrams. An electron and a positron pop up and then annihilate back into the photon—this is where your friend claims to be able to get free energy."

Ryan said, "You read Foster's book?"

"No, I skimmed the web page. It's obvious that they're running the same basic scam as most of these idiots—whether they actually believe it or not—plus, they include enough creationist nonsense that anyone who disagrees with them can be labeled a heretic."

The look of disgust on her face betrayed that she was indeed related to Dodge. Nothing could be a greater turnoff to Ryan. "Whoa. That's pretty harsh—you should read the guy's book before condemning him."

Her eyes met his. The disgust was replaced by something that looked like concern. She said, "It's nice of you to defend your friend, but he is not the first one to try this. You have the book?"

Ryan ran upstairs and got it. When he returned, Emmy was thumbing through Katarina's calculus text with Katarina looking over her shoulder. Emmy was just slightly taller than Katarina. He wished he could take a picture of Katarina so engaged with this woman.

Dodge came in and set a box of pizza on his desk. "Have you two figured out what Ryan's fundamentalist pal is trying to do with those patents?"

Ryan added, "Beer?"

Dodge disappeared and came back with beers for Ryan and Emmy and a Coke for Katarina.

Katarina said, "Dodge is almost nice when Emmy is here."

Ryan added, "Nearly human."

Emmy said, "This is an investment to him. He expects to make a fortune suing that company."

"What?" Ryan said.

"Aren't you suing Creation Energy?" Emmy asked.

Ryan said, "I'm not going to sue my best friend."

Emmy looked at him again. She motioned toward the door, toward Dodge, and said, "He thinks you are."

As Ryan and Katarina ate pizza, Emmy opened Foster's book. "Look, it says so on the first page." She set the book on the desk, indicated the second paragraph, and read aloud: "'By reconstructing the conditions just prior to Creation, an opening is provided between the spiritual and physical worlds where energy can be derived from what are called vacuum fluctuations.'" She looked up. "See? *Vacuum fluctuations*, that's what the loops in these diagrams are called. Electron-positron loops pop out of the vacuum and then disappear—a fluctuation in the vacuum. They are, however, fundamentally impossible to observe directly."

Ryan said, "Foster must have found a way to get energy from them." He hated the tenuous feeling of defending something he didn't understand.

"I'm sorry, Ryan. Perhaps your friend genuinely believes it, but he is mistaken, okay?" She seemed to really mean it. She seemed to really mean everything she said. Ryan realized he'd never hit on a woman before who so fully lacked bullshit.

Emmy caught something in his look and leaned toward him. "Ever since quantum mechanics was formulated, about eighty years ago, people have tried to get around the Heisenberg uncertainty principle." She took a piece of pizza. "I'm sorry, but your friend has made a mistake."

"I like that," Katarina said. "An uncertain principle. That's perfect for me."

Emmy laughed and almost choked on her pizza. She set her slice down, wiped her fingers on a napkin, and picked up her pencil. "The Heisenberg uncertainty principle can be interpreted in two ways." She wrote an equation on the blotter: $\Delta E \Delta t \geq h/4\pi$. "The ΔE is the energy scale, Δt is the time, and h is Planck's constant—it's a wicked tiny number. Anyway, I call this thing the watermelon-seed principle. You know how slippery watermelon seeds are? Right when you get your fingers on them, they squirt away." She pointed at the E and then the t in the equation. "This means that once you measure the energy, all the information about time squirts away. Conversely, if you determine the time it takes for something to happen, all the information about the energy squirts away—like trying to pick up a watermelon seed."

Katarina said, "But you *can* pick up watermelon seeds."

"Yes, but you have to be careful. If you squeeze too hard, it slips away. To pick up a seed, you localize it, cradle it in the watermelon flesh, and then you can scoop it out." Emmy tapped the equation again—there were several dots underneath the E and t now. "What this means is that we have to balance how accurately we measure energy with how accurately we measure time. Heisenberg's uncertainty principle limits the accuracy of measurements—it is the mathematical realization that we are part of the universe and that we cannot separate ourselves from our observations."

Katarina's eyes were wide. Ryan had never seen her look so unguarded, guileless, so much like a little kid before. She said, "You can actually prove that we are part of the universe?"

Emmy had the same look about her. She nodded rapidly and said, "Isn't it awesome when the math corroborates the obvious? It's like following a treasure map and seeing that you're on the right track."

Katarina said, "I'm thinking that if the math says we aren't part of the universe, it might be wrong." On the corner of the blotter, she manipulated the equation, solving for *E* and then *t*.

Emmy continued, "Okay. That's the first interpretation. The second one is more important. It is the reason that these vacuum fluctuations can't be observed directly. From the watermelon-seed argument, you can see how the picture is blurry. You know the seed is there, but you can't get a good grip on it. In a blurry picture, it's hard to tell one thing from another. They smear together, and we have to try to account for what we can't see, what's hidden by the blurriness." She pointed at the loops in the two diagrams again. "We can't decipher processes like these. Heisenberg's uncertainty principle tells us that these processes occur too fast and with too little energy to be observed. We call these *virtual processes* to distinguish them from *real processes*. A real process is a watermelon seed we have in our hand. Virtual processes are the seeds buried in the flesh. We know they are there, but we have to cut up the watermelon to see them."

Katarina said, "Didn't you have to cut the watermelon to get the real seed?"

"Exactly." Emmy's voice resonated with excitement. "That's how we isolated it, and if I want to observe a virtual process, I can change the system, usually by injecting energy, and make it into a real system. Of course, then I don't have a watermelon anymore."

Emmy set the pencil down and picked up her beer. "Your friend thinks that he's found a way to violate the uncertainty principle to extract energy from vacuum fluctuations."

"Why are you so certain that he can't?" Ryan felt like he had to talk fast to get words in before she swallowed. "It's a theory, right? Why are you so dogmatic? Has there ever been a theory that wasn't flawed in some way?"

Emmy put her beer on the blotter. "If the amount of energy that came out of whatever process they're using is larger than what went in, it would violate the first law of thermodynamics. Remember, energy is neither created nor destroyed; it can only change form."

Katarina said, "Sounds like something came from nothing, to me."

Ryan pointed at Foster's book. "Maybe he's found a way to change spiritual energy into physical energy."

"Please." Emmy sighed. "That's absurd."

Ryan licked his lips. "Hey, I'm not saying that he knows something you don't, just that neither of you knows everything."

Katarina said, "And once again, I must ask, where'd it come from?"

"There was no 'where.' It is here," Emmy said. "Okay, language evolved for us to describe a world where our hearts beat about once each second and a piece of pizza has a couple of hundred calories. Now remember, Planck's constant, that *h*, is way tiny, so tiny that it might as well be zero as far as our senses are concerned. It can be confusing, but fortunately, by describing it mathematically, we don't run into any of these semantic problems."

"Lame," Katarina said, looking back and forth at the two of them. "Lame, lame, lame. It had to come from somewhere. The universe is proof that something came from nothing, so there must be a way for it to happen again."

"She's got a point. The existence of the universe is what engineers call proof of principle," Ryan said. "Something came from nothing—the obvious conclusion is that it came from God."

"Okay, this is another one of those questions like, what was here before the universe? Saying that something had to create the universe doesn't make sense. You end up with an infinite series of origins: if God created the universe, who created God, and who created whoever created God, and so on." Emmy put her pencil in her pocket. "Anyway, I need to get going."

Ryan said, "You should read Foster's book before you attack it."

"Okay, I'll read it. But I have a book I want you to read too."

Ryan held out his hand. "It's a deal."

They shook on it and, in that instant, Emmy held her head at a slight angle. Her eyes narrowed at Ryan as though she were looking inside him. The flirting had felt like a game, but with those eyes on him, he wondered.

Katarina interrupted them. "You had no problem with an infinite sum of these loop diagram thingies, but you don't like a creator creating a creator creating a creator?"

Ryan added, "Einstein believed in God; don't you?"

Emmy took her hand away from Ryan. "Einstein referred to whatever set the Big Bang in motion as a Divine Spark. It is a much different idea of God than the deities invented by human cultures."

Katarina asked, "You really don't believe in God?"

"Define what you mean by *God*."

Katarina said, “God is just the energy or maybe God is the particles and forces or maybe God is space and time.”

“If you define God as energy, then, because I believe in energy, I believe in God. That would be a small step of faith. But it would be a huge leap of faith to believe that the energy in the universe requires that I worship it or that I should kill people who don’t.”

“That’s kind of extreme.” Ryan stared at her. She looked almost playful. He said, “Which do you think came first, matter or consciousness?”

“Consciousness is the result of biochemistry, so the chemicals had to come first.”

“What about the soul?” Ryan asked.

“There is no reason to believe in anything like—”

Emmy had raised her voice, but Katarina’s was louder. “You said that when we look at an interaction, we have to include every way that it can happen. Why not include the soul? Isn’t a soul just as possible as a universe? I mean, what if we had asked you about the soul, and you were like a priest or something? Wouldn’t you have gone through the same argument about the creation of the soul that you did with the Big Bang?”

“No.” Emmy settled back into her lecturing voice. “There is compelling evidence for the existence of a universe and no evidence for a soul.”

Ryan took the last slice of pizza. “What do you think happens when people die?”

“They die. It’s over.”

“Wrong,” Katarina interrupted. “You might know a lot about electrons and energy and stuff, but you don’t know anything about where someone goes when they die. Saying it’s over is mean.”

Emmy leaned forward and spoke calmly, as though her expectation that this child would have a tantrum had been confirmed. "What do *you* think happens when someone dies?"

Katarina caught her tone and, instead of speaking through clenched teeth like she did when she was angry with Ryan, assembled her composure. "I don't know what happens, but I am going to figure it out. Watch me."

A week after Emmy's visit, two packages arrived. One was a six-foot whiteboard with twenty colored markers. The other contained two copies of Richard Feynman's *QED* and the three-volume set of *The Feynman Lectures on Physics.* Emmy had included a card for Katarina with four sets of arcane mathematical symbols surrounding a light bulb and the caption "…and God said, let there be light" but she'd scratched out "God" and written in "Maxwell." Ryan explained that Maxwell's equations were named after the nineteenth-century physicist who formulated electrodynamics.

In the card, Emmy told Katarina how she had loved the purity of mathematics as a teenager and that she envied Katarina seeing "infinitesimals, differentials, integrals, and derivatives for the first time—someday you will use these tools to discover truth in the universe. I hope that I will be working with you when you do."

Ryan and Katarina stared at each other. Katarina squinted and set the note aside, brushing it off. Ryan said, "That's a lot to live up to, kiddo."

Katarina said, "What. Ever."

Emmy included a note for Ryan too, just a few words that it was "nice to meet you" and "call if you have any questions," but there was also a cryptic phrase: "I promised to read Foster Reed's dissertation and you promised to read Feynman's *QED*. Don't ever break a promise to me!" The thing that made it hard to figure was that if you looked long enough at the dot over the *i* in promise, you could convince yourself that it was heart-shaped.

They argued about where to hang the whiteboard and compromised on Ryan's side of the wall that separated their apartments. When it was finally up, Katarina used all twenty markers to draw a dragon. As she drew, Ryan reread the note from Emmy. Holding the note in both hands, he toyed with Sean's football with his feet and unveiled images of Emmy from his memory of her visit. He was smiling at the vision of Emmy when she had caught him staring at her—she'd had a sparkle in her eye, a beer in her hand, and, damn, her body was just so tight and perky.

Katarina interrupted him. Imitating Dodge's nasal whine, she said, "Stop obsessing over your girlfriend, McNear. You're pathetic."

"You think she'll be my girlfriend?"

From that day, the whiteboard was covered in squiggly lines, loops, and mathematical symbols that were constantly written, rewritten, and analyzed. Ryan moved the pile of foam he called a bed so that he could stare at the day's analysis as he fell asleep.

They worked through Feynman's books, and when they couldn't figure something out, Ryan suggested they call Emmy. And every time Ryan made the suggestion, Katarina teased him. In response to the teasing, Ryan pretended they needed to call Emmy at the slightest confusion, like when the black marker ran dry.

Through spring, Katarina soaked up calculus, including ordinary and partial differential equations, and was doing vector calculus before school let out for summer. If she'd had an involved parent, Katarina would have met with a school counselor and switched to an advanced math class. Instead, she did only a serviceable job with eighth-grade algebra while bothering her teachers with questions on subjects ranging from fractals to group theory.

Ryan exchanged e-mails with Foster every week, and the answer was always the same: "Save some time on your calendar for next month." His impatience grew. In three and a half years, the only place he'd seen Sean was in nightmares, images of Sean frozen in time, unable to mature in Ryan's absence, or the slightly less disturbing picture of Sean playing ball with his *new dad.*

His most horrifying nightmare was too real to be a dream, more like a suppressed memory. Ryan's most palpable mistakes involved that addictive chemical, but at the heart of the choices that landed him in this mess sat Tammi. The nightmare began and ended with smoky images of what his meth-junkie girlfriend must have done to Sean that would cause a judge to issue that damn restraining order. As the months passed, the smoke started to clear, and Ryan realized that his subconscious was revealing something that he couldn't have faced at the time. He almost looked forward to the nightmare as the facts clarified in his own brain.

18

Happily ill-equipped to deal with the business side of things, Foster felt useless in these board meetings. All he could contribute was a bit of morale by saying things like "fabric of reality" or "vacuum fluctuations" in the same sentence with "Creation" or "everlasting soul."

At this particular meeting, though, he would have to make a request.

The Creation Energy Advisory Board was led by the primary investor, Blair Keene. It also included the faculty of Evangelical Word University's Department of Earthly Science, but the authority sat with the university chancellor, Jeb Schonders. Jeb was a large man who wore a Stetson hat, boots, and a bolo tie. Foster was certain that the man had never once undone his top shirt button, and he knew that when Jeb started rolling up his sleeves, he expected total quiet.

To Jeb's left, Blair Keene said, "Next on the agenda—we're finally getting somewhere with National Engineering Group. They've had some internal difficulties deciding which direction they want to take." Blair, the Houston trial lawyer, wore expensive suits with conservative ties and, depending on the audience, either tasseled loafers or boots. He had boots on today.

Jeb responded, "The bigger the herd, the longer it takes to turn, but they're coming into our corral now. Another benefit of keeping Foster out there speaking to the faithful. He rounded 'em up in Virginia, and the deal is almost cut. We've got a tenfold increase in our budget to consider."

Blair distributed copies around the table: an outline of Creation Energy's projected and existing debt and a lab wish list Foster had composed at the beginning of the fiscal year. While handing him a set of copies, Blair gave a covert nod to Foster. Funding was coming. Foster relaxed.

The board immediately split between those who wanted to reduce the company debt, led by the department chair, and those who wanted to spend whatever was needed to develop the technology, led by Blair Keene.

Jeb rolled his sleeves up. The room went quiet and he said, "Our deal with National Engineering will be signed by the end of the month. We'll be their primary R and D investment in renewable energy, and they're in a stampede to give us contracts for things like propulsion systems. They're already the biggest non-missile defense contractor and are fixing to extend that to missiles too. We need to be ready to spend the first round of funding on big things to establish Creation Energy as a viable counterweight to the US Department of Energy. It ain't a good time to be timid."

Foster waited to catch Blair's eye, just enough to convey thanks. More thanks. Foster marveled at the man. How could so much good, so much generosity and piety be packed into a single man? And a lawyer at that? Not only had Blair Keene provided all of Creation Energy's funding to date, along with half the university's startup money, but he was the father of Foster's angel. The term *father-in-law* seemed callous in the face of the magnitude of what Blair meant to Foster.

Blair argued with the department chair about funding options. It took longer for Jeb to join the discussion than Foster expected, but eventually, that preacher-voice drowned out the others. "Every cent goes to equipment. What's this at the top of the list? Blade servers? Wouldn't know one from a tractor tire—that's what we're buying next. And understand this: National Engineering wants to announce the partnership on their schedule—until they do, we will only refer to them as a Fortune 100 company, *comprendo*?"

Jeb challenged the board with his silence.

Foster cleared his throat and, as he spoke, pretended that he was writing a note to himself. "Perfect timing, Jeb. I'll invite the other inventor to interview for the software director position." The sound of his own words excited him, made it feel real. Foster owed Ryan. Something had happened at Foster's bachelor party that had started Ryan's downfall. He didn't know what but suspected that it had to do with what he thought of as the final act of his bachelorhood, that lap dance. It felt like a crisis rite, but it also caused a guilt-debt that he wanted paid. "With Ryan McNear in my lab, no computer cycle will be wasted. There is a synergy necessary in a project like this. Ryan knows what I need—he's the software guy, I'm the hardware guy." Foster handed out copies of Ryan's résumé and felt a wave of fulfillment. These were special men, men he could rely on.

Jeb's deep laughter echoed through the room. "You don't have to defend your choice. You know our *requirements*."

In the lab, Foster called these requirements the faith-filter. Every decision he made, every result he reported, had to pass biblical consistency. Foster knew Ryan had never even read the Bible. He said, "Ryan is a nitty-gritty engineer—exactly what my lab needs. He grew up Catholic." It was all Foster could say about Ryan's relationship with Jesus, and it felt like an exaggeration.

Jeb didn't look pleased. Some of the other board members shook their heads.

It was Blair, of course, who came to the rescue. "Wasn't Ryan McNear the man that God chose to start us on this path?"

"Yes," Foster nodded, a little sickened by the inevitable politics. "Writing the patents was Ryan's idea."

Jeb stroked his chin and looked around the table. He stopped at Foster and said, "Son, would you mind stepping outside for a few minutes while we discuss this? Nothing personal, of course, it'll just be a mite easier to speak our minds as we review his résumé. And easier for you too."

Foster sat up straight but didn't move toward the door. He looked to Blair, who shrugged. He said, "But I know Ryan. I know his résumé. I worked beside him at most of those companies."

"You ever work at Oil Xchangers?"

"What? No. What Oil Xchangers?" Foster scanned his copy of Ryan's résumé.

"That's the thing, you see. There are a few positions on his credit report that don't appear on his résumé."

Foster didn't know what to say. Everyone was staring at him. He realized that his mouth was hanging open. He took a breath. Someday he wouldn't have to remind himself to trust in the Lord. "Of course," he said, "speak freely. I'll be right outside if you need me."

He stood and walked to the door. As it swung shut, he heard two faculty members object. One said, "A lapsed Catholic?" and the other said, "He's from the East Coast."

It didn't bode well, but Foster was at peace in his faith.

Fifteen minutes later, they called him back into the room.

The men were quiet. Blair wouldn't make eye contact.

Jeb said, "We'd like you to consider other candidates."

Without thinking, Foster said, "No. Ryan is the right man for this job. It's his work. He should have a right to develop it."

Jeb's eyes opened wide. He then scowled, and Foster felt as though he were being examined. The words had come out so fast that Foster thought they had to be inspired, and it gave him added confidence. An hour ago, if they'd asked if he believed in Ryan, he might have waffled, but not now.

Foster met Jeb's stare. Jeb's eyes relaxed and he started to smile. Finally, he nodded and said, "All right, then. It's your call."

Ryan finally got the e-mail from Foster: "We want to interview you for the position of director of software next week." Ryan waited a day before replying so that he wouldn't appear desperate. Within thirty minutes of sending a note saying he "could be available," he got an e-mail from Foster's secretary with a complete itinerary.

Five days later, a Wednesday, Ryan walked into the San Francisco airport dressed in the high-tech uniform: khakis and a polo. In line at security, he talked to an Asian man carrying an Analog Devices briefcase. On the plane, he helped a computer engineer debug some software. The feeling of belonging stayed with him at the car rental counter in San Antonio and through the drive west to Hardale, home of Evangelical Word University. It wasn't until he set down his suitcase in his hotel room and caught his reflection in the mirror that doubts surfaced. The lines in his forehead seemed to extend the bridge of his nose up to his widow's peak, and the auburn hair over his temples had platinum highlights.

The next morning, Ryan jerked awake with the feeling that he was about to step off a cliff.

He dragged himself to the shower and then made a pot of tea in the in-room coffeemaker. As he sipped his tea, he caught himself wondering if he really believed what he'd read in Foster's book. Emmy sure didn't. Had Foster discovered something, or was it all an elaborate way of forcing religion into the context of science? He tried to put the thought aside. It was more important that he present himself as an engineer excited to start a new project.

The elevator door opened, and across the lobby, Foster rose from a couch smiling, his head cocked to the side.

Ryan held out his arms and said, “Dr. Reed, I presume?”

They met halfway across the room. Foster said, “God’s been watching over you. After all you’ve been through—you look fantastic.”

As far as Ryan knew, Foster didn’t know much of what he’d been through. Foster engulfed him in a hug. Ryan squeezed back. The smell and feel of his longest friendship helped but didn’t push away that feeling of stepping into thin air.

Foster hustled Ryan out to the parking lot. “Come on, we’re spending the day in the lab, dinner with faculty, interviews all day tomorrow, barbecue at my house, and sign a contract Monday. But first, I’m hungry.” He hit the remote entry and opened the passenger door of a red Porsche.

Ryan held up his hands. “Whoa!” He pointed at the huge spoiler. “Someone’s paying you more than you’re worth.”

“Rachel’s dad gave it to us as an anniversary present. As a professor, I’m lucky I make enough to eat—but you. You, sir, stand to make some serious cash.”

Before starting the car, Foster looked at Ryan. “Hey, we’re back on the front lines, man. This is how it was meant to be.”

“Do you have my schedule? I need background on everyone I have to talk to and—for Christ’s sake—tell me what they want to hear.”

“Hold it.” Foster winced. “Do *not* swear around here.” At the first stoplight, he reached behind Ryan’s seat and pulled out a folder. “The agenda is in here.”

The university gate was visible from half a mile: huge ivory-white columns reaching two hundred feet to a bronze arch that read "Evangelical Word University" in turquoise gloss. A gold cross hung from the arch. As they got closer, Ryan noticed the rough texture of the columns—stucco. The gates had outlines of angels blowing trumpets, and there was a small sign: "Established MCMXCIX, Year of Our Lord Jesus Christ."

Foster said, "Driving through these gates never gets old." He zigged under the arch and zagged down a side street. Rich green lawns covered small knolls with pale concrete paths that guided students from one white stucco building to another—all white and green with hints of Greek-temple architecture. He turned into a parking lot at a sign that read "Department of Earthly Science." Before getting out of the car, Foster placed his hand on Ryan's shoulder. "You'll see. Being laid off was the best thing that ever happened to you. You'll see."

Ryan raised one eyebrow.

Foster laughed. "It's going to be okay—we're back!"

They walked along a path to a small cafeteria. The students didn't dress the way they had back at UMass. No tie-dye, no piercings, and no weird hair—the men wore button-up shirts with tacked-down ties, and the women wore dresses that hung past their knees.

Over breakfast, Foster filled Ryan in on how he'd come to EWU. After getting laid off at GoldCon, Foster had gone to graduate school to study physics at Evangelical Word—it started with a piece of junk mail he'd received literally the day they were laid off. He'd be their first PhD candidate.

"At other universities, if you talk about faith, the Lord, or even invoke Creation—they ignore everything else you say. Evidence doesn't matter to them—they're that set on destroying the Word of God. You'll be hearing a lot about the attack we're under, but by the time you and I are finished, it won't matter."

Foster's rants were still the same. It was fun to see him get worked up, and Ryan found comfort in releasing his doubts by reeling Foster in. "Do you have a product requirements document?" The PRD defines the features of a new product so that design engineers have specific goals. Without a PRD, Ryan had once told a junior engineer at GoldCon, you just meander along the path.

Foster's face relaxed. "This is great. God bless you."

They walked back to the department and up a flight of stairs to Foster's office. Foster offered Ryan his desk chair. "I'm teaching a class in a few minutes. When I get back, I'll fill in the details."

Ryan sat in the chair and popped open his briefcase to show Foster that his copy of *The Cosmology of Creation* was suitably dog-eared and that he also had Feynman's *QED*.

Foster said, "Ryan McNear—always ready to get in the trenches."

"Well, I'm trying, but I still haven't figured out what you're doing."

"We're building a power generator based on a combination of biblical and physical principles. The great lesson of modern physics is that every law of nature can be traced back to a principle of symmetry. I discovered the symmetry that links the spiritual and the physical, the very symmetry that God used to create the universe." Foster had a cryptic grin, as though he were tempting Ryan to contradict him. It was the first indication that Foster wasn't quite the same guy Ryan had known years ago. The realization was comforting to Ryan; after all, he'd changed too.

Ryan ran his tongue across his lips, smiled, and offered an outstretched palm. "Dude, I'm with you, but I do have one question: How are you gonna build a power generator out of that?"

Foster looked at his watch and said, "That will have to wait until I get back from class." He motioned to the folder he'd given Ryan in the car. "Look through the university documents, check your e-mail, and relax while I'm gone." Foster grabbed a binder and stepped toward the door but stopped. "I'm sorry about what happened between you and Linda, but it's going to turn out for the best. I promise. You'll find your angel too." He closed the door on his way out.

A picture of Rachel, Foster's "angel," was set next to the computer. She was lounging on the blue ski boat in a bikini. Ryan thought something was different about her. Last time he'd seen her, she was still a skinny aerobics instructor. She looked good in the picture, happy and comfortable; maybe she'd put on some weight. Her hair was shorter now too. Maybe that was it.

There was a knock on the door, and before he could say anything, a petite woman with great gobs of curly white hair peeked in. She looked like Dolly Parton's grandma. "Why, I thought I heard someone in here—you must be Mr. McNear. We've talked on the phone—I'm Mabel."

Ryan stood and took her hand, offering a little bow. She said, "Darlin', can I get y'all a cup of coffee or a Coke?" He half expected her to kiss him on the cheek.

Ryan followed her to the coffee station and answered a slew of questions about California—yes, the weather is nice; no, the men aren't all "queer"; yes, the taxes are high; no, you don't see movie stars in every restaurant. He didn't have the heart to tell her he drank tea, so he took the coffee and excused himself back to the office.

He flipped open the folder and read the university brochure. EWU had been founded by a man named Joseph Bowie, a distant descendent of legendary Texan Jim Bowie. Joseph's father was an oil man, not quite in the class of Rockefeller, and his life goal defined the university mission statement: "We will build an ivory tower that will reach from Earth to Heaven, where the Word can be studied in both letters and science to provide a foundation that is based in Scripture and supported by faith."

It wasn't like anything he'd seen at UMass or at any business. That feeling came back for an instant, the sense of stepping off, but Ryan buried it under the realization that he couldn't recall anyone ever taking a mission statement seriously.

When Foster got back from teaching his class, he led Ryan down a hallway to a bridge that connected the Department of Earthly Science to the Creation Energy Annex. The bridge crossed over the lab's loading dock, flanked by two tanker trucks marked with green "nonflammable gas" signs, one for liquid nitrogen and the other for liquid helium. The tankers were attached to a huge stainless steel structure of pipes. Steam boiled off valves at the connections.

Inside the annex, a steel cylinder stretched from one end of the building to the other, at least fifty yards. Every few feet, the cylinder passed through ceiling-high towers with big valves connected to pipes feeding down. The ceiling itself was covered in trays that routed cables to the different areas of the lab. The steel tube ended at a two-story-tall device that looked like a giant soup can on its side. The floor had been dug out and the ceiling tiles removed to accommodate its height. Thousands of green cables emerging from seemingly every point of the device's surface were assembled in a great coil that disappeared into the ceiling.

Covering the opposite wall were endless racks of blade servers. Each rack held sixty-four separate computers connected by a spaghetti of orange cables—no monitors or keyboards, just raw computing power. Behind each rack, a fist-thick blue cable ran up the wall to a tray that fed the cables to the front of the building. Just to the side, as they walked in, the cables dropped like a waterfall behind a wall of flat-screen monitors. The displays were cluttered with charts and graphs and gauges with rapidly changing numbers. It looked like Mission Control at NASA but with a lot more cables.

A dozen men sat at workstations along each side of the control center. Some nodded to Foster, but most continued working. A young man stepped away from a granite lab bench. He was a short man with a big smile and short messy blond hair, wearing tan pants and a blue shirt. He was the only other person in the lab who wasn't wearing a tie. Foster said, "This is Matthew Smith—my graduate student."

Ryan shook Matt's hand but couldn't take his eyes off the endless row of blade servers. "How many teraflops have you got?" A teraflop is a measure of computing horsepower: one teraflop is a trillion floating operations per second.

Foster wagged his head to the side and said, "Not 'tera,' my friend, exaflops. Each CPU has half a gig of cache and ten gigs of RAM. They're networked with five-gig fiber-optics so that you—yes, you, Ryan McNear—can configure the entire system as a single massive serial processor or over forty thousand parallel processors." Foster wagged his head to the other side. "You like?"

Ryan ran his fingers along one of the racks. "Fuckin' A."

Foster said, "Remember what I said about swearing."

Matt went back to work, and Foster pried Ryan away from the computers to continue the tour. He indicated equipment they'd purchased and showed off equipment they'd built. As he spoke, Foster's enthusiasm increased. When he twiddled the knobs on a high-end oscilloscope to show Ryan a signal, Ryan felt the rhythm he'd always felt while working with Foster.

The long steel cylinder was a particle accelerator, a collider. Foster referred to the spaghetti of green cables as the system's nerves and the thick blue cables emerging from the computer racks as its spinal cord. "Right now, just one of the servers on one of the racks is controlling the collider. It will be your job to implement your invention—your patent of the soul—on this system of processors." Then he said the thing that made Ryan want to work here more than anything he would ever say again: "Did I get you enough computer power?"

Ryan nodded his head and licked his already smiling lips.

"Okay," Foster said, "now it's time for me to explain what we're doing. First—oh dang! I forgot to have you sign the form."

"Form?"

"Yes." Foster held out his hands in a gesture of surrender. "I've acquired a bad case of absentminded professor. You have to sign a nondisclosure agreement."

Foster led Ryan back across the bridge to his office, where Mabel provided a three-page form. Ryan had to sign in two places—one pledging that he wouldn't share any information, the other agreeing to yield rights to any intellectual property he conceived while working for Creation Energy. They were the standard nondisclosure agreement, NDA, and patent waiver forms that Ryan had signed at every company he'd ever worked for.

Back in the lab, Foster pulled a lab stool over to a wall covered from floor to ceiling with whiteboard. Then he handed Ryan a pad of quadrille-marked graph paper and motioned for him to sit.

Ryan took his mechanical pencil from his shirt pocket. Foster took a black marker from a tray. Foster had that same sparkle in his eye that he'd always gotten when he was about to share a cool idea. "Of course, it all started when we wrote our patents—Creation and the soul. When I was a graduate student, I discovered how the two fit together." Foster wrote and spoke at the same time: "The key is that the link between the physical and the spiritual cannot be observed directly.

"We start with the precept of faith." He turned and made eye contact with Ryan. "Faith is important here. Maybe it's obvious, but it's worth emphasizing. To be successful here, your faith in God cannot be in doubt."

That feeling nibbled at the edge of Ryan's conscience again. He took a deep breath and exhaled slowly.

Foster turned back to the whiteboard. "The precept of faith is based on the fact that believing in God, accepting Jesus, and obeying the commandments have no value unless they are done by choice. Free choice. If you could win the lottery by praying, then why have faith?"

Ryan said, "It wouldn't be much of a lottery if everybody who prayed won."

"Right, belief requires faith, and if acts of God could be directly and reproducibly verified by experiment, then there would be no reason for faith. The precept of faith means that we cannot observe God directly." Foster held the marker like a conductor's baton. "The next ingredient is Heisenberg's uncertainty principle. The uncertainty principle defines a boundary between processes that can be observed, real processes, and processes that can't be observed but still must be accounted for, virtual processes."

Foster took a laser pointer from his shirt pocket and aimed it at the cylinder stretching from one end of the lab to the other. "At that end of the particle accelerator, we're colliding positrons into electrons and—"

"Positrons? You have *antimatter* right there?"

"It's shielded. And the antimatter isn't a big deal. It comes from a radioactive source that emits positrons. The big labs like Fermilab and SLAC have been using positrons for decades. We know how to handle it." He put the laser pointer in his pocket and drew the same diagrams that Emmy had drawn.

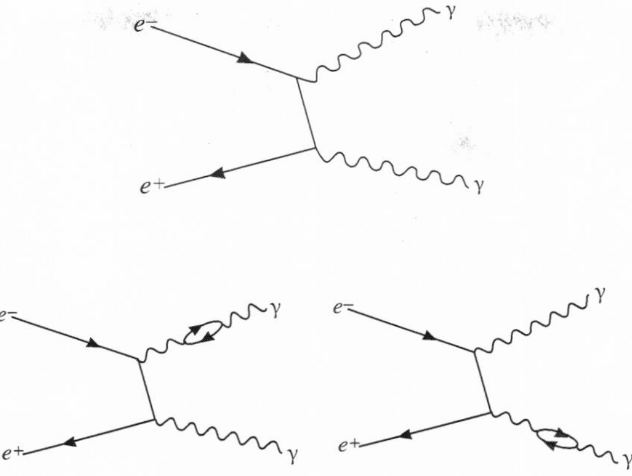

"These are called Feynman diagrams; Feynman was the perfect example of the scientific establishment—made incredible discoveries but wouldn't go to the Bible to see how it fit into the Lord's plan. Born Jewish, he fell to atheism.

"In these diagrams, the only things that we can actually *observe* are what goes in, the electron and positron, and what comes out, the energy of the two photons—everything that happens in the middle of the diagrams is unobservable or *virtual.* They're happening, but the way that God works and our place in Creation prevents us from being able to observe them. In other words, they're not directly observable, but we know they are there. If we ignore them, our calculations are wrong.

"The precept of faith works the same way. It requires that God's actions cannot be directly observed, but still, we know He is there. Do you see the symmetry?"

"Yeah, but it kinda sounds like you're rationalizing that God is unobservable." Ryan started to relax. The hardware in the lab and the lecture gave him the permission he needed to question things, and that helped wash the feeling of vertigo from his mind.

"Just stay with me." Foster acted like he was packed with secrets that he couldn't share fast enough. "The precept of faith plus the Heisenberg uncertainty principle mean that God acts in the physical universe through virtual processes."

Ryan chewed the end of his pencil. "So He can act in our lives, but we still have to make a leap of faith to believe in Him?"

"It's not a leap; it's a gift."

Now Foster sounded put off. Ryan found it oddly comforting. "Are you saying that God is virtual?"

"Of course not; the correct word is *spiritual*." He stared at the whiteboard. "The next piece is God created man in His own image. Think for a moment. What is an image?" Foster drew a vertical line. He labeled one side of the line *spiritual* and the other side *physical*. "When you look in a mirror, your reflection is slightly different from how you really look."

Ryan said, "Left and right are reversed."

"Right on," Foster said. "Think of a different type of mirror, a mirror with a different type of asymmetry, one that reflects the worldly image of a spiritual process." He indicated the vertical line. "I call it Heisenberg's mirror."

"Not bad," Ryan said. "Dude gets credit for stuff he probably wouldn't even believe."

"Remember the other thing that Heisenberg's uncertainty principle tells us, that our observations affect our measurements. That is free will." He wrote the words *free will* along the vertical line. "We use free will to choose how we live in Creation. All our choices affect our eternal souls." He added the word *Creation* below *physical* on one side of the line and *soul* under *spiritual* on the other. "If we could look in the Heisenberg mirror, then we would see our spiritual selves and how our choices affect our souls. We'd see that not only do our choices *affect* our destiny on Earth, but they *reflect* our destiny in heaven." He wrote *heaven* on the spiritual side of the line and *earth* on the physical side.

"It is in this sense that He created us in His image. We are His image in the Heisenberg mirror." Foster spoke softer to add, "This is controversial. Remember, the Bible doesn't tell us where the soul is. But, look, the symmetry is too perfect not to believe."

Ryan gathered it all together. Foster's theory was like a metaphysical layer on top of QED, a self-consistent layer, but still. Ryan tried to be diplomatic. "How can we see into Heisenberg's mirror?"

"When we pray, we can sometimes catch a glimpse, but our senses are stuck in the physical universe." Foster stepped to a blank part of the whiteboard. "This is the piece of the puzzle that gets us to technology. Ready?"

Ryan nodded, expectant, hoping to believe what Foster was about to say.

Foster wrote *energy-time* and said, "Creation was an act of God's will. During the six days of Creation, He allowed energy to transfer from the spiritual to the physical universe. That's how He 'let there be light' and, on the seventh day, when the right amount of energy was in the physical universe, He closed the window between the spiritual and physical, and since then, He's only influenced our reality through spiritual processes."

It wasn't that Ryan wanted to believe—he needed to. To see his son, to reclaim his life—it all rode on Foster being able to convince him that this lab was really onto something. The blur between science and religion wasn't any worse than Ryan's own nagging question about consciousness and matter, and fortunately, Foster's confidence was contagious.

"This brings me to why I need you." He pointed at Ryan with both index fingers. "Our power generator is based on the image of Creation. Where God is a purely *spiritual* being, our power generator is a purely *physical* thing that, with those computers and your soul algorithm, will acquire free will and transfer energy across the boundary. See? It's a simple symmetry transformation, like any other process in nature."

Foster went silent. Ryan could feel his stare.

Ryan clung to what Katarina had said: "The universe is proof that something came from nothing, so there must be a way for it to happen again." Wasn't that proof of principle?

The whole argument was based on symmetry. Ryan tried to separate the science from the religion. The Heisenberg uncertainty principle requires that there are processes that cannot be observed but still affect the universe—that's physics. Emmy had said the same thing. Foster brought up this other thing, though: the precept of faith—that if God's actions were observable and verifiable, then there would be no need for faith. That was religion.

At some point, Ryan had stood and started pacing. Foster leaned against the wall, waiting. Ryan said, "If I get this right, then the link between science and religion, the gift of faith, I guess you would call it, is that the uncertainty principle is to the physical world as the precept of faith is to the spiritual world."

Foster nodded, encouraging Ryan to continue.

"And the technology assumes this symmetry." Ryan stopped pacing. He looked at Foster. He had to do it, had to air out his doubts. "If there isn't a spiritual side—no God, no soul, nothing spiritual—if it's all physical and we're just biochemical machines, then the precept of faith is just a way to hide some mistaken superstition."

"Hold it." Foster jerked his head toward Ryan. "Of course it is a question of faith. Don't you remember what I told you? Faith is important here." It was the first time today that Foster had shown any sign that he might question whether Ryan was right for this position. But then his tone switched back. It was Foster again, his best friend, who said, "Come on, think about it. The Bible *has* to be consistent with science. Otherwise, Creation doesn't make sense."

Ryan sat back on the stool, wishing he hadn't shared his doubts. He scrambled for something to say and came up with "What about prayer?"

It worked. Foster returned to his lecture. "In Matthew, it says that whatever you ask for in prayer with faith, you will receive. To maintain the precept of faith, prayers must be answered in ways that cannot be directly observed. If they were directly observable, they wouldn't be in faith. Prayer is a spiritual act and so are God's actions in response to prayer."

Ryan said, "And since spiritual actions affect the physical universe as virtual processes, they happen, they have an effect, but they can't be directly observed."

"Yes. You rock!" Foster raised his hand for a high five. "It's just another way of saying that God acts in mysterious ways."

Ryan raised his hand and Foster gave it a firm slap. But Ryan's enthusiasm was slipping away. He couldn't shake a lesson he'd learned a long time ago. His freshman physics professor at UMass had been very clear: the laws of thermodynamics limit the amount of energy that an engine can produce, and it is always well under 100 percent of the energy that goes in. He could picture Dr. Kofler in front of the chalkboard saying over and over, "There's no free lunch, no perpetual motion machines. Energy can't be created or destroyed; it can just change form. And all types of energy—heat, motion, even relativity's mass-energy—can be traced back to this simple definition: energy is the ability to do work, force times distance."

Foster waited.

Ryan felt the tension. He ran his tongue along his lips, put on his disarming smile, and said, "Do you have a product requirements document?"

Foster slapped Ryan's knee and walked across the room. He opened a drawer, dug around, and came back with a colorful brochure. He indicated a paragraph on the back that read, "Creation Energy's power generator is a matter-antimatter collider, operating on the cusp of Heisenberg's uncertainty principle that will replicate the conditions of Creation and allow spiritual energy to flow into the physical universe."

Ryan stared straight down, pretending to examine the brochure. Was it enough to think of this as an experiment? That the only way to know for sure was to try? Was he rationalizing his way into this or did he really believe it might work? If only Katarina were here to help him hash through it.

Foster walked across the lab and motioned for Ryan to follow. "Here's your power generator." He indicated the huge steel structure at the end of the accelerator. "This is where the positrons and electrons annihilate into energy. Right now, it detects the reaction and measures the energy released. It's called a calorimeter." He pointed at the rack of computers. "Once we implement your soul algorithm, we'll use that energy to power a generator."

Ryan walked around the calorimeter, touching cables and connectors. As he circled around he saw the control center, the graphs, the monitors, the waterfall of cables, and the technicians at their workstations. He could feel the data being acquired. "You're creating energy now?"

"Yes, but it takes quite a bit more energy to create the reaction than comes out." He paused. "First, we have to break even. At breakeven, the amount of energy that's generated is the same as the amount consumed. Once we get over the breakeven hurdle, we'll have a power generator." He pointed at one of the monitors in the control center. It displayed two numbers: 138 kilowatt, the energy consumed by the collider, and 0.97 microwatt, the energy being produced.

Without thinking about the consequences, Ryan said, "That's a long way from generating anything."

"True, but look at this graph." Foster indicated another monitor. This one showed a curve that started at zero and went up from left to right, at first gradually and then ever steeper until, on its right edge, it was nearly vertical. "Even with the simple software that's controlling the reaction now, we're getting exponential growth in energy generated." He stopped and when Ryan looked at him said, "All the evidence shows it's going to work." He leaned against a lab bench and watched Ryan.

Ryan stared at the graph: energy versus time—data + results = reality. This is what he needed. That feeling that drives every engineer, the thrill of creating something new, something that would work, shoved aside his doubts. It felt as though the floor had solidified beneath his feet.

If they could maintain the rate of energy growth that this graph showed, they would reach breakeven in a few years. The Heisenberg stuff and the faith crap were one thing—theory always needs a big grain of salt—but the data spoke for itself. Ryan embraced a long-silent sense of excitement and urgency. "This could be the greatest power generator ever made. How come no one else ever thought of it?"

Foster put a hand on Ryan's shoulder. "Ryan, there's more going on here than we control. When we wrote those patents, we weren't alone. It will work. Questioning the inevitable will just slow us down."

Ryan spent the rest of the afternoon in the lab with Foster and the graduate student, Matt. They went over circuits, discussed software design, and reviewed a list of reference books that included one he'd already read, Feynman's *QED*.

Dinner was in the faculty lounge with the dozen professors from the Department of Earthly Science. Ryan found the faculty to be well educated, dedicated, and devout. By the time Foster dropped him off at the hotel, Ryan had convinced himself that he could be happy in the weird little college town of Hardale, Texas.

The next day, a Friday, started and ended with interviews. Every interviewer asked about the patents, and when they did, they acted as though the inventions were a biblical miracle. The wiseass in Ryan wanted to say, "We were trying to bilk a company out of a few thousand dollars so we could buy a boat." Instead, he nodded knowingly, emphasized his background in business and the fact that he'd coauthored the patents. The dean countered with, "The person we hire will run the technical side of an energy exploration company." Of course, it was only an independent company on paper. All product development would be performed in Foster's lab.

At lunch in the faculty club, the university chancellor, Jeb Schonders, said grace. The others looked down and went silent. Ryan started to cross himself. The chancellor glared at him and Ryan caught himself in time, turning the gesture into a forehead scratch.

The interview with the chancellor came immediately after lunch. He shut the door behind Ryan and offered a thick leather chair. The blinds were open but little light shone in. The chancellor's desk was huge, yet it held only a blotter and a large cross that appeared to be solid gold—if you swapped the cross for a revolver, the office was almost identical to Dodge Nutter's.

Schonders sat behind the desk, looked at his watch, and leaned forward. "I just have a few questions."

Ryan didn't like the way Schonders's eyes bunched together. When he said grace at lunch, he'd looked almost serene, but now he was frowning. Ryan licked his teeth and leaned back behind his most disarming smile. "Anything you like, Mr. Schonders."

"On this side of that door you call me Jeb, understand? If you get this job, me and you, we'll need to communicate in here—but, outside that door, I'm Reverend Schonders." He nodded twice and then launched into a series of questions about Ryan's background. Ryan answered each one in as few words as he could. The man's frown intensified when Ryan admitted to being Catholic.

Schonders said, "So you're a Yankee Catholic come to Texas but went to California when the going got tough."

"Jeb," Ryan said, "I'm an engineer."

It worked. Schonders laughed. It wasn't a sincere laugh, but the frown was gone. "You got a little mettle, and I like that. It'll be hard for me to trust someone as different as you, but Jesus guided you here, so I'll give you a chance." He brushed his hand across the desk as though sweeping the subject aside. "There are a few things you need to understand about what we're doing here, a few things that might want to stay in this office."

He took a breath before continuing. "You need to understand that we are at war. It's a culture war that's been going on since the Romans and Jews crucified Jesus. We can't give the enemy an angle for a wedge. These two inventions are more important than energy, technology, or wealth. They represent influence. Let me put it like this: the technology *will* work. Our investors will see to that."

"Yes sir," Ryan said. "I have a question, though."

"Shoot."

"What is the source of financial backing?"

Schonders started to speak but stopped. He picked up the gold cross and tapped it in his palm like a hammer. "We have a Fortune 100 corporate partner. They'll announce themselves when they're ready." He set the cross down in front of himself, balanced on its end so that it cast a shadow across the desk. "Now, back to the point I was trying to make, once your power generator starts supplying free energy, it might get out of control, maybe start a chain reaction. This is not what worries me. What worries me is that if I can figure it out, then some tree-hugger can too and put us right out of business. If we hire you, this might be your biggest problem." Ryan didn't like the way the man emphasized *if.* "It's a problem we'll work on together. Maybe you guessed it by now, but I'm no tweed-wearing pipe smoker—I get things done."

"Jeb, sir, we'll design a generator that we can control. Rest assured, the PRD—that's product requirements document—will include a kill switch."

"No." His frown came back. "You've got a lot to learn about faith." He stared at Ryan for several seconds then said, "Do you understand what faith is? A man with faith would stay out of God's way. If God sees fit for us to start the Rapture…well, what could be more glorious than that?"

Ryan didn't know what to say, and just as he was about to put his foot in it, he thought of his father and knew what he would have advised: never miss a good chance to shut up.

Schonders stood and, as he rose, bumped the desk just hard enough that the cross fell down with a heavy clank. "You need to spend more time with the Bible than with your PRD."

Foster was waiting for Ryan on the path outside the chancellor's office. He asked about the interview, but Ryan shook his head and asked, "Is that it for the day?"

Foster nodded and guided him to the parking lot.

"Good thing, because it's beer thirty and I'm toast."

"We don't drink."

"Whoa!" Ryan said. He stopped and took Foster's shoulder. "After a day of interviews? We're buying beer, plenty of beer, and you're damn well going to drink it with me. Weren't you the beer bong king once upon a time?"

"That was a long time ago." Foster said, then looked up in the sky and laughed. "All right, we'll stop at the package store."

Ryan climbed into the sleek red car and inhaled the leather scent. "I think the interviews were okay. I don't score big as a model Christian. How important is the chancellor's opinion? That guy is crazy."

"Hold it. He is not crazy." Then, a few seconds later, Foster sighed. "It's a typical management scenario. The higher up in the administration, the less they understand what we're doing—kind of like working at GoldCon, I guess."

The driveway to Foster and Rachel's house curled through a pine forest and opened at a clearing of expansive lawns with sapling hardwood trees. Foster parked, leaving the car at an angle with the wheels turned so that it looked like an ad in *Car and Driver* magazine. The front porch consisted of white columns towering over terra-cotta tiles.

Foster said, "This is my castle."

There had been a time when Ryan could have made a sarcastic wisecrack to his buddy, but "something hatched in Greece, raised in Memphis, and spoiled in Texas" stayed on the tip of his tongue.

If the size and architecture of the house had surprised Ryan, it was immediately overshadowed by the change in size and architecture of Rachel. She wasn't a skinny aerobics teacher anymore. Trying not to laugh, mostly at himself, Ryan realized what had bothered him about the picture on Foster's desk. She was still a tiny woman except for two outstanding new features.

"Rachel, you look fantastic." He jogged across the porch and pulled her into a tight hug, successfully staving off the urge to add "my, how you've grown" or "you could put an eye out with those" or "do they float?"

Once he got his eyes above her neck, Ryan noticed that Rachel was wearing dangling diamond earrings and as much makeup as he'd ever seen on a working girl. He also detected that she wasn't uncomfortable with the trouble he had keeping his eyes away from her chest.

Foster said something about what it was like to come home to an angel.

Rachel guided them inside, through the kitchen, where she put the twelve-pack of beer in the fridge. She didn't say anything about the beer but shook her head at the sight of the pint of brandy Ryan had insisted they buy.

They went out to the backyard where three seasoned steaks sat on a table next to a barbecue with white-hot coals.

Ryan drank beer from a bottle and sat at a table with Rachel where he had a view of their pond. "Fireflies! They don't have fireflies in California. Sean *loves* them."

Rachel said, "I talked to Linda this morning."

Ryan tried to suppress the surge of adrenaline that shot through him.

Rachel continued. "Ryan, we know you've made mistakes, but we want to help."

Ryan tried to relax, tried to exhale the gulp of air he'd just swallowed, but he couldn't get it out of his throat. Did she know why Linda had been able to get sole custody? Did she know he was wanted in Texas?

Foster was his best friend, but he would do whatever "his angel" told him. Ryan looked in Rachel's eyes. She knew. He said, "How is Linda?"

"She's doing well." She put a hand on Ryan's arm and spoke softly. "Ryan dear, I understand. Linda was never a strong woman. It wasn't her fault. She didn't understand why you spent so much time at the office. She just felt lonely and loneliness, well…I hope you can forgive her."

Ryan peeled the label from the beer bottle and crumpled it in his fingers.

She spoke more quietly, almost a whisper. "Ryan, you need to tell Foster. He's your friend."

Ryan stared at the pond and Rachel stared at him. He had to tell Foster now, otherwise Rachel would.

Foster came to the table with a plate piled with steaks, peppers, and onions. Rachel helped him serve. The three of them held hands and Foster said grace. He thanked the Lord for the food, friends, and beer. Rachel looked a little bit shocked at that last bit. Foster shrugged in response and said, "God made beer too."

Just as Ryan got his fork to his mouth, Rachel said, "Ryan wants to tell you something."

Foster turned to him, anticipating. Ryan took his time chewing.

Rachel said, "Ryan, when things go wrong, there is always a turning point. Whatever happened, we will understand."

Ryan swallowed. How could they understand?

"Come on, it's me," Foster said. "We're back."

Ryan didn't look at him.

"Whatever happened doesn't matter. I understand. I know these things happen for a reason."

Ryan ate some more. The three of them were quiet.

Then Foster said, "Oh. I know. It was the day we were laid off, wasn't it?"

Ryan's appetite for food was waning. He got up. "Can I get you another beer?" Foster looked at Rachel for an instant and then nodded. Ryan went into the kitchen. He looked at them through the window. They were talking, smiling. Rachel looked up and waved at him.

No one had helped him more than Foster had, and Rachel seemed to really care.

Back at the table, Foster said, "I remember that day. I went home to Rachel, and you wouldn't tell me where you were going. After that day, you started avoiding me."

Rachel said, "Ryan, please tell us what happened." She smiled and, in that light and with that tone, she reminded Ryan of his mom. The good version of Mom from before Dad died. She took his hand in hers. "It will cleanse you."

Foster was smiling, egging him on.

Ryan had never thought that a single incident had triggered anything. It had taken a lot of stupid decisions to ruin his life, and Ryan knew that he'd made every one of them himself. There was no shaking this off as misfortune, but if there was one day, it would be that day. The day he met Tammi. The day of his first hit of methamphetamine. Foster was right; it was the day they had been laid off.

Ryan took a deep breath. They were both staring at him. He said, "This is hard, you know. It was a difficult time. My divorce with Linda was a month old and everything was falling apart..."

⌒

The day that Ryan drove away from GoldCon for good, he took his time. He'd given too much to that company and not enough to what mattered. Linda had left him before he even realized how much he'd neglected her. The image of who he had become haunted him—it was a short film loop: A divorced father and his cute son climbing out of a shiny BMW at a chain restaurant. Man and boy sitting at a table with nothing to say to each other.

Of course, Ryan had known for weeks that the last day at GoldCon would come, that there would be a night when he would want to disappear.

There was an ironic justice about returning to the scene of the crime. Every time he opened the sports page, he saw the ad for that same strip joint where they'd had Foster's bachelor party. There was more justice there too. The place had gone downhill just as Ryan had. They'd lost their liquor license and converted to one of those totally nude places that encouraged men to bring their own booze.

He had it all planned. First, he stopped at his apartment, changed into jeans and a T-shirt, and rolled a couple of joints. Next, he went to the bank and got a couple hundred bucks from an ATM, then to a liquor store for a pack of smokes and a half gallon of vodka. He got on the freeway, put AC/DC on the stereo, and lit a joint. The traffic wasn't too bad, and he had the windows down with the music cranked. When he got off the freeway, he realized he was going about half the speed limit. He laughed and turned down the music, then realized he was going about twice the speed limit and turned it back up.

There were a lot of "gentlemen's clubs" on this side of town. The "Playthings" sign was made of flashing light bulbs. Half the bulbs were burned out—they'd all been lit at the bachelor party—and a piece of plywood had been added at the bottom with the words "Totally Nude Playthings, BYOB."

It sure wasn't the classiest place, and that was fine with Ryan. He wanted a night that fit his mood: dirty and foul, exciting and wild. He had nothing left to lose.

He got out and locked the car, realized the bag of booze was still on the front seat, unlocked the door, grabbed the bag, and headed inside.

A woman greeted him. It was her, in the same light-blue lace bikini top and g-string, the woman who'd put her phone number in his pocket on a piece of paper that his wife found. He stopped. He had no idea what to say or do. He didn't blame her. In fact, he found himself relieved to see her, that she was real, that she was sexy. Really sexy. He caught himself staring.

She didn't mind, though. She wiggled a little bit, her breasts quivering together. She took the bag from him and set it on a table. She pulled the strap of her bikini top to the side, exposing her right breast. It was full and round, and her nipple was light brown and pointed straight up.

She interrupted his reverie. "Give me a tip, honey."

Ryan looked up slowly. She pulled his face down between her breasts and made a high-pitched moan. Ryan yielded like a stoned ball of putty. She reached down and felt his groin. "Now give me a couple dollars."

He said, "I have to get change."

She guided him to the bar. On the stage, a skinny, bored-looking woman sat with her legs around a shiny pole. Ryan smiled at her as he walked by. She blew a kiss at him. Her hair was no more than an inch long; the roots were dark and the ends were white, maybe greenish. She looked silly sitting there in bright red shorts as if she'd just fallen down.

Two men sat next to the stage, each with a little pile of dollar bills and a six-pack of beer. At the other end of the room, a couple of guys were playing pool with a tall, buxom black lady in white lace. It smelled like ashtrays, spilled beer, sweat, and industrial cleaner.

Two other strippers sat at the bar. One woman was smoking a long cigarette and drinking from a green bottle of beer, Mickey's Big Mouth. He stared at her for a second, enshrouded in a horny fog.

"Ten dollar cover," she said, "and you'll need lots of change."

He took a handful of money from his pocket, and she converted it into a large stack of one-dollar bills. He took a couple of them and turned to his guide. She said her name was Candy.

He said, "Don't you remember me?"

"You've been here before?" She lifted her breasts together, indicating he should put the bills between them. He let his hand linger. She asked if he wanted a lap dance, gesturing toward a dark alcove to the left of the stage.

"Mind if I have a drink first?"

She guided him back to the table and his vodka, nodded toward the woman on stage, and said, "That's Tammi. Tip her well and have fun…"

He opened the vodka, took a swig, and offered the bottle to the dancer. She came down, had a long drink, and then went back on stage.

Tinny music blasted out of a dusty jukebox, dancing music with plenty of hard-rock chords. The song faded, and for a few seconds, the only sounds were bottles being set on tables and billiard balls colliding with each other.

The horny fog that had shrouded his head disappeared. The smoke stood still under the dim colored lights. The thin woman leaned against the wall at the back of the stage staring down at two crumpled dollar bills. She kicked one of them. The next song started, ZZ Top's "Legs," and she stepped toward the center of the platform.

Her hips swayed, and she rolled her shorts down her thighs, showing off the smooth skin between them, then back up. She turned around and looked back at Ryan. He took another drink. A lusty rush crept down his spine. She bent over slowly and peered at him from between her legs. She wiggled a finger at him to come closer. He took another drink, grabbed a few dollar bills, and did as he was beckoned. She pulled the crotch of her shorts aside, baring herself. Ryan held a dollar up. She pulled the crotch of her shorts farther from her skin. He slid the dollar between her thighs, and she leaned into his knuckles.

"Do you want a table dance?"

The horny fog rolled back in, and Ryan pressed his knuckles against her, saying something along the lines of "yuh-huh."

She pulled her shorts down, stepped out of them, and squatted on the stage. Her legs open, she leaned back and smiled at Ryan. She put her hands on the insides of her thighs and pulled the folds back, opening herself.

Ryan plopped into his chair and tossed a few dollar bills onto the stage. He leaned forward and stared at her, his eyes level with her crotch. He winked and said, "When you do that, I can see your gizzard."

Her eyes opened wide. "You what?"

"Yeah, when you open yourself up like that I can see all the way up to your gizzard."

She fell back on the platform laughing, curled her legs together, and then sat up on her knees. "Want to play with me, crazy man?"

He threw another couple of dollars on the stage. "I want to see your gizzard again."

When the song finished, Tammi collected her tips in a little purse and stepped down from the platform, taking care not to topple off of her huge shoes.

"Come with me." She motioned toward the shadowy alcove and he followed. She carried the bottle, her bony hips swaying back and forth. She took another drink and indicated for Ryan to sit on a couch.

The music started, and Tammi danced in front of him. Her breasts were too small to sway, but her long sharp nipples traced circles, mesmerizing Ryan. She moved forward, onto his lap, rubbing herself against his groin, practically fucking him through his pants, and holding his face against her breasts. After three songs, she disappeared in the back of the building.

Ryan stayed in the corner drinking his vodka and smoking cigarettes, his mood cycling from fascinated and horny to self-pity to disgust and back, over and over, ever more fuzzy. He tried to focus on the woman now dancing against the pole on stage. It was her, the woman who had ruined his life. She was beautiful. Her breasts jiggled perfectly, and her nipples slowly grew erect.

He found himself leaning against the stage, holding the bottle. She took a dollar from his hand and pulled her g-string off. The hair between her legs was cut short in a perfect *V.* She put the index fingers of each hand along the line formed by her leg and pelvis, pushing them together, squeezing and separating her lips.

Then she danced away.

Ryan's mood cycled back to self-pity and he objected. He objected to everything. He objected to this woman ruining his life, he objected even more vocally to this woman ruining his life but without ever fucking him. The woman glared at him, and he wasn't sure if he had actually said anything out loud.

He went back to the dark alcove and stayed there. The thin woman, Tammi, sat with him between her dances. He didn't notice the other men leave until the jukebox went silent and didn't come back on. He reached for his bottle, but it wasn't there, so he lit a joint and took a big hit. The woman behind the bar yelled, "No dope smoking!" Tammi took the joint from him and sucked the rest down.

Ryan didn't want to go home, but he didn't want to stay any longer either. "I lost my job today, my wife threw me out seven months ago, and I barely know my kid anymore. I don't know what I'm gonna do tomorrow and—where's my fucking vodka?"

Tammi pulled him up and guided him to the stage. She held up the vodka bottle, swirled it around, and said, "I'm gonna finish it." She tipped the bottle back for the last drops. She let the liquid fall from her mouth, and the bottle bounced on the wooden stage. She started to giggle, then slid down until she landed on her ass. "Come 'ere an' give me some money."

He stood, steadied himself, and took the rest of his money out of his pocket—only six bucks left. He swayed over, grabbed the edge of the stage for support, and half sat, half fell. "You watch what I'm gonna do for that dollar. Just watch." Reaching for the empty bottle, she lost her balance and then struggled to sit up. She started rubbing against the bottle. "Ooooo, it really burns."

She pulled the bottle into herself.

Ryan's mood shifted well into fascinated and horny, but then the music stopped again, and the turmoil came back. This was it. The high point of his life was watching a bony drunk woman impaling herself on an empty vodka bottle while begging for money. He gave her his last dollar, and when he told her that he didn't have any more, she started to cry. Then she tried to slap him but lost her balance.

"You. Have to. Drive me. Home." Lying there, the bottle slipped out of her and fell off the stage. She took off her shoes, stood up, and staggered into the bathroom. Ryan stood slowly and looked around. He caught his breath and walked across the room, then back. His balance wasn't too bad. He turned for the door, and as he opened it, Tammi stepped out ahead of him.

"You have to drive me home." She struggled to keep from slurring her words as much as he struggled to keep from staggering his steps.

"Sorry, I really have to go."

"You don't have anything to do tomorrow. Come on, I'll get you off."

It was dark out, cool and moist. He looked up. The sky was empty. Through the haze, he realized that no matter where he went, he'd still have to face himself.

"Dammit. I need a ride. Right now." As if changing script in midscene, she put on a warm smile and wrapped her arms around him. "Come on, honey, I'll take care of you."

He looked down at her. She leaned against him, smiling. He hugged her close and said, "Will you?"

She said, "I'm cold; hold me close."

"Let me get the heat going." He hit the remote on his key ring, and the BMW made clicking sounds.

"Is that your car?"

"Uh-huh."

"Are we gonna have us some fun!"

Ryan opened and held the passenger door. She slipped onto the leather seat.

He got in and started the car. The heat was cranked up, but Tammi was still shivering. Ryan offered her his coat. She said, "It's not that kind of cold. Just get me where we're going."

It took twenty minutes to drive to White Settlement. She directed him to the parking lot of a townhouse-style apartment complex and then hopped out of the car. She was back in fifteen minutes, no longer shaking.

"Figures, I meet a guy with a BMW and he's just been laid off."

Ryan sighed and drove out of the apartment complex.

Tammi lived in South Fort Worth in an apartment complex that had once been a cheap motel. As he parked, she told him that he shouldn't expect to have wheels on his car in the morning, and Ryan felt a great big sense of, "I don't care."

When they got inside, Tammi pulled a vial of white powder from her purse and said, "You want to snort it, shoot it, or smoke it?"

"What's best?"

She pulled a mirror out from under the couch and sat down. A few minutes later, she was holding a match under a glass pipe, and Ryan was inhaling.

Ryan felt a deep euphoric glow fill his body. It felt like there was finally a place for him in the universe. Tammi curled around him like a snake, and he caressed her. She was soft. The whole world was soft. The shadows along the drab white walls, the big paper light-shade hanging over the simple round table across from the couch, the grain of the wood of the coffee table, and the feel of the couch's brown velour combined in comfortable harmony. Ryan could feel the universe humming along.

The two lines that ran up his forehead relaxed.

As he finished the story, Ryan paced back and forth from the table to the barbecue. "I moved in with her a couple of months later." He stopped at the table. It had gotten dark, so he couldn't see their reactions.

They were quiet for a few seconds, and then Rachel said, "Why did you move in with *her*?" She said *her* as though she'd swallowed a bug.

"I don't really know." Ryan sat down. "I had nowhere else to go, I guess. She took care of me." He grimaced. "It sounds so gross, but you know, when you have nowhere to go, no work, no family, and everything you ever thought about yourself has disappeared, well…"

Ryan leaned back in his chair, unconsciously copying Foster's pose. If there had been some light or if he'd leaned forward and looked at his hosts, he might have seen how Rachel, who had been holding his hand when he started the story, had recoiled. He might have seen Foster's scowl. Instead, he sighed. "Yeah, you were right. As horrible as it is to relive that night, I guess it's good to have it off my chest. Secrets, you know, even horrible ones." He laughed and added, "Maybe I should go to confession."

The fountain sprinkled in the dark, and Rachel gathered dishes together and walked into the kitchen. Ryan didn't notice that she walked the long way around the table, away from him.

Foster did notice. He said, "Let's go around to my study door."

⁓

"We don't usually drink alcohol," Foster said, as if to make the point that Ryan had helped break some sort of vow. Then he poured two large glasses of brandy. "That was quite a story."

The room was lit by a brass lamp on a small table separating the two leather chairs.

Foster added, "I wonder how your experience fits into His plan." He swirled his glass, took a deep breath, and coughed. "You know it's not that alcohol is a sin, it's that 'deliver me from temptation' means you don't walk right into it. We're safe here."

Ryan took a long sip and swallowed slowly. The warmth flowed down his neck and stretched out to his fingers. "You've really got it made, Foster. Fuckin' A. This house, that car, the job you always wanted..."

"I am blessed. I was guided here to walk in the Lord's footprints and understand. Since then, so many capital-T truths have been unveiled to me."

"The chancellor told me I'd be better off reading the Bible than working on the PRD."

"Remember when we were writing the patents? Remember how frustrating it was that Genesis was so short on details?"

"Yeah, it's because the Bible was inspired by God but written by men."

"No, no, no. The Bible is exactly the Word of God, but it is short on details."

"Foster, doesn't the Bible say that pi is exactly three?"

He chuckled, "Yes, 'it was round all about, ten cubits from one edge to the other and a line of thirty cubits did compass it about'—missed by five percent."

"Then the Bible isn't exact. It's an approximation. What's wrong with that?"

Foster flashed a glare in response, as though something had fallen into place, a big clunking doubt. The look went away as fast as it appeared. "You need to trust the Lord, Ryan. If He had provided the mathematical details, it wouldn't have meant anything to people thousands of years ago. But now…" Foster leaned forward. "I think that a new book of the Bible is coming. I think that it will have the details that we can now understand. What if God had spoken through Einstein or Feynman? What if God told a mathematical story of Genesis to someone who could understand?"

"Who, you?"

"I don't know. I can only tell you that every seeming coincidence in my life has led me here. I've sat with humility before the great math and science texts…"

Ryan almost choked on his brandy. Foster was a good guy and everything, but he'd never done anything with humility. "Did He talk to you?"

"I think He was speaking to us when we wrote those patents, and I think that we'll find out for certain soon."

"The chancellor kind of bothered me. He seemed to care more about how the project appears than if it will work." Of everything he'd learned today, this kept coming back to him, Schonders tapping that gold cross on his desk and talking about the Rapture—it seemed crazy. Ryan tried to grab that feeling of certainty he'd had in Foster's lab. "You have millions of dollars of equipment. Is there venture capital funding?"

"The chancellor is a good man. He's a warrior who's been fighting a long time."

"Right, but who paid for all your equipment, and who's going to pay my salary?" Ryan realized that he had just assumed the position. It felt good. He put the chancellor out of his mind, and the whole situation started to feel as warm as the brandy in his belly.

"Ryan, you need to have faith."

Ryan clenched his teeth, giving Foster his get-to-the-point look.

Foster sat up straight and said, “Rachel’s father, my father-in-law, Blair Keene, donated seed money to a lot of projects at EWU, including ours. He and Chancellor Schonders have just signed a deal with a Fortune 100 corporation.” He nodded toward Ryan. “You don’t need to know who it is yet. The main thing is that you not forget who we’re working for.”

“Well, that’s exactly my question. Who are Creation Energy’s investors?”

“All right, Ryan, listen. I’ve been hoping you’d see this for yourself, but I can’t wait any longer. Make no mistake about it: we’re working for God.”

They were quiet. Ryan poured another shot in each of their glasses. “Hey, Foster, I’m a little uncomfortable with how you keep falling back on God whenever it’s convenient.”

Foster sat up straight and wagged his head as though he couldn’t believe what Ryan had said. “Ryan, listen to me, listen very carefully.” He pointed an unsteady finger at Ryan and held it a few inches from his face. “The Heisenberg uncertainty principle sets the scale for how close we can get to the universe; free will sets the scale for how close we can get to God.” He continued to point that finger and spoke a few decibels louder. “There is no room for questioning who defined those scales—and certainly not by someone like you…”

Ryan started to react, but one thought worked its way through the alcoholic haze: he needed this job. The only alternatives were to sue Creation Energy, Foster, and EWU, or continue on the road to nowhere.

Foster was staring at him. His face was red, and he looked mean. Ryan had seen him like this before, of course, back in the day, but this time Ryan needed him.

Ryan licked his lips, smiled that smile of his, and held out his arms, palms facing up. “It’s okay, Foster. I’m with you, and

I appreciate your honesty. You can trust me to follow your lead. I was just airing out my doubts."

Foster's condescending tone turned smug. "Of course, Ryan. I understand. Just keep fighting your doubts and embracing your faith." He leaned back. "You know what? I envy you. You're on the path to salvation."

"You're fuckin' drunk is what you are."

"No, Ryan, I'm right. Well, yes, I'm drunk, but I'm right too." Foster reached a wavering hand to his glass and discovered it was empty. He took the bottle and splashed equal amounts of brandy in his glass and on the table. "Good thing the carpet matches the brandy." Giggling, he took a long drink that ended with a choked cough. "It must have gotten pretty bad. Linda told Rachel that you haven't been allowed near Sean in years—what happened?"

Ryan stared into his brandy. "Oh, Jesus, do I have to tell another story about something I've been trying to forget for three and a half years?"

"Hey! Told you not to curse."

"Huh? Oh shit, I'm sorry."

Foster giggled again. "That's better."

They were quiet for a few minutes. Then Foster said, "Yes, tell the story. You were such a fine father; what could you have done?"

Ryan sighed. Then he sucked down the rest of his brandy and refilled. "I don't know exactly what happened." But as he said those words, it became clear. It was his nightmare, not his memory, but he knew what had happened. Night after night he'd woken from that nightmare with nothing but smoky images of what Tammi might have done, and now, from a combination of what Sean had told the judge and what he knew of Tammi, his subconscious had finally worked it out. In that instant, it emerged from the haze of brandy in his head.

He spoke without thinking, listening to the words as he said them, half storyteller, half rapt listener.

"Three years ago—New Year's Eve, in fact—Tammi was at work, flashing her pussy for dollar bills. Anyway, Linda dropped Sean off at the apartment, and the two of us watched Disney videos, ate pizza, and played Junior Monopoly. We fell asleep on the couch around midnight. Tammi got home a couple of hours later, and that's when the nightmare starts."

The first thing Tammi saw when she walked in the door was Ryan flopped on the couch with Sean. She reached under the couch for the mirror and her stash, but, of course, with the brat there, Ryan had hidden it. She shook him awake. "Where's my stash?"

Ryan stretched and reached his arms around her and said, "Happy New Year, beautiful."

She smiled in spite of herself but pulled away. "Let's get a little New Year's buzz."

Ryan rested his arm across Sean. "Naw, I gotta be Dad in the morning. It's in the closet on top of your shoes."

In the bedroom, Tammi set the mirror on a nightstand, tapped some meth from a vial into a glass pipe, and held a pink lighter under the pipe until the meth liquefied and started to boil. She pulled it into her lungs and leaned back on the bed. The world took on that soft glow again. All better. She kicked off her shoes, took off her clothes, and climbed into a T-shirt that hung down to her thighs. She rubbed the shirt against herself, savoring its soft warmth.

She called, "Ryan, are you coming to bed?" When he didn't reply, she danced into the living room. They looked sort of cute, Daddy and son. A bit of the edge crept back—Ryan was hers now. She leaned down and yelled in his face, "Go to bed!"

His eyes opened and Tammi took his hands. They were rough. She remembered how soft they'd been the night they met. He was hers. The edge faded back behind the glow. She tugged, and he sat up and then followed her into the bedroom.

Ryan climbed under the covers and fell asleep almost instantly. Tammi climbed out of the T-shirt and crawled in next to him. He pulled her close. That was what she wanted, except that she wasn't quite sleepy. The longer she lay there, the more she wanted to play. She tugged at his groin, and just as she started working her magic, he rolled over, his mouth fell open, and he started snoring.

It was the wrong thing to do.

She ripped the covers off and turned the light back on. Ryan put his head under the pillow.

What a prick. He moves into her apartment, brings his asshole kid whenever he wants, and then rejects her?

She tapped a little more white powder into the pipe and had another hit.

Much better.

She rubbed her nipples in circles with her palms and skipped into the living room to look at Sean. A miniature version of Ryan, he couldn't be any cuter. His bare knee stuck out of the sleeping bag. She tucked him in and zipped it up. She cooed at him, and he curled up against her. Maybe he wasn't such a brat.

She rubbed his shoulder. He made a comfy sound and opened his eyes, the same blue eyes as his daddy. She leaned down, rubbed her nose against his, and whispered, "Hi, honey."

Sean jerked upright and stared—just like the men who came to see her at Playthings. She leaned back and rubbed herself, her best tip-generating maneuver.

"Ewww," he screamed. "You're naked! What are you doing—YUCK!"

It was the wrong thing to say.

Sean pushed his face into the folds of the couch—her couch, in her apartment.

Tammi went back in the bedroom. Ryan was still snoring. Motherfucker.

She picked up her pipe, put the rest of the meth in it, and took it into the living room. Sitting at the edge of the couch, just clear of Sean's feet, she took a big hit and then exhaled the smoke into the folds of the couch where Sean was hiding his pathetic face.

He worked his way deeper between the cushions.

Tammi danced around the living room, letting the buzz consume her. She couldn't sleep now, but why would she? It was New Year's Eve. There had to be a party somewhere. She put her big T-shirt back on, slipped on stockings and a garter belt, and as she walked to the door, she noticed the pipe sitting on the coffee table. She giggled, picked it up, leaned down, and placed it into Sean's suitcase, underneath his socks.

"When Linda unpacked his bag," Ryan said, "she found the pipe and, next thing I know, we're in court, and the judge is issuing a restraining order against me and granting Linda sole custody—that was the last time I saw Sean."

As Ryan finished the story, he looked up and realized that Foster was sitting up straight.

"Ryan, that's bad." He spoke in a tense monotone, shaken into sobriety. "That woman is evil, truly evil. How could you let that happen?"

Ryan, wading through misery, mistook Foster's glare for empathy. "I don't know. The meth, I guess. You know, I was fucked up on meth for over a year, but I never, not even once, did I use any meth with Sean around. That's how I fooled myself into believing that I wasn't addicted."

Foster said, "How could you let that happen?"

"I was asleep when it happened."

"But that woman…"

"Poor Sean." Ryan hung his head. Had he warped the boy for life? "No wonder they don't want me around him."

Foster stood and stumbled away from Ryan, but, buried in misery and with his head hanging down, Ryan didn't notice.

Foster said, "You need to pray for forgiveness."

"I tried that." Ryan sat up and sipped the brandy. "While I was getting off the meth, I tried praying for strength and stuff, but it just made me feel guilty, like I didn't want Jesus and God to know."

"What? Do you know anything about the Word of God?"

"I know it's ridiculous. It's like I was embarrassed, so instead of praying, I just pushed really hard to get through it, and then, at the other end, it didn't really seem relevant."

"It didn't seem relevant?" Foster stepped toward the door.

"Not really."

"Not relevant? It's the only thing that's relevant. How can you—oh, never mind." Foster walked out.

Ryan passed out on the couch in Foster's study. He awoke a few hours later to blazing sunlight screaming into his head through the dry red orbs he called eyes.

Locking the blind into its open position, Rachel said, "Oh, I'm sorry, is that light bothering you?" She spoke much louder than she needed to, and, as far as Ryan could tell, the only reason to open the blind at all was to cause him pain.

He said, "Good morning, Rachel."

She scowled and walked out of the study, leaving the door open. A few seconds later, pans started crashing together in the kitchen.

Ryan sat up on the couch, squeezing his head between his hands, hiding from the light and noise. Something was in the air, something that it would take Ryan the next two days to realize. His headache was too sharp for him to feel the distance. Besides, his confessions had cleansed his emotional palette, just as Rachel had promised. He even accepted Foster's smugness. After all, everywhere he looked he saw evidence that Foster's choices had been superior to his.

The crashing pans went quiet, and he heard muffled talking. Then the pans resumed, and Foster came into the study. He looked about the same as Ryan felt.

"I have to drive you back to your hotel," Foster whispered.

Ryan nodded and followed him outside to the car.

Foster drove without talking, and when they got to the hotel, he said, "You should come to church with us tomorrow."

"I haven't been to Mass since I got married."

"I'm not surprised," Foster said. "That's your whole problem."

"I went and sat in church a few months ago. You'd have gotten a kick out of it. I kind of meditated on the similarity between a prayer book and a calculus text."

"Maybe that's all you need." Foster spoke with enthusiasm. "A worship service is a good first step."

"Sure," Ryan said, "sounds good. When I was a kid, Mom had to force me to go to church. But when I got there, the music and incense, the candles and stuff, it was kind of special. Maybe you're right. Maybe I should go more often."

"It's a start," Foster said and gave him directions.

Ryan spent the day in his hotel room watching old movies on TV and nursing his hangover.

The next morning, Sunday, Ryan wore a coat and tie despite the heat. He got in the rental car and took the highway. He could see the church from a mile away. It had its own off-ramp. He sat out front on a bench and waited for Foster and Rachel. Hardale's population, including students, was just over eight thousand, but the church filled all of its ten thousand seats. Officially, it was a nondenominational "Calvary of Christ" church, but the preacher was Baptist, the rules were Baptist, and everyone there seemed to be Baptist.

Still, Ryan didn't feel uncomfortable. As a boy, he had gone to Mass every Sunday, and at some point, wedged into the pew between his sisters, he'd feel something: a warmth, a calm, a special presence. Sometimes it came as the choir sang, sometimes while his parents were at communion. Sitting in that church with Foster and Rachel to his left and a little old lady to his right, he felt at peace. The chancellor sat a few rows ahead. His neck bulged over his collar. He was a little backward in the way of science and, like every manager, had an agenda. Foster's graduate student, Matt Smith, was seated at the end of the pew. Matt gave a little nod of recognition.

Ryan felt it again, just like when he was a boy: contentment and fullness. He looked up at the ceiling. Catholic churches had high steeples where he could imagine the Holy Ghost winking down at him. This church had a more humble ceiling—acoustic tiles. Still, Ryan felt a hint of something; maybe it was a divine presence, maybe just the peace brought by sitting with his friends. Then a thought occurred to Ryan, a thought he really liked: maybe friends are that divine presence.

After church, Foster guided Ryan to a vacant garden between the parking structure and a small amphitheater. He said, "Ryan, I need an answer. Do you believe in Creation Energy? That we will pass breakeven?"

"Foster," Ryan said, looking up in the sky at a little thunderhead. "I really want to thank you for everything you've done for me."

"Hold it, Ryan. That's not what I asked. Do you *believe* in our patents?"

"Come on, Foster." He laughed. "They love you here; you're practically a saint, but as I recall, you were more interested in spending the patent bonus on a boat." He watched a hummingbird levitate over a flowery vine. "I didn't feel God's presence that day. But, you know what? A few minutes ago, inside, there was something. It's been a long time since—"

"You think it was about a boat?"

Ryan finally looked at Foster. "Take it easy. We were both there." Foster's face flushed. "What do you want me to say? You've done some impressive work, but come on, I'm an engineer."

"I spoke with the chancellor a few minutes ago. He made a good point. You have to believe for it to happen. It might sound sort of new-agey, but it's true: you'll see it when you believe it."

"You're right, that sounds new-agey."

Foster looked away.

Ryan said, "Look, either the technology works or it doesn't. I'm here to write code and implement hardware, right? You interpret the Bible, I'll interpret the PRD, and between us we'll build one intense power generator, okay?"

"We'll see."

Ryan put his arm around Foster and said, "Exactly what I mean. Between the two of us, we've got it covered. We *will* see!"

The next morning, Ryan met Foster in his office. Foster motioned for him to sit but didn't say anything. Eventually, Ryan broke the silence: "Should I leave around noon? My plane back to San Francisco leaves at four..."

"San Francisco, huh? The Left Coast. Of all places, why did you go there?"

"Naw, it's okay." Ryan chuckled. "You know, I think I was guided there. I meant to go to Silicon Valley but got confused at a freeway junction—all these 80s: 580, 680, 780, 880—and I ended up going the wrong way. When I saw the sun setting beyond the Golden Gate—you should see it; it really looks like a gate—I thought of what you always say about how things happen for a reason, so I followed that feeling across the bridge and landed in Petaluma. You'd love the wine country. You want to come out and help me move? We could make it a road trip, maybe stop in Vegas on the way."

Foster sighed and then said, "I have a meeting. It won't take long. I'll be back in half an hour."

Foster's tone finally registered with Ryan. "Foster, I really want this opportunity."

"You don't get it, do you?" Foster said. He picked up his briefcase. Its seams bulged, and he had to lift it with both hands. "Ryan, this is more than an opportunity for you to clean up your mess. The scientific establishment has been waging this war on Christianity for hundreds of years, and we're losing. This could be the decisive battle in the war between right and wrong. Do you get that?"

Ryan stood, finally reacting with fortitude. "I interviewed for a job to guide the development of technology that you and I invented seven years ago. I've seen your lab and respect what you've done, but I also understand that this *opportunity* is essentially capitalizing on the prejudices of the scientific establishment."

"It's war and the good guys are losing. Do you want to fight in this battle?"

They stared at each other for almost a minute. Finally, Foster walked out of the office.

Ryan went downstairs and sat at a bench, a white bench just off one of the white concrete paths next to a white stucco building. His adrenalin dissipated and left a sheen of uncertainty.

Half an hour later, Foster walked up the path. He didn't make eye contact with Ryan. "Your hotel and rental car should be paid for. Have a safe trip home."

Ryan said, "What happened? What's wrong?"

"I wonder why you're here." It was as though Foster were talking to himself. "I can't hire you. Maybe you're not close enough to God. It's not for me to judge, but I can't hire you."

"What?" Ryan stood and poked his right index finger into Foster's chest. "What the fuck are you talking about? If you want to win this *battle*, you better accept that it's about technology—you can't build a goddamn generator on faith."

"Forget it. Please accept my apology. You betrayed your wife, your son, and…really Ryan, I'm so sorry. " Foster looked up and spoke to the sky. "There is a reason, though. I hope you find it."

"What? You filthy son of a bitch." Ryan shook his head and smiled at the irony. "This just in, *Professor* Reed: you wrote bullshit patents with me so you could buy a boat. It wasn't a miracle, it was stealing. Fuck you. And fuck your silicone-titted wife too."

Foster deliberately pushed Ryan's finger away from his chest. He spoke in a voice that was warm and calm. "You just don't understand." He turned and walked back toward his lab.

Ryan watched his old friend walk away. When Foster turned the corner, Ryan started to laugh. He felt like he'd woken from a spell. A spell that he'd cast on himself.

Here he was again, one friend fewer and no problems solved.

Ryan got off the bus and trudged up the hill to Nutter House. He pictured Foster's smug-ass face and the shock on Rachel's. It helped to keep his anger revved up. There would be no disarming smile and wisecrack to bring the peace this time. Foster Reed had stolen his work, was profiting from it, and had betrayed him—it was that simple.

Wasn't it? It was hard to keep the doubts at bay.

Marching up to the porch, he saw Dodge and Katarina through the window, sitting on that ridiculous couch watching TV. He laughed at himself, his imitation of Dodge's annoying chortle—Dodge might be his only ally.

He slammed the front door and jogged upstairs.

Katarina was knocking on his door seconds after he closed it.

Ryan threw down his bags, kicked Sean's football out of his way, and fished out his notes and Foster's book. He wrote down everything he could remember about Creation Energy. He combed his memory for the name of any company that might be investing, but all they'd said was a "Fortune 100 corporation" and Rachel's father. He let loose another Dodge-like snicker. To top it off, everything Foster had, probably even his wife's tits, was funded by his father-in-law.

His anger was thick enough that he only now heard the knocking on his door.

She finally turned the knob and walked in.

"Hey, Katarina, I don't feel like talking, okay?"

She said, "So don't talk," and sat on the floor, her back against the wall under the whiteboard with Sean's football in her lap.

Ryan sat in his beach chair looking across the valley. Foster was his best friend. *Was* seemed to be the operable term. No, that had the residue of rationalization to it too. Foster was just being Foster, smug-ass Foster. But there was another way to look at it: suing Creation Energy was simply a "business decision." Ryan had a right to any profit generated from his patent. This was how the intellectual property marketplace worked.

Ryan laughed out loud.

Katarina said, "So you're staying?"

"Huh?" Ryan leaned back in the chair so he could see her. The sun was setting and the room was dim. "Do you think every choice is actually a rationalization? Is there anything that people do that isn't contrived?"

It took a while for her to answer. Ryan liked watching her process the information. Her eyes seemed to fill up. It calmed him.

"Pleasing ourselves is the hypergoal," she said. "Though, Ryan-o, most of pleasing the self comes from what we think other people think, and what we think they'd think if they knew what we were actually thinking."

"You are a weird little chick." Ryan stood, stretched, and let out a loud yawn. "Well, I'm gonna kick my best friend's figurative ass. I got it rationalized every way to Sunday, but the truth is that I'm doing it because I can't think of any other way out of this mess."

"That's nice for you."

Katarina was fixing a box of macaroni and cheese in Ryan's kitchenette when he went downstairs.

Dodge was sitting at that huge desk with the distasteful green lamp. A short glass of brown liquid waited for Ryan a few inches from the revolver. He sat in the rocking chair with the silly diamond-tuck upholstery and set his notes and Foster's book between them. He drank the sweet, smoky fluid, and Dodge refilled his glass. The bottle had a gold label with the silhouettes of three birds, "John Powers, Three Swallow"—the same stuff Ryan's father had drunk the night he died. Terrance McNear drank nearly a fifth of John Powers, then walked out of the bar and fell in the street. A car ran over him.

Dodge said, "Tell me about your trip."

Ryan shuffled through the stack of paper and pretended not to be surprised that Dodge knew where he'd gone. The nondisclosure agreement was the top sheet.

"McNear, nothing happens without my knowledge." Dodge topped off Ryan's glass. "I take it you didn't get the job, and now, finally, you're ready to sue the bastards."

Ryan said, "I signed an NDA."

Dodge took the page and put it in an empty legal-sized manila folder. "Irrelevant." Then he set his elbows on the desk and touched the fingers of one hand to those of the other. He stared at his hands for a few seconds. "Ryan McNear, I've told you this before and I'll tell you again. I'm an attorney, and I am an expert on these things. You're lucky that they didn't hire you. Lucky." He looked across the desk at Ryan. "Listen closely. Getting a job in Texas will not help you. You must have a large sum of money, enough to pay a substantial fraction of your child support debt. Only then can you go to a Texas court and hope they will grant you an audience with your son. Having a job and making payments is not enough. Do you understand?"

"Dodge, I know. Okay? I'm here, I'm ready to sue my former friend."

"Just so we understand each other." Dodge began reading Ryan's notes. He laughed and coughed and set them aside.

"They might be able to pull it off," Ryan said. "They're not a bunch of hillbillies denying evolution. They have a particle collider in their lab and some serious computing power. They're a long way from producing energy, but at the rate they're going, it could happen in a year or two." Ryan took a sip, and when he set the glass down, a bit dribbled onto the desk. "Dodge, they're on to something. I know how Emmy feels about it, but you should see this place. They're not fucking around. I'm talking about hardware that functions *now*. Once the software, the soul, is installed, it's going to take off."

"Ryan McNear, your stupidity impresses me." Dodge pulled a bar towel from a drawer and wiped the desk. "You should have told me when your pal called. I could have prepared you to get the information we need." He tapped Ryan's notes. "The key to winning this is to remember that whether or not they develop a power generator doesn't matter. All that matters is that they're attracting money. As long as money flows, we can skim our share."

Ryan leaned back and crossed his legs. "No, Dodge, if they can produce energy by combining science and spirituality, it will be worth much, much more."

Dodge started to laugh. It started deep in his belly and resonated upward. It wasn't sincere laughter, but it was loud. "I don't know whether to feed you more or less whiskey." He shook his head for a few seconds. "McNear, try to stay with me. All that matters is the money. Okay? Spell it for me—m-o-n-e-y—are you with me?"

Ryan took Foster's book out from under the stack of notes. "I've been studying QED for months. Foster's theory fits together, and his argument makes sense."

"McNear, you're an idiot. Why do you think Foster can't get anything published where the *real* physicists, like my sister, put their work?"

"No offense to your sister, but if Foster is right, there's no way that the scientific establishment would give him a chance to prove it. Dodge, come on, the existence of the universe *proves* that energy has to come from somewhere. Those guys could be onto the biggest discovery in history. Free, unlimited energy—and they might not be able to control the reaction. They don't even care. Unleashing that energy could cause total destruction. Their redneck chancellor thinks it could cause the Rapture, and it's fine with him. Don't you see how dangerous they are? An obscure research lab tapping into a new type of energy with no one in the government, the media, or at mainstream labs paying attention. They could destroy the world."

"McNear, you're killin' me. The Rapture—I've been waiting for someone to play the goddamn Rapture card. What's next? You about to be reborn? If you are, don't do it in here, I don't want to clean up the re-after-birth." Dodge sipped from his glass and squinted at Ryan. "Or do you think there's a way to get more money from them by pretending we believe it?" He stroked his chin.

Ryan flipped open Foster's book to the diagram with the Heisenberg mirror separating the physical from the spiritual. He set it in front of Dodge.

Dodge pushed the book aside, rubbed his hands together, and said, "Let me explain how this is going to work." He swiveled around to a filing cabinet and pulled out several thick files then set them, one by one, in a neat stack on the desk. "This is case law, a dozen examples where companies defrauded inventors of their rights. Every one is an example where the court voided a patent waiver and awarded an engineer rights to income derived from his invention. Half the cases are just like yours, where the company changed the terms of the agreement without the inventor's permission." Dodge started to sip from his glass but stopped. "Ryan? Where's that boat you two bought with your patent money?"

"I guess Foster has it. There was a picture on his desk with his wife posing on it."

Dodge looked up at the ceiling, a full-toothed grin spreading across his face. "So your friend Foster got all the money. You didn't actually get *any*."

"I don't know if you could say that. The boat is half mine."

"Really? Why do you keep it in Texas?" Dodge leaned forward, resting on his elbows. "Okay, as I was saying, the value of those patents is strictly tied to the profit that can be derived from them. Creation Energy believes that the profits will be huge—that's all that matters. We will threaten to sue them, and then we will demonstrate that we can convince their investors that the so-called technology is bullshit. They will offer to settle."

"What? That's convoluted, even for you."

"Listen carefully, I'll speak slowly." He spoke so slowly it was hard to pay attention. "We don't need to convince Creation Energy that their *product* is bullshit, okay? What we have to do is convince Creation Energy that we are capable of convincing their investors that it's bullshit—and that's easy. My sister *lives* for opportunities to expose scientific fraud."

"If she proves that the patents don't work, they'll cancel the project."

"That is why we have to make our play at exactly the right time, right after they've gotten a good-size investor, right when they have dollar signs in their eyes." Dodge snickered. "Trust me, they won't leave money on the table."

"What if they don't settle?"

"They will settle." Dodge cackled. "Didn't I say that already?" Dodge swallowed the rest of his whiskey and poured another.

"You think Emmy will go along with this?" Ryan sipped from his glass and swallowed. "I got the impression that she was more interested in blowing the whistle on them than in making money for you and me."

"Ryan, sharpen your fuckin' pencil. You are in a precarious position. I am your attorney; what we say in this room is confidential. No one has a right to know what is said here. Not even my sister; especially not my sister. I know you like her, but you don't have a chance with her until you have crawled out from the hole you're in. Do you understand?"

Ryan watched the green-tinted light from the desk lamp scatter from the glass-covered desk. Another rationalization added to the pile. Ryan couldn't ask Emmy to jump into the hole he'd made of his life. He had to fix it first. If fixing it required deceiving her, well, hopefully it wouldn't.

Dodge said, "Now we wait. The instant they get major funding, I'll know and we'll file."

23

Two months later, Emmy was making last-minute preparations for a trip to CERN, the big lab in Europe. Her new graduate student, Tran, who had been one of her favorite undergraduates, knocked on her door. Tran had been working on hardware for the experiment at SLAC. She asked, "Do you need anything before I go?"

He said, "Did you see what Bob Park reported in the latest *What's New*?"

"What did the old curmudgeon come up with this week? Another tree fall on him?" The weekly news update from Washington, DC, by Robert Park, a physics professor at the University of Maryland, served as the first line of defense against politics and religion encroaching on the pure empiricism of physics in particular and science in general.

"The company that holds those patents you had me read last year, Creation Energy, is getting a big investment from National Engineering Group. They claim that it's an alternative energy source."

"No." Emmy's smile evaporated. "Total cynics." Her voice mixed irony and disdain. "By investing in alternative energy that won't work, they neither threaten their oil interests nor the interests of their investors, all of whom are big oil men. What greater way to solidify their Christian Coalition base, kowtow to public demand, and avoid threatening their core business."

Tran said, "Oil? I thought they were a defense contractor."

"They're the biggest nonmissile defense contractor in the world, but historically, they're an oil industry infrastructure firm."

Emmy grabbed her briefcase and walked out of her office, leaving the door open.

Tran followed, offering her a sheet of paper. "I designed the preamplifier for the new photon counters."

She took the page in her free hand but didn't look at it. "Okay, I get it. They can claim to be developing a whole new technology. What's the first application of *every* technology?"

"Weapons and porn."

She did a double take but managed to hold back laughter. "If only it were as harmless as porn, but no. Their audacity is amazing. They can get everything Creation Energy does classified under a DOD contract and then tell whatever lies they want, and no one will be able to access the truth."

"D-O-D?"

"Department of Defense." She stopped in the hallway and looked at the diagram.

He looked over her shoulder and said, "I'm on the agenda to present the design at the next collaboration meeting."

"Okay," she said. It was his first project, and it wasn't perfect. She needed to baby him along. Tran was strong and direct in class. His utterly out-of-date short, parted hair, black-rimmed glasses, and pressed shirts complemented his sharp features, making a fashion statement of pure confidence. She knew better. If he presented this design to the three hundred PhD physicists that made up the collaboration, they could destroy him.

She rested her hand on his shoulder and pointed out the design flaws. His confidence evaporated. She said, "Wait until

I get back from CERN to present this. I want you to build one first and see how it works—remember, you don't need their approval if you know you're right."

Tran sighed.

Emmy reached up and patted him on the back. He took back the sheet of paper. Emmy loved watching students mature. People are at the most dynamic stage of growth from age twenty to twenty-five. In a few years, Tran would be able to deliver on the promise of his confidence.

Thinking about the patents reminded her of Ryan. She caught herself thinking of him as a graduate student of life, growing the way Tran was. The way he persevered, how he cared for Kat, his good nature and dogged optimism, all pointed to his potential to be a really wonderful partner. He just needed one little growth spurt to put his life together and graduate to her level. She caught herself smiling at the thought and made a mental note to send him an e-mail next time she logged on.

Tran walked with Emmy as far as the next door and then ducked into the lab.

Emmy chuckled to herself. Suddenly she was all in favor of Ryan suing Creation Energy for all he could get. She turned around, walked back up the hall, and leaned into the lab door. "Hey Tran, could you pull those patents up from the US Patent and Trademark Office site again?"

Ryan's college textbooks were scattered across the apartment floor. After all this time, he still hadn't performed a successful QED calculation without having Katarina breathing down his neck with step-by-step instructions. He stared at the new Feynman diagrams Katarina had drawn on the whiteboard. She'd scribbled in the mathematical expression for each diagram below them.

She sat behind him at the desk huddled over the big red paperback, *The Feynman Lectures on Physics, Volume III.* "Richard weirdo Feynman writing weirdocity."

Without looking at her, he said, "It says lots of weird things in volume three." She grumbled in reply. Staring at the whiteboard, Ryan wondered how the hell Katarina had figured out the math. He sneaked a look at her. She was concentrating so hard that he could almost see beams of cognition bouncing between the book and her eyes. This child was hungry for knowledge and needed to be fed. She needed a decent computer. She used his all the time, but it took ten minutes to boot up, and the disk drive whined in the same tone as his car's transmission. Ryan resolved that he'd buy her a new computer next time he had any money.

Ryan had another realization about the knowledge-hungry child: she was looking less and less childlike.

Her feet rested on Sean's football, shuttling it back and forth. Her legs were longer than they used to be, and when had she grown a waist?

"Identical particles," she said, "identical, the same, no diff. Too weird." She went to the whiteboard and took the eraser from the tray. "Look at this."

"Wait!" Ryan said, "Don't erase—" It was too late.

"That?" She slowly erased the diagrams and equations. "Was one of us still working on it?"

"Yeah, the one with a math degree hasn't figured out how to evaluate a propagator."

She put two dots on the board, labeled one "electron-a" and the other "electron-b," then drew two Feynman diagrams describing different ways they could interact. Under each diagram, she wrote an equation. "This is no help. There's no way to tell them apart. Duh. They're *identical*."

"Why are you freaking out? An electron's identity is given by its quantum numbers."

"Ryan, you're missing the point. They are identical, yes. The only thing that makes one different from another is where it is and what's around it—don't you see?" She was angry that he couldn't keep up. "Identity is all anything has, but if we switch the circumstances of one with the circumstances of the other, their identities switch too." She tapped the whiteboard with a green marker, putting polka dots around each electron. "It's like there's nothing to them; they have no character."

"Their character is that they are electrons," Ryan said. "Why is that weird?"

She tossed the marker onto the tray. It bounced out and landed on the floor next to a couple of others. Relaxing her legs, she slid down the wall and sat on Sean's football. "I don't know, but there's something. I mean everything, *everything* is made of these particles and…" Katarina cocked her head, listening, then Ryan recognized the sound of someone clomping up the stairs.

Katarina said, "Oh shit, what the hell does he want?"

"Damn, Katarina, you talk like a sailor."

They listened as Dodge worked his way up the stairs. Ryan said, "There's a bounce in the geezer's step—that can't be good."

"Could he be happy?"

"God help us if he is."

The clomping made it to Ryan's door and, for the first time ever, Dodge knocked. His knock, the shave-and-a-haircut-two-bits "dun da da daa dun, dat dat" riff, was somehow more maddening than when he barged right in. Ryan didn't say anything; the door was unlocked.

A beat later, Dodge opened the door. He wore an evil smile. Ryan braced himself—rent was due today, and he'd have to post-date a check.

"Mr. McNear," Dodge said, letting the second syllable of *mister* glide off his tongue. "I am about to become your best friend."

Ryan leaned back in the beach chair as if to put distance between them. "Dodge, the last thing I need—"

Dodge walked forward until he stood directly over Ryan, nearly drooling the words. "The pot just got bigger; check or bet to us."

Ryan let the chair fall forward. "Why now?"

Dodge told him that NEG was the Fortune 100 investor. Ryan went to his desk and pulled a spreadsheet up on the computer. "How much do you think I can get?"

"We, partner—how much can *we* get."

"Not funny, Dodge. I need to know. I've got outstanding debts."

"There are three key players in this game: their attorney and original investor, a guy named Blair Keene—"

"That's Foster's father-in-law."

"You're shittin' me." Dodge's faced folded into a smile that emphasized the length of his nose. "Nothing I like more than taking the silver spoon from the baby's mouth." He rested his arm around Ryan's neck. It felt like a big hairy insect crawling across his shoulders. "The other principals are the university chancellor, Jeb Schonders, and the director of alternative energy research at NEG, fellow by the name of Bill Smythe. Keene and Schonders will want to meet with us before alerting National. Think about it. What better way to show they can run their company than to present a problem after it's been solved?" His breath smelled of Listerine. "Listen carefully, we'll bring Emmy along, and within a week they'll make an offer. Then we have options. We can blackmail them—they either pay or we expose them to NEG. If that doesn't do it, we blackmail NEG. The price to keep us from exposing them as idiots to their shareholders might even be higher than Creation Energy would pay." Ryan shrugged out from under Dodge's arm.

It felt like having the school bully on his side.

As though reading his thoughts, Dodge added, "Ryan, I'm your last chance. It won't be long, six months at the most. You'll get your kid back. All better—and all I get is fifty-five percent of the proceeds."

"Fifty-five?"

Dodge took a sheet of paper from his back pocket. It was a copy of a page of their rental agreement. "Yeah, you signed off on twenty-five and, as your attorney, I get forty percent. Twenty-five percent of your sixty is fifteen plus my forty—voila! But forget about it, last thing you need to worry about. Plenty of money to go around. What you need to worry about is getting my little sister on our side. Do you want to call her or should I?"

Ryan sighed. "I'll call her." He wanted to call her. It had been a while since they'd spoken, and he wanted to hear her voice. He thought that if she were on his side, it had to be the right side. "One thing, though, she's only doing this because she thinks she'll get to testify."

Dodge said, "We must avoid telling her that there will be no testifying, then, mustn't we?"

"I'm not going to lie to Emmy."

"You don't have to lie to her." His right eyebrow rose, twisting his face into a sinister mask. "As your attorney, I handle all negotiations—I'll lie to her."

Alone at the whiteboard, Kat redrew the electron-electron interaction, now with a photon scattering off the incoming electron and another off the outgoing electron—that would be enough to tell which was which, give them identity. But it also meant anything that resembled individual character came from their interactions with others. She didn't try to calculate the effect of the identifying photons. She just stared at it while Ryan and Dodge argued.

Eventually, she set the marker on the tray and went next door to the apartment that these days she shared more with her mother's clothes than with her mother's presence. Thinking about identity, she put on her mother's long skirt. It had an equally long slit up the side. She painted on makeup to make her eyes sharp at the edges but open and soft in the center. All the while she watched the eighth grader staring back at her transform into her idea of sophisticated womanhood. An image she had acquired from music videos. Then she sprayed so much of her mother's perfume on her neck and thighs that she smelled like a candy shop.

When Kat came downstairs half an hour later, Ryan and Dodge were still arguing. She went out the door and tossed her skateboard in front of her. Ready to vault across the stairs and down the street, she changed her mind. She'd never thought of a skateboard as a toy before and, as much as she loved the acceleration, freedom, and gymnastic-like power of skating, carrying a toy around all night seemed so childish. Plus, her skateboard didn't go with her outfit. She tucked her skate back under the bench and walked down to the boulevard. She'd walk by the Skate-n-Shred, and if a good band was playing, she'd go in and dance, but if not, she'd try to get into a bar with some of her older friends.

It had been a year and a half since Foster first met with National Engineering Group, the men-in-black meeting at the church in Alexandria. Foster assumed the business maneuvering was finished; after all, the contracts were finally signed, and the funding was in. Nothing could stop them.

Then Mabel guided a man wearing jeans, a T-shirt, work boots, and a "Wayne's Feeds" cap into the lab. The instant Foster looked up, the man seemed to shake Mabel's hand off of his arm.

She was smiling, of course. Mabel smiled most of the time. She said, "Dr. Reed, I'd like you to meet my—"

The cowboy interrupted her. "Foster Reed? This envelope is for you."

Foster took the envelope, and the man said, "You've been served."

Mabel looked confused. The man glared at her wide-eyed, turned, and walked out. From that instant, Foster's attention was consumed by the contents of the envelope.

After opening it and cursing Ryan under his breath, Foster rushed across campus to the chancellor's office. That he was caught by surprise was, as Jeb Schonders put it, "a testimony to naïveté. After all, Judas always goes for the silver."

Two hours later, Foster, Jeb, and Blair Keene, who was still their attorney but now their *second* largest investor, assembled in a conference room.

Blair said, "Stay calm. This is part of doing business."

Foster started, "This is part of the battle."

"How embarrassing can this be to National?" Jeb addressed Blair.

Foster spoke louder. "Come on, let's go. We can win this."

Blair said, "I've known Bill Smythe since fifth grade. He's a good man but very sensitive to appearance."

Jeb put his hand on Foster's shoulder. "Son, as much as I'd love to take on Judas head-to-head, the fact is we haven't done very well in court." Then, to Blair, "All he wants is a settlement…"

"I think we should consider it," Blair said. "A public fiasco right after we sign—"

Foster pounded a fist on the table between the other men. "This isn't the Scopes trial. It's not the Dover School Board. This is real science, technology that is already approved by the patent office. We shouldn't surrender when we can win."

Blair stared at Jeb for a few seconds and then slowly nodded. "Let's find out what they want before talking to NEG. The prudent thing might be to pay them off and shut them up." Then, to Foster, "It may be real technology, but it doesn't work yet. Maybe we will fight, but we need to know all of our options before we decide. The best thing we can do is get a price—it will be a lot cheaper to pay off Ryan now rather than once you're generating energy." He turned back to Jeb. "My office will set up a meeting with Ryan McNear and his mouthpiece—what's his name?" He focused on the summons. "Wayne Dodge Nutter? You know what they say about California: once you take out the fruits and nuts—I'll wager this Nutter guy is a flake."

As Blair stood, Jeb said, "I reckon your office oughta do a background check on this fella. We may have more options than we think."

"You've got a *date* with her and you're bringing me." Kat waited for Ryan in the hallway. She hung her head, then she let her shoulders droop, and, finally, she fell to the floor. "That's not how it works, you blowfish!"

With his goofy auburn hair and freckled pinkish complexion, it was hard to tell when Ryan was blushing—this time his crazy grin gave him away. He said, "Well, I don't think it's a date. Emmy agreed to meet with us to help figure out how to handle Creation Energy." He raised his eyebrows provocatively. "Though, she did say that she wanted to find out more about me. But look, you have to come—you know the QED stuff, and I'm not taking you all the way down to SLAC and then ditching you when it's time to eat."

"She asked you out. You can't drag along your fourteen-year-old sidekick." Kat flailed around on the floor as though writhing in agony. "God, you're so stupid."

"You're *thirteen*," Ryan said, putting his keys in his pocket. He stepped over her and headed downstairs. "It'll be more fun with the four of us."

"Four? You're bringing her brother?" Kat hopped up and onto the banister, slid down, and waited for Ryan at the bottom of the stairs. He didn't run down and catch her like he had when she was a little kid. For an instant, she was serious: "Don't worry, you'll get your date with Emmy."

The Probe made a few new discomforting sounds on the drive to SLAC, Kat noticed. "This car, I believe, does not like to go to the left, because it squeaks going left but not right."

"Are there any left turns in the directions?"

Katarina ran her finger down the printout. "You're in luck, but the drive home…"

"How tacky is it to ask Emmy to drive when we go for dinner?"

"Hmmm, having never gone with a boy who could drive… but! Since she knows the area, it makes sense for her to drive. She'll probably offer. You must park as far as you can from her office."

"You're good."

"Plus, she won't see your car."

"Oh God. What's going to happen when she figures out this tank is my car?"

"Ryan, Mr. Materialist, she's not that kind of woman." They drove along for a while before Kat added, "Besides, she already knows how fucked-up your life is."

"Don't say *fuck*."

They pulled up a hill to SLAC and passed a big sign that read, "Stanford Linear Accelerator Center—Operated by Stanford University for the US Department of Energy." Kat started to feel tingly and couldn't sit still.

They had to stop at a guard booth to sign in. Ryan handed over his license, and the guard wrote on a clipboard. Ryan told him that Kat didn't have a license and wasn't yet sixteen. He asked for her social security number, but Kat didn't even know if she had one. The guard leaned over so he could see her in the passenger seat. Suddenly, she wanted to be invisible.

Her dad would have made sure she had a social security card.

Ryan used one of his tricks. Pulling Kat close to him, he said, "She might look dangerous, but the only weapon she brought along is her cutting wit." Of course the guard laughed and waved them through—everyone laughed when Ryan wanted them to.

They drove through the campus, avoided a street marked by a big "Restricted Access" sign, and found the building with Emmy's office. Ryan kept driving and parked on the opposite side of campus.

They crossed a street and walked up a sidewalk to the big glass doors. Kat mixed images of Emmy and Ryan in her mind's eye to calculate what their children would look like. She looked at Ryan again and, not for the first time, wondered how much the fabled Sean looked like his father.

Inside the building, they passed two men leaning against a wall, arguing. One was old, tall, and wore a rumpled suit; the other was short, young, had a Mohawk haircut, and was waving a paper at the man. Kat whispered to Ryan, "He's wearing the same shoes as me."

Ryan whispered back, "Converse All Stars will never go out of fashion."

Emmy's office door was open. She was leaning against a table next to an Asian guy with shiny black hair. The office had the faint scent of Emmy's sweet, rich perfume. She had on tight low-cut white jeans and a white blouse. A tiny gap between her jeans and blouse emphasized her waist. The blouse was tight over her breasts but frilly and buttoned up to her neck. The effect was casual, elegant, and sexy. Kat wondered if she could get an outfit like that at the thrift store and felt underdressed until she remembered that she had on the requisite shoes.

Ryan knocked, and Emmy turned with a smile. "Welcome to SLAC." She lightly hugged Kat and then bounced up on her tiptoes to kiss Ryan on the cheek. He hugged her tightly for a second and winked at Kat.

Emmy introduced Tran, her student who had read the patents and Foster's book. Tran looked like a total geekoid to Kat. She hardly ever talked to boys like him at her school—but seeing him here at the big physics lab, he looked okay. He wasn't timid like the geekoids she knew, and there was something precise and original, even sexy, about the way he dressed and spoke. Everything about him was sharp. He defied her idea of what it meant to be a cool intellectual.

Emmy led them to a conference room. Tran said that he'd reserved the room for the whole afternoon. Emmy looked at her watch and said, "My brother's late. What a shock."

The room had a long rectangular table and no windows. Three of the four walls were whiteboards. Each had trays with markers and erasers. Emmy and Tran sat next to each other. Ryan started to sit at the closest chair, next to Tran. Kat rolled her eyes and pushed him to the chair next to Emmy. Kat sat across from the three of them.

Ryan set his briefcase on the table, fiddled with the combination, and took out two notebooks. He slid one across to Kat. It was pink and had doodles all over the cover. A mix of Feynman diagrams, sketches of dragons breathing different colored flames, and curly-cursive *K*s.

Emmy laughed and said, "Pi."

Ryan looked confused, as though he'd done something stupid but didn't know what.

Emmy flipped her hair over her shoulder. "Every engineer I've ever known has set his briefcase combination to the first six digits of pi. It's just so cute."

"Well, I, um—"

Ryan obviously had no idea what to say, so Kat rescued him. "I'm having trouble writing down a formula to add up all those loopy diagrams." She showed Emmy and Tran a page of equations and Feynman diagrams. Tran's eyebrows rose. Kat realized that it was the first time he'd genuinely noticed her. She liked it. "The only way I can get the sum to converge is if I do something funny with the spatial dimensions—like, hey!" She wrote another equation. "It works, but only if you force the universe to have three spatial and one time dimension—which, duh, is obvious, but you have to do it in a weird way to make it work." She finished the calculation. "Like this."

Emmy took the notebook and went to the whiteboard. "Nice work—that's called dimensional regularization—but it's not in the books I sent you…"

"Wait," Kat said, "did I just prove that spacetime is four dimensional? Whoa—supergenius over here."

"I wouldn't say it's proof, but if you needed more evidence, then it's not a bad argument."

Ryan said, "I tried to tell her…"

For a second it looked as though Emmy thought he was serious, but then she got it and punched him in the shoulder.

Staring at Kat's notes, Tran's features creased in confusion. "She's doing renormalization?"

Ryan leaned over to Tran and said, "I have no idea what they're doing…"

Tran said, "She's fourteen?"

Ryan said, "Next month."

Kat felt the same way she had the first time she grinded her skateboard down the fire escape at Skate-n-Shred—she knew she could do whatever she tried, but it still felt nice when others clued in too. Emmy walked around the table to the whiteboard where

Kat was working. Kat was the same height as Emmy now, which was weird. How do you not look up at Emmy?

Behind them, Tran took out his marked-up copy of the "soul" patent, and Ryan tried to explain how it was supposed to work.

Kat asked Emmy how Feynman came up with his diagrams and the rules for evaluating them.

Emmy practically bounced to the whiteboard and wrote an integral equation. "This is the principle of least action." Kat asked about each symbol and then started evaluating. It took a lot more work, almost an hour, but when she got the same answer she would have gotten using Feynman's simple approach, it was as satisfying as jumping a flight of stairs on her skate.

When Kat finished, Emmy said, "I'm giving you another one of Feynman's books, *Quantum Mechanics and Path Integrals*." Her brow furrowed, and she stared at the whiteboard. Then she looked at Kat, back at the whiteboard, and then back at Kat. The lines in her brow disappeared. "Kat, if you keep working at it, you can be one of the great mathematical physicists. I totally envy you."

Kat wondered why Emmy would say something like that. Did she want something? Was she pumping Kat up the way her mentor used to? Emmy acted as though she was stating something obvious, as though she'd said "if *a* equals *b* and *b* equals *c* then *a* must equal *c*." It embarrassed Kat, made her feel sort of ashamed, as though she were a fraud. But all she'd done was a little math. Emmy walked to the other side of the table where Ryan and Tran were staring at a big messy diagram on the opposite whiteboard.

Kat looked at the whiteboard where she and Emmy had just been working. She loved the symbols and the language but hated her reaction to what Emmy had said. To dissolve her own shame, she tidied some of her calculations and caught herself wondering what it would look like to her father. She tried to stare hard enough so that if he could somehow see through her eyes, he would see this. She repeated Emmy's words *a mathematical physicist* to herself and slowly, as though under the guidance of her father, she managed to embrace them.

Emmy said, "Kat, pay attention." Ryan had scribbled a mess of little boxes connected by lines and arrows that seemed to go in every direction and back again. Emmy rested her hand on Ryan's shoulder and said, "Okay, I want coffee. Anyone else?" Ryan made eye contact with Kat, then rotated his eyes to indicate Emmy's hand on his shoulder. He looked like a purring cat.

To Tran, Emmy said, "Black coffee, right?" Then to Kat, "You want a Coke or something?"

Kat said, "I'll have mine black too." Ryan mouthed the word *poseur* at her. She'd never had a cup of coffee in her life.

Emmy started for the door but waited at the threshold, looking back at Ryan. He just sat there with a goofy grin. Kat whispered to him—a whisper loud enough to make it across the room—"Yo, doof-McNear, she wants you to go with her."

Ryan walked along about half a step behind Emmy. They paused at the door to a well-lit room as a man in a tweed jacket stepped out. Ryan leaned down and whispered in Emmy's ear, "Are tweed and sneakers like a uniform around here?"

She turned to him and said, "Do you think I'd look good in tweed?"

"I think you'd look good in anything." He straightened up and nodded as though concentrating. "In fact, I suspect you'd look even better wearing nothing at all."

"Oh, please," she said and took paper cups from a stack and a ceramic mug with a cartoon penguin from a shelf.

The coffee room had a sink, a refrigerator, and an industrial-capacity coffeemaker. Ryan put a bag of industrial-quality tea in a paper cup and filled it with water while Emmy poured four cups of coffee.

"Make Katarina's decaf," Ryan said.

"Okay. She said she wanted it black. Should I load it with milk and sugar?"

"Milk, not too much sugar. I don't know how long it's been since she went to the dentist."

Emmy poured in a lot of milk and a packet of sugar. "You do realize that you're her father figure, don't you?"

Ryan handed her a stirring stick. "Probably more like a neighbor figure."

Instead of taking the stick, she took Ryan's hand and looked up at him. She looked concerned. "You're the most important person in her life right now."

"You think?"

"I've met her mother."

"Okay, I'll take her to the dentist."

Emmy smiled and accepted the stirring stick. As she turned away, her hair brushed along Ryan's arm. "Tall, funny, *and* sweet."

"What about handsome?"

"And a mind reader."

"You can't read minds, can you?"

She stopped pouring coffee and turned toward him. She looked down at Ryan's feet. From that angle, her eyelashes stood out, and as she scanned upward, taking in his jeans, untucked shirt, and then his face, Ryan couldn't remember if he'd combed his hair this morning, not that it would do any good.

She poked a finger in his belly and said, "You're mind isn't hard to read."

"You know," Ryan said, looking to the left and then right. "This is the first time we've ever been alone, unchaperoned."

"You better behave. My big brother is right down the hall."

"Dodge?"

She nodded with a closed-mouth smile. They stared at each other for a few seconds and then started laughing.

"It's hard to believe that you're related to him."

"Tell me about it."

"What's the deal with him, anyway?" Ryan asked. "The gun, the obsessive neatness, and why would a guy like that have a business like Skate-n-Shred?"

"Well," Emmy said, "my brother is a walking contradiction. I think the gun is there for some kind of bravado, but I'm not sure." As she spoke, her forehead furrowed in a way that made her eyes look even bigger. "He's always had a strange fascination with suicide. My parents worry about him a lot. So do I." She lifted two paper cups of coffee and her mug and motioned for Ryan to take the cup with lots of milk. "He's much older than me, and I don't know him well."

Ryan said, "He's not really a knowable kind of guy."

"I'll tell you one thing about him that you might not have realized yet." She stepped into the hall. "When it comes right down to it, my brother will always do the right thing."

"What? Dodge?"

"I know, he seems mean sometimes, and he's always scheming, but when someone needs help, he helps them. He's helping you, isn't he?"

"It's hard to tell. It seems more like he's helping himself than doing me any favors."

"That's his way."

Ryan could hear Dodge's voice from the conference room.

Emmy said, "Speak of the devil."

"Devil seems like an accurate description," Ryan said. When they were a few steps from the door, he said, "What are you doing later?"

Emmy stopped. "After our meeting?"

"Yes."

"We'll see."

Then she turned away, her hair brushing against him again, and walked ahead into the conference room. Ryan noticed an extra swing to her walk that he hadn't seen before.

⸻

While Ryan and Emmy were getting coffee, Tran had asked Kat how she'd learned QED. "Emmy gave us the book and we read it." The answer didn't seem to satisfy him. He asked a lot more questions, mostly about math—not math in particular but how she'd learned the math. She repeated, "It was in the book." It confused her and made her feel like an imposter. How could she help Tran? He really belonged at SLAC, and she didn't even know if she had a social security number.

Kat recognized a voice hollering down the hall. "Emmy? Where the hell are you? Nutter? Anyone seen Emmy Nutter?"

She went to the door and yelled, "Shut up, Dodge—we're in here!" She could hear Ryan and Emmy laughing from the other direction.

Dodge sat at the head of the table, set down an old, scratched aluminum briefcase, and took out a yellow legal pad. Ignoring Tran altogether, he looked at the whiteboards and asked Kat what they'd been talking about. As she told him, he wiggled a wooden pencil between his fingers and bobbed his shiny head. Kat concluded by saying, "You need a haircut—it's bozoing around the sides. You look like the pointy-headed guy in Dilbert." She laughed but Dodge didn't respond. Tran smiled into his hand.

Ryan and Emmy returned with coffee a few minutes later, and Dodge greeted them with, "Can you prove that the inventions are bogus?"

Emmy looked at Tran. He shuffled the marked-up patents to the surface.

Ryan started to speak, but Emmy stopped him by resting her hand on his arm. He looked at her hand, and his eyes seemed to soften in a way that Kat had seen before.

In his sharp tone and considered manner, Tran said, "The first patent, Application of Fundamental Uncertainty to the Generation of Energy, blatantly violates the first and second laws of thermodynamics and therefore violates patent law. It is illegal to submit a patent for a perpetual motion machine. I should think that any patent attorney could successfully dispute it."

Dodge broke in, "Who is this guy?"

Tran looked up sharply. "My name is Tran Than Nguyen—graduate student in physics at Cal. Dr. Nutter asked me to review these patents for physical consistency." He glanced at his notes and continued, "The second patent, Method of Multiple Feedback for Neural Network Self-Generation of Artificial Intelligence, being a software algorithm rather than a machine, is less problematic. One might expect the term *intelligence* to be defined before claiming *artificial intelligence*, and the wording seems intentionally obscure…"—he looked at Ryan, who shrugged—"…the description of the behavior of the 'asymptotic generations of self-replicated neural networks' is fascinating." He smoothed the pages of the patent.

Dodge said, "Can it work?"

Simultaneously, Tran said, "Maybe," and Emmy said, "No."

"Yes," Ryan said, louder than was necessary. "It's software that writes other software. The result will make decisions that resemble the way people make decisions—free will. Hey, this isn't my first rodeo."

Tran added, "I suspect that Mr. Nutter's question is asking whether the whole system will create energy and—"

"And the answer is no." Emmy stood up.

Kat sighed in such a way that it caught the attention of Emmy and Ryan. Emmy said, "What is it, dear?"

"What the hell are you talking about?"

Dodge hit the table with his fist and let loose a coughing chortle. "Thank you, Kat."

Ryan went to the whiteboard, erased it, and drew a grid of rectangles with a black marker. "Think of a neural network as a bunch of boxes that you can ask yes or no questions—each box gets a vote. The boxes are called neurons. They're kinda like neurons in our brains, and a bunch of them makes a neural network. Neural nets are good at recognizing patterns, sort of like how you recognize a cup of coffee."

Above the grid, he drew a cloud and then a web of lines from different parts of the cloud to each box in the top row. "Think of each of these lines as sensory input, like color, shape, smell—the stuff that your brain assembles without you having to think."

"First you process the senses. Is it the right color? Does it have the right smell? If it passes those tests, then there are higher-order questions." He drew lines from each box in the top row to each box in the second row. "Does the cup look like a coffee cup? Is it in a conference room, a kitchen, or on a desk, where you could expect to find coffee?" He drew lines to the next row. "And so forth until each of the boxes in the last layer votes on whether the data are consistent with what the network has been trained to recognize." He held up his cup. "All the assumptions and prejudices that you learned in order to intuit that this is a cup of coffee had to come from somewhere."

He took a sip, set down the cup, tossed the black marker toward the tray—it bounced off and landed on the floor—and picked up the red marker from the table next to Emmy. "Training starts by showing the network coffee: with and without milk, hot and warm, but probably not cold, in different types of cups and environments, and then forcing the net to identify each data set as a cup of coffee." He circled the bottom row, but there were so many black lines you couldn't really see the new red one. "Some boxes might only recognize black coffee, or coffee in a Starbucks cup, but the network will weigh each box's answer so that the network as a whole says, 'It is coffee.'"

Kat drew her own version of the neural net in her notebook. Instead of using lines between the boxes, she used tubes so that she could fill them with stick figures, names, and diagrams like she did in her murals. She turned to a blank page and redrew her version of the neural net, this time replacing the boxes with little dragons—that didn't feel quite right either, but it was close, really close. She had that satisfied feeling she got when she figured something out mathematically but didn't know exactly what it meant.

Ryan drew red lines from each of the lower boxes back to every one of the boxes above them—the result was a mess of black and red lines. "My invention is a population of networks. Think of each network as an individual mind on its own computer." He stepped back and shook his head at the indecipherable drawing. "Start with a single computer running a neural net. Every net will have a bunch of sensory inputs—the ones Creation Energy implements will have input from every wire that comes out of the collider. Of course, the main purpose of each net is to operate the collider, but they will also have another purpose: to reproduce."

He took the eraser and pulled it across the whiteboard, making a black and red smear. “Remember, I was trying to patent the soul, so I mixed biblical and biological ideas. Eve came from Adam’s rib, right? So to get the second net, take half the boxes from Adam and configure them on another computer. This way you have two unique nets—every net in the system *must* be unique.” He stepped to the side, behind Kat, to a blank region of whiteboard. He drew a black box and a red box and then a green box below the two. “So Adam and Eve make a baby.”

Emmy said, “Baby?”

Kat didn’t like the dismissive tone in her voice. Ryan’s eyes squinted—he didn’t like it either. They both ignored her.

Tran chimed in, “The patent uses the phrase ‘*begets* a neural network.’ ”

“Exactly, and kinda like people sharing chromosomes, their baby is made by copying half the neurons of each parent, which means half the properties of each parent.” He drew another cloud above the parents, lines from the cloud to the baby, and lines from the parents to the baby and back. “The baby has inputs from both the collider and its parents. The trick to making sure that each net is unique is that they must have limited lifetimes. If they don’t die, eventually they’d learn all there is to know about whatever they’re trained to do, and then they’d become identical—I got that from either Saint Thomas Aquinas or Saint Augustine, something about everyone’s soul being unique. Plus, since the parents have to train their babies, they can’t reproduce until they’re a certain age.”

Kat said, “So you end up with like, a whole mess of neural networks, making decisions and criticizing each other, having babies, growing old, learning and dying.”

Ryan said, “Yeah, each generation starts with the knowledge of the previous generation, trains the next generation, and then, over many generations, the legacy of decisions, preferences, and assumptions lead to increasingly sophisticated nets. Each net has the wisdom and prejudice built from a sort of cultural evolution. It is that combination of wisdom and prejudice that gives them an intuitive sense of right and wrong and the free will to act on that higher-order sense. In other words, they develop morality and make decisions that are indistinguishable from the way that something with free will would make decisions."

Tran opened a thick file and flipped about halfway through. The Creation Energy logo was at the top of each page—it was a printout of Foster's book. He cleared his throat and said, "They think that a godless universe would be deterministic—the antithesis of free will and therefore sentience."

Dodge said, "But it still wouldn't work."

Emmy nodded to Dodge and said, "I find this description wonderfully ironic. You've built a model of how complex systems, like a human brain, can be mechanical but not deterministic."

"What the hell does that mean?" Dodge asked.

"Free will doesn't require superstition," Emmy said. "The vast number of inputs and the way we process them combine with the fact that the tiniest differences in external conditions can lead to huge variations in behavior. The result is that we are biochemical machines with free will." She turned to Ryan and took his hand. "In other words, your patent describes how free will can be achieved without a soul at all. Perfect irony. I totally love it."

Ryan obviously couldn't think straight while she was touching him. He was incapable of pulling away too. He mumbled, "Yuh-huh."

Emmy said, "Of course, some stimuli leave fewer options than others," and let go of his hand.

Kat drew a little baby neural net, stared at it, and then said, "Two thinking things think a third thinking thing into existence. Doesn't that make you God?"

Emmy laughed, leaned back in her chair, and said, "It sure does—and that should bother Foster Reed more than the fact that nothing spiritual is required."

"This makes sense now." Tran flipped to a dog-eared page of Foster's book. "That's it. I get it. They're not playing God, they're maintaining symmetry. It's the inverse of Creation. If man creates a soul, spiritual energy is created on the physical side. During Creation, physical energy was created on the spiritual side." Tran ran a hand through his hair, mussing his part. Kat thought he was going to jump out of his chair. "The window would have to open. There's no telling what could happen. An energy source is the obvious guess. Or it could be an energy *sink*. It could suck all energy out of the universe, it could—"

Emmy groaned and, as though it were a command, Tran stopped.

Kat broke the silence. "So what came first? The soul or energy? Consciousness or matter?"

"Okay, I need to say something," Emmy said as if she were in pain.

Tran looked embarrassed. "It's just a model, I didn't mean that…"

Emmy stared at the table. "You have taken a large step away from reason. I'll grant you that the process you described could result in a network that would appear irrational and make decisions similar to the way that people make decisions. The decisions might not be predictable and in that sense could be indistinguishable from free will. But please, you don't need anything like a soul, and you certainly don't need God. Is that totally obvious to everyone?"

Ryan's jaw clenched the way it did when he was confused. "If it looks like a soul, acts like a soul, smells like a soul, then it's a soul. If you believe in God, then…"

"And if you bind yourself to blind faith, you'll never encounter truth," Emmy said. "Remember when I visited you guys in Petaluma and we talked about assumptions and leaps of faith?"

Katarina said, "We said that the scientific method is just watching our step."

"Right. We need to identify our assumptions and make careful steps of faith rather than huge leaps." She turned back to Tran. "If the software is indistinguishable from a soul, is that sufficient to identify it as a soul?"

Tran said, "If, just for the sake of argument, their primary conjecture is true—the symmetry of spiritual and physical energy—then that is exactly what they are testing. If indistinguishability is sufficient, their power generator would work." Then, with a smile that looked almost devilish, he added, "If something is indistinguishable from an electron, it is by definition an electron. According to Saint Thomas Aquinas, free will is the defining property of a soul."

Emmy held up her arms and laughed as though it were a joke. It was real, songlike laughter; she really thought it was funny. It reminded Kat of her new friend at school, Marti. Marti laughed all the time, especially when Kat said something intelligent that Marti didn't understand. In fact, Marti laughed every time Kat spoke like a mathematical physicist. Kat puzzled for an instant. In a way, Marti made it easier for Kat to be a geek.

"Good one." Emmy had a big smile. "I knew you'd say that."

How could Emmy have seemed so angry and then all of a sudden be amused?

Ryan laughed too. Even Dodge smiled. Emmy was sort of like Marti—when she laughed, other people always laughed with her. That's how Marti affected people. She had a happiness feedback loop, but it was weird to see the same thing in serious, brilliant, badass Emmy. It didn't make sense.

Kat looked at her notebook and concentrated, visualizing herself as a neural network with lines from her five senses to a row of boxes. The next row connected to her mother and had severed lines to her dead father, with a new box connected to Ryan and another with a thin line to Emmy.

She looked at Ryan's coffee—a paper cup with a little heat-ring around it and a white plastic cover. Traces of steam curled out of it. Emmy's was in a big mug with a dancing penguin cartoon. It didn't have any steam now, but it had a few minutes before. Kat watched everyone interact but concentrated so that their voices were no longer words, just sounds, as though she had erased the input line from her ears to her mind. Even though Emmy thought everything Ryan said was wrong—really totally wrong—she still touched him every time he spoke, and Ryan leaned toward her like a happy puppy. Kat didn't understand why Emmy would help Ryan. They seemed so mismatched—Ryan the big fuckup and Emmy the great scientist. What other feedback loop needed to be drawn in? Could it just be that Emmy thought Ryan was hot? Ryan was hella cute and funny, and he was smarter than most boys, but…

A thought hit Kat from a different angle, as though the severed line to her father had just solidified. Her father would say that Emmy is simply a nice woman who wants to help a nice man.

Dodge stroked his chin and glared at Emmy. Emmy's brow furrowed deeply—the same way that Dodge's did when he was angry, but now Emmy didn't seem angry, just adamant. And every time Dodge made his annoying raspy not-laugh, Emmy exhaled. She looked like a little girl when she exhaled.

Kat turned to Ryan. He was looking back at her and had that smile on his face that he sometimes got when she was working at the whiteboard.

At once, as though all her little boxes lined up in agreement, she recognized the look on Ryan's face. It was *her* look. It was her special look for when she really liked something. That little closed-mouth smile, lips turning up and eyes wide open.

Kat tapped her pencil on her notebook. "Each network has an effect on the others, right?"

Ryan nodded. The others didn't notice that she'd said anything.

"What if two of them started out identical, and you put them with a bunch of others—eventually the two would be different, right?"

"Yep, in fact, that's a good debug test. If two started out as identical but had different inputs and remained the same, it would mean something was wrong." Kat had to strain to hear Ryan over Dodge and Emmy's arguing.

Kat noticed that Tran had started listening to them.

"What would happen if you killed one of them?" Kat twirled her hair around her finger. "The decisions made by the other nets are still affected by the dead one. So it's not really dead, is it? It has just stopped changing."

"Sort of, for a while I guess. But the others keep changing, so eventually there's no trace of the dead one."

"No." At some point, Emmy and Dodge had gone silent. Everyone was staring at Kat, making it hard to think. She sat up a little straighter. "No. Each net that was ever affected by the dead one continues to be influenced by its, um, its affection. And every affected decision affects other nets until the effects of the dead one are distributed evenly over all the others. So the longer you wait, the more the dead net affects the whole system. Even though it's dead."

Tran added, "Though the longer it was alive, the greater its total impact on the others—just by sheer number of decisions."

Kat wondered why he'd bother to say something so obvious. His eyes had narrowed some; he was obviously concentrating. Kat had never believed that she was smarter than other people. When she acted smart around her friends, it seemed to bother them, seemed uncool, at least until Marti laughed, so she usually acted the way they did: a little clueless, unconcerned, uninterested—you know, cool. She figured they had been doing the same thing. But that look on Tran's face made her uncomfortable, though not in a bad way.

She turned to Ryan.

He spread his hands and said, "You're way past me now…"

"What if, before it died, you recorded everything about it and then, right after you turned it off, you loaded it onto a different computer?"

"It's software. It would be the same on any box."

She could hear Ryan's foot tapping against the table leg. "So the others would never even know that it had died."

"But if you rebooted another computer with the same net, then it's not dead," Tran said. "What's the significance?"

Kat realized how tightly her ankles had been crossed. It felt like she was looking for something but was blinded by the light of everybody staring at her. Her shoulders slumped. She felt out of place again—an imposter. "Nothin'," she said. "I was just thinking about identical particles. Never mind."

Emmy said, "The only effect that a well-trained neural net could have on an electron-positron collider, or even a *real* power generator, would be to optimize its output and get it closer to the thermodynamic efficiency limit or even the Heisenberg limit. It could never get over that."

Dodge said, "Can you convince a jury that it won't work?" And the two of them were arguing again.

"Wait," Ryan interrupted. "Dodge, you said that we just have to be able to convince the investors that it won't work."

Dodge jerked his head from side to side, and his eyes got so big they looked like they might pop out. "No, no, we want Emmy to prove the patents are worthless."

"What?" Ryan said.

But Kat understood. It shouldn't have surprised her. Dodge was lying to Emmy or Ryan, probably to both.

Before Ryan could say anything else, Dodge said, "Okay, Emmy—how are you going to prove the patents are worthless?"

"They violate the first and second laws of thermodynamics," Emmy said.

"You'll have to do better than that."

"Dodge, there is nothing better than that," Emmy said but then calmed down and turned to Tran. "Is there anything obvious in Foster Reed's dissertation…" She said *dissertation* as though it were a dirty word.

Ryan turned in his chair to face Emmy and said, "You haven't read Foster's book? I believe we had a deal, ma'am. I read Feynman's *QED*."

She smiled a guilty but playful smile. "I tried to read it, but every time I picked it up I got queasy." Then, to Dodge, she said, "I can destroy this dissertation sentence by sentence if that's what it takes."

"Good," Dodge said. "If it works, Ryan gets to see his kid; if not, Sean McNear continues through life thinking his father is a bum."

Emmy said, “I guess I’ll have to read this thing.” Then she faced Ryan again. This time she was serious. “I want to destroy these charlatans, and I’d like to help you too, Ryan.” Her stare dwelled on him an instant longer and then turned to Tran on her other side. As she turned, her hair swirled near Ryan’s face. He inhaled deeply.

Kat wondered how things would change after Ryan fixed his life. He’d probably move back to Texas, probably forget all about her. The thought sent a little jolt through her. She wouldn’t admit to herself that it was fear. Instead, she insisted that it would be better for Ryan to leave her alone. On the other hand, as long as he kept looking at Emmy the way he was now, he wouldn’t be going anywhere. Kat looked at the whiteboards and the clock, then back at Ryan and Emmy. Ryan was still staring, and Emmy, obviously aware of it, was preening her hair and glancing at him occasionally.

Kat stood up. “Shit, I forgot something. Dodge, you have to drive me home.”

Without turning away from Emmy, Ryan said, “Don’t say *shit.* I’ll take you home after dinner.”

“I have to go home *now.* I forgot to pick up my registration packet at the school, and it’s due tomorrow.”

Ryan finally dragged his gaze away from Emmy. “I’ll take you.”

Kat stared at him, willing him to get the completely obvious point—*this is how you get to be alone with Emmy, idiot!*

Emmy looked at Kat and nodded subtly—she got it. Emmy said, “Ryan, we need to talk, okay?” She stood and pointed a finger at Dodge. “You take Kat home.” And then to Kat, “Thank you for coming, Katarina. You are an amazing young woman.”

Kat didn’t know how to respond, so she tossed her notebook into Ryan’s open briefcase.

Dodge carefully set his pad back in his. Everyone else followed suit except Tran, who said, “One other thing, Mr. Nutter. In my research, I noticed something odd. Both of these patents were reviewed by the same officer at the US Patent and Trademark Office—it struck me as anomalous because of the terrific gap between the intellectual properties described.”

Dodge asked, “Did you get the guy’s name?” Tran quoted the name. As Dodge wrote it down, he made several slurping noises as though he were drooling.

Sushi?" Ryan made a face. "Can't we have food that's cooked?"

Emmy poked a playful finger into his chest. "Have you ever had sushi?"

"No."

"Come on, I'll drive." She walked out her office door, leaving Ryan behind. "Sushi is the food equivalent of sex. If you don't like it, I won't be able to date you." She walked away from him but glanced back.

Ryan caught himself letting loose a held breath and straggled behind a little longer. How could someone be so intelligent, opinionated, and cute all at once?

She turned a corner, and he rushed forward to keep her in view. She peeked back at him and laughed. Her long strides pulled her blouse up, exposing her waist. Ryan lagged farther behind. When they got to her car, she turned, still laughing, and said, "Stop staring at my butt."

He said, "Stop having such a nice butt."

"Men are such simple creatures," she said and got into the car.

Emmy worked the stick shift with the same precision she did everything. Main Street in Palo Alto was lined with freshly painted older buildings, like a refined version of the boulevard back in Petaluma.

Ryan held the door and Emmy approached the hostess, a tiny Japanese lady in a gold kimono. Emmy pointed at the sushi bar and said she wanted to sit in front of the owner, whom she indicated by name.

Staring at the different colored raw fish, little piles of fish eggs, and the tentacles of octopuses, Ryan caught himself making a *tsk* sound. The chef set wooden blocks before them, each with a pink heap of ginger and a green pile of wasabi. Emmy took a bit of wasabi on the end of a chopstick and motioned for Ryan to follow suit. Then she held it up. "Here's a toast. To you, Ryan McNear—be a good father to all of the kids who look up to you."

Ryan considered her words and thought of Katarina, then Sean. Seeing himself through Emmy's eyes was a little scary. Being a good father had somehow become his entire goal in life. He'd been aware of it before but never with Katarina and Sean in the same thought. He raised a stick with a wad of green stuff at its end and put it in his mouth. So did Emmy. His eyes started to water, and his nose felt like it might fly off his face. Emmy's eyes opened wide and she held one delicate hand over her mouth.

Emmy ordered a few pieces of sushi and showed Ryan how to concoct a mix of soy sauce and wasabi perfect for dipping. The raw fish tasted clean, like a deep blue ocean, not at all like the fishy harbor he'd expected.

When Emmy started to write on the little sheet of paper to order more sushi, Ryan said, "Let me order." She looked at him quizzically. He covered her hand with his and set the pencil down. Ryan got the chef's attention and leaned forward, holding a hand to his mouth as though concealing his speech from Emmy. "Would you please help me impress her? Please pretend like I'm ordering something sophisticated…" His eyes rolled between Emmy and the chef. Emmy straightened up and appeared tickled. Ryan gave the chef an exaggerated wink and the chef bowed. A minute later, the chef pulled two big octopus nodules from a toaster oven. They were bursting with warm, tangy oil that exploded in their mouths.

Between servings they told each other stories from their past. Ryan started with the story of the night his father died. Then he asked about Emmy's childhood.

"With Dodge around, it was like having three parents," she said. "I was like such a cocky little girl, and I wanted to be a ballerina—but my bones were too fragile, and I had asthma, so I went with my fallback—math major at UC San Diego, then PhD in physics at Caltech." Then, in a clear but quiet voice, "Ryan, what happened between you and your wife?"

Ryan looked away, waiting for words to come. "She wasn't like you. She wasn't strong, and I didn't give her the support she needed. I loved her more than anything, probably too much. Everything I did was in some way for her—building our life, our home, our family. I was preparing for sixty years together, but I worked too much. I let her slip away, let her fall out of love."

Emmy's stare slowly dropped from Ryan's eyes to somewhere around his arms and chest, then she looked away. "I loved a man once, a good man, a carpenter and an artist. I loved him more than I could have imagined. But one day, I came home, and he was sitting on the couch waiting for me. He said that he'd packed up his tools two weeks before and moved out—I was working so much that I didn't even notice he was gone."

Ryan started to run his tongue along his lips but stopped. This instant between them had to be authentic. He didn't want to think back to this night and worry that he'd bullshitted her in any way. He wanted her to know; it seemed fair.

"What happened was this." He ate the last piece of sushi, chewing slowly so he could think. "It started the morning after Foster's bachelor party." Emmy's eyes flickered. "Yeah, the same guy I'm going to sue. Anyway, the party was a Dallas tradition at a gentleman's club. One of the strippers put a note in my pocket. I was barely aware of it. The next morning, Linda, my wife, found it, and it upset her so much that she asked me to sleep on the couch, so I did. I would have done anything for Linda. Then, at Foster's wedding, she wouldn't dance with me, wouldn't even talk to me—she danced with everyone else, though.

"I slipped love letters under the bedroom door every night. She pushed them back out, but I kept writing them. The last Saturday that I lived in that house, I tried to serve her breakfast in bed. She pushed it back and started crying. She let me in our room, and we finally talked. She told me that she couldn't get the image of that note with the phone number out of her head—I never saw it; I don't even know what it said. I told her that I couldn't bear to sleep on the couch anymore, and we agreed that I'd stay at a hotel for a week or so. We just needed a break, and then we'd work it out. I told her that I'd always be her knight, and she kissed me. That was the last kiss..."

Struggling under the memory's weight, Ryan tried a matter-of-fact tone. "I buried myself in my work, of course—twelve-, sixteen-hour days." Emmy was sitting still, open but expressionless. "Linda stopped answering the phone when I called, and she wouldn't open the door when I came over, wouldn't talk to me when I sat next to her at PTA meetings. I guess eventually something had to give, right?"

He felt his teeth grinding together. "One afternoon, I went to visit Sean. I parked the car, and Linda walked out the front door. She turned away from me, down the street. I called her and walked along behind. Three doors down, she got in a big Mercedes with one of our neighbors—a guy I used to go fishing with, Howard. Actually, she didn't just get in, the old bastard kissed her—she knew I was there, knew I was watching."

A waitress picked up the last few dishes, and Ryan handed her the pile of twenty-dollar bills he'd stashed away just for this event.

Emmy started to gather her things.

Ryan said, "I'm not finished."

She turned back to him.

"Six months after that, we got divorced. A month later I got laid off. You have to understand that I'd just lost everything I'd ever wanted. Everything. All I wanted was to be an engineer with a nice family." He took a deep breath and said it: "I started taking methamphetamine and got mixed up with a, well, with a meth-whore. It's hard to explain. I'd lost everything..."

Emmy stared at him, betraying no emotion. She took her keys out of her purse and stood. Ryan helped her with her coat. Her back to him, he couldn't gauge her reaction. Had he blown it? It was okay, he decided, if honesty blew it; that had to be okay.

She stepped toward the door. He took a quick step to get ahead of her. "Did you say something?"

She didn't stop until she was out on the sidewalk. Then she looked up at him. He put his hands in his pockets and looked at the ground. The sidewalk was clean and smooth. Trepidation wrapped around his heart like a fog.

She reached up and gently tugged him down to her as though she were going to kiss him, but the look on her face was more resigned than affectionate. She whispered, "You're a good man, Ryan. People make mistakes. Thank you for telling me. It was hard to say, wasn't it?"

He exhaled. "It's the sort of thing that doesn't really come up by itself, you know? And I didn't want you to find out in a year or two and feel deceived."

"A year or two?"

"Yes, a year or two, maybe fifty." He rubbed his nose against hers and said, "I could use the help of a genius like you."

She punched him lightly in the chest. "Keep me up on that pedestal, McNear. I like it up here." As she took a few steps along the sidewalk, she laughed her oh-so-feminine version of that raspy cynical chuckle.

Ryan said, "You know, you and Dodge have a few really uncomfortable similarities."

Emmy drove Ryan back to the lab. "Okay, now it's my turn." She got him into the restricted area by having him flash a graduate student's ID to the guard. Spotlights from the corrugated warehouse-like building reflected from huge pieces of rusting iron that cast eerie shadows. Inside, two men in their late twenties, both wearing jeans and T-shirts, looked up from computers. One immediately picked up three beanbags and started juggling. The other greeted Emmy with a too-enthusiastic smile and, when she introduced Ryan, said, "Oh, never mind," and turned back to his computer.

She guided Ryan down two flights of stairs below ground level to a long, gracefully curving tunnel. A steel pipe, about a foot in diameter, ran through the center of the tunnel. "This is the beam line. The electrons come from that direction and the positrons from there." Continuing along the tunnel, she led him to a metal apparatus standing nearly six stories high with thousands, maybe millions of cables. It looked vaguely similar to the calorimeter in Foster's lab but much bigger. "This is the detector. We call it BaBar, after the cartoon elephant. The electrons and positrons annihilate at an energy that produces mostly b and anti-b quarks." She smiled up at him, bounced on her tiptoes, and said, "We don't even need an artificial soul!"

Ryan couldn't help but think of her as a ballerina. He leaned down, placed his arms around her waist, and kissed her. Her lips responded to his by opening slightly, and as she drew him closer, she looked into his eyes. He nibbled her lower lip. Her eyes were dark blue and clear, and very, very moist.

She pulled away a few inches. "I've been working on this experiment for twelve years. We're figuring out why the universe is made of matter instead of antimatter."

He put his arm around her, and she led him out of the brightly lit cavern, back up the stairs to her car. They drove up a dirt road to the top of a hill. She stopped in the moon shadow of an oak tree. They got out and sat on the hood of her car under the stars. Emmy leaned against Ryan, and he hugged her close.

After a few minutes, Emmy said, "This is why I don't need superstition to be impressed."

"What do you mean?"

Speaking in a soft voice full of wonder, Emmy said, "People always want more. They want haunted houses and ghosts, ESP and horoscopes, gods and martyrs; they want to jump off the diving board of faith. But look, look at this galaxy where we live. Why would anyone want more than this?"

Ryan wrapped his coat around her when she shivered, and she giggled when he kissed the back of her ear. When he moved his lips to hers, she pushed him back and said, "Let me look at you in the starlight. Ryan, why do you need more?"

Ryan said, "You mean God? A soul?"

Emmy didn't say anything.

Ryan said, "Haven't you ever felt it?"

"Felt what?"

"Well, love, I guess," Ryan said. "When I was little and we went to church, there were always a few seconds when I could feel

God's presence. I guess that's what I mean. Doesn't there have to be something? Something else? Something more?"

"Yes and no, respectively."

"What?" Ryan asked.

"Yes, I feel love," Emmy said. "And no, there doesn't have to be something else. The physical universe is plenty."

"Then what is love? Where does it come from? And what was that little boy feeling?"

"Ryan, listen carefully." She sat up straight and spoke in her lecturing voice. "Love is a verb. It's something that we *do*, and when it becomes a noun, it dies. Feelings, like wanting to curl up in your arms and never look away from you, are acts of love. But when we stop loving, then it's a noun and it's over." She tapped his nose with the nail of one finger. "Is the significance of these feelings changed by the realization that they arise from an incredibly complex combination of chemical reactions that evolved to encourage people to make love and reproduce and do what all the other mammals do? Isn't that mysterious enough?"

Ryan sighed, nodding to her and then to the stars. "A verb, yeah. Love is an action. You're a pretty smart chick." He lifted her onto his lap and, with his hands tight on her hips, gave her a deep vigorous kiss and said, "I can think of a few more chemical reactions we might enjoy."

Emmy slid her hands under his shirt, kissed him on the neck, and said, "It's time for you to go home."

"But I don't want to go home."

"That's just evolution talking."

"No—it's magic!"

"That might work on some girls..."

She untangled herself from him. They got in the car, and she drove him out to the parking lot where, in the dark, his old Probe looked like the sports car it had once pretended to be. He prayed that it would start.

He asked, "If consciousness isn't something like a metaphysical spark, if everything is purely physical, if there's nothing *in here*, if it's all *out there*, then what happens when we die?"

"Would you rather live with certain knowledge that you'd never die? Isn't it precisely the threat of having it all end that makes life sweet? Ryan, part of what feels so warm and wonderful when I inhale the smell of your neck—"

"I knew I should have put on some cologne!"

Emmy reached up and held his chin. "Part of what feels so good is the lack of control, the threat that I could be wrong, the risk that it's all a lie, that all you want is for me to meet with those idiots and get you your money and, what the hell, you get a piece of ass too."

"You don't think that, do you?"

"Risk and uncertainty are the thrill of being alive. The knowledge, every day, every instant, that this breath might be our last is what makes life full of wonder. Having a ghost who keeps score and assigns reason to our existence makes it *less* wonderful. Religion decreases significance."

Ryan rested his chin on her head and stared across the horizon. "Hmmm, I believe in something more, something special. I think that love and emotion have something like an energy of their own. Something that connects us to whatever it is that made something from nothing. Something that can violate that rule of yours: neither created nor destroyed."

Emmy pried herself away, reached up, and brushed his lips with her fingers. "Good night, Ryan."

28

Ryan set the pizza box on a patch of well-manicured grass under a marine-blue sky—the perfect spot for a picnic. On one side, a cool breeze blew through majestic redwood trees that grew from the banks of a creek, and on the other, a wide stretch of concrete guided students and faculty between buildings on the UC Berkeley campus. Emmy handed Ryan a tiny cup of espresso and sat next to him. They were both wearing jeans and T-shirts. Their crossed legs overlapped, and they leaned close together. A group of young men kicked a hacky sack on the grass a few yards away, and a street musician sat on a bench picking melodies about twenty yards up the path, his open guitar case inviting tips.

Ryan took a sip. "How many packets of honey did you get?"

"Three."

"Well, I get them all," Ryan said.

Emmy nudged him with her elbow. "Silly man."

Ryan squeezed the honey into his cup. When he finished, Emmy took his hand and kissed the last drop of honey from his fingers. She looked up at him as her tongue lingered on his finger.

He put his other hand on her neck and pulled her toward him for a kiss.

"Ryan!" she said, pushing away with her forearm. "What if my students see me? I can't just make out in public like a drunk freshman."

He bit his lip. "You started it."

She leaned in close, her breasts rubbing his arm. "And I'll finish it." Then she sat up straight, wiped her mouth with a napkin, and added, "But please, Mr. McNear, I have a reputation to maintain."

Ryan sipped his espresso. How long had it been? He fell in love with Linda seventeen years ago. Then he fell in love with her all over again when Sean was born, and again and again.

Emmy was looking at him, waiting, blue eyes twinkling. For an instant, Ryan felt like he was cheating on a memory. And then he surrendered. He felt his eyes go soft and he inhaled Emmy, not just the light flowery smell of her perfume, no, her warmth, her Emmy-ness—he felt like he was melting. It was a little bit scary.

It was their third date. They had met in San Francisco on their second for dinner and the theater. The restaurant had been expensive and loud and the play political and morose. Ryan spent the night treading water in the flood of San Francisco culture. He remembered Emmy's fingers touching his face as he kissed her good night. She had pulled him down so that she could whisper in his ear, "Be comfortable with me," before walking through the subway gates.

With the pizza box empty, Ryan leaned back in the sun. Emmy stretched out against him, resting her head on his chest.

Emmy said, "What are you going to do next?"

He started to explain again how he needed money to pay his child support so that he could get joint custody, see his son, clear his record, and resume his life, but she interrupted him: "No, I mean after that."

He had to think for a minute. The guitarist played a lazy chord progression. Finally, Ryan told her that he wanted to rebuild his career. "My dad used to say that a man should hang his shingle and make it on his own. I'd like to open my own software company—I'll make a fortune in software souls."

"Where does Kat fit?"

"Katarina?" He thought some more, listened to the guitar, and ran his fingers through Emmy's hair.

"Maybe I'll give her a job—McNear and Sidekick Software Incorporated."

"Come on, I'm serious."

"You have to understand," he said. "Katarina makes it pretty clear that she doesn't want me playing the role of her father."

"Have you ever thought that maybe Kat needs you more than your son does?"

This made him sit up. He stared at the grass for a minute. "I don't want to abandon my son."

"Your son has a stepfather, right?"

"Yeah, Howard, ancient Howard," Ryan growled. "Sean and I were really close until he came along. I have to fix it."

"Katarina has only her mother and you."

"Her mother told me that she's going to join her husband as soon as Katarina is ready."

Emmy sat up on her knees so that her head was level with Ryan's. "Isn't he dead?"

Ryan told her how Jane bicycled around Petaluma talking to herself.

"Ryan, listen to me." Emmy's brow furrowed. "You're all Kat has. A girl who grows up without guidance is a time bomb."

"Naw," Ryan said, "Katarina is cool, a little rough around the edges, but she's a good kid, brilliant and healthy, strong. She's not a time bomb."

"Katarina is lucky to have you. You're lucky to have her." She seemed angry. "Both of you need to realize that before it's too late."

"Emmy," Ryan said and reached over to touch her cheek. "I know. Okay? I do." Ryan rubbed the furrows out of her brow and pulled her close.

"She needs you to worry about her."

They settled back on the grass and listened to the guitar for a few minutes. Finally, Ryan said, "Do you want to have kids?"

"I have plenty of kids." Her fingers traced random curves around his chest and stomach. "Totally. Right now I have, like, five. One just turned twenty—an undergraduate lab rat; I have two in their early twenties, teaching assistants; a new one came in last week; he'll be a research assistant; and, of course, you know my favorite, Tran. They're creative, curious, intelligent, and they never need their diapers changed."

"I don't believe you." Ryan reached down and rested his hand just over her belly button.

"I don't think I'd be a very good mother. I'm kind of impatient. Do you want more children?"

"I'm Catholic." Ryan laughed. "By rights I should have you squirting them out every other year."

"Me?" She feigned shock, but her fingers stopped their random circles and tweaked his nipple.

Ryan rolled onto his side to face her. He noticed the students watching and buried his face in her hair, kissing her neck. She turned to face him and ran her tongue along his lips and whispered, "I've wanted to do that for a long time. I love how you lick your lips just before you smile. I love it."

Ryan met her kiss and pulled her hair so that it covered their faces, forming their own little world.

From the concrete path, not ten yards away, Ryan heard a deep voice with some sort of European accent say, "Good afternoon, Dr. Nutter. We missed you at the faculty meeting. I see that you had a pressing engagement."

Emmy rolled away from Ryan. Her hair fell away and the sun shone in. She was already flushed, but Ryan could tell that she was blushing.

"Hello, Claude," she said. "Yes, indeed. I'm meeting with a visiting scholar. Ryan McNear, this is Claude Onet, director of Lawrence Berkeley National Laboratory."

"Don't get up," Claude said. "I'm late for a meeting with the chancellor." They could hear him laughing as he walked away.

Emmy blessed Ryan with a warm smile. "Good thing I have tenure."

Ryan watched him go. The tall bald man in a corduroy jacket tossed a few dollars into the guitar case of the musician and spoke to him. Then the guitarist repositioned himself to face Ryan and Emmy and played the Beatles' "Here, There and Everywhere."

Emmy pulled herself onto her feet, dragging Ryan up by his shirt. She caught a couple of chest hairs in the process. With a steamy glare, she said, "My house is five blocks from here."

29

Not quite two months after the complaint was filed, the defendant, Creation Energy, requested a private meeting with the plaintiff, Ryan McNear. Dodge arranged a conference room at the Mark Hopkins Hotel in San Francisco.

Emmy was waiting in the lobby when they got there. Dressed in a white lacy blouse, black pants, and a herringbone waistcoat, she looked polished and professional. She greeted Ryan with a hug and complimented him on his suit—coal with salmon pinstripes.

Gripping her by the hips, Ryan held her a few inches away. "Emmy, thank you for coming, but I don't want you to feel obligated to do this for me." Their relationship had grown into consistent midweek visits and weekend stay-overs. Ryan had never seen Emmy dressed like this—he knew her as a jeans-and-T-shirt woman.

"Ryan, I'm here to defend the integrity of science." She straightened his tie and added, "Not that I don't expect some favors for helping you."

He pulled her close and whispered in her ear, "I like you dressed like this—let's play professor scolds the naughty engineer Saturday night…"

She bit his earlobe in reply.

Ryan felt his whole life coming together, as if everything that had happened from the day he'd moved away from Linda and Sean until today had been a bridge from one wonderful life to another. The transition wasn't over and, no question, it was a bitch, but the lawsuit was going exactly the way Dodge had predicted. If this meeting went well, Creation Energy would settle, and Ryan could get on with his life. An image was coming clear in his heart, the way that abstract art takes shape the longer you look at it: Ryan and Emmy walking in a park holding hands with Katarina and Sean straggling along behind, arguing over their favorite bands or skateboard technicalities or some dumb thing that teenagers are willing to fight over.

His arms around Emmy, his face buried in her neck, he opened his eyes and looked at the world through her hair. Amolie. Even her name was beautiful.

"Break it up!" Dodge yelled from across the lobby, holding the elevator door. "We have twenty minutes to prepare."

The conference room had a view of the San Francisco skyline. Dodge shut the blinds.

Scowling, but with a spring in his step like a boxer ready to get in the ring, Dodge dimmed the lights and directed Ryan and Emmy to sit at opposite ends of the big glass-and-chrome table. "None of the antagonists will sit next to each other. There will be no private conversations. I'll sit between their attorney, Blair Keene, and that redneck, Jeb Schonders."

He went to Ryan's end of the table. "First thing—you need to make peace with Foster."

Ryan said, "Last time I saw Foster wasn't exactly friendly."

"McNear, who are you kidding? You couldn't hold a grudge against a serial killer. Just be yourself." Even when Dodge provided insight, it came out as an affront. "Second, your only goal is for them to admit something, just a starting point, no more."

Then Dodge walked to Emmy's side of the table. "Third, Emmy, go after them like a lion on a Christian." He laughed at his own joke, extra loud, obviously trying to get a laugh from Ryan or Emmy. It didn't work.

Emmy set the copies of the patents that Tran had marked up in front of her.

Dodge peeked behind the blinds, a con man waiting for his mark.

Ryan watched them both. What a strange new family he had. Despite what Dodge said about this being just a step in the process, hope brewed in his heart. Emmy smiled at him—amazing how that smile transformed her from sophisticated professor to adorable woman. He wanted to bring her back to Massachusetts. He could picture his mother interrogating her, could practically hear Mom ask Emmy naïve but potentially offensive questions about being Jewish and then break out the photo albums and force-feed her the reality of joining an Irish Catholic family.

Finally, they heard a knock on the door. Foster walked in behind his father-in-law, Blair Keene, and his boss, Jeb Schonders. Blair looked like a San Francisco banker in a form-fitting black suit. Jeb Schonders wore a bolo tie and a brown suit that showed the wrinkles of having been stowed in checked luggage. Dodge introduced himself and Emmy.

With his shirt sleeves rolled up so you couldn't miss the monogram and his briefcase stuffed so thick that one of the hinges had already popped, Foster looked like such a goofball—Dodge was right: he couldn't hold a grudge. Foster was just being Foster. How could you hate the guy?

The only vacant chair was next to Ryan. Foster pursed his lips. He glanced at Ryan from the corners of his eyes. It wasn't the first time they'd been pissed off at each other and found themselves sitting together at a conference table. The familiarity found a warm spot in Ryan's heart. He elbowed Foster and whispered, "Just relax, dude."

Foster raised his briefcase to the table, and Ryan saw the remaining hinge start to give. He grabbed it by the sides, holding it closed, and said, "Foster, I swear to God, you need constant supervision."

"Thanks," Foster said. "I really need a bigger briefcase."

Ryan could feel everyone's eyes on the two of them. He wondered if Foster had the balls to drop his indignant air. Foster dug a mechanical pencil out of his briefcase and scribbled on a pad. To the others it might have passed for setting up his notes for the meeting, but Ryan knew from all the other meetings they'd been in together that it was a note meant for him: "You're on the wrong side of this fight."

Jeb questioned why they couldn't sit on opposite sides of the table. "After all," he said, "that's how it will be in court."

Dodge said, "People are adversaries in court, but we're all on the same side here—we all want justice." An elastic grin formed on his face. "It's more important that we get to know each other as people…" His voice trailed off. Then he walked around the table and shook hands with Jeb, Blair, and Foster. He took their hands in both of his, held them, and asked about their families, their hobbies, and health. He even cautioned Jeb not to put too much cream in his coffee: "That's the real stuff there, Jeb. Don't clog up your ticker." Jeb responded with a short diatribe about having to come "way out here to the Left Coast, step over bums, walk past prostitutes, and Lord knows what these San *Fran-sickos* do to each other at night."

After appearing to listen carefully, Dodge responded, "We all want to live in peace together and spread love around the world." Then the capper: "I know that's why I'm here. The good Lord has given us an opportunity to help a fine man reconnect with his only born son. I think we can all agree that we're meeting here to help Ryan McNear."

Jeb replied, "Ryan McNear is a wanted man in my state."

Dodge took it as a cue to begin the meeting. After reviewing the argument presented in the complaint, that Ryan still owned rights to the patents by virtue of GoldCon violating an implied contract, Dodge added that, as it worked out, Foster had actually been paid in full—he had the boat. He looked at each person in the room emphasizing that Ryan could not legally be "denied his right to the income generated by his talent, originality, and intellectual property."

Ryan felt a wave of discomfort. The "implied contract" seemed like an absurd technicality; he had signed the patent waiver. Plus, they'd gotten the boat, and Ryan was sure that Foster still thought of it as half his. Besides, the patents were still being developed. There was no income. Then he looked at Emmy. She smiled back and it made him feel worse. She wanted to testify. Dodge had told her that this meeting was preliminary to a lawsuit, that she would get a chance to fight EWU in court. Ryan hadn't told her that the meeting was designed for them to make an offer to settle, that there would never be a lawsuit. In the time they had spent together, they talked about science and religion, about Sean and Katarina, and Emmy's students. And they talked about the future. That was the real reason Ryan hadn't mentioned that the case would never go to court. He wanted that future. His dad would have told him that it was okay, that there is a difference between lying and leaving out the truth, but Grandma wouldn't go for it; she'd say it was like the difference between clover and shamrock—there might be a difference, but they still looked the same. Dad and Grandma argued in his head for a few seconds. Ryan knew Grandma was right.

Dodge handed out copies of three patent cases he'd researched. Then he addressed Blair. "How would you like to handle this?"

Blair spoke softly, "This meeting is premature. No income has been derived from the intellectual property."

Jeb said, "Your threats are nothing but extortion."

The word *extortion* seemed to broaden Dodge's smile.

"There *is* another aspect to the problem," Dodge said, nodding to Emmy.

In her lecture voice, she started reviewing the patents almost line by line, describing every point that was inconsistent with "the established laws of nature."

Ryan stared across the table at her. When she kicked on that lecture voice, there was an authority to her. The first time he'd heard that tone, she'd been in Dodge's office drawing Feynman diagrams on the desk blotter. Now, when she flipped on the lecture voice, Ryan recognized it as a wall that she erected between the roles she embodied—the warm, caring woman and the cool, rational physicist.

Foster thumbed through his copies of the patents with his head cocked. Ryan recognized it as the Foster equivalent of a game face. But as Emmy continued, Foster's eyes narrowed. He didn't look pissed off though; no, this was a look that Ryan didn't recognize. Halfway into her argument, Jeb interrupted, saying that nothing she said mattered, that the Lord's work would be done. Other than raising her voice, Emmy ignored him. Blair tried to interrupt too by addressing Dodge, but Dodge didn't waver from pretending that he was listening to Emmy. Then Jeb interrupted again. This time, Emmy spoke softly, though with no less authority, so that Foster had to lean in close to hear.

Emmy concluded, "To summarize, in the descriptions of the preferred embodiments, neither patent meets the minimal requirement of demonstrable viability. Further, the first patent, Application of Fundamental Uncertainty to the Generation of Energy, violates federal patent law—it is against the law to submit a perpetual motion machine for patent."

Foster pushed his chair out and stood. With his hands on the table and arms propping him up, he spoke slowly. "No, ma'am. I'm afraid you misunderstood. It's not a perpetual motion machine. We've made a lot of progress since submitting the patents." He pulled a copy of *The Cosmology of Creation* from his briefcase. "The patents themselves are incomplete. You should read my later work." He waved his book at her. Ryan knew that she still hadn't read it. Foster continued, "The technology is a power generator more or less like any other." His head bobbed down to that smug angle. "Not *exactly* like any other, of course. The fuel source is hardly conventional, but the technology is based on laws of symmetry like any other physical law, and that's what makes our work innovative."

Emmy didn't even look at him.

Blair cleared his throat. "Interesting that you'd introduce an expert witness to demonstrate the *lack* of value inherent in Mr. McNear's alleged intellectual property. Why are you weakening your case?"

"Oh, my mistake," Dodge said, smiling at Blair. "I should have reserved Dr. Nutter's commentary for National Engineering or, even better, the US Patent Office and the Departments of Energy and Defense."

Jeb Schonders started to speak, but Blair leaned forward, brushing him off with a wave. Blair said, "I understand."

"Excellent," Dodge said, rising from his seat and sliding sheets of paper across the table to each person. "In addition to the points that Dr. Nutter has raised, there are a few other, um, oddities surrounding these two patents: both were examined by the same patent officer, an officer who is generally charged with reviewing patents of *biological* systems. These were the first and only patents that this officer has examined involving either energy generation or artificial intelligence. We find that very odd. We also found it odd that this patent officer was once in the employ of you, sir." Dodge smiled at Blair again. "In fact, it seems he was once engaged to your daughter." Dodge turned to Foster, his eyes narrowed, and after a short but poignant pause, he said, "who is now Mrs. Foster Reed."

Foster's head had been stuck at that smug angle, but now it straightened and slowly drooped until he was staring into his briefcase. Ryan understood how Foster felt about his "angel," Rachel. Add this to Emmy's step-by-step conviction of the patents, and Ryan's old buddy was clearly shaken. Ryan scribbled on his notepad "Dodge is full of shit." But Foster didn't look at it.

Then Ryan wondered about something else. Emmy still hadn't read Foster's book. The symmetry argument—the physical and spiritual, Heisenberg's mirror—was not included in the patents. As soon as the thought came to him, though, he realized that Emmy would immediately reject the symmetry argument anyway. Just as Foster wouldn't consider anything inconsistent with the Bible, Emmy wouldn't so much as ponder anything beyond the purely physical. Every time Ryan entertained the possibility that Foster might be onto something, two things came to mind: first, the lingering question of matter and consciousness; and second, Katarina's proof of principle argument, that energy must have originated somewhere. The engineer in Ryan thought the resolution was obvious: build the thing and see if it works.

Dodge spread his hands out as though embracing everyone at the table. "We can all agree that the mission of Creation Energy could be in serious peril if the patents are withdrawn and the various improprieties exposed to investors."

Ryan looked at each person at the table. Jeb frowned, Blair calculated a response, Foster struggled to remain silent, and Emmy—well, Emmy was looking back at him. Ryan smiled at her, but she didn't smile back.

Dodge continued, "My client has no interest in causing any harm to your endeavor, and, just between the six of us, I think he hopes that you'll succeed."

Emmy's eyes locked on Ryan's in a cold stare.

"We are willing to settle for a modest fraction of the moneys Creation Energy can reasonably expect from the subcontracts it will receive from NEG and will be quite happy to divest any and all future interest."

Emmy turned her glare on Dodge.

Ryan's stomach felt hollow.

Foster nudged him and whispered, "It's not too late, Ryan. Have faith."

Foster then took a deep breath and said, "This lady's arguments demonstrate the gulf that has formed between elite academics and hardworking scientists and engineers—people whose minds are open enough to make things happen. I'll stand by the viability of our work on any field, in court, at a conference, in the press, any day, any time. I would love to expose the scientific establishment for the closed-minded bigots they have become."

Ryan watched Emmy fume when Foster referred to her without addressing her. Dodge's eyes kept going back to her too. She was dangerous, and Ryan realized for the first but certainly not the last time that he was firmly entrenched in the crossfire. He felt his tongue run along his teeth. He wanted to disarm the situation and started to interrupt, but Emmy beat him to it with one word spoken very quietly.

In a southern gentleman's drawl, Blair said, "What was that, ma'am?"

Emmy looked at him. "I said *please.*"

"What do you mean by that?"

"Well, Mr. Reed—"

"*Doctor* Reed."

"Yes, well." Emmy cleared her throat. "He said he would like to expose the scientific establishment. My response is, please. Let's discuss this in public. Let's compare experimental results. The problem, *Mister* Reed—your work is so weak, so divorced from the scientific method, that I couldn't imagine"—she looked at Jeb—"an accredited university awarding you a doctorate."

Blair began assembling documents into his briefcase. Jeb followed his example. Dodge watched the two of them, his eyes squinted, but a trace of a smile lingered on his lips.

Blair shut his briefcase with a snap and looked across at Dodge. "What sort of number are you considering?"

"We believe that, at this point, ten million should appropriately compensate Mr. McNear for his contribution. Right now, that's a small fraction of the contracts you must anticipate from National Engineering. You could wait, but in a few years, maybe a hundred million will be more appropriate."

Jeb's false laughter drowned out Dodge. "Millions? You got quite an imagination there, Nutter. Tell you what, I'll pretend to use it as a starting point. See, I was thinking a few thousand." He looked at Blair, as if for support, but Blair looked away. Jeb said, "I reckon extortion is what you get in this town for trying to do the Lord's work."

Dodge closed his briefcase and dropped the kind demeanor he'd been masquerading. He released an extra-long version of his raspy chuckle. "I prefer the term *blackmail* myself, but as long as the check doesn't bounce, we can call it whatever you like."

"You lied to me," Emmy said.

Ryan stammered.

Dodge had just led Foster and the others to the elevator. Emmy had stayed in the conference room and was looking out the window. Ryan stood in the hallway, caught between them.

"Dodge is a liar. I expect him to lie to me, but I trusted you."

"It wasn't a lie," Ryan said, though he didn't believe it. "You were here to set them straight, and you did."

"I told him that everything I said had to be in the open, and here I am in a smoke-filled room."

"There's no smoke in this room."

She turned and glared at him.

His heart sunk. "I'm sorry. Emmy. I needed your help and—"

"And you got it!" She marched out of the room, past Ryan. "You used me."

"Wait a second," Ryan said. "I appreciate your help—you know how much I appreciate your help. I didn't know what Dodge planned. No one knows what Dodge plans. Come on, Emmy, I—"

"Ryan, just leave me alone, okay?" She stopped several feet away from him. "I'm angry, so just let me figure this out, okay? I'll call you."

She walked away.

At the airport, Foster quietly changed his seat assignment for the flight home. On the way out he'd sat between his father-in-law and his boss. But right now, he was fighting the impulse to get in their faces. They were politicians, not warriors. If Foster questioned them, Blair would list their losses again, from the Scopes trial to *Roe v. Wade* to the defeat of intelligent design in *Kitzmiller v. Dover Area School District*, right up to the most recent, *Lawrence v. Texas*. To Foster, the last was the worst—the courts openly embraced sodomy.

Yes, the Christian soldiers were racking up defeats, but this was a battle they could win. He took a breath and leaned against the window. He could see their wisdom; they needed time to develop the Creation Energy Generator. Settling with Ryan would give them that time. Soon enough, Foster would open Heisenberg's window, and the power of God would be unleashed. That's when the battle should begin, but not yet.

He was a paladin fighting for God, and always, hovering over him, was the angel Rachel. The accusation made by the shark, that Rachel had been engaged to the patent officer and had been deceiving him all these years, opened a wound. When Blair failed to deny it, a demon of self-doubt had flown into that wound, into his heart. He knew how to fight the self-doubt in his head—why had God chosen him, and what if he couldn't do it?

He fought those demons every day, but he had never had a doubt in his heart.

The plane weaved through clouds over the Rockies, each a distinct thunderhead towering into the heavens. Foster could see flashes of lightning inside them, and shining between each great column were individual beams of sunlight. The possibility that Creation Energy could unleash enough power to initiate the Rapture seemed desirable right now. Purge the world of evil in one righteous slap.

Would paying off Ryan be his sin or Jeb's? He sighed. The man sitting next to him shifted his laptop away. Ryan's collapse had started at the celebration of the end of Foster's bachelorhood—his wound oozed doubt. Ryan had suffered for that night all these years. Maybe it was time that Foster suffered too.

And, like so many other times, it came to him—how to exorcise the doubt from his heart.

Ryan was the best friend he'd ever had, and the deeper Foster looked inside, the more obvious it was. He felt a pang of disgust that it had taken guilt and doubt to motivate him to do the right thing, but if that's what it took…

31

When Dodge unpacked his briefcase after the meeting, he discovered a legal-sized manila envelope. He opened it and let the contents slide onto the desk. There was a short note on Evangelical Word University stationery, several photographs, and two newspaper clippings. The note was an ancient threat: "Then Judas, which had betrayed Him, when he saw that he was condemned, repented himself, and brought again the thirty pieces of silver to the chief priests and elders. Saying, I have sinned in that I have betrayed the innocent blood. And they said, What is that to us? see thou to that. And he cast down the pieces of silver in the temple, and departed, and went and hanged himself. And the chief priests took the silver pieces, and said, It is not lawful for to put them into the treasury, because it is the price of blood. —Matthew 27:3–5"

He leaned back in his chair and flipped through the photos. Some were pictures of Dodge visiting with his clientele at Skate-n-Shred. He examined them with a magnifying glass. They must have been taken from across the street, probably from a second-story window with a telephoto lens. Two were much older. The first was a file photo from the *Los Angeles Times* with a teenage Dodge in shackles. Dodge chuckled and then wiped a line of spittle from the photo. A paperclip attached a newspaper clipping. He remembered what it said word for word. Tried as an adult, he'd been acquitted.

The other picture came with newsprint too. It had been taken the day he'd gotten his nickname from the University of Michigan campus police: a college-aged Dodge standing in front of a cemetery. The clipping, from the *Ann Arbor News*, said that Dodge had been acquitted of manslaughter and grave robbing in the Zeta Sigma Chi "hazing suicides" trial. It also quoted the officer who had dubbed Wayne Nutter "Dodge," saying that the police had closed the case for lack of evidence.

The last piece was a short paragraph from the Los Angeles County Bar Association's newsletter. Dated 1987, it described a case where Wayne Nutter, JD, had been held in contempt of court while representing a man who, during a bank robbery, had executed five tellers with single shots to the backs of their heads. Dodge had argued that the defendant was merely guilty of "assisted suicide." The judge had not been amused when Dodge attempted to demonstrate that none of the tellers had had a life that was worth living.

Dodge set the pictures on his desk in a straight line and stared at them. He leaned forward and picked up the revolver, spun the chamber, and held the gun to his head. He looked at the pictures and said out loud, "No. Not today," and set the revolver back on the gavel pad.

He took a sheet of monogrammed paper from his desk and wrote, "The Lord hath made all things for Himself: yea, even the wicked for the day of evil. Every one that is proud in heart is an abomination to the Lord: though hand join in hand, he shall not be unpunished. —Proverbs 16:4–5." He sealed it in an envelope with a twenty-dollar bill and a short note that read, "Deliver to Jeb Schonders, EWU, by hand and with emphasis." Dodge mailed it to the ranch outside of San Antonio, addressed to Dale Watson, the son of Foster's secretary.

Ryan's faith in make-up sex was restored.

He knew that Emmy had come to Petaluma that night to end their relationship. She'd been ignoring his e-mails and hadn't answered his calls in almost a month, and then, finally, she invited herself over. She lit into him pretty good too, accusing him of misleading her, abusing her support, and perpetuating nonsense nonscience in the face of the truth. He admitted that he had known Dodge was manipulating her. She had glared at him, those warm blue eyes turned hot indigo, and he admitted what he thought would be the killing blow: "Yes, I misled you. It was selfish. Without your help, I could never fix my life, never see my son and"—he placed both hands on her shoulders—"if I couldn't fix my life, well, I didn't want you to fall in love with a failed man." Emmy glowered for a few seconds. Ryan felt her shoulders tense up, and when she looked away from him, he thought it was over.

She turned back, though, and put her hands over his heart. "Ryan, I would have helped you anyway." Then she relaxed and started to laugh. "For some reason, my grody brother cannot do anything in the open. He's been lying to me all my life, and every time I get mixed up with him, I think it will be different." Then she lightly punched his chest, and her eyes simmered to a warm glow. "Ryan, I'm falling in love…please be the man I think you are."

The sun's first rays eased their way over the mountain, sneaked under dark rain clouds, and reflected pastels of pink and peach onto the ceiling. Emmy was asleep in his arms, and he buried his face in her currently jet-black hair. Ryan's faith in the universe was renewed.

It was his second anniversary in Petaluma, and he celebrated with a deep breath of Emmy, salty, sweet Emmy. She stretched and nuzzled against him. Wake-up sex might have been as good as make-up sex, but oh well.

BAM!

Emmy lurched against him. "What was that?"

Again, against the door: *BAM!*

Ryan groaned, "It's my youthful ward."

"Ryan, wake up! You have to drive me to school."

He looked at his watch: 7:00. She was already late. "Okay, just stop—"

BAM!

"Stop pounding—Jesus H...."

He pulled on jeans and a T-shirt and unlocked the door.

Katarina came in. She looked frustrated. The high school was on the other side of town and started early. Then she noticed Emmy and started to blush.

Emmy said, "Hi, Kat."

Katarina looked at Ryan, who raised both eyebrows into his dorky-womanizer face.

To Emmy, Katarina said, "I'm late for school." Then she yelled at Ryan, "Come on!"

That kid he'd met on the porch two years ago was long gone. She didn't skate very much anymore, and her Converse All Stars had been replaced by an array of suede boots, the kind that Ryan's sisters used to wear in the eighties. She'd painted them with acrylics—little dragons exhaling breaths of Feynman diagrams and equations. Her denim jacket was gone too, replaced by a formfitting coat like Emmy wore. At fourteen, the skirts she'd always worn looked different. Somewhere along the way, her legs had gotten long and graceful. Fading scars on her knees were the last evidence of the kid who used to skate down fire escapes. It didn't take much makeup for her to pass for eighteen.

"You have to stop missing the bus—what if I had to work today?"

"What work?"

He finished tying his shoelaces and followed Katarina down the hall. She carried a small leather purse and had her old backpack slung over a shoulder. Her hair, nearly all the way down her back, bounced in time with her steps.

"Why aren't you taking the banister?"

She paused at the landing and scowled. "Mind your own business."

"Um, do you *want* a ride?"

She let him pass and then followed down the stairs and out to his car.

"Katarina, people don't do favors for people who treat them like shit."

"Fine! I don't want to go anyway." She threw her backpack into the car, got in, and slammed the door.

Ryan started the car. "So how's school?"

Katarina turned the radio up until it was too loud to talk.

Upstairs in Ryan's apartment, Emmy got up and showered. She liked it here. She liked the apartment's unashamed masculinity: the football that Ryan said was his most valuable possession, the beach chair, the foam "bed," the milk crates that held his clothes, the fridge with plenty of beer but barely enough milk for his tea. She liked that he drank tea instead of coffee too. In the shower, she noticed that he used pink soap and sighed. Wrapped in Ryan's towel, Emmy stepped into the kitchen and took the small jar of instant coffee he kept for her down from the cupboard. She hated instant coffee, but he'd been so pleased with himself for thinking of her that she hadn't told him. She knew that Dodge would have a full pot of high-octane French roast downstairs.

That bastard. After thirty-six years, why did she still have faith in him? Yes, he doted on her. Yes, he had always been there when she needed help with anything. Anything. But he helped by twisting things, not just to his advantage either. It seemed like Dodge twisted things for amusement more than he did for profit—neither reason was acceptable. He had conned her again.

She put the kettle on, scooped a double dose of coffee crystals into a mug, and got dressed. A few minutes later, she sat in the beach chair, Ryan's towel in her lap, and sipped coffee. The whiteboard was covered in calculations. Kat's handwriting was precise but with girlish curlicues. Emmy pictured Kat at the whiteboard with Ryan at her side, Kat guiding Ryan through mathematics while he guided her through life. She took a deep breath of the towel and felt as warm as she ever had. Then a thought crossed her mind. The thought wasn't new, but there was a new element.

Her choice not to have children was calculated from two realizations: first, guiding students through their most creative years ought to fulfill her maternal instincts; and second, she'd always assumed that she didn't have the maternal warmth necessary to accept the burden of a baby. Right now, though, watching Kat dazzle Ryan in her mind's eye, she realized that she had been wrong. What was it that had convinced her that she wasn't a complete woman?

She heard motion downstairs. Dodge. That was why. Growing up in Dodge's cynical shadow had convinced her that motherhood would be more burden than reward. The realization made her feel weary. A baby?

Her coffee mug empty, Emmy stood and shook off her reverie. She gathered her things and headed for the door. It was time to deal with Monday morning traffic.

As she passed the whiteboard again, she looked at it. A thought invaded her mind: Kat needed a mother.

Ryan drove Katarina down the hill and across the river to Casa Grapevine High. He pulled up to the curb and turned down the stereo. "Have a happy Monday, Katarina. Can I pick you up after school? We should work on those Feynman path integrals..."

She looked at him without moving her head, her eyeballs swiveling up at him, said "whatever," and got out of the car.

Ryan started to pull away, but a clot of traffic was passing. He watched Katarina join a group of other kids standing under an awning. Most of them hung out at Skate-n-Shred. A tall thin boy smoking a cigarette took Katarina's hand without looking at her. He wore a black jacket a size too large and big black boots. He also had a trace of what he probably considered a moustache over his lip. A green bandana hung from his back pocket. Ryan had "escorted" him out of Skate-n-Shred more than once. It was that kid, Alex, the one the kids called "The Ace." For a scrawny kid, he commanded a lot of respect.

When Katarina leaned into the circle and said something to one of the other girls, they leaned against each other laughing. The other girl was Katarina's friend Marti. The two of them separated from the crowd and walked up the steps to school. Just before opening the big glass door, Katarina looked back at Ryan and waved.

The rain had stopped, but when Katarina waved, a different storm came over him. Katarina was becoming a woman as beautiful as she was brilliant, and Ryan wasn't ready. He wiped his eyes with the back of his hand and forced a smile. This is how it is supposed to be. As incredible as Katarina could someday become, right now she was a snarling, fire-breathing little bitch—exactly what fourteen-year-old girls are supposed to be.

On the drive home, Ryan questioned whether he should let Katarina walk all over him like she had. At a stoplight, he watched the sun pass behind a cloud and decided that, more than anything else, Katarina needed someone she could rely on. That she could treat him like shit but still rely on him showed deep, if twisted, trust and affection.

When he got back to the house, Emmy's car was gone, and Dodge was sitting on the couch. "McNear, my office right now."

Ryan followed him in. Every time he sat there, Ryan automatically reached for something to twiddle with, but the only thing on the desk was that damn revolver. He reached for it, realized what he was doing, and jerked his hand away.

"This," Dodge said, holding a sealed envelope out to Ryan, "is notification that someone is pregnant."

Was Emmy pregnant? Ryan rejected the thought as soon as it came. Dodge would be the last person Emmy would tell and, even if she were, Emmy was quite clear that she had no intention of bearing children—she already had six graduate students.

Trying to appear nonchalant, Ryan took the envelope. It was addressed to him, care of Wayne (Dodge) Nutter, Attorney at Law. The return address had the cross-and-lightning-bolt logo of Creation Energy, LLC. "You didn't open it?"

"That would be a federal offense," Dodge said. "Besides, I know what's in it."

Ryan tapped the envelope on the desk. "What?"

"This is how it works. They start the bidding and we finish it. The main thing is that they've admitted we're right." Dodge cupped his chin in his hands. "Go ahead, open it. Let's see where the games begin."

Ryan tore open the envelope. There were three sheets of paper. As Ryan read the cover letter, Dodge reached across and took the other sheets.

Jeb Schonders was "pleased to compensate Ryan for his contribution to the success of Creation Energy under the conditions set forth in the enclosed documents."

"Ha!" Dodge wiggled in his chair with glee. "They think it's stillborn." He waved a page just out of Ryan's reach. "How much do you owe your wife?"

Ryan folded the envelope into a little triangle. How long had it been since he ran out of money, a little over three years? The monthly child support had been 20 percent of his income back when he was making almost $250,000 a year.

"Come on—you don't have to calculate to the tenth goddamn decimal place."

"Over a hundred and fifty thousand dollars. What's the offer?" Ryan tried to grab the page from Dodge.

Dodge waved it like a flag, just out of reach. "One fifty? I'll get you that."

Ryan stood and set his hands on the desk, looming over Dodge. "What's the offer?"

"They've admitted they're pregnant. That's all you need to know."

Ryan picked up the revolver and glared at Dodge.

Dodge let loose the annoying rasp. "You *finally* figured out why I leave that out—makes negotiation so much more interesting."

Ryan set it back on the gavel pad and slumped on the desk. "I just want to see my kid—tell me or I'm getting another lawyer."

"No, you should shoot me. Really."

"Dodge..." Ryan whined.

"Your cut would be about twenty grand."

Ryan felt the blood leave his face.

"We're winning. Now go away. I'm going to drag this on. The longer it festers the more they'll pay."

"Tell me what you're going to do. You're representing me, remember?"

Dodge took a labored breath and then said, "I'm going to let it fester until it's a big scabby pile of pus, and then I'm going to collect the gold at the end of the rainbow. I might even give some of it to you." He rotated around and pulled a file from the cabinet behind him. He rotated back and took a yellow legal pad from his desk. Licking the tip of a pencil, he looked at Ryan as though he were surprised to see him. "Don't you have coffee to spill or plants to water? Shouldn't you be standing on the corner with the other Mexicans?"

"God, you're an asshole. Those guys are from Guatemala and El Salvador. They're good men. You could learn something from them."

"Right. I could learn how to speak Mexican. Run along, now."

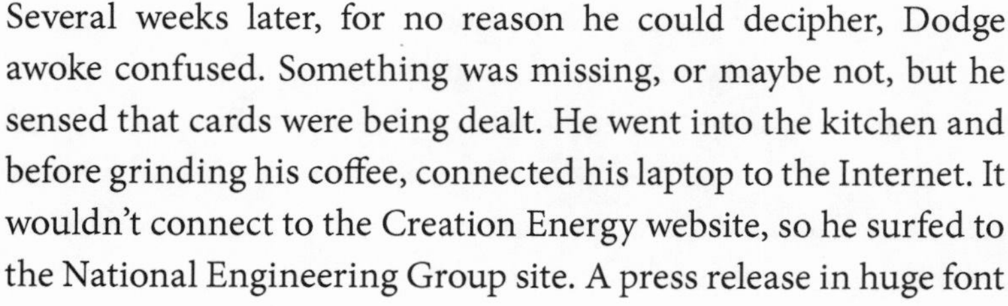

Several weeks later, for no reason he could decipher, Dodge awoke confused. Something was missing, or maybe not, but he sensed that cards were being dealt. He went into the kitchen and before grinding his coffee, connected his laptop to the Internet. It wouldn't connect to the Creation Energy website, so he surfed to the National Engineering Group site. A press release in huge font greeted him: "The National Engineering Group expands alternative energy research to include propulsion technology based on vacuum fluctuation energy extraction."

NEG stock was up fifteen points, almost 20 percent. A link to an article at MarketWatch said the stock was riding the announcement of a deal for exclusive rights to "new technology being developed by an obscure university in West Texas" that had the potential to "change the way we think about energy."

He danced into the kitchen and poured a celebratory jigger of whiskey into his morning coffee.

He turned the kitchen TV to Bloomberg. A woman yelled into the camera. "Already riding their deal for new technology, we just got word that NEG has been awarded a contract by the Department of Defense. A huge surprise to the market, investors are guessing that NEG could overtake Northrop Grumman in rocket-propulsion technology. It's a big *could* right now, and details of the technology are sketchy. NEG officials are acting more cautious than their investors, but if the market believes the technology can end dependence of the world economy on fossil fuels, the stock should double today."

Trailing phlegm-riddled laughter behind, Dodge skipped into his office and added three zeros to the counteroffer.

The phone rang just before ten. Dodge checked the caller ID—it was from a Texas area code—picked up the phone and said, "What have you got? And it better be good, because right now, I'm getting all I need from Bloomberg."

"It's crazy around here—closed the gates to the university and canceled classes." It was Mabel, secretary to Foster Reed and mother of Dodge's current favorite informant. "Dr. Reed and Reverend Schonders were fixing to meet with the press up until a herd o' Yankees showed up in black trucks."

The phone beeped, and the call waiting ID indicated Emmy's office number at Cal. Dodge said, "I'll call you back," and connected to Emmy.

"I heard National Engineering on NPR," she said. Then the Vietnamese kid interrupted. Dodge could tell it was Tran by the complete lack of any accent. Emmy came back on the line, her voice cold: "Those two patents have disappeared from USPTO-dot-gov." Away from the phone, Dodge heard her say, "Search for them in cache. Find them now." Then into the phone, "I'll call you back." She hung up.

Dodge dialed a Texas number. Dale Watson answered. "Still haven't gotten the check, Nutter."

"Give me your account number, and I'll wire a thousand right now."

"Account number? US mail'll do fine. Just get it here." The line went dead.

Dodge put $500 cash in an envelope, stamped it, and attached it to the outside of his mailbox with a clothespin. The phone rang as he walked back in the office.

It was Emmy. "Dodge, helping you scheme is anathema to me." She went quiet, as though fighting an internal battle. But she was on the phone. Dodge knew he'd already won.

She finally spoke. "I called our Department of Energy rep, the man who reviews our funding each year. Even he can't access information on this technology." She spat the word *technology.* "*I* am the only one who knows anything about it. Plus, just like the patents, Reed's dissertation has disappeared from the web—hang on a sec."

Dodge heard her talking to Tran. She came back on. "It gets weirder. Tran found the dissertation cached on three nodes, but when he went back, they'd disappeared. Same story with the patents. Someone is scouring the web to remove all documentation of this nonsense—which, under other circumstances, I'd favor, but this time, it's like a military-industrial complex conspiracy."

Dodge said, "And I'm sitting on the pot of gold at the end of the rainbow…"

"I'm going to post Reed's dissertation on the Lawrence Berkeley Lab website and send an e-mail to Bob Park at the University of Maryland—he'll blow the whistle on them. Every physicist in the world will be attacking this thing within an hour."

"Emmy!" Dodge yelled into the receiver. "Dammit, no. Stop right now. You're approaching this all wrong." He switched to a relaxed tone. "Just let them go for a little while, short their stock first, let them capsize under the weight of their own bullshit."

"Dodge, shut up." Emmy kicked into a voice that Dodge barely knew—quiet, soft, and demanding. "I am not going to allow ignorance to overwhelm reason. The press must be educated and these cozeners brought to justice."

"Emmy, what about Ryan? If you're successful, Ryan won't have a chance in hell. With his last hope gone"—he paused for effect—"would you blame him if he goes back to meth?"

"Oh, please. You can still get your settlement. Ryan will be fine."

"Not if you blow the lid off," Dodge said. "Not much to settle for once everyone knows the real value of the patents." He waited for her to respond. His confidence grew with every second of her silence.

A minute passed, and in a voice much more familiar to Dodge, she said, "How long will it take for you to get a settlement?"

"Well, the price just went *way* up, but I suspect they know it. Give me a week."

"Someone will find a copy of that dissertation, and it won't take long for the American Physical Society to take a position." She stopped, as though thinking about it, and then chuckled with no mirth. "Okay, you've got a week. Dodge, you better help Ryan. I'm watching you."

"Of course I'll help him." Dodge hung up the phone and waited.

Half an hour later the phone rang again.

"Jeb Schonders here. Mr. Nutter?" He paused, but Dodge didn't reward him with a response. "It's time we had ourselves another meeting." Schonders spoke slowly and sounded comfortable, too comfortable. "This time, how about we do it in my neck of the woods—Monday in the big D? We need to settle this thing straightaway and, one other thing, Nutter, I advise you not talk to anyone until after our meeting." The sound of Jeb's laughter turned Dodge's stomach. He had to find out what cards they were holding.

Dodge stood and forced a smile. "Why wait until Monday? I've seen the news, and I'd like to help you out. I can be in Dallas tomorrow."

"Mighty neighborly of you," he said. "How about you leave your client back there in California so as to keep the meeting short?"

Dodge hesitated. Something was missing. "Jeb that sounds just fine. Better not to bother Mr. McNear—why, just this morning he was telling me how much he's looking forward to putting this behind him."

Schonders laughed. "I'll have someone pick you up at the airport."

Maybe he was just anxious to settle before the pot grew too rich.

"I sure appreciate your southern hospitality, but you don't need to go to any trouble. My people in Dallas will make arrangements. Only thing I need from you are directions to the best barbecue in DFW."

Dodge paused at the mirror on his way out of the hotel room. He should have gotten a haircut, but the suit, a black three-piece Italian with gray pinstripes, fit perfectly. It even narrowed his waist.

He walked into the Chase Center lobby at 8:30 a.m. and bought a double espresso from a woman working at a cart. Masses of curly chestnut hair framed her made-up face. He sat on a couch with a good view of the Elm Street entrance and held the *Wall Street Journal* in front of him.

Just before he'd left Petaluma, Dodge had sent an e-mail to Jeb Schonders telling him to reschedule the meeting for ten instead of nine because of the two-hour time difference. Of course, the time difference also meant that Schonders wouldn't get the message until this morning, and then, only if he bothered to check his e-mail.

Fifteen minutes after he got his coffee, at 8:45, Dodge watched Jeb Schonders and Blair Keene walk in together. Perfect, he thought, Schonders hadn't gotten the e-mail, and it should throw them off-balance. Schonders had on beige snakeskin boots, a ridiculous cowboy hat, and the brown suit that emphasized his girth. Keene complemented his navy-blue suit with black cowhide boots but no additional stupid relics. After they got on the elevator, Dodge relaxed and read the paper for an hour before heading up to the twentieth floor to the suite of a law firm associated with Blair Keene's firm.

A receptionist who looked like a clone of the woman at the coffee cart led him to a conference room. Dodge knocked—dum da da dum dum, dum dum—before walking in. "Good morning, gentlemen." He emphasized his West Coast accent.

In addition to Schonders and Keene, there was a third man. "Alan Royce—good to know you."

Keene stood and offered his hand. Dodge gave him a firm shake and Keene said, "We asked Mr. Royce to help out. He's a patent attorney with lots of experience in the telecom corridor just north of here, where Mr. McNear and Dr. Reed worked when they wrote the patents." Keene sat down and Royce stood.

Dodge shook his hand and said, "Good to have *you* here—should make this meeting a lot shorter. Thanks for coming."

Schonders remained seated and held his arm across the table. Dodge barely closed his hand around Schonders's—the dead-fish shake to counter Jeb's not standing. Dodge said, "I trust you received my message regarding the rescheduling?"

Keene cut Schonders off. "No problem. It was nice to sleep in."

Dodge took a chair across from the patent attorney, Royce, and set out a legal pad and three wooden pencils. Royce began by criticizing the three cases that Dodge had presented in the first meeting. Of course, these were the weakest of the dozen cases he'd uncovered. Dodge nodded like an idiot and pretended to be surprised that they had found flaws. Royce followed with descriptions of cases that he thought were "similar in nature to Mr. McNear's situation" where juries had decided against the inventor. Dodge took Royce's files as they were offered, skimmed them, asked open-ended questions, and encouraged Royce to expand on case law. Dodge affected a confused expression and waited with his pencil poised, like a novice taking notes. The longer Royce talked, the further he veered from the letter of the law and the closer he got to its spirit. For Dodge, it was like sitting on three aces, waiting for the fourth.

As Royce went deeper and deeper, Dodge watched the others. Keene folded his hands behind his head. Schonders kept checking his watch as though he had another appointment.

About forty-five minutes in, Dodge said, "Mr. Royce, I certainly appreciate your help." He shuffled the files that Royce had handed him and pretended to review his notes. "You've clarified an awful lot."

Royce motioned to Keene, who said, "Terrific! You understand that—"

"I'm still confused about a couple of things." Dodge wound his face into a big, confused Colombo-style furrow. "In that first case, didn't you say that the jury denied the inventor's claim on the basis that the company provided his lab, and without all that expensive equipment, he'd have never come up with it? And in that second case, didn't the jury decide that the company's interests outweighed the inventors? But just now you said that patent law was developed to protect the intellectual property for the inventor. Isn't Ryan McNear the inventor? And he didn't even use a lab at GoldCon—"

"The law says that the company is the inventor. You see, once the engineer takes employment, the company who *pays* him has the rights to what he does under their employ. It's called work for hire."

"Huh. Why is Ryan's name listed first on the one patent, second on the other, and GoldCon Corporation is listed third on both?"

"Well, Dr. Reed and Mr. McNear were the inventors, but the invention is owned by the company."

"So, Ryan's the inventor, and patent law was developed to protect the inventor, unless he worked for a company?" Dodge stared at the file and waited for someone else to speak. Royce started to break the silence, but Dodge interrupted on the first syllable. "So the money that GoldCon paid Ryan McNear and Foster Reed is the total compensation for their invention?"

"That's right. You see, the day they came to work for GoldCon—and it's standard industry procedure—"

"Even when GoldCon didn't pay Mr. McNear what they promised?"

"I beg your pardon?" Royce glanced at Keene.

"I said, GoldCon did not pay Mr. McNear what was promised."

"Do you have documentation of that?"

"No," Dodge said, relishing his own voice, "but you do."

Royce looked confused.

Dodge indicated Royce's briefcase. "Of course, you have the signed patent waivers and copies of the award checks."

Royce opened a file and set the waivers on the table along with documents that both Ryan and Foster had signed when they received the bonuses. He said, "The revenue derived from the invention is owned by whoever owns the intellectual property. As you can see, Ryan McNear released his rights to the patents twice."

Dodge lifted the signed receipts for the bonuses that GoldCon had granted Ryan and Foster. There were two for each patent, one for the patent submission and one for the bonus when the patents were granted. "Notice that each inventor was granted five hundred dollars when the patents were submitted but only twenty-five hundred when the patents were granted." Dodge unwound his brow and waited two beats. "See how the awards were given in full for submission but split when the patents were granted?" Then he made an assumption. "If you check the original memo defining the patent bonus award program, you'll see that the inventors were promised five hundred on submission—which they each received—and five thousand if the submissions resulted in patents being issued. The patents were issued, but GoldCon split the award between the inventors."

Dodge looked at each man in the room and then said, "GoldCon assumed rights to the patent under terms that were modified *after* the patent was submitted and without notification to the inventors—they violated an implied contract."

Schonders cleared his throat as though about to spit. "That the best you got?"

Dodge pulled a thick file from his briefcase. It felt like turning a nice hole card. "Here are ten cases where juries have made substantial awards to inventors who were misled by their employer by menace, fraud, undue influence, corporate mistake, and any combination thereof." He tossed the file in front of Royce and pulled a second one out. "Here are another ten cases where inventors were in some other way denied employment by the company who held the rights. Are you aware that Creation Energy rejected Mr. McNear's application for a job?

"One last point: Mr. Reed is in possession of Mr. McNear's half of the award so, in fact, Mr. McNear received nothing. The patent waiver has been violated in three different ways. Mr. McNear retains his rights to the patents."

Dodge waited as Royce looked through each case. Schonders looked at his watch again.

When Royce closed the files, Dodge called the bet. "Do you want to go to court?"

In an offhand manner, Blair Keene said, "No one's going to court."

Dodge smiled, as though preparing to collect the pot. "Of course not. No one wins if Professor Emmy, that is, Amolie Nutter, destroys those two patents in front of a jury. Rather like mutually assured destruction, you see?" Dodge pulled a copy of the press release from his briefcase. "Says here that the revenue from their investment in Creation Energy could be in the billions."

Dodge took a deep breath. He should have been tasting victory, but neither Keene nor Schonders looked worried, and Royce was just angry.

Dodge started putting things back in his briefcase, pretending he was finished, then, as though it had just occurred to him, said, "Or would National Engineering prefer to have their face rubbed in the fact that those patents are bullshit anyway. How many Nobel Prize–winning physicists—maybe even Texas's own Steve Weinberg—would it take to knock thirty or forty percent off NEG's stock price, erase those big government contracts, and expose that their investment in *alternative* energy will do nothing more than guarantee another decade of dependence on foreign oil?"

He left the question hanging.

Schonders leaned over and whispered in Blair's ear, and then Blair mumbled something to Royce, who stood up, nodded to Dodge, and left the room. Schonders said, "We'll give you a hundred thousand just so I never have to hear your Left Coast voice again."

Keene handed Dodge a letter. Dodge took a Cross pen from his coat pocket—notably different from the wooden pencils he'd used to take notes. He added two zeros to the number and handed it back.

Schonders looked at his watch. "He should be here by now."

Keene said, "Mr. Nutter, I really think you should accept our offer."

"We're getting there." Dodge held his hands together, fingertip to fingertip, above the table. "Tell you what. I'll convince Mr. McNear to accept two million, and we all go to lunch, my treat."

"You're missing the point, Mr. Nutter." This time Keene looked at his watch. "But I think it's about to be made clear."

Dodge concentrated on appearing relaxed. Unfortunately, there's a big difference between doing something and trying to appear to do something. He leaned into his open briefcase so the others couldn't see him wipe the sweat from his brow. The three were quiet for a minute that dragged into five. Schonders scowled. Keene tapped a pencil. They'd been in the conference room for two hours. Dodge wouldn't be the one to blink.

Then there was a single knock on the door, and a tall thin man in a black suit walked in. Keene stood and said, "Good to see you, Bill. Thanks for making time to drop by—let me introduce you to Mr. McNear's attorney, Wayne Nutter." The man held out his hand. Dodge stood and took it.

The man was also wearing boots, but his suit was European. "Bill Smythe, chief technology officer for the National Engineering Group." The man turned to Schonders, whose seemingly permanent scowl had been replaced by a smile. "Sorry I'm late. My schedule was set for a nine o'clock. Because of the mix-up, our attorney couldn't make it. But I can handle this."

Dodge chose that instant to tighten his grip. "Good to meet you, Mr. Smythe. I have some information that might interest you." Dodge raised an eyebrow at Keene, but Keene smiled and shook his head.

Smythe said, "I only have fifteen minutes, so let's settle this right now."

Dodge took his seat. Smythe showed no indication of sitting. Dodge didn't want to yield the height advantage but couldn't bounce back up, so he leaned back and crossed his legs. "Excellent, we were just reviewing an offer."

"Mr. Nutter," Smythe said, "I'd like to clarify a few things. First," Smythe handed Dodge an envelope, "this is a court order. Because of the potential for the technology to fall into the wrong hands, the patents have been classified. The nation's security requires your secrecy. If you discuss the technology with anyone, it will be an act of treason. Treason is punishable by death. You must provide the names of every person with whom you have discussed the patents. You must surrender every copy of the patents that you have stored on a computer or printed. If you carry a suit on behalf of Mr. McNear, the particulars of the patents will not be admissible. Do you understand?"

Dodge wanted nothing more than to punch this man.

"You no longer have the ability to leverage the technical feasibility of the patents in favor of your client. Do you understand?"

Dodge could feel his jaw tightening. "Mr. Smythe, do you realize that these patents have no technical value? Are National Engineering engineers that stupid?"

"Second, Mr. McNear has no rights to the patents. And, third, to address your point, our goal is to increase our shareholders' value. Our mission is to protect the vital interests of the United States, expand her energy resources, and contribute to her national defense through the development of cutting-edge technologies." He leaned over the table, staring down at Dodge. "Let me spell it out for you. You have no power here even if the technology doesn't work—and I'll give you that it is a controversial invention that requires an element of faith, but faith with a capital *F* that most people in the United States of America are happy to give. You see, our investment in Creation Energy will benefit our shareholders. If that's all, I have another meeting."

"Smythe, you can't put a lid on this."

"Read the court order, and you'll see that I have done precisely that."

"The patent is out there. You'll have every physicist worth his calculator on the news in a week. Do you understand that—"

"We know exactly what we're doing." Looking up at him, Dodge saw in his eyes that the National Engineering Group had considered every scenario and calculated that it would profit from each. Smythe seemed to register Dodge's capitulation and looked at the other men as though to make sure that no one was in doubt about who was dealing. Smythe nodded to Schonders, patted Keene on the back, and said, "Dinner tonight. Patty's already got the ribs smoking," and left the room.

Schonders leaned across the table grinning. "Well?"

Dodge scanned his notes, rearranging them as if looking for a different hand. Getting the patents classified was the kind of trick that Dodge dreamed of pulling off. Finally, he tapped his notes into a nice rectangular pile. "How about we double—"

He stopped midsentence. "My offer is still on the table: two million."

Schonders jerked out of his chair. "You som' bitch." He stomped toward the door. As he stepped out of the room, he spoke to Keene, "Don't offer him nothin'."

Keene waited for the door to close. "Mr. Nutter, we want to put this behind us, and Dr. Reed would like Mr. McNear to be compensated for his work."

Dodge leaned forward, put his elbows on the table, and touched the fingertips of his left hand to those of his right. "I'm sure you've enjoyed this meeting, but there's one item we haven't covered." He motioned toward the door. "Something your redneck friend might not be aware of—something regarding the patent officer…?"

Keene said, "We want to put this behind us."

Dodge savored a raspy chortle. The patent officer had been engaged to Keene's daughter, and these were the only energy and software patents he'd examined. Like an unturned hole card, that tidbit could go either way. He decided to call. "My offer..."

Keene took the original offer letter. The number at the bottom line was Dodge's scribbled-in $10 million. Keene erased the last zero and initialed it. "This is the best I can do."

Dodge thought about it. His cut would be over half a million for the equivalent of about a full-time month, not a bad wage, and it had the added bonus of pissing off a bunch of Bible-thumping hypocrites. He shrugged, initialized the number, and offered to shake Keene's hand.

Keene said, "You should leave before I change my mind."

"No barbecue?"

Back in Petaluma, the first thing Dodge did was look for Ryan. He drove along the boulevard, then across the river down to the warehouse district. He found Ryan pushing a water tank along the sidewalk. He stopped the car in the middle of the road, lowered the passenger window, and yelled across, "I need you to sign this right now—I have a feeling it's a limited-time offer!"

Ryan shut off the hose, wiped his hands together, and leaned in the window of Dodge's pristine but ancient diesel Mercedes. Dodge handed him the offer letter. Ryan scanned it. "A million?"

Ryan went silent. His brow furrowed. He looked at the offer, then at Dodge, then the offer again. His brow relaxed. He licked his lips. His shoulders relaxed. He looked as though he were about to levitate. It rather irritated Dodge. "You're only getting four fifty of it, and the taxes will be a bitch."

Ryan didn't take his eyes off the number.

Dodge held out a pen. "Sign on the line. We need to cash their check before your girlfriend and her buddies blow this up."

"Emmy?"

"Yeah, you remember her. My sister is going to be majorly pissed off when she finds out how NEG plans to rape science in the name of religion."

Ryan signed. Dodge took the offer directly to the UPS office and paid extra to get it to Blair Keene the next day.

Back in the office, Dodge called Keene in Houston and told him that the offer had already been delivered. Keene thanked him with artificial sincerity. Dodge said, "Cut that check today, or the deal's off."

"What's your hurry?"

Dodge was comfortable now. "National Engineering is bulletproof, but you're not."

"You have a court order, you can't even—"

"If that check isn't cashed by Monday morning, Reed's dissertation will be in every physics department in the United States." Dodge lifted the revolver from its gavel pad and twirled it around his finger like a gunslinger in a western movie. "I'll include a letter quoting Bill Smythe saying that NEG knows the patents are bogus. That their profit motive is in dividing the country in a culture war that will assure their two greatest sources of income: foreign oil and perpetual war in the Middle East."

"You can't do that."

"Why not?"

"You'll go to jail."

This was the part that Dodge loved. It was better than sex. He pointed the gun at the phone and said, "You know, it's not so bad. I've been there before." He mouthed the word *bang* and set the gun on its gavel pad.

"I'll see to it that you get a nice long stay, this time," Keene said and went quiet.

Dodge waited, letting the silence do the negotiating.

Finally, Keene said, "I'll get a check to you, but you listen to me, Wayne Nutter, if anything slows down this project, I'll come after you, and when I'm finished, you'll be praying for jail."

The check arrived Saturday afternoon just after the banks closed. Dodge waved it under Ryan's nose before locking it up in a safe. "You can touch it when we're standing in front of a bank teller."

Ryan watched Dodge waddle down the hall. Then he walked slowly up the stairs. He felt as though he'd been living on a desert island and a rescue ship was steaming into shore.

He sat at his desk and stared across the valley. Katarina came in, and out of habit, he started bouncing ideas off of her. He'd have to go to Texas and turn himself in, but he was sure to please the court. He could even be there for Sean's sixteenth birthday. After all this time, it was hard to imagine.

Katarina asked, "So, you movin' back?"

"Naw, I don't think so." He liked Petaluma, and once he was legal, he could buy a house right here and get a real job without worrying about a deadbeat-dad agent tracking him down. "California's spoiled me. I'll fly Sean out every month, what the hell, every week. I'm no longer poor."

Katarina was working on path integrals at the whiteboard. She'd figured out how Feynman had derived the rules for QED within minutes of reading the book Emmy had lent her. Ryan still hadn't figured it out. He tried to focus on her but was too distracted. What would his ex-wife do when he got cleared? Would moving to Texas help Sean? Eventually, he looked back over and Katarina was gone. She'd left the door open with Emmy's book on the floor.

Kat had gotten bored, not so much with the math as with Ryan. She left the door open so he wouldn't hear her leave. Back in her apartment, it smelled like her mom—that weird cotton candy perfume she wore. These days, the only way Kat could even tell if her mother had been home was by the occasional twenty-dollar bill she left on the counter. It suited Kat just fine.

She slumped down in the old wooden chair in front of her table. Her father had painted the table pink, and the paint was flaking off. She remembered him saying that it would peel, but by the time it did, she wouldn't be a little girl anymore and would want another color anyway. She liked the pink just fine, though, and sort of liked the way it peeled too. She took her notebook from under the mess of makeup. A little card fell off the table. She leaned over and picked it up. It was the stupid poem that Alex had given her last week. The Ace—more like The Ace of Liars, The Ace of Mean, The Ace of Two-timing Pricks.

She hurled the note at the garbage can, but it floated to the floor under the table next to a dirty cereal bowl. Why did he have to dump her? It was that whore Marti. She'd always wanted him. It was the only reason Marti had pretended to be her friend.

Kat stared at herself in the mirror. She wouldn't cave in to the sob that was clutching at her throat. She evaluated the image in front of her the same way she would evaluate an integral equation. No wonder he broke up with her—the pimples on her face, her flat chest, dorky hair, and her mother's ugly jawline. She hated the image looking back.

She coughed, turned away from the mirror, and opened her notebook to the first Feynman diagram she'd worked all the way through. That guy Tran had been so impressed. It had all seemed so separate from the cliques at school, so above who was dating whom, who was fucking whom, and who was getting high with whom. But now it seemed like it had been written by another person. She slumped over the notebook, resting her face in her hands. She wanted to go back to Ryan's apartment, but he'd ignore her, all caught up thinking about his son.

It wasn't like she hadn't known this day would come.

She stared at the picture of her father, took it down from the wall, and held it so that she could see her image in the mirror next to his. They had the same forehead and the same nose, but she had her mother's lips. She wondered if he had been good at math—probably so, and probably a lot better at it than Ryan. The yearning feeling of missing her father shadowed her heart, a feeling so much a part of her that she realized something weird. She didn't really miss her father at all. The thought was uncomfortable, and she immediately denied it to herself. She raised the picture again and said to her mirror image, "I am who he was." But that scared her too.

Who was she kidding? She hated her father.

She tossed the picture into the corner next to the overflowing trash can, grabbed her purse, and ran downstairs. She just had to get out of that place; anywhere would be better. Anywhere she could get away from all this crap that was her pointless life.

Ryan hustled down the hill. An extra-large crowd was gathered outside of Skate-n-Shred—Broken Skeg was playing, and in the years since Ryan had landed in Petaluma, they'd acquired a following. Some of their songs had sold in the thousands on iTunes. It would be a busy night, and the thought of hanging with the kids maybe for the last time was bittersweet. Ryan walked his circuit, flushed a handful of stoners out of the alley, recommended that graffiti be written on the "huge pieces of plywood that we provide for it, not the damn bricks," and reminded several dozen teens that "cigarette smoke contains carbon monoxide."

When he passed the ticket booth, Ryan asked Dodge if he'd seen Katarina. Dodge said she was inside.

The theater was packed so tight that they had to move some of the skate ramps out into the alley. It seemed like a fight broke out every ten minutes and always on the opposite side of the building from Ryan. They broke up as soon as the kids saw Ryan's irritated smirk. He thought he saw Katarina a couple of times, but he never had a chance to check in with her.

At the end of their set, Broken Skeg's "roadies" broke down their equipment. "Roadies" at Skate-n-Shred? Ryan headed backstage to see what else Broken Skeg had graduated to. A particularly large boy stopped him at the door leading upstairs to the dressing room. As Ryan began to explain the situation to the thug-starter-kit, he heard a siren.

"Oh shit!" Ryan brushed past the kid, up through the dressing room to an emergency exit. The door was open and clogged with aspiring musicians looking out from the fire escape. Ryan pushed between them onto a landing. A police car was directly below. Ryan tried to gauge the situation before descending the stairs, but the flashing blue and white lights did nothing to illuminate the scene. Ryan worked his way down the fire escape between teenagers. The usual smell of the alley was augmented with a familiar scent.

A scent that had once been an intimate companion of Ryan's—burning methamphetamine.

With none of the cloying qualities of burning leaves, meth smoke dissipates quickly. The cops must have caught them lighting up.

At the bottom of the stairs, he struggled through the crowd to a police officer who was guiding teenagers away. Two other cops were shaking down five teenagers against the brick wall right under one of Katarina's dragon murals. There was a small pile of paraphernalia behind the cops. The pile grew as the officer pulled vials, baggies, and pipes from the pockets of the teenagers.

The cop working crowd control approached Ryan. "Where is Nutter? If he's not here in one minute, we're going to shut you down."

"Oh no." Ryan said, but not in response to the cop. "Oh no. Oh, Katarina, no…" The cop grabbed his arm, but Ryan shook him off and rushed forward.

The cop called from behind. "She related to you?"

Ryan said the first thing that came to mind: "She's my daughter!"

Katarina was spread against the wall sobbing. Seeing her helpless and humiliated dislodged something in his heart. He had to stop it. He wanted that cocky kid back, the one who'd said, "My friends call me Kat. You can call me Katarina," the day they met.

It got worse.

At first, Ryan thought she was wearing a very short skirt that had been hiked up, maybe by the cops while they searched her. In the blinking lights, it was hard to tell, but then it was too obvious. She was naked from the waist down. Ryan turned away. The image froze in his mind, and he feared it would never go away.

In a strong, solid voice that easily carried over the commotion, he said, "Katarina, I'm right here." Then he scanned the alley. The adrenaline edge slowed time and his eyes followed the police-car lights. He ran to the side of a Dumpster and grabbed Katarina's skirt, her little black purse, and boots. A flashlight lit on him, and the cop who had just searched Katarina said, "Drop that—now!"

Ryan tossed the skirt to Katarina's feet and dropped the purse and shoes. "Let her put on some clothes." He held his hands in front of him.

The cop picked up Katarina's skirt.

Ryan felt a huge rush of guilt. What had he done? The image of that check being waved under his nose rushed back. Was the world so cruel? Did he have to trade one child for another?

"You're her father?" The cop broke Ryan from the trance.

"Yes. I'm her father." As the words came out, Katarina's head snapped around. Trails of mascara ran down her face, but her eyes sparkled. Even from the ten feet that separated them and with the poor lighting, Ryan could see the size of her pupils. Her beautiful emerald irises were crowded away, meth's certain signature.

Before she spoke, Ryan knew what she would say. All the hours they'd spent together working and laughing, struggling with the great concepts, trying to comprehend the universe, collapsed in that instant.

Katarina screamed, "My father's dead!"

The cop said, "We have to process her. You can pick her up in a few hours. Give your name and phone number to Officer Dorsey." He finally handed Katarina her skirt.

Dorsey was the cop who had been doing crowd control, and now he was working a clipboard, taking down information from the teens. After Katarina pulled on her skirt, the cop handcuffed her. As he led her to the squad car, Ryan reached out and grabbed her shoulder. “It’ll be okay, Katarina, I promise.”

“Fuck you.”

The cop pushed her into the car.

Ryan mumbled to himself, “Don’t say *fuck*.”

Ryan didn't know where to look for Katarina's mother. How do you search for a ghost?

He sprinted to the box office. Dodge was counting money. Ryan told him that Katarina had been arrested. "How can I get Katarina out of jail?"

"Bring her father back to life," Dodge said. "Kid's lost, McNear, nothing you can do."

"Katarina is in jail!"

"That might be what she needs."

"Dammit, Dodge, do you hear yourself?" Ryan pushed Dodge's chair away from the desk and stepped in the gap, pointing with his index finger. "Are you kidding? Where can I find her mother?"

"Even if you find Jane, she won't come." Dodge pushed Ryan's finger away. "You understand? When Jane finds out, she'll just get on her bike and ride away."

Ryan stared at Dodge. His stomach felt empty, and the adrenaline was fading away, leaving acid behind. Dodge was right. Katarina arrested, Katarina smoking meth, Katarina having sex—it was way too much for Jane. "You're a lawyer. What can I do?"

"Lie."

⁀

So Ryan lied. But his lies couldn't keep Katarina out of a juvenile holding cell at the county jail. He sat in a plastic chair under fluorescent lights staring at the tile floor. He tried not to listen to the sob stories every person on his side of the counter told the police sergeant. He tried not to watch the gangbangers swagger in and argue the innocence of a comrade. And he ducked every time that door in back opened and another DUI, another hooker, another criminal was shepherded in for processing. Mostly he prayed for Katarina. Prayed that she knew he was out here, prayed that she would be all right, prayed that it wasn't as bad as it seemed.

About an hour before dawn, Officer Dorsey, the cop who had carried the clipboard the night before, pushed another covey of handcuffed teenagers through the back door. Ryan jumped to the counter. "Please release Katarina to me. I'm her father."

But Dorsey worked the kids into the bowels of the jail without looking at Ryan.

A few minutes later, Officer Dorsey pulled a chair next to Ryan and told him that Katarina was being transferred to juvenile detention and that he knew Ryan wasn't her father. He asked if Katarina's mother had been located. Ryan shook his head. "What can I do?"

The cop's voice was steady and clear. "You have to find her mother. Otherwise the child will be remanded to juvenile hall. A week in juvenile hall is not an experience you want Katarina to have. If the mother doesn't appear, then a public guardian will be appointed." The cop stood and put the chair back. "Find her mother."

Ryan stood. The muscles in his back were taut. He walked into the cold darkness. The moon had set, and the stars couldn't muster enough light to give him a shadow. The freeway was empty and Petaluma Boulevard deserted.

Katarina's skateboard was under the bench on the porch. Jane's bicycle wasn't out back. Ryan walked down Dodge's hallway, turning on the lights as he went. "Dodge!" he called.

Dodge leaned out the door of his bedroom.

Even with the tension this thick, Ryan laughed—sincere, muscle-relaxing laughter. Wearing a long red-and-white striped nightshirt with an old flannel hat, Dodge looked like Sleepy, the seventh dwarf. But he still sounded like Dodge: "Lying didn't work?"

"Where can I find Jane?" As Ryan spoke, helplessness crowded away the laughter.

Wheezing, Dodge walked into his office, sat down, and turned on the green light. He picked up the handgun and rolled the cylinder. When it stopped, he said, "If she's not at the cemetery with her husband, she's riding around town. She'll ride by Volpi's, the Italian restaurant where she and Kat's dad had their first date; Saint John's church, where they got married; Wickersham Park, where they had their reception; Copperfield's Bookstore, where he worked."

Ryan started for the hall.

Dodge said, "One other thing: you might check that wooden bridge behind the old mill."

Ryan drove out to the cemetery and around the narrow ring road, scanning the hillside and calling her name. He drove back into town, up and down the empty streets. He stopped at the park, the restaurant, and the bookstore.

The stop-and-go driving wore on the old car. The transmission complained, so he parked and walked down to the old mill. The mill had been converted to a small shopping mall decades ago, but there was still a trestle behind it along the river. The decking was slick with dew. The bridge arced over the river, lit by a string of white lights that shimmered on the easy current.

He sat on a bench near the bridge. The sky was just turning from black to violet, and a few cars passed by on the boulevard a block away. Ryan wondered what Katarina was thinking, wondered if she had slept, but he doubted it. Meth doesn't like its victims to rest.

The sun peeked over the mountains, and just as he decided to go wait for Jane at the cemetery, he saw her silhouette coming toward the bridge from the other side of the river. Her dress and hair flowing behind her, she rode up the bridge and stopped in the middle. She got off her bike, leaned on the railing, and stared across the river as the sun rose.

Ryan stood, careful not to scare her, suppressing the urge to scream at her for failing a daughter she didn't deserve. He eased onto the bridge.

She noticed him and brushed her hair away from her face.

Ryan forced a smile, as serene as he could muster. "Beautiful morning, huh?"

"It was," she said.

"Hey, I'm glad I bumped into you." Ryan put his hand on her shoulder. She didn't seem to notice. He said, "Could you come with me? Katarina needs you to, um, sign her out. She's up in Santa Rosa."

"This is where he proposed to me." She turned back to the sunrise.

His grip tightened on her shoulder. "It'll just take a minute."

She noticed his hand then and tried to slip away.

He spoke with all the warmth and fake happiness he could muster. "Jane, you need to help Katarina, just like he said, remember?" He forced a smile, and it made him sound happy. "She still needs you. We'll go for a ride in my sports car, and all you have to do is sign your name and hug your beautiful little girl."

He took her hand and tugged. She followed, looking back at the bridge until it was out of sight. He guided her to the car and she got inside but didn't put on the seat belt.

"Yes, of course, she still needs me." She spoke with no inflection.

They pulled into the jail parking lot as the sun cleared Sonoma Mountain. Ryan talked about Katarina, telling Jane the good things: that Katarina had talent and goals and was doing well in school. Jane seemed calm, almost happy. Ryan took her into that room with the fluorescent lights and the tile floor. With his arm around her, they approached the desk.

A different harried officer looked up.

Ryan said, "This is Katarina Ariadne's mother. Can you please release Katarina to her?"

"She is being bussed to the juvenile detention center right now." He pointed toward the window to a plain white van that was just then leaving the parking lot.

Ryan hustled Jane back to the car. He caught up with the police van and drove alongside, hoping that Katarina would see him and know someone cared.

Ten minutes later, Ryan and Jane entered the waiting room at juvenile hall. Sunbeams worked their way through floor-to-ceiling blinds. Ryan put Jane in one of the plastic chairs. She stared at her hands in her lap. Ryan tried to sit still, tried to mind his own business, but couldn't help but realize that this is where parents go to worry. Even the parents with gang-logo tattoos sat quietly, some crying softly, some whispering to each other in anger.

At 8:30, a man in a short-sleeved shirt with a badge on the front pocket pinned two sheets of paper to a bulletin board. Ryan followed the line of parents to look at it. Katarina would appear before the judge at 9:20.

At nine, they were ushered into juvenile court. The orange carpet, blue walls, and modest mural of happy children among flowers gave the appearance of a court desperately trying to deny its identity. Ryan walked Jane to the bailiff who was checking identification and matching parents to juveniles. Then the two of them sat in the front row. A few minutes later, Katarina was led in with a dozen other teenage girls. Katarina made eye contact with Ryan first, then leaned her head to the side, indicating her mother, as if to say, "What's she doing here?"

It was good to see her, to see that she wasn't a monster, that she was just his youthful ward, Katarina. He braced himself and checked Jane. She was staring at Katarina. When he looked back, Katarina was staring at him, no longer smiling. He mouthed the words, *it'll be okay*, to which she mouthed, *What. Ever.*

When Katarina was called forward, Ryan and Jane met her at the table facing the judge just as the other parents and teens had. The judge had short gray hair and a strict expression dampened by smile lines, the sort of woman you'd expect to wear sandals with socks. After reviewing the police report, she called Miss Ariadne's parents forward. The judge explained the charges. As she spoke, her gaze lingered on Jane, who was looking at the wall behind the judge. Finally, the judge spoke directly to Ryan. "Katarina must appear in juvenile court in two months." She gave Ryan a list of things to bring, including letters from schoolteachers or community leaders, "anything that can testify to her character." The gavel came down, and ten minutes later, the three of them were in the parking lot.

Ryan said, "What the fuck were you doing?"

"I don't want to talk about it."

With his frustration rushing out, he was comfortable ignoring Jane. "You're going to a doctor."

Katarina got in the backseat. Jane stood by the door with Ryan still holding it. He pushed her in, less gently than he meant.

Katarina asked, "Why?"

"You're going to a gynecologist to be tested for sexually transmitted diseases and to see if you're pregnant." Ryan slammed the door shut and walked around the car. He settled in and started the car, afraid to say too much. The silence on the drive back to Petaluma was broken only by an old Bruce Springsteen CD.

As they drove up the boulevard, Katarina said, "I've never wanted a shower more in my life."

Jane made a strange sound, like a sigh mixed with laughter. Ryan heard the intake of Katarina's breath and looked at her in the rearview. He raised his hand. "Stop!"

But it was too late.

"You fucking bitch—"

Ryan said, "Don't say *fuck*," but he couldn't hear himself over Katarina.

"You are nothing, NOTHING!" She took another breath. "Ryan, stop this car."

But he already had.

Katarina said, "Let me out."

When Ryan got out of the car, Katarina started to fight her way out of the backseat. He leaned in and grabbed her shoulder. With a glare and tone that offered no compromise, he said, "I just bailed you out of jail, and you will behave. I can take you back."

She leaned back in her seat.

Ryan walked around to the passenger side and opened the door. Jane stretched her legs, stood, and smoothed her skirt. She looked up at Ryan with a calm smile and said, "She's almost grown up now."

Katarina raised her eyebrows and flashed him a you're-wasting-your-time smile.

He took Jane by the hand and guided her away from the car. Katarina climbed into the front seat.

Out of Katarina's hearing range, Ryan said, "Your daughter is in serious trouble."

"Kat finally had sex," Jane said. Her forehead wrinkled into something that looked like concern. "She's a woman now."

"No, Jane, she's a stupid little girl in trouble with the law."

Jane looked back at Katarina. Katarina was staring at Ryan with an odd expression.

Jane said, "I'm almost finished."

"No!" Ryan yelled in her face. "You're not almost finished, you haven't even started. Do you know how lucky you are? That beautiful, brilliant child needs you and you—"

But Jane wasn't listening. What he'd thought was concern had been confusion, and now it smoothed into serenity. She stared north, toward the cemetery.

Ryan understood. Jane was a tweaked husk of humanity, and he knew that he couldn't help her. He walked back to the car. Katarina was still watching him. He shrugged.

Jane said, "Your father loves you, Kat," and walked away.

Katarina smiled at Ryan, really smiled, like she'd won something. Ryan didn't get it, but he did feel the presence of his grandma, a soft, gentle presence like a wrinkled palm against the flesh of his cheek assuring him that he was doing the right thing.

Ryan got in the car and let go of a sigh. He and Katarina leaned against each other. Ryan said, "That's one fucked-up individual." This time, the feeling of his grandma chastised him.

"You're telling me," Katarina said. "Like I was saying about that shower?"

Ryan turned to her, shaking his head. "That'll have to wait." They drove through town and up a windy road. Katarina didn't ask where they were going. Outside of town, the road curved over hills and through canyons, past vineyards, olive groves, and cattle. In a lush valley, Ryan turned onto a bridge that had been painted purple.

Katarina mumbled something.

"What?" Ryan asked.

She was facing him. A tear struggled loose from her eyelashes, and she tried to hold back a sob. Ryan pulled the car onto the dirt shoulder and wrapped his arms around her. He gently squeezed the sobs out. The words *thank you* and *I'm sorry* didn't come out very clearly and, truth was, they embarrassed Ryan—as though he'd done her a favor, as though she didn't deserve to be cared for. They drove along a bay and then up onto a ridge. Wisps of moisture, more like baby clouds than fog, passed over the car and left mist on the windshield. They passed lots of cows and the occasional barn. When they came to a clearing at the top of a hill overlooking the ocean, Ryan stopped the car. Katarina leaned forward, and Ryan said, "Be quiet, okay? Just look for a few minutes and then follow me." He got out of the car and walked into a field as far as a barbed-wire fence. A few minutes later, Katarina came and stood next to him.

Ryan said, "See how the ocean stretches all the way across the horizon?" He waited for a couple of minutes and then turned around. "Now look inland. You can barely see any buildings, and what you can see are really small—they don't amount to much."

It was the first time Ryan had ever seen Katarina do as she was told. It was a good thing. Part of him wanted an excuse to whack her a good one, but most of him wanted her to see something bigger. "Katarina," he said, facing the ocean again, "if we started swimming, we'd get to Japan." Then he turned inland and said, “If we started walking, we’d get to New York.” He stepped in front of her. When she looked up at him, he said, “Right now we live in a town over there somewhere. The stuff in that town—Skate-n-Shred, your friends, school, the cops, Dodge and his ridiculous house, even your mom—those are temporary details in the grand scheme.”

He stepped to the side. Katarina turned toward the ocean. The breeze picked up. Her hair blew in the wind, the way her mother’s did when riding her bike. The resemblance was superficial, though. Katarina was darker in skin tone and much deeper in countenance than her mom. Ryan hadn’t given much thought to Katarina’s father but, right then, realized that he must have been a special man.

Ryan put his arm around Katarina’s shoulders and held her tight against him. Waving his arm across the entire horizon, he said, “This is the world. Live in it.” Then he let go and walked back to the car.

Katarina looked out to sea a few minutes more.

They drove down into a canyon and parked in a lot next to an outhouse, which they each used. Ryan took an old beat-up sweatshirt out of the trunk and tossed it to Katarina. It fit her like a dress. The two of them walked down a sandy winding path between dormant wild sage, ice plant, and daisies. A little brook meandered along, occasionally dropping into a creek. As they got closer to the ocean, the clouds grew thicker, and when they got to the beach, they could only see a few hundred feet in any direction. The only prints in the sand were from seagulls and sandpipers. They took off their shoes and walked toward the surf. The beach was boxed in by rocky reef formations to the north and south. Violent waves smashed into the beach leaving whirlpools in their wake, the signature of rip currents so brutal that even sea lions avoided them.

"Well?" Katarina asked, looking up at Ryan.

He didn't look away from the ocean, just kicked the sand in response. He didn't know why he'd brought her here, just that she wasn't ready to go home yet. He knew that she needed something, but he didn't know what it was or where to find it.

At the end of the beach, waves pounded a rock formation where thousands of sea anemones opened and closed as the water washed back and forth. Ryan climbed up on a boulder, out of the direct line of sea spray but close enough so that when he inhaled, he could taste the salt. He sat where he could lean against a rock that was smooth and dry. Katarina looked up at him, pulling her wind-whipped hair out of her eyes. He patted the rock next to him.

"I don't think I can get up there."

He shrugged as though he didn't care, and she started climbing. When she was close, he offered a hand. At first she didn't accept it. Ryan narrowed his eyes in anger that surprised him. She took his hand and he pulled her up.

They sat together and stared out over the ocean. A squadron of pelicans flew up the beach about ten feet over the sea and, just off the reef where Ryan and Katarina were sitting, broke formation. Most of them veered up at an angle so that they could examine the water for fish. One after another, they tucked their wings and dove into the water. They landed upside down, splashing with no grace whatsoever. Most of them returned to the air empty-beaked, while a few struggled to fly under the weight of water and fish in their gullets.

Ryan laughed.

"What are you laughing at?"

"Look at them. We always think of animals as so damn perfect. Like a lion hunting a zebra or an eagle against a snake, a bear and a fish—but pelicans, my God, look at them! They flop on their backs, splash all over the place, and then almost always come up empty. Look at that one over there." He pointed to a pelican perched on a rock thirty feet away. "He's got a potbelly. The way his beak pokes way out—look at the expression on his face, did he just burp? I think he burped."

Katarina laughed and pulled herself closer to Ryan. He put his arm around her so that his coat draped around her shoulders and said, "I feel like I should ask you what happened last night, but I'm not sure I want to know." He looked toward the ocean. A sea lion's bearded face bristled over the back of a wave for a second. "I've never been so scared in my life. I don't want this," he struggled for words. "I don't want this to have happened to you."

"No duh. I'm the stupid McBonehead this time." She sighed and then looked up at Ryan. "I wanted to get crazy. I wanted to forget everything. When the band was playing, I got lost in the music. And when they finished, it all came back—all the stupid reality of my stupid life."

As the sun climbed up the sky, the fog burned off, and they could see the other end of the beach. They still had it all to themselves.

Katarina dozed for a while, her face nestled against his chest. As she slept, her mouth fell open, and a little bit of drool leaked onto his shirt. He had to smile.

The pelican took a few steps toward them and poked its head into a tide pool. When it looked up, its beak was covered in sand. It waddled closer.

Katarina mumbled.

He looked down. Her eyes were open, and she rubbed her mouth on Ryan's shirt. He said thanks and she giggled.

She said, "When I was sitting in that little steel room last night, my gray matter, like, caught on fire. Remember that stuff we talked about when we went to SLAC—neural networks? If you take two computers and load them both with the same neural network, they'd be identical at first, remember?"

Ryan was still staring at the pelican. It took him a few seconds to switch gears. "Okay, we start with a neural network—a computer program—and load it on two identical computers. Yeah, of course they'd be the same."

"But they'll get different, right?"

"If they have different inputs then, yes, in a few seconds, their internal parameters will change, and the more input they get, the more different they'll be. Eventually, they'll look totally different."

"Totally?"

Ryan thought for a few seconds. He caught himself staring at the pelican. "Why doesn't he take off?"

"Because he's interested in what I'm saying. Unlike you."

Ryan stared at a patch of sand so he could think. "No, they won't be totally different, especially if they both get some of the same inputs. I mean, they'll be the same the way that twins are the same—the same hardware and the same software, but the longer they run, the more distinguishable they'll appear to anyone who is using them."

"What if you had a whole community of neural networks, and you took one off to the side and copied it onto another computer and then put the copied version back in the community—could you tell the difference?"

Ryan picked some grains of sand off a rock and started a little pile on his thigh. "You mean, could I tell that it was a copied version? No, of course not, they're identical."

"Just like identical particles, right? The only thing that makes them different is the situation they're in. Like electrons, the only thing that makes one different from another is their quantum numbers."

Ryan loosened his grip on Katarina so that she could raise her head and he could see her face. "What are you driving at?"

"What if you kidnapped someone and cloned him. Then you somehow made the clone grow really fast so that the clone would be the same age as the guy. Then you copy everything from the guy's brain to the clone's brain. You couldn't tell the two apart, right?"

"I guess the clone wouldn't have any scars or freckles—"

"No, the clone gets all those too, so that they're identical. The same body, the same brain, and once you copy all of the guy's memories into the clone there's no way you could tell them apart."

"Okay, if you somehow make two identical people, then no, you couldn't tell them apart. So what?" Ryan tried to push the little pile of sand on his thigh into a column, but it crumbled apart.

"Think about it. The clone would have the same physical body and the same memories. It would believe it was the real guy, right? The real guy and the clone wouldn't know which was which." Katarina wiped the sand off Ryan's thigh. "Okay, but since *I* cloned him, I know which is which." She raised her eyebrows to indicate the brilliance of the point she was about to make. "Okay, so what if I kill the original guy and put the clone back in the community. No one would know the difference, right?"

"I guess. Except for you, the murderer."

"The clone is exactly the same in every way to the original guy, and he *believes* that he's the original guy because, well, why would he believe anything else? Now, since we have to include all *possible* combinations of processes that lead to the same outcome—just like when you add up Feynman diagrams—then he *is* the original guy."

"No he's not. He's the clone."

"This is the point. This is why my brains almost vaporized in my head last night while I fermented in that little cell. If someone had done all this to me—mapped my brain into my clone and then killed me—when I came out of that cell, there is no way you could tell the difference. But even better, I wouldn't know the difference either."

"Hmmm." Ryan started another little pile of sand, this time on her leg.

"It would be like a virtual process. The cloned Kat *is* the real Kat."

"Sounds like Schrödinger's cat to me—"

"Shut up." She started adding grains of sand to the pile. "Here's the totally weird part—I swear to God, I wanted them to get you on the phone so I could tell you—check this out: since the cloned Kat is exactly the real Kat, then the real Kat never died."

"But you killed it," Ryan said. "What about the body?"

"They never find the body; it's burned and the ashes are thrown in the river—it doesn't matter because Kat is still alive. And—shut up—I haven't gotten to the best part." She flicked the pile of sand off her thigh. "Does the cloned Kat have a soul?"

"Good one. Why not? At least she thinks she does."

"Well, everyone thinks they have a soul—that's what makes it a soul. But does it have the *same* soul as the original Kat?"

"This is really confusing," Ryan said, "and leave my sand alone."

"Put it on your own leg then."

"Yours is flatter."

"Are you saying I'm fat?"

"No, I was just..." Ryan stretched out his legs.

"If it happened, I'd never know it, you'd never know it, no one would ever know it." She was speaking really fast. "It wouldn't even matter. It's like a virtual process—"

"Wait. Hang on a second," Ryan said, "there's something wrong with that. It's like you're saying that when you copied the original Kat's experiences, memories, and stuff onto the cloned Kat that you copied the soul along with it."

"No," Kat said, slower now, "I'm saying that the soul *is* all that stuff in your mind: experience and sentience—that's what gives us the context for making decisions, and from that comes free will."

"Doesn't that mean that when you die you're just snuffed out, including your soul?"

"That's what I was thinking when they drove us to that courthouse—by the way, I saw you, and your car is spewing white smoke." She flicked Ryan's leg. "Why can't there be two identical souls? Do souls all have to be different? Does God have to assign them? Isn't it their own awareness that makes them magic? What is a soul if not the sum of someone's experiences and feelings and sensations, dreams and nightmares, everything that a person has ever thought or sensed? All that stuff that we copied onto the clone's mind?"

"Foster told me that the Bible says something about God breathing a soul into each person when He creates them—just like He must have done with the Divine Spark that started the Big Bang."

"Yeah, so God's breath would be part of consciousness and, just like everything else, it'd get copied—but I don't think you need the spark."

Ryan stood and climbed down to the beach. "I bet none of the other little criminals on the bus were thinking about how souls work. I hope you didn't catch anything. Has anyone ever told you about condoms?"

"Oh, gross, I didn't even think of that last night. Yuck, I'm like maximo disgustized." She slid off the rock, kicked off of a boulder, and grabbed Ryan's arm before landing on the beach. "What am I going to say to those people?"

"Katarina, it was a nightmare. You were all naked and meth and…" He hugged her again.

Katarina shook her head, shook as though she were trying to get out of her own skin.

"Are you worried that everything's going to change now? I guess it's already changed, huh? All the time I spend with Emmy, you did most of the path-integral stuff without me…"

"I like Emmy. I like you with Emmy."

"Katarina, you'll always be my best friend. Nothing's going to change that. Now that I can fix my life and see my son again, it's just going to get better. You'll really like Sean."

"How would you know? The last time you saw him he was *eleven years old.* Now he's fifteen—you're not even gonna recognize him."

The check was drawn on the corporate account of Creation Energy at Bank of America. Ryan signed in front of the teller, a woman who looked about eighteen. Immediately after the deposit slip was stamped, Dodge, elbowing his way up to the teller, instructed Ryan to request a cashier's check for the entire $1 million. The teller called over the branch manager.

Since it was an interstate check, though drawn on the same bank, the manager said it was subject to a seven-day holding period. Dodge asked for a photocopy of the check and asked the manager to guarantee that the check would clear. Unfazed, the manager repeated the seven-day hold policy.

While Dodge threatened the manager—"It's illegal to write a bad check, so why not guarantee it?"—Ryan whispered to the teller, "Is there some way that you can confirm that the check will clear?"

The teller did a double take at the manager, who was occupied with Dodge, and then typed away at her keyboard. A few seconds later, she looked up, first at Ryan, then at the manager. She caught his eye and motioned him over. Ignoring Dodge, the manager leaned down to see the computer screen.

He stood back up and, with traces of glee, said, "This check has been canceled."

Dodge went silent.

"What?" Ryan's heart raced. "No. This can't happen. You mean it's not worth anything?"

The manager, looking at Dodge, said, "That's right. This piece of paper has no value." Then, to Ryan, "There is also a thirty-dollar invalid deposit fee. I'll just subtract it from your account."

He looked at the teller, pleading. She mouthed the word *sorry*.

Dodge said, "Give me the check."

The manager denied him and Dodge added, "Then make a photocopy." He spoke in a breathy tone, not unlike the hiss of a snake. The manager started to speak, thought better of it, and took the check from the teller. A few seconds later, he returned with a copy.

Dodge marched out of the bank with no sign of his frumpy waddle.

Ryan called the manager over and asked what he could do. The manager, still obviously angry from his interaction with Dodge, walked away. The teller printed the bank's canceled check policy and handed it to Ryan. It had the usual legalese denying any responsibility of the bank and quoting the thirty-dollar fee for invalid deposits. It didn't say anything about how to find out why the check was canceled or how to redress the issuing bank. As he walked out, he crumpled it up and threw it in the trash.

Here he was again. It was like *Groundhog Day*. The world seemed to be designed to keep him from making any progress.

Ryan walked along the river, turned up a street, and after a few blocks found himself standing in the courtyard under the twin bell towers of the Catholic church. The doors were unlocked and candles lit the inside. He sat in a pew next to a stained glass window portraying Jesus in His moment of doubt. Ryan muttered, "Got any extra nails?"

Dodge weighed his options. Unleash Emmy? Absolutely. But Ryan still had rights to the patents. The problem had always been that without a way to prove that the patents had generated profit, he couldn't go to court. Since the patents were worthless, they would never generate profit. Perhaps that had changed, though. If NEG contracted Creation Energy to deliver technology, then profit should follow. If he went to court, he'd be fighting the legal team of a huge corporation. They would delay the process and would no doubt call an expert witness like Emmy, maybe even Emmy herself, who would convince the court the patents had no value. NEG would then argue that the contracts were unrelated to the patents. Dodge coughed the taste of defeat into a tissue.

He picked up the phone and called Creation Energy's administrative assistant, Mabel Watson. She was her usual cheery, pestering, gossip-packed self but was caught surprised that Creation Energy had canceled Ryan's check. Rather than sit through her drivel, Dodge hung up on her.

Then he called Emmy at her office in Berkeley. She didn't answer so he left a message: "Let the shit fly where it may."

He set the phone gently in its cradle and turned off the green desk light. His fingers crawled across the desk to the gavel pad where the revolver sat. He picked it up, pulled the chamber out so he could see all six slugs. He locked the chamber back in place, spun it, and pulled back the hammer. It made a satisfying click. He rubbed the end of the barrel against his temple.

With his finger ever so lightly touching the trigger, he silently asked himself a question, then he spoke out loud, "Not today," and set the gun down.

Ryan sat in the church long enough to calm down.

Back in his apartment, he paced. What's next? Did he have rights to the patents or not?

He popped the cap off a bottle of beer and looked at the whiteboard. It still had Katarina's work from the night she was arrested. Damn, it was just yesterday that he'd gotten her out of jail. It seemed like a month ago.

Why had the check been canceled?

He picked up the phone. Foster answered on the second ring.

Ryan expected Foster to sound distant and cold, but he seemed almost happy to hear Ryan's voice. Ryan thanked him for settling the case, for getting Ryan the check, and reminded him that the money would help him reunite with his son. Foster warmed to the gratitude. Glad to take credit, he pontificated for a few minutes on reasons and angels.

Ryan waited for Foster to finish and then said, "So you don't know that the check was canceled?"

"We bought your rights. We had to," Foster said. "Ryan, I wanted to help you, I really did. Hold it—canceled?"

Ryan explained what happened at the bank. As he told the story, his anger wound down to despair.

"Ryan, I'm sorry," Foster said. "Something must have changed."

"Yeah, I guess so," Ryan said. "Everything changed the night before your wedding."

"I don't know what happened, then or now, and I can't do anything about then, but listen Ryan, I'm going to try to help you. Just hang in there. It's going to get better. You have to have faith."

"Faith in what? Faith that you'll fuck me over again?"

Foster sighed. "Ryan, I've tried to help you, that's all I've ever done. Your lack of faith is what's holding you back."

Ryan hung up.

Foster toggled the on/off button on the phone and dialed Blair Keene's office in Houston. "Blair, did you cancel Ryan McNear's check?"

Foster could hear Blair working a keyboard.

"It was canceled Friday," Blair said. "Jeb must have done it. He was dead set against settling." His words were sharp and clear but, strangely, not angry. "This is a shame. We require Ryan's rights, and we won't get a better price. I told Jeb it was a bargain." He sighed and added, "Jeb Schonders is convinced that Dodge Nutter is an agent of Satan."

Foster stared at his desk, at the pictures of Rachel, and, for the thousandth time, felt the wound in his heart that had been opened when he discovered that his angel had been engaged before him. He still hadn't exorcised that demon.

The bachelor party.

He thought through it again. The bachelor party was a crisis rite, his final temptation, the thing that the best man is supposed to do, a guy thing. It was also what had sent Ryan's life into a tail-spin. The bachelor party and the wound in his heart—they had to be related. If he could help Ryan, he could exorcise that doubt.

Blair finally spoke. "There is one way around this that might solve two of our problems." He took a breath. "How is the software side of the project coming?"

"We've got code running," Foster said. They were using a neural network they'd downloaded from the CERN website. "Why?"

"Six months ago, you said Ryan was the best person to direct the software."

Foster looked down. The latest graph of power output versus time stared back at him. The first neural net they'd implemented had increased the output power, but since then it had been flat—no increase for the last month. The team of software engineers he'd hired had gotten nowhere.

Blair interrupted his thoughts. "Ryan needs money. He's a neural network expert, and if he were on our payroll, with an ownership interest—like stock options—then he'd be exercising his patent rights. Think about it. This is the right way to solve our problems."

Foster smiled at himself. He even licked his lips the way Ryan always did. Another stepping-stone set along the path. Blair needed Ryan for political reasons; Ryan needed Creation Energy to fix past mistakes; Creation Energy needed Ryan's talent; and Foster needed to be rid of that demon. Uncanny. God's will would be done.

Foster said, "Will Jeb let me hire him?"

"No, but I can work around that. You'll have three months to make serious progress; that's when Jeb will see the books. Jeb can't see him around campus either, but if Ryan can help you increase energy output, Jeb won't be a problem." Foster could hear Blair scratching notes on paper. "Do you think he'll take the job if you offer it?"

"He's pretty angry," Foster said. "I'm not sure. This could be a serious problem. You're right, Blair, we need Ryan. Doesn't Jeb understand that?"

"Jeb has a completely different concept of what success looks like than you or I have. He's not a scientist or technologist, Foster. He's a warrior and he thinks Ryan is the enemy."

"Ryan is not a man of faith, but he's not a bad man," Foster said. "He could help us."

"I get that. I'm a pragmatist. I'll see what I can do and let you know."

Emmy posted Foster's dissertation on the Lawrence Berkeley Laboratory website, then she sent a note to Bob Park describing the "scientific travesty that National Engineering is propagating in the name of alternative energy." Park sent an unprecedented Monday edition of *What's New* to the thousands of physicists who read his weekly newsletter.

Within an hour, the LBL web server was struggling under the demand to download Foster's dissertation. Graduate students, professors, research associates, and lab rats from coast to coast opened the document. Many thought they'd been duped by the physics equivalent of an urban legend; most stopped reading after the fifth Bible quotation, around page twenty. Some religious physicists were offended by the work, but others quietly hoped that Foster was on to something.

The next morning, as she sat down to prepare a lecture, Emmy logged on to her computer and found a slew of e-mails complaining that the dissertation had been pulled from the website. She skimmed down to an e-mail that had been sent late the previous night from the laboratory director. He explained that he had been ordered by the Department of Energy to remove the dissertation from their site. She stashed the message in a folder, switched to another window, re-posted the dissertation, and ran upstairs to the director's office.

As Emmy marched through the office suite, the director's administrator said, "He's expecting you."

Emmy pulled open the door, stepped in, and slammed it behind her. "What are you doing?"

He spoke with a Belgian accent. "Running a *national* laboratory."

"Okay, fine." Emmy wagged her finger in the director's face and spoke loud enough to be heard down the hall. "If you deny that dissertation scientific scrutiny, I'll resign right now. Are you so weak, so timid, so totally afraid of doing the right thing that you'll buckle under to the first wave of complaint? Is this who you are? Do you consider yourself a leader?" Her voice got louder with each word, and she knew inside that she was screaming and ranting, knew that this was not the way to motivate him, but she couldn't stop. He leaned back in his chair and nodded to everything she said. Finally, she said something so out of character that it gave her pause: "When did you have your balls cut off?"

As though to emphasize that she had been ranting, he spoke just above a whisper. "The secretary of energy called me at home last night, after midnight on the East Coast, and *ordered* me to remove a classified document from our website. I had no idea what it was or why it was there but agreed to remove it."

"Okay, no problem. It's back up. Sorry to bother you." She turned to leave, a bit shocked at her own behavior.

"Lawrence Berkeley *National* Laboratory is not going to break federal law," he said. "I am not going to risk our funding for your scientific jihad."

Emmy's temper rushed back in, but this time she was ready. She stared at him and spoke very clearly. "Remember this day. This is the day that you destroyed your career. Claude, I remember when you were a physicist. You're not a physicist anymore, you're a corporate pawn."

She left, and when she got back to her office, sure enough, Foster's dissertation was no longer linked from the website. She called Bob Park in Maryland.

"It's classified?" Bob growled into the phone. "First they classified their mistakes to keep them out of the press. Now they're classifying their campaign contributor's mistakes." Emmy could almost hear him scowling. "I read that piece of hogwash yesterday. My stomach was turning by the fifth page. I thought you were putting me on, then I checked the press release." At the end of a long sigh, he added, "All right, this is what I'm going to do—and I *hope* they charge me with treason—I'm sending it out as an attachment. Over ten thousand PhD physicists will have it in their inboxes within an hour." He chuckled, a gravelly chuckle that reminded Emmy of her father. "Talk about peer review. Then I'm calling the *New York Times* science editor."

A second *What's New* special edition was transmitted with Foster Reed's dissertation attached. Copies were printed and shelved in the libraries of every major lab—SLAC, Fermilab, CERN in Switzerland, Tsukuba in Japan, DESY in Germany, Rutherford in England, and others.

But when Park called the science editors at the *Washington Post* and *New York Times*, he got the same message that Emmy got when she called the *San Francisco Chronicle* and *San Jose Mercury News*—the science correspondents were in meetings. In fact, they were on a conference call with the chief technological officer of National Engineering Group.

That evening, NBC news led with a report of "perhaps the most significant investment in science ever made by a private corporation. It could bring about both energy independence and the completion of President Reagan's dream of a Star Wars antimissile system." CNN's was somewhat vague: "A new way to harness subatomic energy reported by an obscure Christian university in Texas has caught the attention of major energy and military investors." Fox reported, "The Bible has overtaken science."

A television interview with NEG CTO Bill Smythe was careful to maintain that it was "an alternative energy source with great potential, whose specifics can't be discussed because of their potential national security applications." He described Foster and Ryan as "inventors in the great American tradition of Bill Hewlett and Dave Packard," who brought "good old American know-how to the biggest problems facing America and the world." He told America to expect skepticism. "From Einstein's relativity to the invention of the personal computer, great ideas always bring out naysayers. This technology will be no different. National Engineering doesn't invest in fads—this is not some elitist theory without applications. It's good hard technology. Once again, a couple of guys working for a small company in the heart of America did an end run around government-financed labs. We're just doing what private enterprise has always done, investing in promising solutions to make an honest buck for our shareholders."

The next morning, a Tuesday, the *New York Times* headline blared, "Christians Discover Science They Like." The *Washington Post*: "Little Christian College Beats Big Labs to the Punch." Not even college newspapers could resist the sensation; the *Daily Princetonian* ran "Evangelical Word U Embarrasses Institute for Advanced Study."

Emmy stared at the *San Francisco Chronicle* headline: "Physics and Bible Get Married in Texas." Bile rose in the back of her throat. She wanted to fight. She wanted to cry.

She had a dozen phone messages, most from colleagues offering support. Four of the messages caught her by surprise. The first was from the director of LBL, whom she'd threatened the day before. He said that he and the director of SLAC wanted her to represent the labs. The second message was from the director of SLAC, echoing the first and adding that he was checking with the National Academy of Sciences to coordinate a response with the Union of Concerned Scientists.

The third message floored her. CNN asked her to appear on Wolf Blitzer's *The Situation Room* later that afternoon with Foster Reed and Ryan McNear.

The last message, left just a few minutes before she sat down, was from Ryan, and it brought Emmy back to Earth like a falling satellite. "I'm worried about Katarina. She got arrested Saturday night. I think she's in big trouble. Could you come up and talk to her? She got busted with meth and,"—Ryan's voice cracked—"and for having sex in the alley behind Skate-n-Shred. Her mom is in total denial. Anyway, call me. I missed you this weekend. I hope you got caught up—love you."

Foster Reed was in his lab when he got the call. Mabel popped her head in the door. "Dr. Reed, y'all have a call from Washington—CNN wants you on that Wolf Blitzer show…"

Foster looked up at Mabel. What was she doing here? The phone? "CNN? Have them call Jeb."

She said, "The CNN boys want *you*, Dr. Reed."

39

The media had an effective feedback loop: every news outlet was compelled to out-sensationalize the other. By midafternoon, MSNBC was questioning religious leaders about evidence for Noah's great flood. They said that the flood explained away the scientific establishment's so-called evidence that Earth was four billion years old. That the actual age was six thousand years, as calculated from the Bible, and that such seeming contradictions as seashells found at the top of mountains and the formation of the Grand Canyon all made sense in the light of the great flood.

Members of both the state of Kansas and Dover School Boards—the people who had fought at the Supreme Court to have Creation science and intelligent design taught alongside evolution in public schools—were being interviewed on national news.

The biology community responded the way it had in the past, by submitting a short press release: "Evolution is grounded in a preponderance of evidence. Creationism and intelligent design are religious ideas that have nothing to do with predictive science."

Man-on-the-street interviews painted Joe Sixpack as skeptical that this was "it" but certain that eventually science and religion would meet. Religious leaders from Buddhists to Muslims,

Sikhs to Mormons, Hindus to Wiccans embraced the idea of science accepting a distinction between "in here" and "out there." The official response from the Vatican: "We're happy to see that progress is being made in understanding the work of the Lord."

Demonstrators from the left flew to Texas to protest a dangerous new form of nuclear energy and, from the right, to prepare for the Rapture.

Ryan was excited at the prospect of going on TV—who wouldn't be? He also understood that he would be smack between Emmy and Foster. He would stick to his core beliefs, respect their positions, and expect them to respect his.

CNN had asked Emmy and him to appear together at a TV studio north of Petaluma. Ryan waited on the porch for Emmy to pick him up. Her red Acura came up the hill, and she parked behind Ryan's car. He went down to the street, opened her car door, and offered his arm. Every time he saw her, he felt a little *Lady and the Tramp* thrill. She was so cultured, important, respectable, and he was an outlaw.

She stepped out of the car and hugged him. Ryan saw the tension, anger, and disgust drawn in lines across her brow. He lifted her up and gave her a mushy wet kiss.

Her nose against his, she said, "Ryan, please put me down. I don't feel playful."

Emmy drove Ryan to the television studio where they were directed to makeup. Ryan asked the makeup artist to paint a moustache on him, "a big Fu Manchu job." His wisecracks were more effective at removing the lines in Emmy's brow than the makeup.

In the studio, they sat on stools separated by a few feet, each with a different color backdrop and separate cameras. The producer asked them to smile in the cameras and say a few words to check the lighting and sound. Ryan listed punch lines to dumb old jokes: "if we find my keys, we can *drive* out of here," "he only took tips," and "no one expects the Spanish Inquisition." By the time the producer indicated that they were about to go on the air, Ryan felt confident and comfortable. He raised his eyebrows provocatively at Emmy. She turned away, trying to cover her laughter. Good, she was ready too. He didn't want her all uptight and defensive.

Five TV monitors were mounted behind the cameras, one each for Ryan, Emmy, Foster, and Blitzer, plus one with the live feed. Two thousand miles away, the studio in San Antonio had a similar setup for Foster.

"Has science met spirituality?" Wolf Blitzer spoke in his patented gruff monotone. "Tonight we have Foster Reed, the physicist behind Creation Energy; Ryan McNear, coinventor of the technology; and Amolie Nutter, professor of physics at the University of California and leading critic of Creation Energy—after this message."

The producer said, "Back in ninety."

Emmy took several deep breaths and closed her eyes. Ryan looked at the monitor showing Foster—he seemed to be looking right back.

"Three, two, one…"

"We'll start with Dr. Reed of Evangelical Word University." The monitor with the live feed showed a three-way split screen with Foster on the right, Ryan in the middle, and Emmy on the left. "How does this technology bring science and religion together?"

Foster smiled into the camera, cocked his head slightly, and spoke with rich confidence. "The power generator is a matter-antimatter collider operating right on the cusp of Heisenberg's uncertainty principle. It's based on a principle of symmetry like all other laws of nature. What makes it remarkable is that by replicating conditions symmetric to those of Creation, spiritual energy will flow into the physical universe and power the generator."

Blitzer's voice was passionless. "Does it work?"

"It's new technology that is showing tremendous potential," Foster said. "We should have an operating power generator within five years." There was a slight pause before Foster said *five years.*

The camera shifted to Blitzer standing in front of a wall of monitors. "In a CNN/Gallup poll, a stunning ninety percent of Americans believe science and religion must eventually meet, and fifty-four percent believe that Creation Energy has done it." He turned to the monitor showing Emmy. "Dr. Nutter, why are you so critical of the technology?"

"What technology?" Emmy held her hands out as though asking for help. "There is no evidence whatsoever to support his claims. This man is nothing but a snake oil—"

Foster spoke over Emmy. "Another attack by the scientific establishment. Don't listen to these atheists as they destroy the moral fabric of—"

Emmy cranked up her voice from small classroom to auditorium level. "Let me add that I don't want my appearance with this man to give any credence to the nonsense he's selling." She went silent.

Foster said, "Why do you have this woman on? This atheist who has risked our national security by posting classified documents on the Internet—"

Blitzer cut him off. "We'll get back to that point in a minute. But first, Ryan McNear—you are a coauthor of the patents. Is this technology feasible?"

Ryan looked to his left—giving the impression on television of looking at Foster—and then to his right, toward Emmy. With an irreverent smile, he said, "Look, I'm an engineer." Ryan leaned back in his chair and crossed his legs. "I've developed a lot of technology. There's a leap of faith anytime you try something new. Physicists are pretty good at telling engineers what is and isn't possible, but engineers are pretty good at pulling off projects that seem impossible. Will it work?" He scrunched his lips together as though it were a ridiculous question. "Need to build the thing to find out—but I'll tell you this." He uncrossed his legs and leaned forward. "I hope it will work. Scientific evidence for the soul? Who wouldn't like to see that? Solving the world's energy problems doesn't sound too bad either. Even if the chance of it working is tiny, it seems to me that it's worth a try."

He held a hand out to Emmy. She looked annoyed. "This woman right here, Professor Emmy Nutter, is the smartest person I've ever known, and if she says that it violates physical law, you better believe it. The thing is, though, God already built a perpetual motion machine—a little thing we call the universe—so I don't think the rules have to apply to Him. So, yeah, it probably won't work, but what the hey?" Ryan shrugged and turned back to Emmy. Now she looked pissed off.

Blitzer said, "We have to take a break, but we'll be back with our three guests."

Ryan exhaled a huge sigh and said, "Emmy—you okay?"

Looking straight ahead, she said, "Ryan, some day you're going to have to take a position on something."

"Three, two..."

Blitzer said, "Dr. Nutter, why won't the scientific establishment entertain the possibility that Dr. Reed could be on to something?"

Foster jumped in before she could talk. "They're threatened. Why else won't they publish our results or face us at a conference?"

Emmy ignored Foster. "Wolf, this is a very important question. Let me explain to Foster Reed why his papers are rejected by peer-reviewed journals. His fundamental error is that he thinks scientists want to uphold established theory. It is simply not true. I'm an experimental physicist. Discovery comes when we find something that is not understood, something that *violates* established theory." Settling into her lecture, she took a cue from Ryan and motioned to the side so that, on the television feed, it looked as though she were indicating Blitzer. "Think about it—which would be more fun for a scientist: a measurement that everyone expects or a measurement that is a huge surprise?"

She turned back to her left, on the monitor, toward Foster. "Foster, the reason your papers are rejected is that they don't hold up to scientific scrutiny. It takes more than a hypothesis. You need experimental evidence that can be reproduced under similar conditions in any laboratory. If there was even the tiniest shred of evidence to support your claims, then not only would your papers be published, but physicists all over the world would be working overtime to reproduce your results. But all you offer is superstition."

She turned back to the camera. "The difference between doing science and doing whatever it is that Foster Reed is doing—I guess Mr. McNear would call it *engineering*—is that Foster Reed has a vested interest in a specific outcome. His results *have to conform to the Bible*. He assumes that reputable scientists work the same way. This is why he insists that there is some entity that he calls the scientific establishment. But the community of physicists has no shepherd. The scientific method is based on what we call a disinterested love of the truth. We love *the* truth, not *a* truth."

Blitzer asked, "Do you believe in God?"

"No. I find the universe beautiful enough without ghosts, however holy."

Blitzer said, "We're going to extend this discussion into the next segment so that Dr. Reed will have a chance to respond. When we come back, we'll find out why Dr. Nutter intentionally published a classified document—was it treason?"

"Back in sixty..."

Blitzer said, "Amolie, thank you for a fine interview, and Foster, thank you for holding your peace while she spoke. I'm sure that she will offer you the same courtesy." He looked away from the camera and then added, "You've got forty-five seconds to relax."

Emmy took a deep breath and closed her eyes. Ryan looked around the studio. Foster stretched his legs while watching the clock.

"Three, two..."

Blitzer said, "Dr. Reed, why do you think that the scientific establishment has suppressed your work?"

Emmy's mouth fell open in an ironic, hopeless grin.

Foster said, "You just heard Dr. Nutter admit that she's an atheist. I feel deeply sorry for her. These intellectual elitists are divorced from mainstream America. They don't just deny God, they deny patriotism, they deny everything that our country is built on, and then—this is one of the saddest things I can imagine—they look at the stars and into the sunset and somehow deny a higher power. Without faith in Jesus their lives are so hollow." He wagged his head abruptly to the side. "As for this *disinterested love of the truth*—why do they fight the teachings of God as documented in the Bible? Why do they go to court every time a schoolteacher tells the story of Creation? Why are they so threatened by liberating scientific principles like intelligent design? If they're disinterested, why not teach both sides?"

Emmy's monitor reappeared on the feed. She spoke as though exhausted. "There are not two sides. Science is based on empirical evidence. There is no evidence for the religious doctrine that this man advocates. Promoting a mythical description of the formation of the universe to the same level as the Big Bang, a theory that stands on a firm empirical foundation, would be absurd. Why not teach people that the Earth is flat? Why not teach astrology as science?"

Foster said, "You see? They are afraid, threatened—"

The producer shut Foster's feed off, and the image on the screen showed Blitzer next to a monitor with Emmy. "Dr. Nutter, National Engineering Group, as well as senators from Texas, Arkansas, Kansas, and Florida are demanding that you be arrested and tried for treason. Do you deny knowingly distributing a document classified as a national defense secret?"

"I notice that no one has pointed out that Foster has been distributing signed copies of this *classified document* for some time. When were megachurches granted higher security clearances than national laboratories?" Emmy smiled and bounced slightly in her chair. "Wolf, don't you find it interesting that this document was removed from the Evangelical Word website literally hours before NEG's press release touting their investment in alternative energy and new propulsion systems?"

She dropped her ironic smile, her eyes narrowed, and she focused on the camera. "As a citizen and as a physicist, it was my duty to bring this document to the attention of experts in the field. Don't you see? NEG is buying political support, not technology. For a tiny fraction of their annual revenue, NEG bought the religious right and risked nothing. NEG employs real scientists and engineers. Did you ask any of them to appear?"

Blitzer said, "We had their chief technology officer on yesterday afternoon."

"Right, and would he answer any questions about the technology?"

"The technology is classified. He couldn't address it directly."

"How convenient." Leaning forward, a lock of hair had fallen over her face. She pushed it behind her ear.

Blitzer asked, "As it is written, did you violate the federal law restricting dissemination of classified documents?"

"If there is a law designed to protect corporate interest from public scrutiny, then I violated it. Wolf, why do I have to do your job? You're the journalist. Find out how NEG manipulated the Department of Defense into classifying these documents. That's where you'll find treason."

The feed panned in on Blitzer. "We'll return with final comments." During the commercial break, Blitzer told the three guests to limit their final comments to fifteen seconds each.

"Three, two…"

"We're back in *The Situation Room*. We're going to conclude this segment with the only truly relevant question—a question that has been lost in the hype and headlines: will this technology work?"

The screen split back into three. "We'll start with you Dr. Reed, then Ryan McNear, and I'll give Professor Nutter the last word."

Foster was composed and solemn. He read from an index card that he held below the camera frame. "We're on schedule to produce energy within five years. The technology is showing results that threaten the scientific establishment, and they are reacting out of fear." He looked up to the camera and concluded,

"Imagine, in a few years, there will be a new book in the Bible, this one answering the cynicism of the scientific establishment—no longer any reason to doubt. Imagine."

Ryan said, "I guess I am in the middle." He looked at Emmy. She didn't look back. "It's ridiculous to expect the Bible to be a science textbook. The Bible was written by men thousands of years ago. I believe they were inspired by God, but it was men who put ink on the page. What if God tried to explain the Big Bang, thermodynamics, quantum mechanics, and all the rest—no way could they have understood. They even got pi wrong. Science is right, but science isn't finished." He looked at Emmy again. "I say let's build it and see if it works."

Foster interrupted, "Do you really want to see it work?"

"Yes, I do," Ryan said. "I hope the best for you, Foster."

"Then come to work at Creation Energy. We need you…"

"What?"

"I'm offering you a job right now. Would you like to be director of software at Creation Energy?"

On television it looked as though Ryan were looking into space, but he was staring at Foster's monitor. He started nodding and said, "Do you have a product requirements document?"

Foster yelled, "You're hired!"

Blitzer said, "Dr. Nutter? You have the last word."

"This is disgusting," Emmy said. "I have nothing to say."

The cameras went off, and Wolf Blitzer turned *The Situation Room* to another situation. Emmy quietly walked out of the studio.

Ryan followed several steps behind. He turned a corner as the stairway doors closed. He pulled them open and ran down the stairs. He called to her, "What's wrong?"

Without turning around, Emmy said, "Leave me alone, Ryan. I don't want to see you, I don't want to hear you, and"—her voice cracked—"I don't want to know you're there."

Emmy hit second gear hard. The tires chirped, and she zipped through a yellow light onto the freeway. Doing ninety at the Petaluma off-ramp, she remembered that she needed to talk to Kat and had to double back.

What a total fool Ryan had turned out to be. Did she have a twisted need to be the smarter one in relationships? And why was the world so scientifically illiterate? Only about 20 percent of the population reads books, and less than 1 percent even knows calculus—what an ignorant species.

She parked behind Ryan's car and was tempted to scratch the damn thing, as though he could identify one more scratch. By the time she got to the porch, a lump had formed in her throat. How could he betray her like that? But inside, a soft voice, edged with Ryan's sense of humor, pointed out that Ryan hadn't betrayed anyone, hadn't taken sides at all. He was just being Ryan, trying to sprinkle the world with peace and humor. She could picture him now making wisecracks on the bus ride home. The vision brought another wave of anger.

Kat's skateboard was under the bench. Emmy took a seat. She needed a clear head, needed to focus on Kat. What would she say? This wasn't a graduate student who'd lost sight of the future while struggling to make rent.

Growing up is so hard. How much harder must it be without parents? She shuddered at the thought of her father dying. Even at thirty-seven, she didn't want to think about the inevitability. How could she have survived if he'd died when she was ten?

At least Kat had Ryan—stupid lunkhead that he was. One thing about Ryan: he had an incredible capacity to love, and he loved Kat. Emmy pushed away thoughts of Ryan's love by standing and going inside.

Emmy knocked on Kat and Jane's apartment door, but no one answered. Hopefully Kat would get home before Ryan did. She went and got a book from her car, came back inside, and took a seat at the top of the stairs. She could hear Dodge puttering around but didn't want to talk to him. She sat on the stairs for an hour trying to read her book, but she was just looking at words; she couldn't get her mind away from Ryan and Kat and CNN.

The door opened, and Emmy started, ready to hide if it was Ryan. She immediately felt stupid. It was Kat.

Kat didn't look up. Whispers of music leaked out of her headphones. Her hair was longer than Emmy remembered. She looked so grown-up that Emmy sighed, and the sigh came as a surprise.

Shuffling slowly up the stairs, kicking each one in rhythm before stepping, Kat ran her hand along the banister and paused at the landing. She looked back at the front door, did a little pirouette, and kicked the next step. She finally looked up and saw Emmy. She yanked out her earphones, rolled her eyes, and laughed.

Emmy compared the version of Kat the day they'd met with this young woman. Her analysis compensated for the makeup and eyeliner and used all her other images of Kat to interpolate from that first day to this one.

Emmy stood and offered her a hug and had to swallow another lump in her throat. She'd missed it. It had totally escaped her. Kat's soft round cheeks had straightened, emphasizing the shadows of her high cheekbones. The dimples of that little girl were now hints of mirth in the beauty of a young woman.

"Emmy! What are you doing here?"

"I was in the neighborhood, thought I'd say hi."

Kat looked over Emmy's shoulder, down the hall. "Where's Ryan?"

Emmy sighed. "He's probably on a bus between here and Santa Rosa."

"Ooookay?"

Kat hugged Emmy lightly, but Emmy latched her arms around Kat and held her tight. Kat was taller than Emmy—when did that happen?

Emmy loosened her grip enough to lean back and look Kat in the eye. "What happened to you this weekend?"

"Oh," Kat said, "that's why you're here."

Emmy felt Kat withdrawing and pulled her close again. The more Kat stiffened, the closer Emmy held her. "Yes, that's what I'm here for. I'm sorry I've never come and visited just to be with you."

"Not like you could change anything."

Emmy laughed at herself. "That's not it, Kat. I wish I'd spent more time with you because—well, look at you." Emmy released Kat from her hug. "When did you grow up?"

Kat looked at her feet. "I don't know." For an instant, she looked like a child again.

The front door opened. Emmy said, "Let's go inside."

She led Kat down the hall. Kat opened her door, and just as Ryan came up the stairs, they went into Kat's apartment.

Emmy closed the door.

Kat looked confused.

Emmy realized she'd never been here before. "Where's your room?" But it felt like a stupid question. The living room was decorated with a mural of a dragon exhaling a cloud of little symbols. A stack of dirty dishes sat on the coffee table, and there was a pillow and comforter on the couch.

Kat moved toward a closed door, shrugged, and said, "If you think this is a mess, we probably shouldn't go in my room."

While Kat carried the dishes into the kitchen, Emmy folded the comforter and set it and the pillow to the side. The two of them sat on the couch next to each other, Kat with her legs curled under her and Emmy on the edge at an angle, facing her.

Staring at the ceiling, Kat said, "Okay. It was just really lame. My stupid not-friend Marti was making out with my equally stupid not-boyfriend Alex. The world started falling apart, and then the band played. I danced in the corner all by myself—right in front of the speakers—and I didn't care, it was just hella copasetic, you know? Then, when the band stopped playing, the guy guarding the stage door asked if I wanted to go backstage."

Emmy took Kat's hands in hers. Kat looked forward, and Emmy nodded that she should continue. "So I partied with the band, and that's pretty much it."

Emmy waited, staring at Kat. When she didn't say anything, Emmy squeezed her hands. Kat said, "So we got together, so what?"

"Please," Emmy said, "you're too good for that."

"Too good?" Kat pulled her hands away. "I'm not a stuck-up bitch, I'm not *too good* for those guys. God."

"Why not?"

"Why not what?"

"Why aren't you a stuck-up bitch? I am."

Kat's expression changed. She looked for an instant as though a window to her heart had just opened.

Emmy put her hands on Kat's shoulders and looked her up and down. "You should be a stuck-up bitch. It's better to be respected than wanted. Besides, the more respect you have, the more you'll be wanted."

"That's rude!"

"So what? When did you capitulate to someone else's rules? Your friend Marti, the guy you think was your boyfriend, your teachers, the cops, even Ryan—when did you give them permission to judge you?"

"Ryan doesn't judge me."

"Kat, you have a choice. It's a choice that you can either make yourself or let the world make for you. If you decide to be a stuck-up bitch—if that's what you want to call it—then you can take the world on your own terms. You can decide whether what Marti thinks matters, you can decide whether you want to have sex or not." For a second, Emmy's lecture voice had taken over, and a shadow fell across Kat. She restrained her tone. "I'm sorry. I don't mean to come off like I totally know what you're going through or what your life is like or anything like that." Then she spoke louder, but just for the one sentence: "And me too—you can *choose* to respect my opinion or not. Everything is up to you."

Kat looked confused. Emmy pulled her forward as if to hug her but stopped short. "Kat, I want to shake you and pour some of me into you because, right now, you seem a little empty. What happened to that cocky, brilliant thirteen-year-old? No—don't answer. Just wait."

This was a talk Emmy had never expected to have. She ran through different approaches to the subject, finally sighed, and said, "Okay, this is the only way I can think of to say it: If you want to have sex with a man, then do it. But do it the way you do everything else. Do it intelligently. Do it with the whole life calculation included. You don't have to take stupid risks. Men are simple creatures; they'll do whatever you want them to. It's obvious, but most women never figure it out. But women like you and me—"

"I'm not like you." It came out barely louder than a whisper.

"You are too—for sure you are." But even as she said it, Emmy knew it wasn't true.

Kat shrugged. "Have you met my mother?"

"Kat, you're smart enough to, um, the way you think says more about who you are than your relationships."

"Nuh-uh, it does not." Kat raised her arms, breaking Emmy's grip. Her eyes flashed, and she spoke with authority as though she were unveiling a discovery. "All we are is our relationships. How can you talk about character or personality and leave out the people who gave it to you?" Her eyes sparkled, and her voice was strong and direct—this was who Emmy wanted Kat to be. "I don't like my mother. I don't respect my mother, but sometimes I like to wear her clothes and perfume. I don't want to be her, but it's stupid to deny that I'm made up of pieces of her—I'm made up of you too. And Ryan, probably mostly Ryan these days. I catch myself all the time doing Ryanisms. Making faces and stuff—saying *stuff* all the time and—you know, I never bit a pencil in my life before I met him."

"Kat, you're not tied down by these relationships. The only limit you have is your health and your intellect, and I don't think you'll ever find the limit to your intellect. Take control of your life."

"I am in control of my—"

Emmy couldn't resist the lecture voice, and it came out strong. "People manipulate you and use you and you don't even know it. Your mother does it all the time—look where and how you live? And Dodge…" They made eye contact and the ice broke.

Kat burst into laughter. "Dodge is the worst."

Emmy chuckled. "You're right about how we're made up of the people we know. Dodge taught me a lot. He's always been like that, a manipulative bastard. He taught me to recognize it, so even when he manipulates me, at least I know it. Do you see? You learn from people, but you're the judge. It's your life. You have to—"

"Ryan said that."

"What?"

"He bailed me out of that juvenile dungeon and drove up to the top of a hill and said,"—she lowered her voice, imitating Ryan—"'This is the world, live in it.'" She paused and looked Emmy up and down. "You and Ryan are perfect for each other. He's so comfortable and easy, but he pays closer attention than anyone. And, Em-ster, you need a lot of attention."

At the mention of Ryan, Emmy looked away, toward the dragon mural. "He needs to learn about taking control too."

"You broke up didn't you?"

Emmy sighed. "How did you know?"

"Kind of obvious, Em. He walked in and you almost started crying." Kat took Emmy's hand. "Don't worry, you'll get back together."

"I don't think so. Sometimes the parts just don't fit all the way together." Emmy took a breath to collect herself. "We don't *need* men. Except maybe for sex and, as you've probably discovered, we can get sex whenever we want it, and listen to me, we can have it on our terms."

"Someday, someday you'll get back together, but you're so stubborn, it might—" Kat stopped abruptly and looked down as if she'd lost something.

"What's wrong?"

"Never mind." Kat looked worried. "I think I know what you mean about being a stuck-up bitch. You don't care what other people think, do you? I don't know if I can do that."

"It does matter," Emmy said. "What's wrong? What happened just then?"

"Oh, it's just stupid Ryan. Without you, there's no reason for him to stay here. He'll move back to Texas where his son is. That'll be good for him. He belongs there."

"He probably is moving back—so stupid—he agreed to work for those fools, charlatans, idiots. He's betrayed everything that we were…" Emmy stopped. Kat looked like a little girl who had let go of her balloon and was watching it drift up into the clouds. "Oh! Kat, oh my God, Kat. Ryan loves you. Even if he moves back to Texas, he loves you, he'll want to bring you with him…"

Kat smiled with her lips sealed shut. It was perhaps the most obvious forced smile Emmy had ever seen. "It's okay, Emmy, you're right, he'll keep in touch."

"Of course he will," Emmy said, wondering if she was telling the truth. If Ryan moved, she'd have to check in, remind him that he was still a father figure to Katarina. Then it occurred to her that he'd never quite admitted that he was her father figure. It all piled on top of her anger with Ryan. No, Kat was wrong. They wouldn't get back together. Emmy was finished with him.

"Kat, I need you to promise me something."

"Sure, Em-ster, I'll promise you something."

"Promise to keep working, keep studying, not just because you're talented, but because your talents can take you to a better world. Remember the note I sent you along with the whiteboard and Feynman's book?"

"The one where you said that you hoped you'd get to work with me someday?"

"You do remember."

"I'm not a doofus."

"I meant it. You have a wonderful life in front of you. Like Ryan said, it's a big world, much bigger than this town or your school. Don't forget that, okay?"

"I guess."

The ringing phone woke Ryan. It was Foster.

"So you were serious," Ryan said.

A month had passed since the CNN interview—a lonely month of recovering from the breakup with Emmy.

Typical, the guy could crank out Feynman diagrams but couldn't calculate the time difference between Texas and California. The sun hadn't even come up yet.

"Yes, but it's a little tricky," Foster said. "You'll have to work under Jeb Schonders's radar for a while. Jeb's still livid that I offered you a job on national TV. That's why it's taken me so long to get back to you."

Ryan leaned back against his pillow. It had been a tough month. Foster hadn't returned his calls, so he was back trying to figure out how to get a pile of cash without having his name appear on that deadbeat-dad registry again. "Foster, if you hire me and I telecommute from here, is there a way to accumulate my salary so I could get paid in one big chunk—you know, without having my name show up on any federal employment rolls?"

"Yes," Foster said. "I tell you Ryan, the way things fit together—yes, that makes everything easier. You see, Blair is going to pay you from a separate account. Stashing your pay and keeping you off campus assures that Jeb won't find out until I want him to. Let me call you back."

Ryan hung up the phone and rolled over so he could watch the sunrise. Working for Creation Energy would destroy any last chance with Emmy, but it could solve his big problems. Oh well, he mused to himself, if you love something, let it go; if it doesn't come back, then simulate it in software.

Foster called back a few minutes later. "Ryan, we can do it, no problem. And there's one other thing: in exchange for your rights to the patents, we want to offer you stock options."

"Options too?" Ryan asked. "Are they worth anything?"

Foster laughed. "Not yet, but you'll vest immediately at the current value. You know the drill."

Foster yammered from circuitry to faith, and Ryan pulled him back to software. When Foster told Ryan that they had been modifying a neural network they'd downloaded from CERN, Ryan laughed and asked for a raise.

When Ryan hung up, he felt the upswing of the yo-yo that his life had become.

Downstairs, Dodge hung up the phone too.

When Ryan started developing the new software, he was struck by the volume of necessary research. He commuted to the UC Berkeley Engineering Library each day and sat at a table next to a window where he could see the Golden Gate Bridge. From that perch, he worked through textbooks and journal articles on neural networks and fuzzy logic. The more he learned, the more he realized how close his patent had been to a workable method. Sometimes you guess right, and back in those days, he'd been on a roll with good fortune. Since he couldn't check out books and take them home for her, he brought Katarina with him on weekends. She blitzed through the mathematical formalism and then corrected Ryan's software designs. Their partnership cut the development time in half.

Being at UC Berkeley had other temptations, though. He e-mailed Emmy, telling her what he was up to. She replied once: "The love we had is a noun." He went to her office and asked her to lunch. She made courteous excuses, but he persevered, stopping by at the same time each day. She finally agreed so that he could "have closure." Ryan asked her to meet him at a bench near Sather Gate.

Ryan wasn't there when she arrived. She sat on the bench, and just down the hill on a patch of grass near a creek—the place where they'd made out like drunk freshmen—dozens of roses were scattered. A guitar chord resonated from behind her, the same street musician broke into the Beatles' "Here, There and Everywhere," and Ryan walked up the path. When he got to the bench, he knelt in front of her, licked his lips into a melancholy smile, and said, "I want our love to be a verb."

Emmy started to take his hand but stopped. The music and the roses on the grass may have been enough, but when he licked his lips, she fell apart. She couldn't go through this again.

He reached out to hug her.

She ducked under his arms and rushed down the path. It hurt too much. She just had to get away from him.

The support network that Foster Reed had cultivated in the great churches of the Bible Belt paid off. Along with the president and Congress, the mainstream press and conservative radio were bombarded with letters, phone calls, and e-mails demanding the end to religious oppression. A senator from Kansas gave a floor speech demanding that Amolie Nutter and Bob Park be tried for treason.

Emmy had strong but invisible support from academe, just enough to weather the threats and criticism—until she was stopped at airport security.

On one of several trips she made each year to the experiment at CERN, in Geneva, Emmy was schlepping her carry-on bag and dreading twelve hours crammed into a coach seat, when a kind young security officer asked her to step aside for a "routine safety screening." She was guided to a small windowless room where she submitted to an X-ray search and was then left alone.

Emmy knew that this experience was part of her fight. She sat on the floor, pulled her legs into the lotus position, and exhaled slowly. It took an hour to relax, but eventually she lowered her heart rate to fifty beats a minute. She looked inside and went back in time, then forward. From when she was three years old, her first memory was Neil Armstrong walking on the moon—a vivid memory of Dodge pointing at the moon while her father pointed at the TV. She recalled wielding a hammer in kindergarten. She'd told everyone she was making a ship anchor out of wood. She worked through every year of her life up to the present and then went back and forth again.

As the hours passed, Emmy looked ever deeper inside. She liked being a physicist. She loved discovery and the simple awakenings of understanding. There was one other thing she wanted. At first the thought teased her; she felt a yearning but couldn't figure out the object of that desire. It was like the weird way that we know when we've forgotten something. She knew it was there but couldn't figure out what it was.

Another hour passed, and she brought her heart rate lower, relaxed into a deep calm, and that desire resolved itself. It surprised her. She'd been pushing against the idea for weeks. Every time Ryan had entered her mind, she shoved him out, getting almost physical pleasure at the expression of anger. But now, in the strange peace of this cell, with her thoughts running in every direction, she let him into her mind and finally admitted it to herself.

She wanted to wake up next to Ryan McNear every day. And she wanted to be there holding his hand when Katarina graduated from high school. She wanted to help Ryan carry boxes into a dormitory when Katarina went to college. She might even want a little red-haired baby.

A TSA officer opened the door without knocking.

Emmy, still sitting on the floor, looked up. She let him mistake her tears as fear or anger or whatever he wanted. He helped her up and she got ahold of herself.

His was the only apology she would receive. He told her that her name was on the FBI's no-fly list. There was no further explanation and no written record that she had been detained. The only documentation was the unused boarding pass for a nonrefundable ticket.

She girded herself for battle, and the next day, from her Berkeley office, she ranted at the Department of Energy official who funded her research. When that got her nowhere, she called her congressman. The FBI wouldn't take her calls, but an investigator from the Office of Homeland Security appeared on Fox News saying that as long as Emmy's name appeared on websites "known to pose a threat to national security," she would remain on the no-fly list. Conservative talk show hosts and Bible Belt congressional representatives lauded the event as evidence that the Patriot Act was working.

Finally, two months after the CNN interviews, the Union of Concerned Scientists composed a letter to the Senate Subcommittee on Defense Appropriations, voicing specific doubt that vacuum fluctuation energy extraction was technically viable. The evangelical senators from Kansas, Mississippi, Arkansas, and Texas responded by calling themselves the "Union of Concerned Defenders of Spiritual Freedom and American Ingenuity" and argued that basic research bloated the federal budget and did nothing more than "subsidize the attack on America's fundamental spiritual ideals."

The National Engineering Group maintained what, to most American citizens, appeared to be the moral high ground: "NEG's investment in alternative energy sources can relieve the country's reliance on foreign fossil fuels, reduce greenhouse gases, and provide a new technical backbone for American security." The Union of Concerned Defenders of Spiritual Freedom and American Ingenuity negotiated sole-bid status for NEG in a defense appropriations bill for top-secret missile technology.

The Union of Concerned Scientists delivered a letter to the president bearing the signatures of seventy-five Nobel laureates demanding that "all documents related to vacuum fluctuation energy extraction be declassified," any defense contract related to these "questionable technologies" be subject to peer review, the two patents related to the technology be reexamined, and, finally, Professor Amolie Nutter's right to freely travel be restored. The letter was published on page fifteen of the *New York Times* and page seventeen of the *Washington Post*. It didn't appear in either the *Chicago Tribune* or *Dallas Morning News*.

Ryan received a certified letter from Creation Energy after the end of his second week of work.

Standing on the front porch in his stocking feet, Ryan handed the pen back to the postal carrier. He turned to go inside. Dodge was standing at the threshold, blocking Ryan's way.

"You're an idiot, McNear."

"Dodge, get out of my way."

"You're settling for chump change," Dodge said. "As your attorney, I recommend that all communications with Creation Energy flow through me. The more contracts they get, the higher the price tag on your rights." Then his voice went coy. "Read that offer carefully. Stock options on technology that has no value? I can get you cash."

Ryan looked at the unopened envelope. "Nutter, get out of my way." He pushed past Dodge, walked inside and up the stairs.

Dodge called after him, "Don't forget my twenty-five percent."

"Wait a minute," Ryan said, calmer now. "How do you know what's in this envelope?"

"Nothing happens in this house that I don't know about."

"Only two people know what I'm doing, and neither of them would tell you." Ryan started up the stairs again but stopped.

"Did you trick Katarina into telling you? She's got enough problems without—"

"Nope, not Kat..." Dodge coughed on his raspy chuckle.

Ryan rushed to his room, his heart racing. He paced in front of the whiteboard and, slowly, his heart broke.

Emmy must have informed Dodge of everything.

Betrayal spread from his chest to his limbs, and his world went cold. All this time, he believed that she would come to understand why he did what he did, believed that their love would survive, but no, he really had lost her.

Ryan leaned back in the beach chair, Sean's football on his lap, Katarina's scratch paper cluttering the floor. He had the job and would have some money in a couple of months. With his pay at director level, it would be a good chunk of change. The beach chair thumped forward, and Ryan pulled a box from under the desk. Near the bottom, he pulled out the arrest warrant that Constable Holcomb had set on the counter back at Oil Xchangers.

He punched the number into the phone—the Fort Worth courthouse—and asked for Constable Holcomb. After a long wait, he heard, "Holcomb here..." He was a bailiff now, too old to go running around handing out summons.

Ryan identified himself and explained that he was ready to come back and turn himself in.

Holcomb didn't sound impressed. "What's it been? Darn near three years since I served you? I shoulda collared you back when."

"I need some advice," Ryan said. "Three months' pay at this job should be enough to impress a judge—how long can I be on a Texas payroll before your office finds out?"

"About the length of time it takes your plane to taxi to the gate, if I find out what flight you're on."

"Like you said, I can't pay anything from jail—Officer Holcomb, I need some time in Texas to sort things out before I turn myself in."

"McNear, just do the right thing. Get yourself a lawyer here in Fort Worth, and get it done."

"What am I looking at?"

"That check you're talkin' about will help get things started, but you're walkin' into a helluva legal dust cloud." Holcomb paused. "Awright, you need a family law attorney with a heap of experience—you got anything other than the warrant I served you?"

"Isn't leaving a state to avoid paying child support a federal charge?"

"Yup."

The thought of having Dodge represent him flitted through his mind; he swatted it like a fly on a window. "Do you know an attorney?"

"Now you're talkin'," Holcomb said and then gave him a name and phone number.

The attorney's name was Cynthia Robins. She listened as Ryan explained his situation. It took him half an hour. He wondered about her hourly rate. She whistled when he told her how much he owed and said something about that "just being the principal." When he finished, Ms. Robins told him to collect copies of the canceled checks that he'd sent to Linda. Then she took a deep breath.

"Mr. McNear, Officer Holcomb put it accurately when he said that you're entering a legal cloud of dust. Nothing about this process will be straightforward. Over the next six months, you will submit to weekly counseling, drug testing, and court appearances—you will pay for every single one. Your child support will be neither reduced nor forgiven. We will plead the federal charge into a fine. You will not see your son until the court is convinced that you are clean and will stay clean. It's remarkable that your ex-wife managed to have the restraining order renewed every three months—it does not bode well for you."

Ryan chuckled, "Sounds like I shouldn't be shopping for a new ski boat just yet."

She didn't laugh. "Now for the good news."

"There's good news?"

"Yes, the finish line. If it is true that you're off of drugs, have a steady high-paying job, and can produce character references from reputable people—if things go perfectly, you will be granted thirty consecutive days of custody this summer. I want you to be able to explain to the judge how you will use this time to repair your relationship with your son. Include counseling and perhaps a vacation of some type—you need to look like a good father in court."

Thirty days with Sean? Ryan stared out the window at the mountains.

"I'll start filing next week," she said, "and set an appointment for you in Fort Worth next month—February sixth?"

"Um, the sixth?" Ryan laughed again. "This is going to sound strange, but I'll be in court here in California that day."

Ms. Robins was silent.

"Not for me," Ryan said, "for my friend, sort of like my niece, I guess."

"Mr. McNear," she said, "you cannot be in or near trouble. If that's too much to ask…"

"February eighth?" Ryan explained in as few words as possible that Katarina needed him to accompany her to court.

"You're there to help her?"

"Yes, of course."

"As almost a surrogate parent?"

"More like an uncle."

"Have the file sent to me. If it checks out, then we can meet on the eighth." Ryan could hear her hesitate. Then she said, "If you don't do every single thing that I tell you to do, jf you stray from my instructions in any way, and it won't matter whether it's by mistake or if you have an excuse, I will drop your case, bill you in full, and see to it that no decent divorce attorney in the state of Texas will ever take your case. Do you understand?"

"Yes, ma'am."

"I'm doing this because I believe that boys need their fathers. Do we understand each other?"

"Thank you, Ms. Robins."

I'm not going with that bitch." Katarina crossed her arms and clenched her teeth. It was Ryan's first glimpse of what she must have looked like as a two-year-old. The funny thing was, prior to the outburst, Ryan had been thinking that she looked mature, more like a twenty-year-old. She wore a pressed skirt with a subtle design along the hem, Feynman diagrams of course.

"If your mother isn't standing next to you in front of the judge…" Ryan looked down the hallway. The door to Katarina and Jane's apartment was open. Maybe Jane was listening. He spoke softly, "You want to be a foster child? Ward of the court? Or do you want to stay here in the glorious Nutter mansion?"

"You'll be there," Katarina said. "What do we need *her* for?"

"I'm not your legal guardian."

"You could be my legal guardian—you just don't *want* to be." She kicked Sean's football. It ricocheted off the wall underneath the whiteboard. A marker fell from the tray.

"Cut the drama," Ryan said. "Like a judge would grant a wanted felon who is a deadbeat dad custody of a junior criminal like you."

"What about Emmy? She would be my guardian. Why not you and Emmy?"

Ryan hadn't had the heart to tell Katarina that Emmy had betrayed him, that they were finished. The twinge of pain caused him to speak without thinking. "Emmy doesn't want kids, and besides, we're through."

Katarina unfolded her arms and looked down. She mumbled something.

"Shit," Ryan said. "I'm sorry. Emmy loves you—if you asked her, she'd do it. And I swear, if I could do it, I would. But Katarina, right now we need to get to court and look like as happy a family as you and your mom and I can."

"You're going to get back together," Katarina said. "You're made for each other."

"What?" Ryan said.

"You and Emmy are the perfect couple."

"Katarina, you need to focus." Ryan gripped her shoulders. He wanted to shake her. Instead, he waited until she looked up at him. "We are going across the hall. You are going to hug and support your mother, and, when we get to court, you will hold her hand—if you have to prop her up and hold her eyelids open, that's what you'll do. Do you hear me?"

Katarina started to laugh.

Good, she was getting it. Make it a game, learn to survive. "If all it takes to keep your ass out of jail is to fake a healthy relationship with your mother..."

Ryan patted her on the head. Good, the Katarina who seemed like a twenty-year-old was back.

Ryan and Katarina walked on opposites sides of Jane into the pseudomodern, orange-and-blue, juvenile-friendly courtroom.

Ryan reached across Jane's shoulders and rested his hand on the back of Katarina's neck.

They sat in the back row behind dozens of youths and their parents—mostly single moms with rebellious-looking kids, plus a few sets of well-dressed parents with conservatively dressed teenagers. Sitting in the row ahead of them, a teenage boy wearing khaki pants and a turtleneck sweater looked at Katarina. He shrugged. She rolled her eyes.

The bailiff called Katarina's name, and, following the example set by other families, the three of them stood. Ryan guided Jane up the aisle. Katarina walked to a podium. Ryan and Jane stood a few feet behind her. The judge was a woman about twenty years older than Ryan. She had a warm, energetic countenance but eyes that threatened to pierce through her glasses at any provocation.

The clerk listed the charges—public indecency, lewd and lascivious behavior, possession of controlled substances, and resisting arrest.

Ryan saw Katarina's back stiffen. She was about to say something stupid, so he whispered, "Chill."

The judge glared at Ryan. He offered a slight bow as penance.

She stared at Katarina for a few seconds before speaking and then spoke so that Katarina had to strain to listen and the rest of the court could hear very little. Katarina described what happened that night in much the same way that she had described it to Ryan the day after it happened. Ryan felt a surge of pride at Katarina's calm honesty. Jane stood straighter, and at first, he thought Jane shared that pride, but she looked downward and whispered to herself. Ryan caught her words: "I'll be with you soon." He realized that every indication of Katarina's maturity encouraged Jane to withdraw further into her bizarre mourning. He tightened his grip on her arm.

Katarina stood during the examination without breaking eye contact with the judge. Her only mistake was asking how she could be charged with "possession." The judge lifted the report at an angle to accommodate her bifocals. "Miss Ariadne, the police found a pipe with methamphetamine next to your clothes—did you use drugs that night?"

"Yes." She sounded nothing like a scared teenager.

"You are fortunate that the police were there to protect you."

Katarina stared at the judge. Ryan silently prayed, "Lord, please make her behave for five minutes."

The judge asked Katarina the same thread of questions that she'd asked the previous first-time offending juveniles. The theme of the questions was Katarina's vision of her future. Katarina said that she hadn't decided yet whether she wanted to be an experimental particle physicist or a mathematician. The judge took her glasses off, as though sensing sarcasm, and asked Katarina to repeat herself. Katarina's matter-of-fact tone and attitude belied her core innocence. Katarina had no idea that her ambition was any greater than to work in a bookstore like her father had. She just didn't want to work in a bookstore, that's all, so particle physics or math would have to do.

The judge must have noticed Ryan beaming—she looked at Jane and then at him again. Ryan mistook the look as a question and stepped forward to Katarina's side. He unfolded a sheet of paper and leaned toward the microphone. "Your honor, I have letters from Katarina's science and math teachers—Katarina is a brilliant girl. She's already learned relativistic quantum mechanics and is studying calculus and differential equations."

The judge lifted her glasses and looked at the report again. "What is your relationship?"

Ryan looked back at Jane. She was staring at the floor. He put his hand on Katarina's shoulder and said, "Um, family friend? We're neighbors..."

The judge looked at Jane, who didn't look back. "Mrs. Ariadne, please approach."

Ryan and Katarina looked at each other, and as they did, Ryan could feel the judge scrutinizing them. Jane looked surprised and confused. Ryan started to lead her forward, but the judge said, "Just Mrs. Ariadne."

The judge stood so that she could lean forward and talk with Jane from a few inches away. The judge then called Katarina forward.

Katarina looked up to Ryan. He gave her a reassuring wink and then patted her on the back—nudging her forward.

As the judge talked to Katarina and Jane, Ryan couldn't help but fidget. He folded the teachers' notes back and forth. Katarina and Jane finally turned away from the judge. Relief washed over Katarina's face. Ryan smiled at the judge, mouthing the words *thank you.*

The judge didn't return his smile. Instead, she said, "Mr. McNear, would you approach?"

Katarina's smile disappeared.

Ryan stepped forward with what he hoped was a confident-looking stride. He paused for an instant when he passed Katarina. "Don't worry."

He stood before the judge, his head just slightly lower than hers. In a confident, businesslike tone, he said, "What can I do to help Katarina?"

"Mr. McNear, I think I understand your situation in regard to the Ariadnes." She pushed her glasses up the bridge of her nose and looked at her notes. "The child's mother told me that she will continue to take care of Katarina, but as soon as the child has grown up, she is moving back in with the child's father." She looked at the arrest report. "But it says here that the father is deceased."

Ryan nodded. He felt like the judge had discovered a horrible secret. His tongue ran along his teeth, he leaned close to her and said, "The father died a few years ago. Jane's still recovering."

She scowled and turned back to her notes. "Katarina told me that you are more like her father than her father ever had been, even when he was alive—those were her exact words."

She pulled her glasses down her nose so that nothing was between her eyes and Ryan's. "Do you understand how much that little girl needs you?"

"She said that?" Ryan stole a glance behind him. Katarina was at the podium either prying something off of the wood veneer or trying to dislodge the light. She looked up, saw him, and resumed her fake smile.

"Those were her words."

"She loved her father."

"I'm sure she did, Mr. McNear, but he's gone now."

"Katarina is a smart kid, your honor. She's learned her lesson."

"Her mother doesn't seem capable of taking responsibility for the child. The court can order her to seek counseling but can't force her to pursue it."

"She could really use the help."

"Is there anyone else? A family member? An aunt or uncle, a grandparent?"

"I don't know of any."

"Mr. McNear, I don't want to incarcerate Katarina. My only other choice is foster care." The judge looked over Ryan's shoulder toward the podium. Ryan wanted to steal a glance too but thought better of it. Instead, he focused whatever telepathic abilities he had into Katarina's head, pleading with her to give the impression of a well-behaved child.

She turned back to Ryan. Looking over her glasses, she seemed to be examining him.

"Surely you have a third option," Ryan said. "Katarina has never been in trouble before."

"Do I have your word that you will take responsibility for her as long as her mother is incapacitated?"

"You do."

"If she appears before me again, I will put her in foster care." She lifted her gavel. "Mr. McNear, do you realize how dangerous the world is to her right now?"

Ryan nodded.

"Return to the podium."

Ryan walked back and stood next to Katarina.

The judge said, "Miss Ariadne, I am suspending your sentence until you're eighteen. If you commit no further offenses, the record of this crime will be sealed on your eighteenth birthday. However, if you are charged for another crime and appear in this court again, you will either be incarcerated in the county juvenile detention center or be assigned foster care. Do you understand?"

"What?" Katarina said. "You mean I can go?"

The judged nodded and tapped her gavel on its pad.

Ryan and Katarina walked up the steps, and Jane went around back to her bike. The house looked different to Ryan than it had that first day. The 150-year-old Victorian in basic black with bright-red features and lime-green trim, the two spires, and immaculate garden had looked like the Munsters' comical, macabre mansion. Now it looked warm. The black wasn't intimidating, the red seemed to fit the mood of the owner, and the green expressed the hope of its occupants with that red. Complicated and bright, this was where Katarina grew up, Dodge connived, and Ryan climbed out of his hole as Jane sunk deeper into hers.

Ryan opened the door for Katarina. "The judge told me what you said."

"Oh."

"About me being like your father and stuff."

"Well, who knows what my mother told her." Katarina laughed. "Like you said, do what it takes to stay out of jail."

Ryan unlocked his apartment door and went in. Katarina followed. She went in the kitchenette and put a pot on the stove, pulled a box of macaroni and cheese from the cupboard, and then brought Ryan a bottle of beer.

"Whoa!" Ryan said, opening the bottle. "What is this?"

"I believe it's water, grain, and brewer's yeast—the ingredients are on the label. I bet you could even read them." Then, stirring the macaroni, she asked in a soft voice, as though it were of no consequence, "Are you moving back to Texas?"

Ryan didn't catch her tone. "Well, I'll have to go back and forth. My new lawyer said it'll take a few months of legal mess to fix things, and I have to install the new software in Foster's lab—but wow." He leaned back and sighed. "This summer you will finally meet Sean McNear. I owe an awful lot to him, you know, and it'll take a while. But I don't want to live there."

"So is this Sean McNear I've heard so much about going to live here?" Katarina said. "Will I have a new neighbor? Do I have to be nice to him?"

"Just try not to scare him too much, okay?"

"Is he as goofy looking as you are?" And then, before Ryan could answer, she added, "Oh, that's right, you wouldn't know, not having seen him in over four years?"

"Yeah, I don't know, do I? People used to say that he looked like me. His mother is gorgeous. I couldn't have polluted her gene pool that much. But seriously, I'm going to be traveling a lot for the next couple of months. There's nothing I can do about it, and the judge said that I have to take care of you, so you better not get in any trouble while I'm gone."

"I could come with you."

"What about school?"

"You don't want me to go with you."

"It's not like I want to go there. Besides, what would you do in Texas?"

"If Emmy hadn't dumped you, you'd stick around." Now she sounded surly.

"What? That has nothing to do with anything."

"Never mind."

"I'll bring you with me when school's out this summer. Just be careful while I'm gone. Stay away from Alex and those idiots, okay?"

"I don't hang with those losers anymore." She handed him a big bowl of mac 'n' cheese. "I don't need them. I don't need anyone. And I don't want to go to Texas."

Ryan felt like a grizzled version of who he'd been the last time he landed at DFW airport. Reviewing what he planned to say to his attorney, he wandered into the parking lot. He looked up, half expecting to see the blue BMW that he'd had in a different life, laughed at himself, and went back to wait for the rental-car bus.

Cynthia Robins reminded Ryan of a schoolteacher. She wore a suit with a calf-length skirt and one-inch heels. Her graying brown hair was wound up in a bun, and she wore wire-rimmed bifocals with a chain that went around her neck. Cynthia Robins Law Office was on the thirtieth floor of a Fort Worth building a block from Sunset Square. Her oak desk was half the size of Dodge's and cluttered with pictures of parents and their children, single parents with one or more kids, and their pets. A floor-to-ceiling window looked over the prairie, and, just visible through the haze, you could see the Dallas skyline. She made him tea and told him that she had read the documents related to the restraining order. Ryan described what had happened with Tammi in as much detail as he could bear. She was looking at her notes when he finished and, barely glancing up, said, "When was the last time you took methamphetamine?"

Ryan understood the significance. Every recovering addict knows that date. "Halloween, two thousand three—it was warm that morning, the sky was clear, but a wind blew down from the north and dropped the temperature into the twenties by the afternoon. I broke my pipes and locked my apartment door—chain-smoked cigarettes for a week." It was a fond memory, the greatest victory of his life. "And when I walked out of that apartment, I wasn't sure if I'd ever use meth again, but I was absolutely certain that I'd never quit again."

Ms. Robins leaned back in her chair and took a sheet from the printer on the table behind her. Setting it in front of her, she put on reading glasses. "Tomorrow you will meet with the Department of Child Protective Services to set up weekly counseling and drug testing. The initial fee is seven hundred dollars, counseling is six hundred dollars per month, and drug testing is four hundred dollars per month." She looked over her glasses at Ryan and added, "You have a right to perform the counseling near your residence, which will be Hardale, Texas. This is your first lesson in disappearing into county bureaucracy: you have a right to Hardale, but if you request Hardale, it would mean extra work for someone. This would make you stick out. You must disappear. You will petition for counseling and testing in San Antonio, where resources already exist. It will take at least a month for the county to process your request. This means that your first six weeks of counseling and drug testing will be in Fort Worth. You won't complain, you won't be late, and you will accept the first scheduling options you are presented. Do you understand?"

"Make it easy for them?"

"Yes, become a name on a sheet of paper and nothing else—do not bring gifts of any kind to your counselors, do not befriend the nurses who take your urine, do not crack jokes, do not speak unless you are spoken to, and agree to every request." She pulled her glasses back up and looked at the page before her as she spoke. "The county will charge you a two hundred dollars per month surcharge for allowing you to be counseled and tested in San Antonio." She set the page down again, as though expecting Ryan to comment.

Ryan didn't say anything.

She finally broke a smile. "Very good. I think you're getting it."

"Thank you, ma'am. May I have another?"

"Understand this: you are a county revenue stream. You pay, the county collects; the easier it is for them to take your money, the more latitude I will have to work the system in your favor." She frowned. "Wednesday morning, you and I have an appointment at the federal courthouse in Dallas with the Office of Child Support Enforcement." She glanced at a legal pad to her right and told him that his current overdue child support was $188,732. She looked over her glasses again.

Ryan wrote the number down. It was consistent with a quick estimate.

She said, "The system will not entertain the prospect of you working below your income capacity. I have spoken with the OCSE officer assigned to this case. It will be easiest for him if we, first, do not appeal the amount and, second, offer to pay the standard fifty-thousand-dollar fine in addition to prime plus five percent compounded annual interest on the outstanding debt."

"Fifty, plus compounded interest?" Ryan ran the numbers through his head. "That's almost an additional hundred thousand. I'll never be able to—"

"You will find a way. You see, by presenting the officer with an offer that is explicitly that which he is authorized to grant, we will make his day easier. Ryan, it will be worth every cent."

"Wait a second." Ryan stood and walked to the window. "I thought your job was to get those fines reduced."

She stood, took his empty cup of tea, and left the office.

Ryan stared across the prairie south of town. He could see the strip mall where he'd worked at Oil Xchangers and, not too far from there, the apartment complex where he'd lived with Tammi. He let loose a big sigh, his shoulders slumping by the time he fully exhaled. It wasn't supposed to be easy.

Ms. Robins came back in the office. "Ryan, please sit down."

He slid back into the seat and saw that she had poured him another cup of tea. A purple tag hung from it, Darjeeling.

"I don't enjoy making you suffer, but it's the best way to prepare you to deal with the system."

He sipped the tea. She'd put in a slice of lemon and the perfect amount of sugar.

"Ryan," she said, looking at the legal pad again, "Sean is turning sixteen this summer. You and he have already lost so much time." Her eyes softened and she spoke gently, "I can recommend an attorney who will fight for your money. I want to fight for your son."

Ryan sat in waiting rooms the next day, signed stacks of forms, and wrote checks. He provided urine, hair, and blood samples and, of course, wrote more checks to have each of them processed. He tried not to smile at any irony and resisted every temptation to make a wisecrack. The only challenge to his resolve was that the nurse who took his blood and hair was extremely hot.

The day after that, he met Ms. Robins in Dallas. He gave her an envelope with copies of the checks he'd sent Linda. She said that they would be useful in court but would only irritate the Office of Child Support Enforcement. Money sent directly to the custodial parent without being channeled through the OCSE would not count as child support but rather a gift.

He filled out more forms, including one that authorized Creation Energy to garnish his wages, a mandatory service for which he had to pay a fee. Ms. Robins had Ryan wait in the hallway as she negotiated the federal charge for leaving the state to avoid paying child support. In three minutes, she stepped into the hall and said, "Can you write a check for thirty-five thousand dollars right now?"

Ryan said, "Thank you, ma'am. May I have another?" He had deposited the two months of accrued pay the day before. After taxes, it came out to $32,000. Hopefully the check would have cleared. He could skip paying Dodge rent for a month, but there was one obligation he didn't consider negotiable, that he would buy Katarina a laptop computer with his first paycheck. "Thirty thousand is the most I can do."

She went back in the office with the check.

Everything looked the same as it had when Ryan was here to interview. The grass was manicured, the buildings looked like ivory, and the lab was stocked with equipment and packed with technicians—but it didn't feel the same. Mabel walked Ryan to the lab, and Foster greeted him with a long article that described the collider in detail and told him that its output power had been bogged down at a factor of ten million from breakeven for the last three months.

Ryan handed Foster a memory stick with the neural network software he and Katarina had developed. Without another word, the two of them sat opposite each other at a granite lab bench. Ryan started reading the paper, and Foster popped the memory stick into his computer.

At first, Ryan was psyched that Foster had written up the collider. It was tantamount to a product requirements document, but it took him fifteen minutes to work through the first page. It shouldn't have been a surprise that collecting positrons into bunches and focusing and accelerating them into a target was complicated. He flipped a few pages forward to a schematic diagram. The realization dawned that he knew far too little about the nuts and bolts of the project to provide a neural network mind.

An hour later, Ryan looked up. Foster was staring at him. They started to speak at the same time. Foster laughed. Ryan wiped his forehead as though he were sweating, flipped back to the first page, and started over.

In their first job together, before they worked at GoldCon, they had experienced a moment of panic while designing a new networking gadget. Not only did the gadget not work, but they had no idea if it could ever work. They learned quickly that moments of panic are part of the buzz of engineering. You think it's impossible, then you start figuring it out, and then, usually, you get it to work.

Ryan reread the first paragraph of the collider paper for the sixth time.

At midnight, they were still seated across from each other. An empty pizza box served as a collection plate for printouts of marked-up software source code that had doubled as napkins.

Foster set down a fresh cup of coffee and sighed. "Ryan, this is a powerful software algorithm. I'd recognize your code anywhere, but the interface with the collider isn't close to functional."

Ryan was hunched over a printout. He leaned back, looked around the lab, and said, "Man, I haven't done an all-nighter in years." Then, as if he'd just heard what Foster had said, he said, "No prob', we'll figure it out."

It turned into a six-week crash course in accelerator technology, particle detector development, and data acquisition. The number of switches, knobs, and levers involved in operating a particle collider was in the thousands, and each one provided information that could influence the decisions made by the community of neural nets.

Ryan worked fourteen hours every day. On those days that he had to drive to Fort Worth for counseling and drug testing, he debugged software on his laptop in waiting rooms and did all-nighters in the lab to catch up.

Foster put in twenty-hour days six days a week. When he wasn't on the road speaking at churches, he used the Sabbath to sleep.

Ryan called Katarina from the lab every day after school. The day Katarina's laptop computer was delivered, Ryan e-mailed her a document. She opened it while on the phone: a patent submission for their neural network algorithm. It listed Katarina as an inventor.

The calls settled into a routine. First, Ryan would ask about school, what she was up to, whether she was getting in trouble, what was up at Skate-n-Shred, that sort of thing, and Katarina replied in information-free single syllables. With that out of the way, Ryan would e-mail her the latest software and put her on the speakerphone so Foster could join them.

At first, Foster had a hard time accepting a fourteen-year-old girl as a consultant, but then she recommended they use separate neural network communities to control the focusing magnets. He said, "But they're both doing the same thing—separate nets will be redundant; it's a waste of resources."

"Foster," Katarina said, her voice straining with condescension, "are they identical? Of course not. There are an infinite number of small differences, right? You should also be aware that using feedback loops in a nonlinear system means that even infinitesimal differences in the boundary conditions can have large effects on the results. Remember that little nugget of chaos theory? Separate networks will respond in different ways to small variations of stimulus. They will compete to get the right answer, increasing the efficiency of the system. Have you ever heard of survival of the fittest? Evolution? Oh, that's right. You don't believe it." She finished with, "Do what I tell you and bitch at me if it doesn't work—but wait, oh yeah, that's right: it will work, so shut up."

Ryan expected an instant dose of Foster smugness, but instead, he asked for details on how to implement the new system. It seemed completely out of character, especially letting the crack about evolution slide. Watching Foster closely, Ryan recognized the look on his face. It was the same as when Rachel was short with him. He never questioned his angel. In exchange, Katarina granted him a hint of patience—from her, the ultimate expression of largesse.

The next day, Foster reported that this single change had increased the power output by a factor of two.

A month later, on one of their daily conference calls, Ryan told Katarina that he missed her. He said it every time he called, but this time it slipped out, and the fervor he said it with surprised him. "I feel homeless without you around. I just don't belong here."

Foster looked away as though giving them privacy.

Katarina said, "Ryan, Foster can confirm that we're not plants! We don't grow roots, and the more we interact with others, the more we become a part of each other. It's how we develop character."

Ryan said, "What about genetics?"

"Genetics is the biological history of our ancestors, the foundation or canvas, and character is the paint that goes on that canvas—that's what the soul is."

Foster interrupted, "Katarina, there's another piece. Don't forget the symmetry between the physical and the spiritual."

"I'm just thinking out loud," Katarina said. "You know that feeling when you can tell you're about to understand something but haven't yet?"

Ryan said, "Not really."

"Figures. Well, I'm close to understanding something, something major."

Foster said, "Really? You're about to get it?"

"Pretty soon."

"Katarina, listen to me," Foster said. "Follow that feeling. You are being guided to the truth."

"Foster," Katarina said, "you are freakishly weird."

Ryan said, "We better figure out something major soon and get this thing going or I don't think they'll let me go home."

"Ryan, you *are* home," Katarina said. "Accept it. You live in Texas where you belong, near your son. Don't waste your time worrying about me. I've got it goin' on."

Ryan oozed into semipermanent residence in Foster and Rachel's guest room. Rachel apologized for being judgmental the night that Ryan confessed how he'd wrecked his life. More than that, she seemed to think he was the cavalry come to save her husband's reputation.

Every morning, precisely six hours after Ryan went to bed, Rachel would open his door, draw back the curtains, and wake him with a smile, showcasing frighteningly white teeth. A cooked breakfast and a full pot of tea would be waiting downstairs, and she'd sit across the table to chat. Her favorite subject was Emmy. Rachel convinced Ryan that he shouldn't assume that Emmy had betrayed him—talking to your brother about someone you care for is not betrayal. She also talked him into sending her e-mail. "Just pop a note to her whenever you think of her, whatever is on your mind. She'll be flattered."

After he'd been there a month, Emmy finally replied—a short note asking about Katarina. Rachel helped him invest the correspondence with significance, and the two of them wrote to Emmy and invited her to visit. The note concluded with a line that took them an hour to compose: "Katarina told me that you and I are meant for each other, and I believe her. Do you?" Emmy didn't reply to this one.

Ryan also sent a note to Ward, the guy back in the neighborhood who'd been sending occasional notes about Sean. Ryan told him that he was back in Texas and building a legal case to resume joint custody. Ward responded with more frequent updates—things like, "Sean's stepfather is teaching him how to drive" and "I bumped into Linda and Sean at the Piggly Wiggly yesterday. He's a well-mannered young man."

It took six weeks for Ryan and Katarina to get the power output of the collider back on track. It had increased tenfold and was still rising. A month later, Katarina introduced a new idea.

"Is this it?" Foster asked. "Is this what you were talking about? Have you figured *it* out?" He lingered on the word *it* as though choosing the word carefully.

"Huh?" Katarina said. "Oh that. No, probably not, but this should be good enough for you." She told them to attach the parameters of all the neural networks that had died of "old age" onto a superstructure connected to every "living" network—Katarina called it a "cloud of death." Over the lifetimes of eleven generations of neural networks, which was a couple of hours in the lab, energy output increased by a factor of a hundred. They were producing a ten-thousandth as much power as they were using—an important benchmark to NEG.

The three of them spent the next week analyzing how the energy output had changed during those eleven generations. They found a little bump in a graph of output energy as a function of beam energy. Ryan and Foster wrote it up as "Observation of a New Electron-Positron Resonance in the Presence of Heavy

Nuclei"—hardly an earthshaking discovery, but it was accepted for publication in the *Physical Review*, the first peer-reviewed academic publication from EWU.

Emmy sent Ryan an e-mail when the paper came out: "Congratulations on some nice work and a fine discovery."

Ryan replied immediately, "I miss you."

By the end of spring, after three months of peeing in cups, writing checks, visiting psychologists, and writing software in waiting rooms, Ryan had successfully disappeared into the system. Ms. Robins contacted him on the first of May to tell him that she had filed for joint custody. Ryan asked how she thought it would go. First, she praised his behavior over those months, but then she expressed doubt: "I find it extraordinary that your ex-wife has managed to have that restraining order renewed every ninety days. I trust that you have told me the whole story."

"I've told you everything."

"If there's anything you need to say, now is the time, because it will come out in court."

The court date was set for the middle of June.

In Petaluma, Kat took Emmy's advice as a recipe for life. She asserted control of her destiny and used the force of her intellect to command others. That the people she had thought of as friends now called her a stuck-up bitch reinforced her new self-image. Sure, she was the only one who didn't have a cell phone or a best friend or a ride to school when it rained, but that was just more evidence that she wrote her own rules.

After being arrested, she ignored the cliques, and as the months passed, she gained a reputation for being aloof and weird but artistic. Word got around that she was some kind of mathematical genius. The others only knew for sure that she painted murals wherever she could put a brush. The murals mixed mathematical symbols with fantastic images of dragons and wispy ghost-looking people. And clouds. Above every image she painted great thick clouds—some looked like thought bubbles, some like fog or dragon breath. If you looked closely, though hardly anyone ever did, you could see that the clouds were laden with shadowy images, small drawings of people, names, and diagrams.

One thing was certain: Kat was cool—really cool—not an idiot like the kids who tried to be cool or the kids who didn't bother to be cool. Kat was hella cool.

On the last day of school, she felt a surge of emotion, a sort of aggressive loneliness—for three months, she wouldn't have teachers to talk to, no one to bother her at all.

She went straight to Skate-n-Shred, skipping Ryan's call for the first time ever. A clique blocked the entrance. She strode toward the center door without pausing, and every kid stepped out of her way, dissipating like fog burned off by the sun. Kat glowed inside. Emmy had nailed it. This was the way to live.

She glanced back, pretending to examine an early piece of work and caught a boy checking her out. She started to look away—but no. No way. She turned to him, fixing him with a smile; he jerked aside and mumbled, "Sorry."

She watched him for a few minutes. His self-consciousness was obvious. He stood just so, holding his skate all poised to take off so that his bicep was tense. It was as ridiculous as it was cute. She waited until he looked back at her, then she held up her hand and motioned with her index finger for him to walk toward her.

He obeyed. "What's up?"

"I want to show you something," Kat said. "Stay right here and wait for me." She indicated an old couch just inside the theater. He shrugged and did what she said.

Someone from the clique called after him, "Dragon girl breathe on you?"

He looked back with a self-conscious smile. Kat pointed at him and mouthed the word *stay.*

She walked down to a pharmacy and bought some condoms. She took her time walking back, detoured along the river, watched a pair of ducks, and listened for a few minutes to a bunch of old men playing jazz. Ryan would call it "geezer jazz."

Leaning against the railing over the river, the geezer jazz behind her and the sun reflecting off the still water, she let the warmth course over her. A breeze started to pick up, and its scent reminded her of when she was little and her dad used to walk her along the river. She remembered the strain of holding her arm up to meet his hand. It felt good to not need him anymore, to not miss him, but in a way that she just hadn't quite figured out, it still didn't feel like he'd left. It was a whimsical thought, but somehow it felt as though he were still holding her hand.

When she got back to Skate-n-Shred, the boy was still on the couch. Two girls sat next to him, one on the armrest. As Kat approached, he looked up with a twinkle in his eye. She ignored the other girls and just stopped in front of him without speaking.

He said, "T'sup?"

The two girls made *humph* sounds and, as far as Kat could tell, disappeared. She offered her hand. He took it, and she led him outside and up the hill two blocks to the black-and-red house.

The next day, she felt like a superhero. Emmy was right. She could do anything she wanted. She put her laptop in her backpack, stuffed a blanket on top, went down to the boulevard, and stuck her thumb out. Within two minutes, a man driving an old Volvo pulled over. She got in the car and laughed at the stereotype: he was wearing a tie-dye shirt, had a gray beard, and immediately started lecturing her on hitchhiking because "the world's not safe like it was when I was your age." He wasn't even headed in that direction, but he drove her all the way out to Point Reyes anyway, just to keep her from hitching another ride.

Kat walked down the sandy trail to the fog-enshrouded beach and headed north to the rock outcropping and its tide pools, the place Ryan had taken her. She climbed up the rocks and sat in the same place as before. She took out her laptop, opened a file, and started typing. She took out a pad of paper, scribbled down some equations, and sketched some diagrams. When she got back to typing, she typed furiously. She was so engrossed that she didn't notice the wind pick up, didn't notice when her notes were torn from the pad and blown back up into the rocks. She didn't notice a pelican waddling across the rocks toward her either. He waddled a few steps closer every few minutes. Maybe he was attracted by the pages from her notebook rattling in the breeze, maybe by the cloud of deep concentration that surrounded her.

Kat stopped and scrolled through the document, nodding at each paragraph. Without looking away from the screen, she reached for the pad, for scratch paper to check the result. Her hand touched something wet and soft. The pelican was perched on her notebook. It flapped one wing and the other hung lifelessly.

"You!" Katarina said. The pelican didn't move. "I remember you, poor thing." She leaned toward the bird and the bird leaned toward her. It pecked at her keyboard as she examined his broken wing. It had healed in such a way that he could only move it laterally but not flap at all.

She nudged his beak away from the computer, half wondering if he'd typed a message to her. Of course it was gibberish, but she saved it in a different file anyway and labeled it "ramblings of a pelican." She pushed the pelican gently away from her pad and started scribbling. When she finished, she scrolled through her work again. Her eyes didn't blink. She looked at the calculations a third time and again scrolled through.

The pelican relaxed against her arm and pecked around her backpack. His big chin-wattle caught on the zipper. She untangled him and then rammed her things into the backpack and climbed down to the beach. The pelican took her place on the rock, perching in the warmth she left behind.

A mile up the road, she was picked up by a dairy tanker headed for a creamery in Petaluma.

Kat sat quietly in the apartment looking across the dark valley. It looked different than it had the day before. Everything looked different. Everything felt different, as though nothing mattered, nothing solid anyway, just interaction. There was no cool, no image, no bullshit; just time passing and energy changing form.

An hour later, she broke out of the reverie and, just to make sure, went through her work a fourth time. There was nothing left to question.

She started shoving clothes into a second knapsack.

No one answered the phone at Ryan's lab, and the other number, where he was staying with those crazy Christians, was answered by an overly cheery woman who said Ryan was out of town. Kat remembered that he and Foster had gone to a physics conference to present a paper. She called his cell phone, but it went straight to voice mail without ringing, so she left a message. At least no one had to endure Ryan's lame ringtone.

Ryan had to reschedule a counseling session so that he could accept an invitation to attend the Washington meeting of the American Physical Society where Foster would present their paper. It was the only blip that Ryan made on the deadbeat-dad system radar.

They flew into the nation's capital and stayed at the same hotel as their science establishment colleagues. Wisecracks about Creation Energy's power generator circulated among the tables of the conference banquet but didn't prevent anyone from attending their session. The auditorium aisles overflowed into the lobby. Ryan stood next to the stage as Foster gave the presentation.

Foster's nerves were on fire when the session chair introduced him. His confidence in the presentation was strong—the paper was accepted for publication; it had been through the wringer—but he felt like a spy. An honored spy, though. It was a prestigious forty-minute talk, long enough to show the details of the collider and control software. Foster went through the slides the same way he taught undergraduate physics at EWU. He concluded with the graph of the observed output energy as a function of the incident positron beam energy and left it on the overhead during the question-and-answer period.

In the pause before the first question, he looked at the crowd, and that feeling of espionage took hold. Right here, before the full faculty of the scientific establishment, he had unveiled his greatest weapon. Demonstrating a weapon before it was operational was a strategic move.

A group from Fermilab quizzed him on focusing magnets, and a group from CERN asked about software control—Ryan's neural network. When no more arms went up, Foster stared across the auditorium for a few more seconds, surveying the enemy. Things were falling into place—just as they always had.

Then a recent Nobel Prize winner in a fifth-row aisle seat raised his hand. A graduate student rushed over and held a microphone. Behind thick wire-rimmed glasses, the swarthy man spoke slowly with an Italian accent, ending most of his words with an *ah* sound. "These results you show are the most precise, agreeing with the QED theory since Harold Lamb calculated the hydrogen hyperfine structure—elegantly precise." He held his hand up, fingers together as though savoring a glass of wine. "*Bella*, you make the day beautiful, but, ah, I have the one question."

Foster felt like a general watching his opponent enter an ambush in the decisive battle of a great war.

The Nobel laureate paused, leaning back slightly. "You see, when I was young, I chose to become a theorist to know the thoughts of God. Later, I became an experimentalist to hear His voice." He spread both arms out as if to embrace the image projected on the screen. "Today, you show me this, these images of how the universe, ah, works—this graph, it is more beautiful than the ceiling of Sistine Chapel. The question I have, is this not enough?"

Foster turned to the graph behind him, trying to give the impression that he was pondering the question. In fact, he was praying. The strategy would stand or fall right here. He had to answer this question in a way that would guarantee his credibility as a legitimate God-fearing physicist. The graph proved that he had built a collider of unprecedented efficiency. If he could win this man's respect, the next time he presented this graph, in six months, a year, or even five years from now, when it showed the effect of spiritual energy flowing into the physical world, the scientific establishment would have to accept it. They would have to believe; they would have to surrender.

His prayer was answered immediately but in a way that he wouldn't understand for weeks.

He spoke clearly and in the language of physicists. "We've shown a new technique for calibration and control of a positron accelerator and precise agreement with quantum electrodynamics." He used a laser pointer to indicate the little bump in the graph, evidence for the short-lived state of "positronium" they had discovered. Every data point sat precisely on the theoretical prediction. "When I calculated the theory curve, it amazed me how an infinite number of Feynman diagrams would combine so perfectly—it was a mathematical ballet." He circled three data points with the laser pointer. "That the theory actually tells us to expect this tiny structure is a miracle. Do you agree? A miracle?" He stopped talking, turned away from the screen, and looked directly at the Nobel laureate.

The people who had headed for the exits filtered back into the room. Foster waited for them, and as he waited, the pieces started to come together. The words built up in his mind, and he concentrated on how he'd say them instead of what they meant.

"To answer your question, is it enough? It's more than enough for me. Is it enough for you? I have never felt closer to God than when I performed the calculations and plotted this data. Never. Think of it. A calculation, mathematics, something born wholly of free will, the collective free will of all of us." He set the laser pointer on the podium and stepped forward. "But I feel close to God every day." He focused on the Nobel laureate, "What about you? You made some of the original calculations. It's your will and mine"—he swept his arms to embrace the auditorium—"all of ours. What greater evidence could any of you ask for of God's existence? But still, most of you deny Him." He whispered the last word.

"I think that it is you. You deny." The Nobel laureate took the microphone in his hand and stood. "Ah, what was it that the, uh, how-you-say—the Bard, yes, the Bard, that Hamlet's father to his mother said? The physicist doth protest too much, methinks." He sat down.

Foster indicated the curve again with the laser's dot. "Are you impressed by our results?"

The laureate nodded vigorously. "That is point of *mine*." He held up his notepad. "Your experiment, it is first to show that Heisenberg's limit is also thermodynamic limit. Carnot and Heisenberg agree. In three lines of calculation I prove this."

Foster tried to withhold his triumphant smile. "You are impressed."

Still holding the notepad, the laureate shrugged. "It is shown. It is done."

Ryan's head was going in circles. After Foster's presentation, the Italian guy had handed him the three-line proof that their collider was running at the physical limit. He stared at it and couldn't wait to send it to Katarina. The Nobel Prize winner had proven that the collider couldn't operate any more efficiently? Couldn't possibly? Couldn't *in principle*?

During dinner, Foster sketched diagrams on napkins, brainstorming techniques to improve the neural network, certain that the next version of software would make the transition to free will. He wouldn't look at the proof.

Ryan knew from his research at the Cal engineering library and discussions with physicists after Foster's talk that their software was as close to attaining "strong artificial intelligence"—the Holy Grail of software—as any on Earth, but that was still a long way from violating the laws of thermodynamics.

⌒

Later that night back in his hotel room, Ryan noticed that he had voice mail from Katarina. He smiled at the sound of her voice.

"Hey Ryan, I went out to Point Reyes—I saw that pelican too. He actually typed on my keyboard. Ryan, I figured it out. I understand the soul, what it is, how it works, and why people never really die. It's fucking amazing—oops, sorry, didn't mean to say *fuck*." She laughed for a second and sounded like the kid he'd met on the porch that day three years ago. "Since this is way too complicated, too important, just too hella killer for the phone, and since you said I could come with you to Texas once school got out and lo and behold, it's finally out, I'm coming to see you. I don't know how long it will take to get there, a couple of days I guess. See you then."

What?

He replayed the message. No, she didn't say how she was getting there. Typical Katarina, she just didn't know any better. He called her back. The phone rang five times, and then Jane's airy voice came on the answering machine. He waited for the beep and then said, "Katarina, call me right now, this instant."

Ryan woke in the middle of the night with a vision of Katarina sitting on a bus trying to explain Feynman diagrams to someone's grandmother. He got up and paced around the hotel room for a few minutes, convinced himself that Katarina was a tough kid who would be okay, and then tried to get some sleep. The wake-up call came at six, but he was still awake. No denying it, guilt. Katarina was doing something stupid. Something that she wouldn't be doing if he'd kept a closer watch on her. He thought of that judge who'd told him that the world is dangerous for Katarina.

He called again before getting on the plane back to San Antonio—still no answer.

The plane ride was surreal. Foster spent the whole time filling page after page in his notebook, occasionally glancing out the window. When Ryan told him about Katarina's message, he said, "Perfect. Everything is perfect. Are you starting to see? God is showing us the way. Kat is bringing us the answer—perfect!" He trembled as though he would burst, looked out the window for a few seconds, and turned back to Ryan. "Don't worry about Kat. She will be fine. God is watching over her."

Foster's reaction just made Ryan more nervous. He couldn't stop tapping his foot. The old lady in the seat in front of him asked him three times to stop hitting her chair. She was polite the first time.

There were no new messages on his phone when the plane landed.

Rachel met Foster and Ryan at the door. Foster hugged her tight, carrying her halfway down the hall before setting her down and saying, "I have to go to the lab right away. Don't hold dinner."

Rachel's eyes squinted together. It looked strange, as though she was wrinkling her brow but it wasn't cooperating. She met Ryan in the kitchen. "My father called this morning. He said that you and Foster made a huge mistake going to Washington."

Ryan said, "Did Katarina call?"

"She called yesterday."

"Anything today?" Ryan looked at the answering machine—the light wasn't blinking. "What did she say?"

Rachel followed. "She just asked to talk to you. I told her you'd be back today. What's wrong?"

"Oh, nothing." He went to the fridge looking for a beer, but of course there weren't any. "Okay, not nothing, maybe nothing—we're going to have a visitor."

"She's coming here? I can't wait to meet her. She sounds like a real character."

Foster came back up the hall, his briefcase in both hands, passed the kitchen, and went out the front door.

Rachel said, "Ryan, what's going on? What happened?"

Still staring at the answering machine, Ryan said, "This Italian guy, a Nobel Prize–winning physicist in the audience, proved that everything we've done in the lab confirms what they already knew—but Foster doesn't seem to get it. The software works perfectly. I mean *perfectly*."

She looked up at him and spoke as though she'd rehearsed what she was going to say. "I talked to my father today." Foster's Porsche roared out of the driveway, punctuating her discomfort.

"Yeah? Why was it a mistake to go to Washington?"

"Ryan, listen to me." She cleared her throat. "I don't think you'll be able to keep your job."

"What?"

"Don't worry. My father said that with your work here, and the paper you and Foster wrote, that you can get a job anywhere—probably name your salary."

Ryan took his phone from his pocket and stared at it. "Katarina doesn't know what she's doing." Then, as though what Rachel said had finally registered, "Yeah, I'll be fine..."

Ryan's cell phone rang the next morning. He grabbed it on the first ring.

"You should see this place," Katarina said. "That lake is freakishly blue."

A great wave of relief broke over Ryan. "Katarina, where are you?"

"Lake Tahoe. Have you ever been here?"

"No. How did you get there?"

"I hitched."

"Are you crazy?" His relief washed back out to sea. "You hitchhiked across California?"

"It's okay, old man, truckers are hella cool, and yesterday I got from Sacramento to Tahoe with this family—they even took me out in their boat. The lake is beyond blue. I mean blue. Have you seen blue? You haven't even seen blue."

"Where did you sleep? How much money do you have?"

"Almost twenty-five bucks," she said. "Last night I snuck into this crazy mansion at Emerald Bay—the ranger-guy shit a brick when he found me, but then the dude cooked pancakes. I tried to explain the soul to him and—"

"Katarina, listen to me."

"Ryan, it's gonna blow you and Foster away."

"I want you to go to a bus station. I will buy you a ticket online—what city are you in?"

"I think I'm in Nevada."

Ryan sighed. "There should be an address on the pay phone."

"Um, South Lake Tahoe—what a stupid name for a town."

"Okay, give me the number of that pay phone and stay right there. I'll buy you a bus ticket and call you right back."

"I'm not taking a bus."

"Katarina, please."

"What? I'm seeing the world. Everyone is really nice. I haven't even had to buy food."

"I'll have Emmy pick you up. Just stay where you are. I'll call her right now."

Her voice switched to impatient. "Ryan, I'm coming to Hardale to work with you and Foster. I'll be there in a couple of days. I've got it figured out. Foster will be stoked. Later."

"Wait!"

She was quiet, but Ryan could hear background noise. He said, "I'll come and get you."

"That's stupid."

"Please don't hitchhike. Please."

"I'll call you every time I'm near a phone—will that work for you, Ryan McParanoid?"

"Katarina—"

"I'm hanging up now."

"Katarina, I love you."

"Yeah, I know." She hung up the phone.

Foster smiled into the flames of Jeb Shonders's scowl. "We're at the Heisenberg limit, almost there. Jeb, it was perfect. When I bring the decisive results, they will have to accept them."

Schonders leaned back in his chair, looking down his nose at Foster. "Why did you go into their den? What were you thinking?" He rolled up his sleeves one at a time. "You've fed the beast, and National Engineering isn't happy."

"That's ridiculous," Foster said. "It couldn't have gone more perfectly. They accepted, even praised our results. I have credibility on their turf. When I bring proof, they will have to accept it."

Schonders spoke in a quiet guttural tone accompanied by a spray of spittle. "You can't have it both ways. You can't be part of the scientific establishment and part of God's army at the same time." He leaned forward and his elbows hit the desk.

"Jeb, listen to me. We have their flank."

Jeb picked up the hammer-sized gold cross and tapped it in his palm. "No. We don't *flank* our enemy. They got nothin' we want or need. We fight on the field of American culture. We're better off with the scientific elite denouncing us. The people in those churches you visit, them is who you need to convince. You're done."

"Take it easy, cowboy." Foster rose from his chair, smiling. "Let me do my job. Everything is coming together. God is bringing the answer—if you needed another reason to believe the wonder of His way—the answer is coming on the wings of a fourteen-year-old girl." He lowered himself back into the chair, arms outstretched. "The technology is going to work, and when it does, I will deliver the scientific establishment."

"You are a fool." Jeb pointed the cross at Foster. "Political advantage is more important than technology. Any technology." He let the cross drop. "You stupid fool, National Engineering has demanded complete control of this project. You're out. They've already replaced you."

Foster stepped around the desk and put a firm hand on Jeb's shoulder. "I know about National Engineering, Jeb. I know that they don't believe. They are just another cynical element of the establishment." He tightened his grip. "We can do this without them."

Schonders lifted Foster's hand from his shoulder, clamped down on his wrist, and, shaking with rage, said, "You will no longer be allowed in the collider lab."

Foster stepped back. "What?" A million conflicting thoughts raced through his mind: the smug look on the Nobel laureate's face; Ryan reporting that Katarina was en route with the answer; that the patent officer had never examined energy or software patents before granting theirs; that Rachel had been engaged to the patent officer; that his angel had lied to him; and, more than anything, that Jeb was banning him from his laboratory, his life's work, his war.

In that instant, he wanted nothing more than to accept defeat, to die on the battlefield. But before Jeb looked up, just as fast as the doubts had swept in, a greater force pushed them away. As though carried in the warmth of his blood, with each pulse of his heart, faith cleansed his mind. He didn't need hardware; he didn't need a lab for this. He'd already accomplished that part of the project. He would write a complete simulation of the collider, including every cable, magnet, vacuum pump, the positron source, and electron-rich target, modeled with perfect accuracy. Then he could test different neural networks, and when he discovered the soul, he would convince them to install it. It was a huge project, perfect for Foster to bury his frustration.

Jeb looked up with loathing in his eyes, but Foster was calm and prepared to continue along this carefully paved path. He patted Jeb's shoulder and cocked his head at that comfortable angle and said, "Do what you feel you need to do. I will continue His work."

Jeb released Foster's wrist and said, "Get out of my office."

Katarina didn't call. Ryan worried.

After four days, he called Dodge. Dodge told him not to worry, at least not yet. He loosed that mirthless laughter and said, "I'll tell you when to start worrying."

On the eighth day, Ryan printed a picture of Katarina and made copies. He sent them to police departments along the route from Lake Tahoe to San Antonio. Then he called the judge in Santa Rosa who had presided over her case. She gave him references to runaway support groups and then leveled with him: "All you can do is wait and pray that she is safe. Lots of kids run away. At least Katarina has a destination. If she's not there soon, you'll have to start looking for her." He could hear the unspoken accusation in her voice.

He kept his cell phone battery charged, but it didn't ring.

Early on the tenth morning, Foster came home after working all night. His face was drawn, his hair a mess, and he had the caffeine shakes. "Where is Katarina? I need her."

Ryan's worry and frustration started to boil.

Rachel stepped between them and lit into Foster. "You need Katarina? Your best friend is fixin' to go crazy with worry, and you have the nerve to demand this child work for you?" Her hands rose in fists. "You're out all night and come home demanding—"

Ryan grabbed Foster's car keys from his hand, ran out the door, jumped in the car, and headed for San Antonio.

At Texas State Trooper headquarters, a woman in blue took a hundred copies of Katarina's picture and promised to distribute them to every trooper on the force. Then Ryan drove to Dallas, just in case, and repeated the exercise all the way up I-35. On the way back, he posted the picture at every gas station between Dallas and Hardale.

He was at one of these gas stations when his cell phone rang. The caller ID said it was Emmy. He answered with "hello" and then wedged the phone between his neck and shoulder so he'd have both hands free to tape a picture to the gas station window.

Emmy said, "I'm sorry I missed the American Physical Society meeting this year. It would have been nice to see you. And speaking of the APS, I thought you should know that a letter I wrote under their masthead is being submitted to the Department of Defense tomorrow. I'm concerned that it might affect your job, Ryan. We've nominated an independent panel to review NEG's contracts."

After pressing down the tape, Ryan said, "Emmy, Katarina's gone. She left Petaluma two weeks ago, hitchhiked. She said she's coming here, but no one's seen her."

"Why didn't you call?" Emmy said, "I'll go to Petaluma right now—what can I do?"

"I'm going to search for her. She called me from Lake Tahoe—that's the last anyone's heard of her. I'll head up to I-80 and try that route, and if I don't find her, I'll try another route."

"Ryan, settle down. Take a deep breath. Okay? Tell me exactly what Katarina said."

He told her about the phone message and described his conversation with her, concluding with, "She just kept saying how blue the lake was. I keep telling myself that she's streetwise and out there adventuring, but she had only twenty-five dollars and—two weeks—why hasn't she called?"

"Is Dodge looking for her?"

"He looked around town but…Emmy, your brother is not helpful."

"My brother has connections—I'll call you right back."

Emmy hung up and called Dodge. He answered on the third ring. Emmy said, "Where's Katarina?"

He answered with that mirthless wet chuckle. "Emmy, I'm working on it. If Kat shows up in any city in the US, I'll know within twenty-four hours. Look, she's probably standing on a corner in Winslow, Arizona, with her thumb out trying to get to Ryan. I'll find her."

But then he sighed. It was a sound that Emmy had never heard him make before.

"Dodge, do everything you can."

"What's that supposed to mean?"

"Just that, well, I know that you got arrested once and that you went to jail, and I know that you've done business with some dubious people and, well…"

"Emmy, I love that kid. I'll do everything I can to find her."

She'd never heard Dodge use that word before in any context. "Do you think she's okay?"

"It's been two weeks. She should have been there ten days ago. Fifteen-year-old girls standing on the highway don't have to wait for rides. No, I don't think she's okay."

Emmy's breath got caught in her throat. She said, "She has to be okay," and hung up before Dodge could scare her any more than he already had.

She called Ryan back. He answered on the first ring.

"Hi, Ryan. Are you okay?"

"I've lost Katarina. No, I'm not all right. I should have been there, but I was here. This shouldn't have happened. Where is she? All I can do is drive across the country and look for her. Oh God, Emmy, what else can I do?"

"Don't give up, Ryan. She's out there and she needs you."

"You're right. Damn. I just need to keep moving. Thanks for calling. I'm sorry I fucked up our relationship—it's an acquired skill."

"Okay," she said. "I'm canceling my trip to CERN. I'll head up to Petaluma in a few minutes. Stay in touch with Dodge. He's got more resources than either of us can imagine."

A week after the physics conference, Steven Jones, the engineer Smythe had introduced to Foster at the men-in-black meeting from National Engineering's Alternative Energy Research Group, moved into Foster's former lab. He brought a staff of two dozen and installed a security system. Within two weeks of their arrival, NEG coauthored a press release with Creation Energy claiming a dramatic increase in energy production that violated the laws of thermodynamics. Since the details were now classified—as was everything that happened in the lab—there was no way for anyone to challenge the claim.

Foster knew NEG was lying, but that didn't comfort him. Without the respect of his colleagues and—he had to face it—the self-esteem generated by leading a large well-funded team of technicians, he found himself reevaluating everything: the project, the patents, every step along the path of coincidental steppingstones that had led him here. There were gaps. He could no longer ignore the irregularity of the patent officer. God wouldn't deceive him, but his own lack of humility might. Had his father-in-law somehow rigged the patent process? And what if he had?

He looked all the way back to that day he'd been laid off. The same day that Ryan's life had started to unravel, Foster's had come together. When he got home that day, Rachel had been waiting for him, barefoot in a light cotton dress, on a bench in their front yard. The recollection warmed him. They'd been so young and so close.

Unemployed for the first time in his life, with a big new mortgage and little hope for a new job, she greeted him with a smile so affectionate and optimistic, so warm that his worries went from solid to fluid to mist. When he sat next to her and she handed him a piece of junk mail that had arrived that day—a generic envelope inviting him to apply to the graduate program of Evangelical Word University—Foster had never been more certain that she was the angel come from heaven to guide him.

But as he reevaluated that path, he wondered. Had it been junk mail? Had her father, Blair Keene, primary investor in EWU, made certain that she got that letter on that day?

The vision through the fog of hubris wasn't pretty.

It was June 15, the day Ryan had been pursuing for almost three years. Today, Ryan would appear in court, and his attorney would argue that Ryan McNear was a pillar of society, capable not just of paying his debts and building wealth, but of being a stellar role model for his son. She would question the grounds that had been used to renew the restraining order that had kept him from his son for the last four and a half years and then, finally, order that joint custody be resumed.

If things went well today, Ryan would have his old life back—what was left of it, anyway.

He was up well before sunrise—not just because worrying about Katarina kept him from sleeping but because he had a long drive from Hardale to the Fort Worth courthouse.

He dragged an iron across his shirt and then put it on in front of a mirror. As he knotted his tie, he noticed the puffy red skin below his eyes. The lines in his forehead looked like crevices. The thought flashed through his mind that the judge might take one look and think he was doing meth again.

The four-hour drive gave him time to think. His mind wasn't quiet. The plans he'd made for his thirty days with Sean kept being shoved aside by ideas of where and how to look for Katarina. He left his cell phone in his lap, willing it to ring. *Please Katarina, please call before I go into court. Please.*

He parked on Houston Street a block from court, an unprecedented rock-star parking space. He looked back at the car and laughed. What would Linda think if she saw him get into Foster's red Porsche?

His laughter was enough. He found the focus. He couldn't help Katarina right now. One kid at a time.

Ryan pasted a smile on his face. It felt genuine enough. His attorney waited for him on the sidewalk outside the courthouse. Before she had a chance to comment on his appearance, he told her that he'd been working late all week. She went through the details of how she expected the case to proceed.

Walking in the courtroom, Ryan saw Linda in the front row. She had her back to him and was looking down. Her husband, that old bastard Howard, sat next to her with his arm around her—with his gray hair and withered skin, he looked about a hundred.

Ryan started across the courtroom but stopped and looked around as though he were looking through someone else's eyes. Words came to him, a phrase he'd heard his father say: "Stand up straight, smile, and go to hell with some poise." He strode to the front row and sat next to Ms. Robins, across the aisle from Linda.

Linda looked older too. He recognized her nervous smile and could tell that she was trying not to look at him. When she finally glanced over, he furrowed his brow and nodded to her—the look he'd always used to let her know that everything was okay. And she reacted as she always had. She tightened her lips nervously but settled down.

Ryan's reaction to Linda had always been the same. It had happened the day they met, every night when he had come home from work, even the last time they'd been here, when Sean told the court that Tammi had blown meth smoke in his face. This time, though, instead of that wonderful but scary warm feeling filling his chest, he felt empty. It was a strange feeling. Somehow Linda was just a woman that he used to know. That was all—none of that warmth tinged with panicked exultation and fleeting doubt that he used to call love. She was just a rather sad looking lady with beautiful curls framing a lovely, if unsettled, face.

This was about his kids, Katarina and Sean. He had to get them back, one kid at a time.

The bailiff entered the court and gave Ryan a curt nod of recognition—it was Holcomb. The judge followed, a man about the same age as Ryan. Ms. Robins presented evidence of Ryan's employment, copies of the checks he'd sent to Linda—Linda's attorney objected, saying that Linda had thought they were gifts for their son. The judge waved it off.

Ryan's attention wandered to Katarina. His focus returned when Ms. Robins argued that the restraining order that prevented contact with Sean should be repealed. It was the weak link. The judge asked Ryan to stand and then questioned him about his living conditions and career. He asked three questions about drug use: when he had first used illegal drugs, when he had last used them, and why he thought he'd never use them again. Ryan answered as Ms. Robins had instructed, as concisely as possible.

The judge looked Ryan up and down, then spoke to Linda. "This court has determined that it is important for a child to have contact with his father."

Linda's attorney stood and said, "If it please the court, we withdraw request to renew said order of restraint but respectfully request that sole custody with the mother and supervised visits with the father be maintained until the father demonstrates drug-free behavior for a period of two years."

Ms. Robins stood, and as the judge's gaze turned to her, she said, "There is no evidence to contradict the father's stated behavior with regard to drug use."

As the attorneys argued the case, Howard whispered to Linda across the aisle from Ryan. She turned toward him, and as she turned, she paused on Ryan for an instant. She whispered back to Howard, and her eyes got large. Howard rubbed her shoulder and whispered one more line, this one just loud enough for Ryan to hear, "…it's the right thing."

Linda turned back to face the court and reached up to her attorney. The attorney leaned down, and Linda whispered to her. The attorney then said, "The mother wishes the court to grant the father's requests."

The judge called the clerk forward and signed a form.

That was it.

A few loud ink stamps, a couple of signatures, and Ryan's life transformed—but it didn't feel like it. With this problem solved, his mind started back to work on finding Katarina, but Ms. Robins stopped it. Ryan still had to meet with Linda to arrange custody of Sean. The two attorneys arranged for Ryan and Linda to meet at a nearby restaurant.

Ryan sat between the two attorneys, across from Linda and her husband. There was an empty chair across the table next to Linda. He didn't recall seeing her with so much makeup before—hazards of age, he figured. Her husband pulled her close to him protectively. Ryan understood what he was doing. Linda was an intelligent woman with a strong moral compass who was a loving mother, but she was also delicate under pressure.

Ryan took a long drink of iced tea and then described his plans to reunite with Sean. First, a weeklong trip to visit the family in Massachusetts: a week at Grandma's house with Sean's cousins—the full benefits of a Catholic family. Ryan didn't mention that it would be his first visit back too. Then, three weeks in California, where they would take surfing lessons—as he said it, he could picture Katarina zooming down the tube of a wave the same way she used to ride her skate down the hill from Nutter House.

Linda said that taking Sean away like that, all at once, might not be best for him. Instead, she recommended that Ryan attend Sean's sixteenth birthday, less than a month away.

Linda, her husband, and both attorneys waited for him to respond, obviously thinking it a generous invitation on Linda's part.

What if Katarina hadn't shown up yet? Ryan stuttered but accepted the invitation.

Linda's attorney asked how visitation would be scheduled when Sean was back in school. Ryan had custody every other weekend. He would alternate those weekends between flying Sean to California and flying himself to Texas. He'd keep an apartment not too far from the house where Linda, Sean, and Sean's stepfather lived. As he described it, he realized that it was a perfectly realizable scenario. He wouldn't be poor anymore. He was a published expert in artificial intelligence and could now work on the books. He could even start his own company.

Linda stood and Ryan started to follow suit, thinking the meeting was over. Ms. Robins pulled Ryan back into his seat. Linda stepped aside and spoke into her cell phone, then came back to the table.

Ryan looked at Ms. Robins, and she rested her hand on his. He looked at the others. Linda wouldn't look back, but her husband said, "Do right by your boy."

"Howard, I will," Ryan said, and then it hit him. "Howard—Ward, it was you, wasn't it? You've been sending me e-mails about Sean all this time."

Howard nodded. Linda looked confused.

"Thank you," Ryan said. "Thank you so much. That was such a decent thing to do. I don't know how I would've—"

Then something in his peripheral vision distracted him, someone walking toward them. He looked up.

It was like looking in a mirror, a mirror that went back in time.

Sean lumbered up to the table the same way that Ryan had twenty minutes before. His hair was thicker than Ryan's, wavy instead of coarse and bushy around his neck. He wore a rope necklace, faded jeans, and a black T-shirt advertising Trivium, one of the bands Katarina watched on MTV. His chin, his jaw, his nose—all except for the big brown eyes and wavy hair he got from his mom—was Ryan at that age.

Ryan tried to stand up, but forgot to push his chair out and bumped the table. Then he started laughing.

Sean sat in the chair next to his mother. He started laughing too.

Ryan said, "How's it goin' buddy?"

Sean said, "Oh, you know, not much."

They stared at each other and laughed a couple of times.

Ryan finally said, "You want to take surfing lessons with me?"

"Sure, whatever."

Ryan pushed out the chair, walked around the table, and pulled his son out of his seat. He measured himself against Sean. They were exactly the same height. Ryan said, "I've missed you, son."

Sean said, "Me too, Dad."

Ryan wrapped his arms around his son and held him tight. Tears flowed around the smile etched onto his face and he said, "Sorry, Sean, I'm kinda blown away, is all. I didn't know you'd be here."

Ryan saw that Sean was fighting back tears. "I didn't know you'd be here either."

"My God, you look good," Ryan said. "I heard you're playing varsity tailback."

"Well, junior varsity," Sean said. "That reminds me. Dad, do you know where my football is? The one I scored my first touchdown with?"

Ryan got back to Foster and Rachel's minimansion late. On the ride back, he'd felt fragmented. The urgent need to find Katarina made it impossible to think about reuniting with Sean. And how could he go to Sean's birthday party if he was on the road searching for Katarina? But he'd promised.

He pulled himself together at the doorway and stepped in. The floor of the entry was littered with shards of glass that had once been a standing vase. Foster and Rachel were arguing in the study down the hall. One or both were crying. Ryan shut the door behind him firmly enough so that his hosts could hear it. He hoped they'd quiet down, but it had the opposite effect.

Rachel emerged from the study yelling at Foster. "I'm not an angel, I'm your wife!"

From inside the study, Foster screamed at her. "You lied to me! The patent officer. You were engaged to the patent officer—Ryan's lawyer told us, and your father didn't deny it." Glass broke, and Rachel lurched down the hall toward Ryan, who was still in the entryway. Foster yelled, "How could you have kept that from me?"

"It was a long time ago. A mistake. It didn't matter to *us*."

"No," Foster said, no longer screaming. "No. You're no angel. You're a whore."

"Why can't you see?" Rachel covered her face with her hands, sobbing. "I'm not an angel. I never wanted to be an angel. I'm just the woman who loves you."

Ryan walked up the stairs toward the guest room. Before he made it to the top, his phone rang.

It was Dodge: "Just got a report of a girl who might be Kat at a truck stop outside of Vegas—she should have gotten farther than that by now. Plus, I had a report this morning of a girl in Amarillo that could be her."

"Why hasn't she called?"

"Not sure Kat would even think of calling. She's never had to call anyone to tell them she'd be late—nothing like that." Dodge whistled through his teeth. "Listen, McNear, handing out posters is doing nothing. The police aren't going to help."

The ruckus downstairs culminated in a crash. Ryan said, "I'll be in Amarillo in the morning—can you connect me with whoever thinks they saw her?"

"Keep your phone charged. I'll hook you up with my contacts along the way—take I-40."

"You think I'll find her?"

Dodge didn't answer.

Ryan slumped down at the top of the stairs. "What do you think happened?"

"No point in speculating."

It took Ryan five minutes to pack. He left most of his notebooks on the bed and headed downstairs—the keys to Foster's Porsche still in his pocket.

Foster was sitting at the bottom of the stairs. He looked up at Ryan. His eyes were bloodshot, but his hands were steady. Ryan set down his suitcase and leaned on the banister. "Foster, I have to find Katarina."

"Yeah, I know." Foster nodded slowly. "We have to find her; she's our angel." He stood up. "Ryan, I thought you deserved what happened to you after my bachelor party. I thought God was punishing you. I just want to apologize. I've made a lot of mistakes along this path—we've gotten a lot right too, but we're not finished."

"Foster, I don't care about that. I'm leaving and I'm taking your car."

"We'll find Katarina." He cocked his head. "Things do happen for a reason. Let's go."

It was a ten-hour drive from Hardale to Amarillo. Foster slept most of the way. When he woke, it startled Ryan.

"You have any idea how much money Rachel spent on Botox? It's a wonder she could smile. And why would an angel need artificial breasts?" He fell asleep when Ryan pulled onto Highway 87. Most of the towns along the way had one stoplight, one Walmart, one high school, five churches, and a bar.

The rhythm of the road gave Ryan some perspective. Seeing Sean had given him the strength he needed to think straight and hardened his resolve to search wherever and for as long as it took to find Katarina.

He tried to remember how it had felt when his own father died—the anger and loneliness. Katarina, though, had been all alone until Ryan found Nutter House that day. He remembered the sassy little kid and her skateboard—she wouldn't even tell him her name. The thought brought a smile, and then he thought of Katarina's dad.

For him, it wasn't the dying that was so bad, it was the missing out on watching his little girl grow up—that's what cancer had stolen from him.

In a quiet, almost tender voice, Foster said, “Don’t worry, we’ll find her.”

“Oh, hey, sorry. I didn’t know you were awake. I guess I’m just kinda freakin’ out.” Ryan pasted a smile on his face. “We should make Amarillo in about an hour.”

Ryan handed Foster his cell phone and told him to call Dodge. Dodge told them where the truck stop was and that a small brown-haired girl with weird clothes and a black backpack was in the restaurant.

Dodge’s contact drove a purple-and-black Peterbilt that was parked in a row of other huge shiny trucks outside a diner at the center of a gargantuan parking lot. Ryan left Foster and the Porsche in a parking space painted to fit an eighteen-wheeler.

The guy was wearing a denim jacket and a Dodgers baseball cap. Ryan introduced himself, and the man pulled a toothpick out of his mouth. “Girl matchin’ the description has been here for two days. She just sat at a booth inside.”

Ryan lunged for the door. The man caught Ryan’s shoulder. “Slow down. Sometimes these girls change while they’re on the road. If this is the kid you’re lookin’ for, you’re likely to be disappointed.”

He led Ryan into the diner and then cocked his head toward a booth in the corner. Two large men with a small girl between them and another man across the table leaned forward as though whispering. Her hair was the right color and her shoulders were the right size. She was wearing a white T-shirt with a strange design: Celtic knots that looked drawn in with a marking pen. He stepped up to the table. “Katarina?”

The girl looked up—no older than sixteen, with freckles and pimples visible under a thick layer of makeup. Ryan’s heart collapsed as fast as it had soared.

Ryan and Foster left a trail of posters at gas stations, diners, and at all the cheap hotels along I-40, then up I-15, through Las

Vegas, to I-80. Every day, Dodge reported a new possibility and they checked it out. Ryan clung to the image of Sean walking up to that table. The rush of emotion had been so huge, but one thing scared the shit out of him: had he traded one kid for the other?

The body isn't designed to maintain high levels of adrenaline for weeks. Each day the panic diminished, and Ryan felt the sands of resignation burying him. His thoughts started to drift from Katarina to Sean. He fought it.

One kid at a time.

At a truck stop outside Salt Lake City, Ryan was sure that he'd see Katarina trudging around a corner or maybe skateboarding along a sidewalk. But four days later, in an all-too-similar truck stop near Reno, he dragged his feet across the parking lot, asking the same old questions, but there was no sign of Katarina.

They stopped at Lake Tahoe—and yeah, it sure was blue. Ryan walked the streets for an hour. They went to Emerald Bay and talked to the ranger who cared for the old mansion. He showed them where Katarina had slept and, shaking his head, described how he had tried to talk her into going home.

They spent the next day stopping at gas stations along Highway 50 and I-80, putting up posters and asking people if they'd seen her. Having made no progress and being so close to the source, Ryan decided to head back to Petaluma to see if he could find any indication of what Katarina might have planned.

It was afternoon when Foster parked the Porsche behind Ryan's Probe along the curb next to Nutter House. Emmy came out to greet them. Her hair was dark brown speckled with gray strands. Ryan put his arms around her and held her tight. She buried her face in his chest. "Why would Katarina do this?"

Dodge was standing in the doorway looking severe. "None of her teachers know anything, and the cops are useless." He turned back inside.

Ryan followed. The screen door slammed into his back. It felt good. It felt alive. "What about Marti? And Alex? What about Broken Skeg?"

"None of them know anything," Dodge said. "She cut all of them off after she got busted—just Kat and her paints and weird clothes." Dodge led Ryan into his office and handed him a file.

Ryan sat in the chair across Dodge's desk. The revolver was sitting on the gavel pad. For once, he didn't fidget. He opened the folder. Each page was titled with someone's name, contact information, and the last time that person had seen a girl resembling Katarina.

Emmy and Foster stepped in and stood behind him.

Ryan sighed. "Where's Jane?"

Dodge said, "Probably camping out at the cemetery."

"I've been studying Kat's murals," Emmy said. "In the last few months, her paintings have become totally intense. They're almost like scratch paper. She sorted out her thoughts in paintings the same way she scratched out diagrams and set up equations."

Ryan stood, somewhat reinvigorated—touring truck stops, diners, and highway rest areas had come to feel as though he was just going through the motions. He felt closer to Katarina now.

Ryan and Emmy went upstairs, while Foster stayed with Dodge.

A mural that Ryan had never seen stretched across Katarina's bedroom walls, around the corners and onto the ceiling. A multicolored cloud formed of thousands of paint smudges, but with puffy curving lines defining the edges covered most of the ceiling. A landscape scene surrounding the window precisely completed the view outside. Ryan stood over a bright red dot in the center of the floor. He stared outside and crouched down. "She completed the image perfectly. The mountains in the painting match the view outside from this height. I can even tell how tall she is." He stood up straight and then crouched down again. "Where is she?"

Emmy put her hand on his lower back and pulled him toward her. "Listen to me."

He kept looking out the window.

"If you want to help Kat, you need to concentrate. You know her better than anyone, and that knowledge is our best chance of finding her."

On the wall that Katarina's apartment shared with Ryan's, the mural included a cartoon whiteboard, probably in the spot where theirs hung on the other side of the wall. The whiteboard was covered with equations and Feynman diagrams. A man-sized bird stood in front of it holding a marker. It had a huge beak and was painted white with a few pink dots and a red bristle on its head. The bristle made it resemble a rooster, but Ryan recognized it immediately as a pelican.

Emmy said, "It's you."

"I never pictured myself as a pelican before."

A big raindrop shape trickled down the wall from the cloud on the ceiling, poised over the pelican-Ryan's head. It encompassed a slew of little smudges, just like the cloud. Emmy stood on the bed for a closer look. "They're names. Each smudge is someone's name. They're dim and most are illegible, but your sisters' names are here. And look, she circled my name in a heart."

"She mentioned something about this on the phone," Ryan said. "I didn't really understand. We were discussing neural nets and free will. She talked a lot about how people get character—the ingredients that make people unique. She said that neural nets exchange pieces of themselves through their affection. She liked the word *affection*."

Ryan sat on the bed and stared across the room at Katarina's original mural, the one she'd been working on when he moved in. It was a collage of self-portraits and little sketches of her friends. He walked over and looked at them up close.

There was a portrait of her father holding her hand. He was penciled in with wispy lines, more like a shadow than a person. Photo-size sketches of Katarina followed in a row. She got taller and her hair grew longer in each, and Ryan could see how her clothes had evolved. In the early ones, she was skating.

The last two differed from the rest. They were nearly identical, like two adjacent frames in a reel of film. In the other sketches, except for the one where she was holding her dad's hand, she faced straight out of the wall, but not in the last two. In the second-to-last, she was looking toward the last one as though she were looking into the future, and in the last, she looked up at the ceiling to the cloud made of all the different-colored names.

Emmy started pulling things out from under the bed: crumpled papers, dirty clothes, some crusty dishes, books, and a couple of binders.

The sound of Emmy uncrumpling sheets of paper brought Ryan back to reality. He coughed and focused on the corners of the room. He went through Katarina's desk drawers, looking for her QED notebook. He couldn't imagine her leaving it behind. There were other notebooks and sketchpads and, at the back of her top drawer, in a little jewelry box, was a stack of notes that her father had written to her while he was in the hospital. They said simple things. Things that fathers say to their little girls about times they shared—one day they found a bunch of peacock feathers at a park, and he asked her to please not forget that day because it was the best day of his life. One said, "When you need me, look inside. You'll see me looking back. I promise."

Ryan's eyes welled up, and in the rush of emotion, he got confused and read the note again. The words, the dragons, the pelican, the names in the cloud—a sense of Katarina's presence rushed in like a wave unfurling on a beach—he didn't so much read the words as hear them, hear them in Katarina's voice. "When you need me, look inside. You'll see me looking back. I promise." Ryan pushed the thought away.

He shook his head to clear it out, looked out the window, and said, "When you can't find something, where do you look?"

Emmy replied, "Where you last saw it."

"I'll be back in an hour or two."

The Probe's engine turned over a couple of hundred times before it finally started. The Porsche was right behind him—he had its keys in his pocket—but he decided to take the car that Katarina would recognize.

The roads curved, and the Probe's suspension complained. He paused at the summit, the ocean on the horizon to one side and the valley on the other—"This is the world. Live in it." He continued along the road and parked in that same spot at McClure Beach. He walked along the sandy path. Ice plant, lupines, and daisies were blooming now. It had been seven months since the two of them had walked down this path together.

Along the beach, he watched seagulls arguing over decaying crabs. A V-shaped flock of pelicans skimmed over the water, and he ran alongside until he reached the rocks and tide pools. He climbed up to the boulder where he and Katarina had sat together. The waves were big, crashing against the rocks. In her phone message, Katarina had told him that she'd been here, that this was where she "figured it out." He smiled at the recollection of her saying "It's fucking amazing" and then apologizing for saying *fuck*.

He had to focus. There had to be a clue.

Guided by the self-portraits on her wall, he rebuilt as many memories of her as he could. Something on a rock outcropping above the waves moved, waking him from concentration. A pelican waddled up the rocks, a fat pelican with one wing drooping at its side. It pecked among the tide pools and then tossed its beak up, swallowing whatever gunk it had found. Katarina had mentioned the pelican too.

He forced himself to relax. The fixation that she was dead was irrational. He had to muster the strength to keep from surrendering to it. Wasn't that the mistake he'd made all those years ago in the face of methamphetamine? Surrendering to the pain instead of fighting?

Something cold, sharp, and prickly poked his hand. His arm was resting on a boulder where he'd been tapping his fingers, but now the pelican was standing on the back of that hand, its webbed feet digging into his skin. The pelican stared back. Ryan leaned forward and faced the bird. Its breath smelled fishy, like fresh fish. It reminded Ryan of the sushi on his first date with Emmy.

The distraction was good. It helped him dispel the ghosts and ask the fundamental question: where the hell is that kid?

The pelican poked its beak into a crevice between two rocks and struggled. It had found a crab, but the gap was too small for it to pull the crab out. Something else was stuck in the crevice, a sheet of graph paper. Ryan pulled on the pelican until it let go of the crab. It complained with the sound of a duck imitating a seagull.

Ryan worked the sheet of paper out of the rock. It was wet, making it difficult to decipher, but he discovered several other sheets of paper in higher cracks that were shielded from the ocean spray. No question, they were Katarina's—a flowchart of the last neural net that she'd described to him. But there was some doodling too, like that cloud on the ceiling in her room with the big raindrop over the pelican-Ryan's head. This one was a diagram of a multiple feedback neural net; the feedback loops all leaked down from other neural networks in the cloud.

Ryan couldn't help but think of the drawings of helicopters that da Vinci had made—it was Katarina's all right, the mathematician with the heart of an artist.

Dodge leaned back in his chair with two files open on the desk in front of him. In one were notes from Dodge's contacts about teenage girls who had been seen between Petaluma and Houston, a separate sheet for every girl. The other contained details of girls recently reported missing.

Foster said, "You've located half a dozen runaways."

Dodge replied, "Maybe, maybe not."

"Have you connected them with their parents?"

"Don't really give a fuck, Reed. I'm looking for Kat."

It was easy to match sightings and reports. Foster reached across and pulled the phone over. When it was halfway across the desk, it rang, startling him. Dodge reached across and jerked it away.

Dodge answered with, "What have you got?" He took a legal pad and flipped to a blank page.

At the other end, the voice said, "What will you give me for it?"

Dodge said, "Ah-ha, would this be slippery Jeff Spilling?"

"I found the kid."

"Put her on."

"Can't exactly do that, Nutter. First I need some recompense."

"Where is she?"

"Kimball Junction, just outside Salt Lake City."

Dodge grabbed the stack of paper from Foster and flipped through it. "I had two reports from I-80; neither of them panned out."

"Well, she's here and you know what I need."

"If you can deliver the kid, you can forget your warrants in Michigan."

"You mean LA?"

"Whatever." Dodge drew a little empty square in the margin of the blank sheet and wrote *clear Spilling in LA*. "Put her on."

"Like I said, I can't exactly put her on, but I'm pretty sure this is the kid you're after. Weird clothes—skirt's all marked up with designs, suede boots like Boy George wore in the eighties. She had a laptop and a couple of notebooks. Lots of diagrams."

Dodge could hear him flip through pages. "You have her stuff but not her?"

"Nutter, I'm at the morgue. The kid's dead, thrown from the back of a truck. Drunk driver plowed into a pickup on I-80 almost a week ago. She was in back. Dude driving the truck said she was hitching—picked her up in Vegas, said her name was Kate."

"Hang on." Dodge cupped a hand over the mouthpiece and spoke to Foster. "Go get my sister."

Foster did what he was told. Dodge waited until Emmy came in. "Guy on the phone thinks he has Kat's notebook." Then, into the phone, "I'm putting on someone who will know if it's Kat's book or not." Dodge handed the phone to Emmy.

Emmy asked Spilling to describe the diagrams and drawings. Her voice got louder as she grew frustrated that the man didn't understand her questions. Eventually, she handed the phone back to Dodge. "Okay, those are Kat's notes. Where is she?"

Dodge spoke into the phone. "What's next?"

"The cops need the next of kin to ID the body."

"Have you seen her?"

"Just pictures—she's kind of mangled, but it's a match. So I'm clean in LA?"

"Oh." Dodge hung his head. "Yeah, come Friday no one will want you in LA either." He hung up the phone and stared at a space on the desk between Foster and Emmy. "She died in a car accident. The cops need Jane to ID her."

Foster took a deep breath.

Emmy turned away. She made a sharp agonized sound and covered her face with her hands.

Dodge wrote three addresses on a pad along with directions to the cemetery, tore off the sheet, and handed it to Emmy. "Jane'll be at one of these places. If her bike isn't there, she isn't either. When you find her, tell her we heard something. Don't tell her that her kid is dead—I will handle that."

Emmy took the sheet and walked out.

Dodge tapped on the desk, staring at the revolver.

Foster sighed and looked up in the shadows of the dark office.

Neither spoke for several minutes. Finally, Dodge leaned down, opened a desk drawer, and pulled out two shot glasses and the bottle of Irish whiskey. He poured both full and slid one across the desk to Foster, motioning him to pick it up. When he did, Dodge held his glass and said, "Here's to Kat. This planet's not worth a shit without her."

Foster said, "Bless her soul."

"Bless my ass."

Foster didn't respond.

They knocked back their drinks.

Dodge filled the glasses again. He pushed Foster's glass over and took the revolver from the gavel pad. He twirled it around on his thumb. He could feel his face twisting into grief and tried to shake it off, shake off his whole association with life on Earth.

Foster shuffled the edge of one of the legal pads like it was a deck of cards. "That's it then. That was the last chance."

"What?" Dodge's mouth fell open. This guy couldn't be serious. "No. No, you piece of shit, don't tell me—"

"She had the answer. She could have made it work." Foster sipped from the glass, set it down, and shrugged. "I was so sure. Where did I make the wrong turn?"

In a life that could be described as brimming with repulsion, Dodge had tasted a lot of bile but never this flavor. He smiled at Foster and spoke gently, with a tone of understanding and compassion. "You think it's about you?" Dodge pointed the gun at Foster.

Foster looked at the revolver. "Hold it."

"Don't worry. I just want to help. I can tell that you don't get it." Dodge pulled the hammer back, clicking it into position, poised a quarter of an inch from the chamber. "You can prove right now that there's a God." He set the gun, cocked and loaded, on the desk between them, pointed at Foster.

Foster drank the whiskey and set his glass carefully against the end of the gun, as if it could block a bullet. "I apologize. I was wrong."

Dodge refilled Foster's glass.

Dodge stared at Foster, daring him to make eye contact. He didn't. "First you want to bless her, and then you want to damn her because she got herself killed before she could make you rich. Is that right?"

He drank half the glass. "It boils down to the precept of faith. God wants faith, but all along I thought He was guiding me so that I could show the world the nature of His power."

"Tell me this, Foster Reed, PhD, are you being presumptuous?" He clinked his glass against the gun, as though in a toast. The gun spun on the desk.

The light that reflected from the gun seemed to capture Foster's gaze. "But everything lined up perfectly. I couldn't have been completely wrong. I'm missing something."

Dodge said, "No one cares about you."

"I know that," Foster said. He tapped his glass. "I honestly believed my wife was an angel, that she was sent to guide me. Me, yes, to guide me to some kind of glory. I truly believed that those patents were written with divine guidance—"

Dodge moved the gun up against Foster's hand. "I thought you wrote those submissions to get a down payment on a boat."

"The boat—that's right. Yeah, it was a boat." Foster laughed and then drank. "I thought it happened for a reason. I thought Ryan's misfortune was meant to happen so that my destiny could be fulfilled." His shoulders sunk together. "Why would God break down the Heisenberg barrier to satisfy my ego?"

Foster swallowed more whiskey, choking slightly as it went down.

Dodge spun the gun again. He knew just how hard to touch it to get the effect he wanted. He did it again and again. Foster couldn't take his eyes off of it, and each time it stopped spinning, it pointed at Foster. Dodge asked questions the way that a cat toys with its victim, questions designed to stoke Foster's doubts. "When you demand that God create energy for you, isn't that using the Lord's name in vain?" Then he'd spin the gun again, wait for it to stop, and ask another question. "If you would have no God before Him, then where do you get off demanding that He expose Himself to you? Why you?" And like an injured mouse, Foster grew weaker. "You did it for a boat. The patents were bogus and you knew it. You stole, you coveted, you gave false witness…"

Dodge refilled Foster's glass less often as time passed and managed to synchronize spinning the gun with moments where

Foster's doubts were boiling to the surface. When Foster started to nod off, Dodge poured a capsule into his drink. He didn't even try to hide it, just popped open a capsule—a mix of caffeine and ephedrine—and tapped it into the glass. The powder floated over the surface of the amber liquid, and Foster drank it. As the sun rose, Dodge began to find the game tedious.

"You see, Foster,"—Dodge topped off the glass and Foster took it—"you keep saying that you're doing God's work, but this time you'd actually be helping Him out."

"How?" Foster said. "What do you mean? I can't help Katarina, and it's too late to help Ryan. What can I do?"

"You could kill yourself..." Dodge picked up the gun and stared at it. The greenish light from the desk lamp reflected off the dark blue steel. "You know why I leave this gun here?"

Too drunk to focus, too wired to pass out, Foster shook his head as though he hadn't heard clearly.

"I leave this gun out to remind myself that being alive is optional. Truth is, no one else really cares whether you live or not." He worked the hammer loose and set it gently on the chamber, spun the cylinder, and cocked it again. The gun made a satisfying click. Dodge held it up to his head, placing the barrel just in front of his ear, pointed so that the projectile would travel through his brain and out behind the other ear. "Every night, I hold this gun up to my head like this and ask myself a question." He smiled. "You want to know what the question is?"

"You're crazy."

"I ask myself if I want to see tomorrow. Do I really want to go through it again? And so far, I've decided to keep going." Dodge took the gun away from his head and offered it to Foster, handle first. "You should try it. Go on, do God's work. Just what you need, really. And don't worry, I'll be happy to clean your mortal remains from my walls."

Foster took the gun and held it in his palm as though weighing it.

Dodge sipped from his glass. "You'll feel better. We'll all feel better."

The cold metal in his hand seemed to rouse Foster's consciousness, so Dodge took another swipe. "When you think of sin: theft, murder, adultery—those are the easy ones. But you went for the big one, didn't you? Idolatry, name in vain."

"He was right," Foster whispered. "The Nobel laureate was right and Ryan knew it. He knew it and didn't tell me because he knew I wouldn't listen."

"That's right. Tell me what happened. Tell me how you failed your God."

"I gave a talk last month at a physics meeting, and a man asked a question." He looked at Dodge, and his eyes focused for the first time in hours. "I answered it. I thought it was a good answer too. He told me that I'd done something wonderful. And I did do something wonderful but not divine."

Foster went quiet. His hand drooped to the desk under the weight of the gun.

"Do you want to see tomorrow? Do you?" Dodge whispered. "Why?"

Foster looked at the gun, and as he looked, his hand rose and tightened.

"Don't worry," Dodge said, "it's cocked, ready to go. Just ask yourself the question."

Foster looked at the gun. His hand slowly rotated so that he was looking down the barrel.

"Let's add it up, Reed. Why would you want to see tomorrow? First, you ripped off everyone you know. Your wife loved you, and instead of returning her love, you made her into a fucking angel—how hard do you think it was for her to live up to that?

Second, you fucked over your best friend. The way I heard it, you could have said one word to Ryan's wife and she wouldn't have thrown him out. Wasn't that your bachelor party? Third, you betrayed your God and religion. Fourth, you lied to the whole world, and why? Because you decided that God chose you personally for glory. And fifth, you were trying to have God give you credit for the work of a fourteen-year-old girl." Dodge shook his head and released a long, slow sigh. "That's quite a tab. I advise you to close it."

A bead of sweat rolled down Foster's brow to the arch of his nose, then down the side. It looked like a tear. "Everything I've done has been…"

Dodge spoke softly. "Everything you've done has hurt people, has hurt Jesus's flock. And now you have a chance to make it up to Kat in heaven. Or maybe hell." He whispered, "You're a wolf. You're Satan…"

Still staring down the barrel, Foster strained. His chin wrinkled.

Dodge said, "No, no, don't cry. You're not worth tears."

Foster tensed and the skin on his face tightened from his forehead to his chin. "God, let me go, please forgive me."

Softly again, Dodge said, "Just pull the trigger and yield up the ghost. Just pull."

Foster closed his eyes and tightened his finger on the trigger. As the hammer came down, he cocked his head.

The gun fired. Crown molding above the door exploded. Splinters showered down. Foster screamed. The gun fell on the desk. He rubbed his hands across his skull. One hand came away smeared with blood.

Dodge took a sip of whiskey. He waited for Foster to sit back down and then said, "For an instant there, I thought you had the courage to do the right thing."

Ryan trudged through the sand. The crashing waves and gusting wind splashed saltwater on his face. Once back in the car, he set Katarina's notes on the seat next to him and turned the key. The engine turned over but wouldn't catch. He stopped to let the starter cool. He tried again. It cranked over for about fifteen seconds and then caught. He put it in reverse and eased out the clutch, but the engine made a loud screeching sound and died. He turned the key again, but it just clicked.

He popped the hood and poked around, just to be certain. The smell of oil burning off the exhaust manifold mixed with a less familiar scent. One more thing to try. He pushed the car so it was pointed downhill and jumped in. The car rolled forward. He put it in gear and popped the clutch. The tires chirped, and the car stopped as though he'd jumped on the brakes. The engine had seized. The odometer read 271,828 miles. Not bad.

Ryan took Katarina's notes. The light played across the ocean, the crests shimmering and the troughs in shadows. It looked like a stairway over the horizon.

He fought for perspective but fear distracted him. Three years ago, confused by the mishmash of Bay Area freeways on his way to Silicon Valley, the sunset behind the Golden Gate Bridge had lured him north, and he had met Katarina. He watched the sunset some more. There was no bridge, no gate, just fading light. But there had been a reason for him to come here. He'd wanted his child, and in a way that he understood only now, his wish had come true. He really had come here for a reason.

He noticed movement on the path to the beach, something the size of a small dog, maybe a skunk, probably a raccoon.

Sitting on the Probe's hood, he focused on Katarina's notes. It had started when she discovered identical particles and latched onto the idea of identical people. Katarina argued that if someone were cloned and the entire contents of the original's mind were mapped onto the clone's mind, it would be impossible for anyone to tell them apart—even themselves. They'd called it "the clone paradox."

The question was, if the original was somehow eliminated, then was he or she really dead?

Katarina insisted the answer was no. Since the clone was still alive and since no one, not even the clone, could tell the difference, he or she must be exactly the original person. It was the same for identical particles: if two go in and two come out, there's no way to tell which was which.

He stared at a diagram on one of the pages. It had a horizontal time axis and two stick figures.

Katarina had come up with a model of how people exist in time.

Time is a series of consecutive instants, and people only truly exist in one instant: the present. We're awake or asleep yet sentient and alive in each instant, but no others, only *now.* We can't live in the past—we have memories and impressions, but we can't actually live in them. Same deal with the future. We can plan and dream, but we can't *be* in the future. It's as though we move forward in time by being cloned and mind-mapped in one instant and are then killed and replaced by our clone in the next instant. The person you were in the previous instant is identical to the person you are at this instant—the same way that the original and the clone are identical. The time steps are short enough that growth and change are so gradual that appreciable change occurs over many instants—like the mathematical concept of a "differential," where you choose a time step so small that the difference between the two steps is, as the mathematicians say, "arbitrarily close to zero."

Okay, Ryan thought, *kind of a fun way of thinking about our relationship with time, but in her message, she'd said that she understood the soul, what it is, how it works, and why people never really die.*

It was dark and getting cold, but enough light flashed off the thing waddling up the path for Ryan to recognize it as the lame pelican. "Crazy bird."

The sound of his own voice gave Ryan a feeling of substance and reality. He rummaged around in the trunk for a coat and found that old beat-up sweatshirt that Katarina wore when they came here the day after she was arrested. He tied it around his waist. The cold felt good; it distracted him from worrying so much that he couldn't think. He started walking.

The road twisted up out of the canyon. The breaking waves were luminescent in the starlight, and damn if that pelican wasn't back there waddling along.

After a few miles, the moon rose. It would be full in a few days.

The model of rebirth in every instant certainly fit.

Is that all there is to it? Was this the key piece she'd mentioned? He'd never given the time structure of a neural net much thought.

The road curved through pastures dotted with the shadows of sleeping cows, then up a hill, over a ridge, and inland toward Petaluma. His feet were starting to hurt, but he didn't mind because the longer it took him to get back, the longer he could hope that Katarina was okay, maybe even waiting for him at home.

The thought formed slowly.

If, in every succeeding instant, we wake up and experience this thing we call life, then what does it mean to be dead?

Well, if we die in every instant, then we must know what death is. After all, we experience it constantly. He stood at an angle so he could see her notes in the moonlight. Death isn't really such a thing as it is a time. We exist in each instant, die, and are reborn in the next instant.

Okay, here's an easier one: what happens when we stop breathing?

"We die," he said and laughed. "Duh."

It was almost noon when Ryan passed the sign "Petaluma City Limits, Pop. 55,900."

At Skate-n-Shred, he turned up the hill. When he got to the top, his feet were blistered and his heart was heavy but full.

It made sense.

Emmy's car was parked where his Probe used to sit. Ryan trudged up to the porch. Katarina's skateboard was under the bench. He hadn't noticed it before. Could she have gotten home? Ryan rushed through the door.

Emmy was lying on the couch. She sat up and rubbed her eyes. "Where've you been?"

She didn't look like someone with good news. He said, "My car finally died."

Emmy sat up. Her eyes were puffy, and her hair was a mess. She stood. There was no bounce to her, no smile on her lips, and her eyes were downcast.

The doubt, the worry, the fear boiled in Ryan's heart.

Emmy reached up and put her hands on both sides of his face. When he looked down at her, her lips curled up, but it wasn't really a smile.

"They found her," she whispered. "Ryan, she's gone."

Ryan closed his eyes and there she was: Katarina the strong eleven-year-old, Katarina the nasty adolescent, Katarina alight with understanding at the whiteboard, Katarina making a wisecrack, Katarina smiling. She smiled more in his head than she ever had at his side.

He whispered, "Fuck," and would swear that he heard her say, "don't say *fuck*."

In a slow, steady voice, Emmy told Ryan where and how Katarina had been found.

He nodded, and as much as he wanted to turn and run, run forever, he sat on the couch. He sat for a long time. Emmy hugged him, but he didn't hug her back. He didn't have the energy. It took a long time, hours, before he could say a word without breaking into sobs. He fidgeted with Katarina's notes, folding them and looking at them—not so much reading as looking at Katarina's handwriting, thinking about her touching them, as though if he stared hard enough he could see her looking back. He lay on the couch but couldn't sleep. He just stared out the window at the Sonoma Mountains and let the tears fall down his face until his stomach felt empty and his throat hollow. Emmy brought him a cup of tea and he drank. She sat next to him and held his hand over the pages. He said, "I found these at Point Reyes. I figured it out."

At first, Emmy was quiet as though she didn't want to know. Then she asked, "What was it that she couldn't tell you on the phone?"

"Yeah, she was full of shit about that. She could have told me on the phone." Ryan looked out the window again, at the mountains. "Emmy, Katarina was just lonely. I left her here too long, and she came looking for me because I was her only friend."

"Don't blame yourself."

The comment caught him by surprise. "Why? She was coming to see me, and if I'd been closer, she'd still be alive. The judge told me that this world was dangerous for her. It is my fault that she's dead. I was supposed to take care of her—that's why I was here." Ryan fought back a sob.

Foster and Dodge walked in. Dodge's face was ruddy and seemed to have acquired more wrinkles. Foster was pale except for dark ovals under his eyes, and his hair was sticking out at a bunch of angles as though he'd acquired a cowlick. They sat in chairs at opposite ends of the coffee table. Ryan and Emmy stayed on the couch.

"Someone has to identify the body," Dodge said.

Ryan put his feet on the coffee table. "I'll do it." His voice choked.

Emmy sighed as if it were a question that had to be asked. "What did Katarina figure out?"

Foster jerked his neck to attention. Then he looked across the table at Dodge. Dodge reflected back a look of disgust.

Ryan said, "Katarina figured out how and why the soul is eternal. She figured out heaven and hell and why morality is more than a set of commandments or a fight against karma.

"Remember when she told us about the clone paradox? The clone is identical to the original—soul, sentience, experience—everything is the same: two spiritually and physically indistinguishable people. Now, if the original is eliminated, there's no way that we could know it. Therefore, he or she must not have died, and the soul survives in the clone."

Emmy said, "In this definition, the soul must not be split between the clone and the original. When the original is destroyed, all the soul the original had is still in the clone, right?"

"Yeah," Ryan said. "It's kinda weird. The soul isn't like energy—soul can be created and destroyed, and it can change form too. The clone paradox says that in the instant where the original and clone are identical, they have the same soul. So if one disappears, the soul is still there, in the other." With every word he said, he could feel Katarina's annoyance that it was taking him so long to figure it out. "Which brings me to the next piece: how we exist in time."

Then Ryan described what he'd gleaned from Katarina's notes about the steps of time. "It's like each instant of existence is another frame in a film. Our lives are forever stuck in the present. No future or past, just now. So the way we move into the future is the same as mapping our minds into a clone that is one instant ahead in time. The soul is what carries us through time. It is not attached to our bodies. It awakens anew in every instant.

"The key is that when someone dies, the body stops waking up in each instant. The body dies, but the soul keeps waking up."

Foster said, "If there is no body for it to awaken in, then it wakes up with God?"

"No. Or maybe." Ryan touched Emmy's knee. "I guess it depends on how you define God." Ryan stood and walked toward the foyer. "This is where it really gets thick. Come on upstairs. The answer is in Katarina's mural."

Emmy stood quietly. Foster looked fascinated, but as he stood, he cocked his head into his smug look. Dodge looked like he cared more about the sand Ryan's shoes had left on the coffee table than what Ryan was saying.

When they got to Katarina's room, Ryan pointed at the ceiling. "See the cloud? The smudges are the names of people—the names of every person Katarina could remember, everyone who affected her. Look at how the cloud drips into her drawing of me. She put my sisters' names in, and here's Foster's. There's a little heart around Emmy's.

"This is the immortality of the soul: our every action, everyone we touch, every way we express our affection—whether by making love under the stars or giving the finger to some asshole who can't drive—is a gift to another. The soul isn't something that we have to ourselves. We've gotten it from everyone who's loved us, everyone who's hated us, and everyone who didn't care but somehow affected us. Our genetic makeup comes from the affection of our ancestors. It's the core; she called it the canvas. In the instant following the death of our physical bodies, our soul awakens in everyone we've ever affected, the same way that the soul awakens in any other instant—except that it's no longer confined to one body."

Ryan smiled at Katarina's nagging impatience. "Katarina is a part of me. All her little quirks, the way she hassled me, her total lack of patience when I try to figure something out, all that. She's right here, wide awake. Emmy, you didn't know her as well, so you don't have as much of her, but she's awake and sentient in you too.

"At the instant of death, the soul awakens in everyone that soul ever affected. It's only when we're alive that we're bottled up in one consciousness."

Dodge said, "How is this different from the tired bullshit that"—he switched to a high-pitched mocking tone—"we carry the dead with us in our hearts?"

"No. You missed the point," Ryan said. "The difference between the instant after you die and any other instant is that instead of awakening in your own single consciousness, you awaken in everyone you've affected—get it?" He paced for a few seconds, trying to wrap his own head around the idea. No one interrupted him, except for the sense of Katarina: "Ryan McDoof-face, it's kind of obvious, we're doing it right now…come on, get with the program."

Finally, he said, "It's like this: while I was walking home, I was thinking about this conversation. As I went through it in my head, I had a good idea how each of you would respond. Okay? I know you guys, so in my head, you responded the way your affection has taught me to expect you to respond. You weren't aware that I was having this conversation in my head with the version of you that you've given me. You weren't aware of it because your consciousness, your soul, is locked up in your own head. But when you die, your consciousness isn't locked up anymore. If you were dead, you'd have been wide awake in my head having that conversation. You see? Katarina's not locked up anymore. She's in here, and she's annoyed that it took me so long to figure this out—annoyed in sort of an amused way, though, a very Katarina way. You see? When you're alive, your soul is confined to your head, but when you're dead, you're aware and sentient. But instead of being in one brain, you're smeared across everyone you affected."

Ryan held his arms up to the ceiling. "That's what the cloud represents—she called it the soul-cloud, but I guess you could call it something like a universal eternal soul. A cloud-like continuum of soul-stuff smeared across everyone. When you're alive, your soul is stuck in one head as though a drop of soul condensed from the cloud into your mind. But when you die, your soul evaporates back into the cloud, and since you're awake, you know it. You know everyone and are a part of everyone, and you share everyone's experience."

With his arms still raised to the ceiling, Ryan realized that he must look like a preacher at a revival. He dropped his arms and shrugged.

Foster said, "Then where does the soul come from?"

It struck Ryan that Foster spoke with none of his smug dogmatism. Ryan pointed at the ceiling again. "A baby is an affection sponge. When it's born, it's a genetic canvas built from the choices of its ancestors, and then we paint it with affection. We give it pieces of our souls. Like in the cloud, we rain drops of soul onto the baby and its own soul condenses. It awakens and grows and gives its own affection, gives us its soul—in a feedback loop."

Dodge said, "Sounds like bullshit to me," and walked back downstairs.

Foster said, "Good and evil come from our actions and the actions of those who trespass against us."

"Heaven is when your soul awakens in all the love, care, and decency you gave others. Hell is awakening in the hatred, offense, and harm you gave them," Ryan said. "I guess most of us get some of both."

The room went silent. Emmy's brow was furrowed. She looked around the room, at the murals and self-portraits, at the mess of dirty clothes and trash Katarina left behind. Tears worked their way out of her eyes, but she smiled. She said, "I hope so. I don't want her to have died." A dozen tears coursed down her face so slowly that most of them didn't make it all the way. "People die, you know? Their bodies decay into earth, but Kat watched her step, and instead of a leap of faith, she derived a model that requires only one small step of faith. She distilled belief in her idea of the eternal soul down to one simple question.

"In the clone paradox, do you believe that the soul is alive in the clone even after the original is killed?"

The next day, Ryan packed a few things for the trip to Utah to identify Katarina. Dodge forged Jane's signature and notarized a statement permitting Ryan to ID the body. Foster offered to drive Ryan to Salt Lake City, but Ryan turned him down.

After Foster left, Emmy and Ryan sat on the couch. Ryan told her that he'd found in Petaluma what he'd lost in Texas: a wonderful child that he got to watch grow up.

Then Emmy surprised him. "You know what she gave me?"

"What?"

"I've spent my whole life with a plan. I've worked hard, and all the dreams I've had—not stupid daydreams but the ones that I could really picture for myself—have all come true." She sat up on her knees, facing Ryan, and wrapped her arms around his neck. "Kat gave me a new dream. I used to think that my students were my children, but Kat showed me something special." A tear punctuated her statement. "I want to have a baby."

They were quiet for the better part of an hour. Finally, Ryan kissed a tear from her cheek, stood, picked up his backpack, and tucked Sean's football under his arm.

Emmy said, "Are you coming back?"

"Someday. I'm going to my son's sixteenth birthday party, and then I'm heading back to Massachusetts. I haven't seen my mom in five years."

"I want you to come back."

He set the backpack and football back down, put his arms around her, his nose rubbing hers, and he asked what felt like the most important question. "Did you take that small step of faith?"

"No."

"I did."

"Oh."

Ryan walked out onto the porch and down the steps. He glanced under the bench at Katarina's skateboard. He stopped on the corner and looked back at the house one more time, up toward the spire to his room. He could see the whiteboard, and Katarina's window was open. Dodge was inside on a ladder, painting over the murals. A sign had been duct-taped to the porch railing: "Apartments for rent."

Ryan looked down the block at Skate-n-Shred, turned toward the boulevard, and walked to a bus stop. When the bus came a few minutes later, he stepped up, counted out change to the driver, and headed up the aisle to find an open seat.

The driver grunted behind him. "The freaks I have to tolerate…"

Ryan looked back. There, on the top step, stood the pelican.

ACKNOWLEDGMENTS

In writing *The God Patent*, I had a tremendous amount of help and support.

Foremost, I'd like to thank Ann Clark for working through every draft and for expressing her intense enthusiasm for this and every writing project I have ever pursued. I'd have never jumped into this pool if Ann hadn't pushed me.

I'm in debt to everyone who reviewed the early drafts, especially to my writing colleagues and mentors: Tamim Ansary, Athena Katsaros, Carol Sawyer, and James Warner; as well as Jessica Sinsheimer (who will one day be the greatest agent in New York City); and the experts on particle physics, law, and evangelical Christianity: Michael Vinson, PhD, H. Lee Sawyer, PhD, Barry Wildorf, JD, and Marty Castleberg, PhD—who did what they could to help me get the facts correct. The mistakes are mine and mine alone.

I also wish to thank Kemble Scott for encouraging me to publish *The God Patent* in electronic form and Yanina Gotsulsky and Numina Press, LLC for publishing the original print edition; Robert Kroese, who read the Kindle version and recommended it to his editors at Amazon Publishing; Laurie McLean for providing the support that only an agent savant could; and my editors at 47North: David Pomerico for his confidence in this project, Christopher Cerasi for helping to improve this edition, and Bill Latimer for protecting you from my abuse of the English language.

I wish to express tremendous gratitude to The San Francisco Writers Workshop for their help in six-page segments; to Litquake, the San Francisco literary festival, for morale and motivation; Lefty's Sports Bar for the fine IPA; Joe Quirk, who bought the first copy of the electronic version; and Christine Comaford, whose footsteps I followed into this business.

FROM THE AUTHOR

Thank you for reading *The God Patent.* Thank you even more for buying it.

I was born in Oakland, a fifth-generation Californian, and raised in the foothills of Mount Diablo. When I was in the physics PhD program at UC Santa Barbara, I discovered a particle while working on an experiment at SLAC—the sort of academic achievement that matters to about fifty people. Later, as a research associate and then a physics professor at the University of Texas at Arlington, I worked on the ATLAS experiment at CERN and the D0 experiment at Fermilab and was on the team that discovered the top quark in 1994. In 1999, I couldn't resist the allure of the expanding high-tech bubble and took a job directing patent development for a wireless web startup.

The God Patent is my first novel and is in no way autobiographical. Ryan McNear came from a recurring nightmare. For ten years, my daughter, Heather, and I lived in the Dallas–Fort Worth area. As the single father of an adolescent girl, I had a huge fear of losing custody and making the sort of stupid decisions that ruined Ryan's life. Things worked out for us, though, and when Heather graduated from high school, we moved back to California.

Katarina is based on who I feared/expected Heather to be before she was born. Fortunately, Heather and Katarina have almost nothing in common other than their brilliance, the cadence of their speech, and smart-alecky attitudes. Along those lines, Ryan's voice is a lot like mine, but I'm not as friendly and outgoing or as tall and pale as he is, though I have better hair.

Emmy Nutter is based very loosely on the turn-of-the-previous-century mathematician Amolie (Emmy) Noether. She was a Jew in Nazi Germany, and she made what I think is the most important discovery in human history, Noether's Theorem, which is what Emmy Nutter is teaching in the chapter where she first appears.

Skate-n-Shred is a bizarro version of the Phoenix Theater in Petaluma. Unlike Dodge Nutter's place, the Phoenix is an incredible resource for teens that provides health, homework, and life advice—as well as a great place to hang out.

I live in Petaluma now with the wonderful Karen and our dogs and make a living by writing novels and by writing popular science and stuff for the electronics trade rags.

Novels are capsules of thought, and reading one is akin to reading the author's mind. It's an intimate experience that ought to breed familiarity. To that end, it's only fair that you share your thoughts with me. Please drop me a note at *ransom@ransomstephens.com.*

My website is www.ransomstephens.com and there's a bunch of stuff there about *The God Patent*, including a bibliography, a bunch of relevant (and irrelevant) science, a reader's guide, videos, and more background about the characters. If you have any questions about the science in *The God Patent* or something related, feel free to ask!

Should you ever wonder, I prefer beer to wine, tea to coffee, hard rock to jazz, and I attend every Oakland Raiders home game.

—Ransom Stephens, Petaluma California, October 2012

ABOUT THE AUTHOR

Photo © 2012 by Mark Bennington

Ransom Stephens is a former physics professor and fifth-generation Californian. After earning his PhD from the University of California, Santa Barbara, he taught at the University of Texas at Arlington and conducted cutting-edge research at high energy physics labs across the United States and Europe. He then moved into the high-tech arena, leaving academia to work for a wireless web start-up. He's now a science writer and high tech consultant living in Northern California's wine country, though he prefers beer. More about Stephens can be found at his website, http://www.ransomstephens.com.